PURSUITS UNKNOWN

PURSUITS
UNKNOWN

AN AMY
AND LARS
NOVEL

ELLEN CLARY

SPARKPRESS

Published by SparkPress, a BookSparks imprint,
A division of SparkPoint Studio, LLC
Tempe, Arizona, USA, 85281
www.gosparkpress.com

Published 2019
Printed in the United States of America
ISBN: 978-1-943006-86-1 (pbk)
ISBN: 978-1-943006-87-8 (e-bk)

Library of Congress Control Number: 2019930388

Interior design by Tabitha Lahr

For my parents, who taught me to keep trying, to believe in myself, to push back against obstacles, and to slay the dragon of uncertainty.

CONTENTS

CHAPTER 1:

———

The Call Comes In

HARRIS SAID, "Incoming missing-person report. We have a disoriented elderly man who has wandered off, and they haven't been able to find him for more than four hours."

Amy hopped up from her desk inside the Locate and Investigate office that they all just called LAI. "Me, me, me. Pick me."

Looking over from his own desk across the common area between all four agent desks, Harris said, "Okay, I just sent you the details about Herman McConnell and the home address."

Amy looked at her handheld and confirmed the address. It was in Evergreen, but at the edge of town. Evergreen was medium sized, beside the Grebe River about five miles from the ocean. Its gentle rolling hills were green with just enough rain, though it had the occasional summer brown. Despite its name, Evergreen was actually a mix of evergreen and deciduous, and many of its residents called it Semigreen; Amy's coworker Steve called it Evergrebe.

She and Larson hustled over to one of the Locate and Investigate (LAI) vehicles. Amy slid her five-foot-seven self into the driver's seat, adjusted the mirror while moving her wavy caramel-blonde ponytail out of the way as she settled in, and plugged her handheld into the docking port to download the address to the

1

vehicle. The car purred to life and when she buckled in, it headed off. She extracted her handheld from the dock so she could go over what little they knew.

They had a few minutes before they reached their destination. Amy said to Lars, "You ready to do some searching?"

/Search! Search!/ he said mentally back to her.

"Good thing."

Reading the initial call report told her that Herman, who was suffering from the devasting disease of disorientation, had gone missing about five hours ago. They normally would choose to wait a little longer before doing a serious search, but in the case of a child or a sick or injured person, they tended to move much more quickly. Disorientation was a brain disorder where the brain no longer functioned as it used to. Memories got scrambled, or forgotten, and reasoning ability was severely compromised. These days, Amy would search for the elderly as often as she searched for children.

Amy looked at the surrounding area. Yolanda, another coworker, had been campaigning for them to learn to identify plants and trees, as it was more useful to say "I'm in a stand of birch trees" than "I'm in a bunch of white-barked trees." Oak trees flourished here along with pines, birches, and the occasional maidenhair. It was early spring, so most of the trees agreed that green was the operative color, except for the occasional white or pink blossoms. Trees in Evergreen were spaced well enough apart that hide-and-seek was a real game, and not a battle over detangling one's feet from the branches of a manzanita or rhododendron. It also made Amy's job of chasing down lost people easier, though not a cinch by any measure.

After they arrived, with Lars armed with a sample of Herman's scent, they headed off into the sparsely wooded, hilly area that bordered the property.

Lars raced ahead.

Amy ducked under a sagging oak limb, its scent ripe with musty, matted leaves underneath. She said, "Slow down. You'll miss something and we'll have to do this all over again."

ELLEN CLARY

Lars urged: /Here. Here. Here./

"Lars, will you let me catch up? It looks bad when you're just careening around like you're chasing a rabbit."

/Rab—?/

Amy remembered they had been working on that word in the Canine Language Project, but he probably didn't know it yet.

Lars was a kelpie/shepherd cross, with the svelte kelpie body and face and the distinctive golden eyes, but he had the sturdier, wider look of a shepherd, though he was only forty-five pounds. Amy called him a stealth kelpie, because his fur, though not as long as a typical shepherd's, was longer than a kelpie's and he was tan on his lower body with a heavy dusting of black along the top.

"Never mind, just go search."

/Search!/

He charged ahead and Amy raced behind him. She noticed that he would sniff the ground every so often, but he was also smelling the bushes and air scenting.

She raced over a small rise and nearly collided with him. His nose was buried in the ground.

"Nice to see you, too."

Lars walked in a couple of circles, the second one wider; then he decided and headed off again. Breathlessly chasing after Lars, she got her comm out, trying not to drop it. "Hello, Central?"

Harris came back, "Yes, Amy?"

"This guy is moving right along for an older guy."

"We heard back that he's actually in his fifties and this is a case of early onset disorientation."

"Oh great, we could be at this for a while. Talk to you later."

"Good hunting."

They crashed around for what seemed like hours over hill and dale. Enough for Amy to realize she had no idea what a dale was, but she was sure she had been over at least three of them. She broke through some low holly and found herself looking right at Lars. He was sniffing the ground right beside a paved road. He said, /Here./

3

Ah ha, she thought.

She got on the comm. "This is Amy. We've come to a road-side. I think our vic was picked up by a car."

Harris said, "I'm requesting a police car over to that location right now."

Amy looked up to find Lars wandering down the road.

"Lars, you can't track a car. Stop. You did great."

He kept going.

"Lars. Hello?"

Lars was mentally making that dog-thinking sound which a human would call "hmmmmm."

"What is it?" Amy asked.

/Hmmmm./

Lars had his nose jammed up on the ground.

"May I see?" He looked up, making a deliberate sniffing-in sound. Amy asked, "Do you know what you found?"

/Mmm,/ he said, making a sound that meant he didn't know the word he wanted to use.

She got the handheld out and held it over the spot so it could take a sample. It said: *Preliminary Analysis: Blood*

Amy said, "Central, Lars has found a blood spot."

"Roger." That had to be Harris again.

Looking around, Amy saw broken branches and bent grass that suggested a body hitting the ground, but there also appeared to be signs of someone getting up.

Lars followed the track back into the woods, climbing up a small hill.

"Central, I need this area cordoned off so I can search it further for other scents. The vic has continued on and we're following that."

"Okay. Roger, Amy."

Lars kept on going.

Chasing after him, she said, "Oh great, now you really are looking for a rabbit. I need to report specifically on what we're doing, and if what you're looking for has two long ears, we are both are going to have some explaining to do."

Lars ran up a short rise and disappeared around a leaf-covered boulder about twice his size.

/Here,/ he said.

She couldn't see him, but it was such an unlikely place. "You're kidding."

/Here—/

When Amy got up there, she saw Lars pulling at a leafy branch on the hillside. There seemed to be a hole underneath it.

She got her headlamp out. She could see there was quite a large hole.

"Central, Lars has found a sizable hole in the side of a hill that he says the trail leads to. I think it's a cave entrance. I'm going to check it out."

Harris asked, "Do you need backup?"

"No sign of trouble. I'm sending a photo."

Amy, with Lars assisting, pulled the branch back. With effort, she struggled in, finding herself in a cavern. Her breath caught when she shone the light around. She saw dozens of reflections, the beam catching unexpected, beautiful glimpses of what she realized were hundreds of gray, white, and cream–colored crystals dancing in the light. Stalactites dripped in frozen animation all over the ceiling, some extending down more than a foot. The air had a long-undisturbed quality, but she could see that some dust had been stirred up.

She noticed that Lars had his nose on the ground. Footprints.

"Central, we have footprints in this incredible crystal cavern."

There was no response. She realized she needed to poke her head out of the cave to transmit; she did so and repeated her transmission.

Amy thought, *How could Herman have found this? He must have come here as a kid.*

Back inside, Amy called out, "Hello! Hello, Herman, are you here?"

"Yes, I'm right here," said a soft voice.

Squinting into the gloom, she could see there was a light from a small flashlight. She could see a figure sitting on what looked to be a very old bench that someone had fashioned many years ago. It should have fallen apart long ago, but the cavern's atmosphere must have been a protection. Amy carefully approached him. Shining the light on his face, she could see blood on his temple. "Herman, how are you doing?"

"Mary Ann, I'm so glad you could make it."

"Er." *Time to wing it,* she thought. She reached down to her handheld and switched on the recorder and the night vision.

"And look, is that Freddy? He's gotten to be such a big dog."

/Freddy?/ Lars asked.

Talking mentally just to Lars, Amy said, /Just go along with it. Wag your tail and look happy./

Lars wagged his tail.

"Mary Ann, come sit beside me."

"Okay, Herman. How are you?"

"Oh, I'm fine, just tripped over something."

"That looks like someone hit you."

"Oh no, just me."

"You didn't see anyone just recently?"

"No."

"You were running here, do you remember that?"

"I wanted to get here for our meeting."

"Herman, what is the meeting about?"

"You know, it's our usual club meeting that we always have. I remember how there was this big debate among the boys to figure out if we were going to let you in."

Amy brought the handheld closer. Thinking again, she realized this would be easier outside.

"Herman, do you want to go outside, so we can look at your wound?"

"Oh, it's nothing."

"I'd love to see it better."

"You like it?"

"It's quite the shiner."

"Okay."

Herman rose and walked carefully back to the entrance. Amy took a moment to make some video of the cavern.

Once they got outside, Amy asked, "Herman, could you sit down on this log here?"

Amy knelt down in front of him. Herman had a light build, dark tan skin, and a soft, almost baby face with just a hint of a five-o'clock shadow. His light brown eyes had that faraway look of someone who is seeing something else entirely. She noticed the gash on the left side of his face and the start of a black eye. Blood pasted his brown hair down and the wound was starting to dry in an ugly way.

She took a photo of it and ran the scanner over it. The scanner indicated that it found something embedded. She took some pre-medicated gauze out of the med kit. "Okay, Herman, you have quite the gouge here. I'm just going to hold this cloth on it, which will help it staunch the bleeding and make it hurt less."

Herman said, "Don't worry about me."

"I am worried about you, Herman. Just let me help you."

He seemed to acquiesce.

Amy placed the gauze on his face. He stiffened at first and then relaxed.

"Who hit you, Herman?"

"Who? No one, I just tripped, I think. I'm trying to remember what we were going to be talking about. Did we decide what to do about the Walton boys down the street?"

Looking right at Amy, but still not really seeing her, he said, "They were pestering you something terrible after school."

"I think I'll be okay, Herman."

"You sure?"

"Yeah, I have this big dog now."

Lars wagged his tail and came wriggling in. Herman joyously petted him.

Lars said to Amy, /Smells strange./

She replied, /Well, he's been through a lot./

/Smells strange./

Amy asked Lars, /What do you mean? Are you sure you're not smelling the stuff I put on him?/

After a pause, Lars said, /Different./

Pleasantly surprised at his language improvement, she said, /Hey, you remembered 'different.' Good boy./

Amy made a note to include the funny smell in her report.

"Central, Herman was hit with something. I think just a fist, but I took a sample to see if we can find any foreign material."

Amy heard approaching voices. A woman that she hadn't yet met exclaimed, "Herman! Where have you been?!"

He said, "I'm right here. We were just having a club meeting."

"What happened to your face?"

"I just fell."

"Oh, I think not," she said.

"No, really."

She looked at Amy.

Amy extended her hand. "My name is Amy Callahan with Locate and Investigate. Someone did hit him, and we're going try to figure out who it was. Is he missing anything?"

Herman said, "But how could that be?" He didn't appear to think that anything unusual had occurred.

"It happens, Herman," Amy said, feeling just a little out of her depth, but trying to cope.

The woman, who was just a little shorter than Amy, but with much darker walnut brunette hair and a concerned expression, said, "I'm Carolyn, his wife." She started to carefully examine his pockets, her hands moving in a well-practiced, familiar fashion. She embodied that competence that longtime partners have around each other.

Amy watched her, wondering what it was like having someone you love slip away from you. The drugs for disorientation were way better than they used to be, but the early onset cases were the most stubborn, though there had been miraculous reversals.

Carolyn said, "He's missing his wallet, but I don't know if that means anything. I give him some cash and a credit card with a set limit. He can't remember ID numbers so he doesn't get a debit card. I haven't switched him over to the fingerprint authentication as they don't have a way to limit how much someone can have yet."

Amy examined Herman's hand closely. "Carolyn, there is some fluid underneath Herman's fingernails. May I run a scan on it?"

Carolyn consented and Amy took her handheld a little closer.

"Supplemental recording of an interview of Herman McConnell: this is Amy Callahan with Herman and his wife Carolyn."

"Herman, I just want to take a look at your fingernails. It won't hurt."

Herman looked hesitant, but then relaxed a little.

Amy swiped her fingers a few times over the screen and brought the edge right up to his index finger. After a moment it beeped and she repeated the process for his thumb. Another beep and she gave him back his hand. She stared at the screen for a while with a thoughtful expression.

Carolyn said, "What is it?"

Amy replied, "It is telling me it's fingerprint solution. Unusual because it's not usually needed unless you want to get the maximum quality contact between the finger and the handheld screen."

"Well, that's kind of left field, isn't it?"

"My thought, too."

Amy cleared the screen and picked it up, looking back at Herman.

"Herman, did you see anyone when you were on that road before you went to the cave?"

"Oh no, I was on my way to our meeting. I did stumble on a branch on the way."

Amy paused a moment, considering. She picked up his hand again and brought the handheld over.

"Did anyone do this?" She took his thumb and pressed it onto the handheld like she was taking a thumbprint.

Herman's eyes widened and he breathed in suddenly. "Yes . . ."

"Can you describe them? How many people?"

"Three, but there was one in particular."

"A man?"

"Yeah."

"What did he look like? Was he tall, short?"

"They were all tall, but they were standing over me."

"What color was his skin?"

"Oh, you know, tan, but a little pale."

"What color was his hair?"

"Kinda brown. Real short hair."

"Was he fat?"

"No, he was thin."

"What did he sound like?"

"Kinda like everyone else, but he was bossy and he did sound like he was from somewhere else, but not that far away."

"Did they get out of a car?"

"Don't know, they just appeared."

"A van or a truck?"

"Oh wait, there was a white van."

"Where they in a hurry?"

"Oh yes, they didn't want to even chat or say hello. I thought it was the Payton boys down the road, but I didn't recognize them and they were too big."

"Were they rough?"

He seemed to hesitate. "Kinda."

"Did they hit you?"

Herman looked a little blank.

Amy looked at Carolyn and said in what she hoped was a reassuring tone: "Don't panic." She stood up over Herman and raised her arm, hand in a fist about to strike.

"NO! No, don't do that again please. What do you want?"

Amy dropped to the ground in front of him, her hands flat and on his arms.

Carolyn rushed in, too.

"Is that what those men did?" Amy asked.

"Yes." Herman was gasping and he shook.

Carolyn got a hold of his shoulders. "They did that? They hit you?"

"Yes."

Amy asked, "What happened after that?"

"I don't remember. Next thing I remember is the cave."

While Carolyn was rubbing Herman's shoulder, Amy asked her, "What did he do for a living?"

"He was a scientist at Nanology," she said, referring to a biotech firm known for creating extremely small, smart medical devices that acted like biological repair robots.

"Do you know what he did?"

"He said it was mostly what he called 'peaceful plowshares' stuff, but there was some hush-hush stuff that he didn't discuss."

"Something where knowing someone's fingerprints might be useful?"

"I don't know," she replied.

Amy made a note on her handheld and said, "Well, thank you both, you've been very helpful and we need to get a medic to treat that gash. It's going to bruise and could get infected."

"Thank you, too," Carolyn said.

"Give me your messaging address and I'll send you our contact info and the case number for this."

She did and they finished up. Amy sent the data back to Central.

Amy radioed for a medic. Lars got some final pets from Herman and she and Lars headed off.

CHAPTER 2:

Second Scent

AMY HEADED back to the area that she had asked to be cordoned off. A uniformed police officer was just finishing the taping.

"Hi, I'm Agent Amy Callahan and it's my fault that you're out here tromping around in the woods."

She replied, "It's okay, some nice fresh air, no mutilated body. Works for me."

Amy said, "Just a little blood, but no mutilation fortunately." Holding up her handheld she said, "Hello, Central. I'm back at the cordoned-off area and we're going to see if there's any evidence to collect."

"Roger," came the reply.

Amy looked at the scene again. They needed to find a human scent that was different from Herman or herself. This was going to be a challenge. She and Lars had been spending time working on the concept of different, but it was pretty abstract.

Looking over at the kelpie, Amy said, "Lars, I want you to find human scents that you haven't found before."

Lars looked at her and inclined his head in that 'Really?' expression.

"Lars, do you remember when we were working on same and different? These four blocks are the same and this ball is different?"

Lars didn't say anything but she could see recognition in his eyes.

"Now this is harder. We're looking for a different smell than Herman's but I don't know what it is to begin with. I have Herman's smell here in the sniff-o-meter, but we're wondering if a different person was chasing him."

/We chase him./

"I know, but someone else. Do you know what that means?" She realized that this was going to be a stretch for his understanding.

Lars had that noncommittal look. Amy reminded herself that they had nothing to lose by being out here and that if it didn't work they would still be fine.

He put his nose to the ground and after a few moments said, /Here./

Amy held the sniff-o-meter, which they used to record synthetic approximations of scents, over the spot. "That's Herman. That's the guy you already found. Are there other scents?"

Looking at the ground, he said, /Rabbit./

"You probably meant squirrel. I'm interested in human smells."

Lars started to walk in an S pattern, going back and forth along Herman's path.

He stopped, drilling his nose into the earth.

"Don't go too far away."

Lars pulled up an acorn that a squirrel had probably buried.

"I'm so sorry, but those are poisonous to you. Here, trade me." Lars brought over the acorn and Amy gave him a chicken dog treat, which he happily gulped down. Amy tossed the acorn into the woods. "You know the squirrels bury these to find later when there aren't a lot of acorns around." She decided not to bother mentioning that he would have to eat several of them to get sick.

Lars shrugged in a way that only a kelpie could do.

"You're so sensitive to the needs of squirrels."

/Huh?/

"Never mind. I'm not going to explain sarcasm."

/Sar—/

"Sar-nothing, keep searching." Amy could see the officer trying not to laugh.

Amy realized there was a breeze, which could easily move the scent around. She wished she could just wave the sniff-o-meter scent storage device around and find things, but it was pretty useless without a specific location to check. Using an expert like a dog was the best way to pinpoint things, even with the communication barrier.

Lars swung his head around and pointed out a different spot. After checking, she laughed. "That's my scent, silly. Was there anyone else?

He went wider and said, /Here./

Amy, with low expectation that it was going to be anything different, headed over to the spot. It was different. Likely human. Lars followed the track back to the road and she found a better sample. There were prints, too. "Central, Lars has found evidence of one assailant. We're going to check Herman's path before hitting the road to see if there was a different pursuer."

There was. Now she had evidence and a theory. One person had chased Herman to the road, where another person assaulted and thumb-printed him. *What a lot of trouble to go through,* she thought as they walked back to their vehicle.

CHAPTER 3:

Back at the Office

AMY AND Lars wandered back into Central. Amy tossed her bag down on her desk. Lars flopped down on his dog bed, underneath her desk on the right-hand side.

"Harris, do you have a second?"

He swung around in his chair. "For you, I have two, maybe even three."

"What do you know about nanoelectronics?"

Harris laughed, which lit up his olive-skinned face. He had chin-length, dark brown, straight hair which was at a length to be constantly getting in his face. He kept threatening to cut it, but wanted to go back to having a ponytail again. "Of all the things you could have asked me, that is not what I was expecting."

"Sorry."

"No, no problem, it's just so off the wall."

"That it is. Anyway, this guy Herman—the one with disorientation that we chased down today. Well, he was a scientist who worked in nanoelectronics, and today he was mugged. They took his thumbprint and roughed him up some."

Harris leaned his head forward, looking intrigued. "His thumbprint?"

"Yeah, I verified that he had the solution under his fingernails, the stuff that's used to get an accurate scan. Plus, he was able to recognize the motion when I held his hand."

Steve, who had been half-listening, piped up, "Aww, you were holding hands."

Amy said, "Steve, don't you have a rhinoceros you need to go carry off somewhere?"

Steve, at six feet with a medium-heavy build and in excellent shape, could lift most anything. "I'm just jealous, that's all. I always fingerprint the people I mug."

Harris looked at him thoughtfully, with one hand holding an errant lock of hair. "Good point, the mugging was probably just for show."

Amy added, "He was also chased to a spot where his assailants were waiting."

"Oh, this is getting even better," Harris said. "This is weird, no one uses solution anymore unless it's for . . ." He trailed off, looking into the distance. " . . . extremely accurate prints that go beyond just using them for ID."

"Lost me there," Amy said.

Harris looked at his own thumb. "Think of writing instead of reading. Like if you wanted to create a hand."

Steve held out his own hand. "I think you're reaching."

Amy groaned. "Rhinoceros, Steve, a rhino has to be just outside waiting for your reaching arms."

Steve stood up with both hands reaching out at Harris.

Harris said to Steve's dog, "Pearl, help, help. Your person is losing his mind. Go see Steve."

Both Pearl, Steve's yellow Labrador retriever, and Boomer, Harris's Portuguese water dog, leapt up and ran over to Steve to see what the game was. Petting both dogs and looking over at Harris, Steve said, "I will get you some day, you know?"

"Contrary to common belief, I am fully capable of running away."

"You're going to sic that fake hawk on me that you keep trying to build, aren't you?"

"It's a spy pigeon that listens and records, and he's just going to learn enough to blackmail you."

Steve waved his hand dismissively. "As if. We work with dogs here remember?"

"Do you pay attention to pigeons?" Harris said.

"No, but you can't blackmail me since I have nothing to hide." He blew a kiss at him and Harris looked at the ceiling.

Amy cleared her throat. "Um, boys, I thought we were talking about fake hands and fingers."

"Pigeons don't have fingers," Steve said.

Amy flung a dog toy at him, sending all three dogs scurrying.

Looking at Steve, she asked, "What could someone do with a physicist's fingerprints?"

"Sounds like identity theft."

"Well, his only credit card is a physical card with a small, set limit. It doesn't use bioidentity."

"Maybe open a new account?"

"Aren't there checks for that?"

"Yeah, there was a lot of that sort of theft going around, so you have to be physically present in some way or at least have a verifiable video connection or have a notary present, but with the right connections they could still pull it off."

Amy said, "Sounds like a lot of trouble and I don't think this was a coincidence."

"You think he was tracked?"

"I'm starting to wonder that."

"Maybe take the sniff-o-meter and Lars back out there."

"I already entered Herman's general smell and his footprint smell, so I could rule out duplicates."

"Assuming you didn't go running by any spice mixes that can really confuse it."

Amy smiled, remembering. "Yeah, what was that case? We were trailing a cook who had spilled curry powder mix on herself and then went through her garden. We couldn't get a solid read on anything. We had to go to the other side of the garden, and start from there."

"Poor sniff-o-meter."

"Harris, what's a sniff-o-meter really called?"

Looking up from his scheduling, Harris said, "Olfactory reflectometer."

Steve and Amy looked at each other and, at the same time, said, "Sniff-o-meter."

Harris looked back at his work. "Suit yourself. The search engine will hate you."

"Technology hates me anyway," Steve replied.

Amy retreated into one of the shared private offices that was on edge of the common area to dictate her report.

"Lars, you said something about Herman smelling strange?" /Weird smell./

"Who taught you the word 'weird'?" Opening the door, she called out, "Who taught my dog the word 'weird'?"

Steve called out, "Oh, that was me."

Amy looked at him, a little startled.

He continued, "All out loud, no voodoo. I was just talking to him and was telling him that cats are weird. Delivery people in funny uniforms are weird. Flowers can smell weird."

Amy, still looking at him, said, "That's quite a leap you're describing. Dogs generalize poorly. I could make this my Senior Project if I didn't already have one."

Steve said, "I tried with some smells, but he likes smells that we think are weird. I tried my feet, but he liked my feet as far as I could tell by how deeply he was breathing in."

"You're better off with lilies; I know he doesn't much like them."

She shut the door of the office and continued her report.

CHAPTER 4:

Beth Speaks with Amy

AMY WAS back at her usual LAI desk when her handheld buzzed. It was Beth Hanscom, the detective looking into Herman's case. Beth appeared on the screen. "Hi, Amy."

"Hi, Beth." Beth's sweet, cherubic, welcoming face did a nice job of covering her raw determination in solving cases. She did not give up easily. While she wasn't in the same excellent physical shape as her more active peers, she still managed to get herself where she needed to go, and to get others to go with her as well.

"I've been going over the Herman McConnell case and I'm thinking I'd like you and Lars to go visit the other affected person." She paused and Amy could see her looking at some notes on the monitor. "Lincoln DeLaVitt is his name."

Puzzled, Amy asked, "Um, sure, but how come?"

Beth continued, "Early-onset disorientation is relatively rare. The odds of two coworkers getting it is a little off the charts, which is prompting further investigation. The Center for Disease Tracking is interested, but they're letting us do the legwork for right now."

Amy just looked back at her, waiting for the other paw to drop, giving her that 'And?' look.

Beth said, "We need to chase down every lead that we have."

Amy continued to stare, a very slight frown appearing on her brow.

Beth looked up, catching her expression, and smiled. "You're wondering why I'm talking to you, in particular, aren't you?"

"Er, yes, I feel like I'm missing something obvious."

"Well, you should ask your dog."

"What?"

"Because you reported that he said that Herman smelled funny."

"Yeeesss," she said slowly.

"I want him to meet Lincoln, too."

"To sniff him out?"

"Yes, and you can store his scent in the olfactory reflectometer along with Herman's, so we can see if there is anything in common."

"Well, you know the scents are mostly fake, recreated molecularly. There's no guarantee that you can draw any conclusions from them."

"No stone unturned," Beth said, smiling with that won't-take-no-for-an-answer look.

"Okay, when?"

"Got time tomorrow?"

"For you? Anytime."

"Okay, I'll come by and pick you up in an unmarked dog carrier car at 11:00 a.m."

"Okay, see you then."

Beth cut the connection. Amy announced, "Well, this should be strange."

"How strange?" Yolanda asked.

Amy looked over at the other LAI agent. While she hadn't been involved in the first search for Herman, Amy really wanted her insight. "Beth wants Lars to check out the other vic in this early-onset disorientation case. Lars said that the one guy, Herman, smelled funny and she's wondering if there is anything in common between the two."

"Sounds like a stretch," Yolanda said, running her hand over her close-cropped black hair.

"Yeah. Lars won't even know what he's looking for."

"Does Lars know how to fish?" Steve called out.

Amy said, "What are you talking about?"

"Fishing is when you want to catch something, but you don't know what you're looking for," Steve added.

"He won't understand fishing without having a goal."

Yolanda shifted in her chair, swiveling around, trying to sit up a bit taller than her five-foot-four-inch body would allow. "Why do they call it fishing I wonder? Real fishing has this goal called fish," she said, making a swimming motion with her hands. "This type of thing is more casting a net and seeing if anything swims into it."

"Fish at least have a smell," Steve said.

"This one probably has a smell, just not one he likes," Amy said.

"What are they looking for?" Yolanda asked.

"Any kind of connection that would suggest something more than two ill employees from the same company."

Steve and Yolanda looked at each other and then back at Amy and said, "Fishing."

CHAPTER 5:

Meeting Lincoln

BETH PULLED up in the grey SUV. Amy opened its back door and said to Lars, "Okay, hop in."

Lars jumped up and went into the crate. He flopped down in that thunking way that was half "I'm getting comfortable" and half "Game on."

Amy got in while Beth told the car about their destination. The car located the address and started off.

Amy, settling in, said, "So tell me about Lincoln."

Turning to face her, Beth answered, "Well, he works in the same facility as Herman doing similar work. A few months ago, he started forgetting things and was having trouble focusing. Small things like what day it was or having to be reminded to go to a meeting. Then suddenly he couldn't remember the details of what he was working on and he went on disability. He's been getting worse; now he has trouble with speaking and writing and communicating with both humans and computers."

"And you think meeting with him is going to help?"

"Well, it couldn't hurt, and then Lars gets to get a sniff too and we'll get Lincoln's data also."

"I feel like we're on a therapy visit."

"Well, you can make it that way if you like."

Amy said, "Thera-visits are so rewarding sometimes. Some people, who won't talk much to a person, will tell a dog anything. They want to touch the dog or cat or rabbit so much. Lars likes the attention, though the hugging and the thumping pats on the head can be a bit much for him."

"The willingness to talk is useful with crime victims, too," Beth said.

They talked about doggy therapy, mountain climbing, flying planes, and what it might be like to skydive until the car pulled up to Lincoln and Laura DeLaVitt's home. It was a well-kept, vintage Spanish-style stucco house with a red tile roof.

As they got out, they met a muscular, college-age man who was digging in a front planting area. He introduced himself as Darin and said he was their son. Amy found the way that he smoothly stood up and, while smiling, shook hands using a powerful but gentle grip more than a little distracting, but she tried her best to focus.

After their greetings, Beth, never one to miss an opportunity to get another perspective, said, "While we're here to talk with your father, Lincoln, I was wondering if you could give us your take on how he's doing?"

Darin's smile faded into a sadder expression. Looking at the ground and shaking his head, he said, "He's nothing at all like he was." Reaching down for a weed that he had just pulled, he clenched it in his fist and continued, "He was brilliant, and talkative, and completely annoying with his incessant curiosity. Mom and I were forever saying, 'Give it a rest, Dad.' Now I regret ever saying that."

"I'm so sorry, Darin," Amy said.

Beth said, "The CDT, sorry, I mean the Center for Disease Tracking, is asking us to investigate further. It's more than a little unusual for two people in the same workplace to come down with early-onset disorientation."

Darin's gaze intensified. "You mean this was caused by something external?"

"No, we mean we don't know but want to look for any data we can find."

"Come on in," said a voice from the front step of the house.

Looking up, Beth said, "You must be Laura. Hi, I'm Detective Beth Hanscom and this is Agent Amy Callahan."

"And this is doggy Lars," Amy added.

Laura was petite. She held the door open and shook their hands as she ushered them in. Laura looked at Lars with concern, so Amy said, "Lars is very friendly and can be very polite when I ask him to be. Lars, can you sit?"

Lars sat, looking expectant. Laura said. "I've had big dogs run me right over, so I'm sorry if I'm a little hesitant."

"He only knocks people over that we ask him to," Amy said, hoping that was going to be taken the right way.

Laura laughed and said, "Okay, big guy. May I pet him?"

"Of course. He likes it best on his neck and sides."

"Not on the head?"

"It's not his favorite, but he's okay about it. A lot of dogs don't like it though."

"Really? I didn't know that." She reached out and tentatively touched his neck. Lars extended his neck and leaned slightly into her touch. Working her way into a full-on petting, she said, "Oh you like that, don't you?" Lars groaned in obvious happiness and leaned into the petting.

"Yes, he does, and he'll let you do that all day."

They stepped up into a bright foyer with surprisingly high ceilings. The oak floor had darker maple or walnut trim around the edges.

Beth, noticing that Lincoln wasn't in the room, said, "We were just asking Darin for his opinion on how his dad was doing. Can you tell us what you're seeing?"

"Well, there's not much to tell. He's not himself, but he seems fine in a way. But he no longer understands his work, which is weird because that was his passion. He's over in the next room watching TV."

They entered a living room with two black leather arm chairs and a rose-colored sofa with beige throw pillows. A red and white hand-woven rug on the floor had a geometric pattern woven with intricate stick-figure symbology. Lincoln, who had been slouching in one of the arm chairs with his leg over the arm, stood up immediately.

Lincoln was of medium height, somewhat thin, with hair just below his ears that was just starting to curl at the ends. He had a boyish appearance with a genuine, open smile.

Reaching out his hand, he said, "How do you do? My name is Lincoln." He shook hands with both Beth and Amy and then knelt down to greet Lars.

"Hello, Lincoln. I'm Detective Beth Hanscom and this is Agent Amy Callahan."

Lincoln looked askance at the titles, so to lighten the mood, Amy added, "And this is Lars."

Lincoln, talking to Lars, said, "Pleased to meet you." Then he turned to the women and motioned to the chairs. "What brings you out on this fine day? Please have a seat."

They sat, with Lars sitting beside Amy's chair.

Laura slipped in and sat on the sofa beside Lincoln.

Amy noticed that, unlike Herman, Lincoln seemed aware of his surroundings and understood that he was meeting someone he hadn't met previously.

Beth asked him if he knew about something that happened yesterday, and he was able to say what year it was. He didn't seem at all like Herman.

Beth said, "Your wife, Laura, tells me that you're having trouble understanding your work."

"Are you a doctor?" he asked, sounding hopeful.

Beth angled her head. "No, but your colleague Herman has similar symptoms, and a coincidence is not very likely."

Lincoln shook his head. "I wish I understood what's going on with Herman. He doesn't even know he's here. He doesn't recognize us, keeps talking about his childhood like he's there."

"Tell me what's going on with you, Lincoln."

Lincoln shrugged, looking at Laura who patted his back in encouragement. "I look at my work and I just don't get it. I remember it used to make sense, but it doesn't anymore. I can read and understand the news, but not my work. My doc says this could be an early onset of disorientation, but I don't feel that disoriented."

"Has anyone you don't know asked you for a thumbprint?"

He frowned. "No, definitely not."

"And no one has threatened you physically?"

He smiled, "I think I'd remember that."

Amy got the sniff-o-meter out and called up the smell that Lars had keyed on.

She held it out to Lars who breathed in deeply.

"Lincoln, is it okay if my dog sniffs at you some?"

"Er, sure. It won't hurt, will it?"

"Not a bit."

She said to Lars mentally, /Could you see if this man, Lincoln, smells like this scent?/

Lars got up and walked over to Lincoln. He took two sniffs and said, /Here./

Amy asked him, /The scents match?/

/Yes./

Amy said to Beth, "We have a match. The smell that was on Herman matches Lincoln."

Laura said, "What?"

Beth said, "Really? Hmmm."

Amy walked over with the meter, held it up to Lincoln, and said, "I'm taking a sample of what Lars is smelling. There appears to be something that both you and Herman were exposed to."

"Really?" Lincoln said, looking a little shocked. "What is it?"

"That's what we have to figure out. Have you noticed anyone following you around? Anyone closer than you would expect?"

"Not really. Darin says he noticed a car nearby that caught his attention, but I didn't notice anything."

"We'll talk to Darin again on the way out. In the meantime, try to have someone with you when you're out and about. I don't want you to be assaulted."

"Laura and Darin have been tailing me around everywhere."

"Good for them," she said, standing up. "We'll be in touch." She gave him her contact information.

They shook hands again and parted ways.

———————

DARIN WAS outside cursing at a plant that he was trying to pull out.

Beth said, "Hi, Darin. One quick question."

Darin stood up, kicking at the uncooperative plant. "Yes, anything before I get violent here. Or can I say that?"

Smiling, Beth said, "Yes, you can say that to plants. Your dad says you noticed a vehicle that seemed to be following you?"

Darin nodded. "Oh heck yeah. We're walking along the street to dinner and this white van cruises by real slow. I'm closest to them, and as soon as I stare at them, they speed up, but after dinner, I saw it parked further up the street. My dad thinks I'm just being paranoid, but it didn't feel right."

"Did you get a look at the people inside?"

He shook his head. "No, it was getting dark."

"Trust your instincts in these cases. It can't hurt to be cautious." She reached out her hand. "Thank you for watching out for him." She gave him the same contact info that she'd given Lincoln.

"Oh no problem, I don't mind spending time around him. Is he in danger?"

"We don't know yet, unfortunately," Beth said.

CHAPTER 6:

———

Exploring Herman and Lincoln's Lab

AMY WAS working on one of their Public Relations articles when her incoming call message light flashed. It was Detective Beth Hanscom again. Amy answered the call and Beth appeared on the screen. "Detective Hanscom, how are you?"

"Hello, Agent Callahan, and please call me Beth," she said, smiling.

"Only if you call me Amy. What can I do for you?" she said, relaxing into her chair. "Oh, if this is sensitive, I can put a headset on."

Beth was looking at something just off the screen. She looked like she was reading. "Don't worry about it. I just got a report that there's been a break-in at Nanology, where Herman and Lincoln worked."

"Uh-oh." Amy brushed back her hair.

"I thought you would find it interesting that someone got in using Herman's thumbprint."

Amy frowned. "I don't have a good feeling about this."

"I didn't think you would. They stole a couple of data units using his thumbprint to release them from their dock."

"Must be some thumb, and I assume that Herman wasn't on another walkabout?"

"Nope. Not one, but two alibis. The break-in happened around 9:00 p.m. Herman was at home watching a paid movie from one of the studios with his wife, and he called one of his kids later."

Seizing on the random detail, Amy asked, "Herman was watching a movie?"

Beth laughed. "I think it was Carolyn doing the actual watching, but she says he was there."

"But somehow I think that's not why you called."

Amy could tell Beth was gesticulating with her hands, even though she couldn't see them. "She gets it in one try! Before I send a team in, I'd like you and Lars to take a sniff around to see if you can find any olfactory correlation, if I'm using my terms correctly. Do you have time?"

Putting on her jacket, Amy said, "You have just saved me from my treatise on interspecies dog–human communication."

"I'm sending you the address."

"We'll be right there."

––––––––––

AMY AND Lars pulled up at Nanology. Like LAI, it was a two-story structure, but larger, with a more guarded appearance. Smaller windows looked out of dark red, stone-like walls. Carefully placed maples stood by the entrance where Beth was waiting.

Inside, they were met by a young, serious-looking woman who had the distracted appearance of someone whose day had been completely rearranged.

Beth showed her ID and shook hands. "You must be Ann. Karen told me you're the IT person who would be meeting us."

Ann smiled and shrugged, rearranging her black hair with one hand. "Yes, I'll be taking you back into the scientists' work area. We will be walking past the labs, but we won't be going in them so we don't have to change clothes or put on coats, masks, or caps—which is a relief."

Beth said, "And while the opportunity to play dress-up would be fun, that's not why we're here."

"And you probably don't have Lars's size anyway," Amy said.

Ann looked down as if she hadn't seen him before. She smiled and said, "No, I think not."

THE LABS were behind full-length glass partitions, and they could see people working inside. Amy had only paid partial attention in her high school chemistry class, so while she could recognize hoods, flasks, beakers, and (after a moment's reflection) pipettes, she wouldn't have been able to say what the overall meaning of it was. They continued past the labs, went around a couple of partitions, and came to a separate area that had Herman's and Lincoln's names on a sign. Each space had a desk, a display, and a couple of old keyboards. Lower down on the floor was a place that had a connection bed where equipment could be docked.

Amy noticed that Ann was carrying a cube of something with her.

Beth said, "So it's my understanding that you had a couple of data units stolen last night."

Ann nodded, showing them the cube. "Yes, this is a similar one. They disengaged them from the dock with Herman's thumbprint."

"Herman, who we know wasn't here. Is there any video?"

"Just on the outside of the building, and they were hooded."

Beth said, "Back up a second. When they're here working what does it look like?"

Ann said "Well, they—either or both—would be at their desks with their tablets or handhelds or whatever they were using. They might be talking or using a stylus or one of those ancient keyboards they're so fond of. Their data is stored on these encrypted data units and we swap them out once a week."

Beth asked, "So the thieves have the data?"

"No, actually they have the encrypted data. The thumbprint will allow the disk to be swapped out, which is what we do in

IT, but to actually decrypt the data there is a second level of authentication."

Amy was wishing they had Harris around to help with the Technese. "Authentication?"

Ann paused, searching the room for another word. "Er, like verification, permission. A second way of checking that this person is really who they say they are."

"So what do they have now?" Amy asked.

"Pretty much nothing. A lot of gibberish," Ann said.

Beth said, "And some angry burglars. Amy, can you have Lars take a sniff?"

Amy put down her bag and removed the sniff-o-meter.

Tapping on the display, she told Lars, holding out the meter, "Two scents this time. One." Lars sniffed in. "And two." He gave a second snort. "Go search."

/Search!/

Lars strode out into the room sniffing the floor and the chairs and on top of the desks. He kept coming back to the places where Herman and Lincoln sat. He said, /Funny smell./

Amy said to Lars, "I know you've smelled that one before, but keep looking for the other smells."

As Lars kept sniffing around, Amy said, "He doesn't appear to be finding a correlation."

Beth said, "Our burglars might have been using different people, but I don't like how this implies lots more people involved."

Lars was checking out Herman's desk again. He was standing in front of the dock for the data unit when he swung his head over to the leg of the desk and then stopped at a spot. /Here./

"Really? He found something on the leg of the desk. Good job, Lars. Cookie and a ball for you later."

Lars jumped up and down, nearly hitting his head on the desk, front feet leaving the ground, hitting the floor, and bouncing up again. /Cookie!/

"Good boy," Amy said. "Come here." She gave him a dog treat. "Wait here."

Beth and Amy bent down to look more closely at the desk leg. Beth looked over her shoulder and asked Ann, "If I were taking out a data unit, would I be kneeling in front of it?"

"Sure, if you'd never done it before."

"And if I lost my balance a little while I was trying to figure it out, I might put my other arm right there," she said, pointing to the place that Lars was indicating. "Amy, can you check if there's any DNA?"

Amy already had her handheld out. "Checking for DNA." She held it over the spot. It had already been programmed to ignore anything left by an overenthusiastic canine. "Yes, there's enough. Taking a sample."

"Excellent."

———

CHAPTER 7:

Herman and Lincoln are Ill

AMY RECEIVED a call that Herman and Lincoln were in the Riverview Hospital, an imposing building further up the river. While there was indeed a view of the river, Amy thought the view was mostly for the family and friends.

Amy was directed up to the pair's private room in Intensive Care and Intervention. They were unconscious. Above each bed was a colorful display showing vital signs like pulse, heart activity, blood pressure, and respiration. There was another graph displaying what the label said was brain activity.

Beth was there with a doctor whose name tag said "Thelms." He was wearing that concerned, professional look.

Amy, who had trained as a basic Med Tech, looked at the display and said, "I'm not a doctor, but that doesn't look good; it looks like a kid with a crayon."

Dr. Thelms said, "We think it's the nanobots."

Amy did a double take. "What? Slow down for me. You mean the very small molecular machines?"

"Yes, there are nanobots in their bloodstream. We tested for them."

"In their bloodstream? How?"

"It's possible someone gave them doped drink or food," he said.

33

Amy gave the doctor a dubious look. "I thought that nano-bots were given one job to do like grow a certain type of tissue or help knit a bone."

"These appear to be creating their own special version of bodily chaos."

Detective Beth said, "I was making a timeline for Herman and Lincoln. Lincoln told me that they were at the tavern watching the Neutrinos win the playoffs."

Amy said, "Sure, everyone watched that game, so?"

"Lincoln told me that someone bought Lincoln and Herman's table drinks, even handed the glasses to them. Lincoln drank some of his and Herman downed his. They're doing further testing, but it's possible those nanobots could be causing the disorientation symptoms. There is previous evidence suggesting that—and," she did something that looked like a *ta-da* motion, "a strange, distinctive, subtle body odor."

Amy looked thoughtful. "That unusual smell that Lars was noting?"

Beth said, "It's likely we won't know for sure, but it is one more bit of information."

Amy looked at the doctor. "And you think doping their drinks was possible?"

Thelms inclined his head. "It's a stretch, but it certainly is possible. All it would take is someone with a small doping pipette."

Amy looked at the display of brain activity. She was looking at something more like an electrical storm rather than what she would expect from someone who was unconscious. She looked directly at Thelms. "How are you treating this?"

"Sedation isn't working very well," he said.

Amy asked, "Gods, what are they doing? The nanobots, that is."

Thelms said, "They are triggering release of adrenalin and other hormones that raise the heart rate, BP, and brain activity."

Amy asked, "What's controlling them?"

"Well, we're not sure, but it could have been initially controlled from outside. We've enabled an electromagnetic field barrier around this area. When the EMF is active, there are no signals in or out. If you notice, your handheld isn't receiving a signal."

Amy glanced down to see an unhappy device. "Yep."

Herman's wife, Carolyn, was there, wiping Herman's forehead with a towel. Then, she would wipe her tears with the other end of the towel. Amy admired her precision under stress. Carolyn asked, "How long can he and Lincoln continue like this?"

"We don't know, we've never seen it before," Thelms answered.

A nurse, whose name tag read "Louise," entered, looked at the displays, and made notes on what Amy presumed was a mobile data chart. Amy thought that was odd since it had to be recorded by a computer, but she figured having someone record it meant someone was actually paying attention rather than just relying on the auto alarm; besides, the barrier probably disabled the feedback to the computer. Herman's blood pressure seemed elevated, but it was not killing him. His heart rate was definitely much higher than resting. His eyes were shut and creased at the corner, and his forehead had that dull-but-shiny look of just-wiped sweat. His head would jerk to the side from time to time. This was a man under stress. She looked over to confirm that Lincoln was going through something similar.

Someone opened the door. "Beth Hanscom, your office wants you to contact them as soon as possible."

"I can call them in a second." Beth got up and said to Amy, "I think I'd like you to come with me."

"Er, okay."

Amy rose and followed Beth out. In the hallway, she picked up her phone and said, "This is Beth." There was a pause as she listened.

"Really? . . . Oh no. That's really not good. . . . And that's even worse. . . . How much time do we have? . . . Oooo. . . . Okay, I'll have them take it down. But we need to meet with the concerned parties to come to some agreement. . . . Tell them we're taking it down and considering their offer."

Amy, who had been watching the news monitor, turned quickly to look at Beth.

Beth hung up. She inhaled and let out a long breath through pursed lips. "Wait here one moment."

Beth hurried down the hall and Amy could hear her telling the staff to please disengage the EMF shield and, yes, that she was sure.

Amy reentered Herman and Lincoln's room.

Beth came back in holding a second device. "As you may have guessed, my commander has heard from our bad guys. Without outside control, the nanobots are programmed to overwork the brain circuitry until it dies. Herman and Lincoln have maybe thirty minutes tops. If we take the control down, the nasty dudes can control the bots better."

"Through hospital walls?"

Beth continued, "I guess. We need to find a way to buy more time and we're not sure how to do it."

"What haven't you told me?" Amy asked, looking directly at Beth.

Beth paused for a moment, inhaling and then exhaling. "Our bad guys have figured out that the data units are encrypted and they want the decryption code. Nanology does not want to give it to them."

Amy, trying to remember what Harris had taught her, said, "Don't the data units have self-destruct options? Can't we just lower the EMF shield and send a nuke signal?"

"Yes, but our bad guys also have what appears to be a basic type of security to block outside control signals."

Amy said, "That's not fair."

"Little is in this shadowy world," Beth said.

Amy looked thoughtful and said, "Can our computer whiz-kid Harris get around it? Too bad there isn't a dummy code."

"He might be able to, but there's not a lot of time. Nanology is checking for something that would give out some information, but not all of it. I'm not even sure if Nanology has the decrypt code. It's possible that only Herman and Lincoln have it."

Amy asked, "'How the heck are we going to find these people?"

"That is the billion-dollar question, isn't it?" Beth said.

CHAPTER 8:

Demands

AN OFFICER walked in and whispered to Beth. She stood up stiffly, phone in hand, and motioned for Amy to follow. Amy thought, *I've been doing a lot of this today.*

Beth said to her phone, "Put them through."

Amy could tell it was an audio-only connection, as Beth put the handheld up to her ear.

Beth looked at the floor, her free arm wrapped around her body, listening and hardly breathing.

Then she sighed and looked up.

"Look, you can't do that to these men, no matter what you want. If they die, you're out of luck. They're both good men, loving husbands and fathers, well-liked members of the community. If you hurt them, you're going to make a lot of people very unhappy and you still won't get what you want."

Amy noticed that during this short monologue Beth had been pressing buttons on her handheld, and she realized that Beth must have been setting up a trace on the phone conversation.

"You want the encryption decodes for the units you have? We can talk about that. I don't have them, but I can ask the people who do. But you have to stop mistreating these men or nothing is going to happen, and we'll be coming after you for murder. . . . Yes, really. Stop with the nanobot attacks and we can talk further. Yes, we know that's what's happening. You need to stop this. Nothing happens until you do."

Beth moved closer to the room where she could see the stricken men through the window.

Amy could see Herman's brain activity readout still looking like a hyperactive child's scribble. Then after a moment it started to settle down. Beth leaned to look at Lincoln's and Amy could see over her shoulder that his had also quieted. Then Beth held up the other gadget she had been holding. Amy hadn't seen anything like it before. She watched Beth push a button on it. Nothing happened except for a quiet beep and a single red light.

Amy could hear the person on the other end of the phone yelling and cursing in a funny voice that must have been disguised. She figured that Beth had turned the electromagnetic field blocking back on.

Beth, the picture of calm, said in an ever-so-slightly elevated voice, "Yes, the signal is now blocked. This is so we can better talk without having them muddling the picture." She paused, listening. "I'm sorry this upsets you, but you still have the devices and we can negotiate over those. No, this isn't bad faith, it's more balancing the playing field and it's the humane thing to do—isn't that what you want?" She paused again and Amy could see her almost smile. "Threatening me will do you no good, I assure you. I will pass on your requests for the encryption codes. Can I reach you at this number? Good. And I do so hate those voice scramblers. You sound silly."

Hanging up, Beth said, "I traced the caller's location. I should have sent you when I was talking, but I wanted another person present." Amy's handheld beeped. "Harris has tracked the signal to where the phone is right now and he sent the coordinates to you. Could you and Lars join Steve and Pearl at that location to see if you can figure out who is on the phone? The phone is still on, but they could turn it off any time. There will be backup present, but I've told them to keep a low profile."

Amy said, "Yes, Lars is waiting in the car."

Amy charged out to her vehicle, jamming the handheld onto the docking station and telling it to go to the location indicated. She added to the car's instructions, "Hurry, LAI code 3, no siren," and the car sped off with lights flashing.

She said to Lars, who was wide awake, "We're going on a Search."

He barked and said the equivalent of: /Hooray./

The phone's location was Quincy Park, only five minutes away. When they got close, Amy put the car into manual mode, turned off the flashing lights, and drove slowly around, looking for anything obvious. The park was near the river and there were other people around. Parking the car, they got out. "Okay, Lars, we're going on a walk."

/Walk!/

"But we have to look casual."

/Huh?/

"Walk slow, and sniff things."

/Oh./

Seeing Steve in the distance, she put the micro-transceiver in her ear.

"Steve, can you hear me?"

Steve's voice in her ear said, "Hey there. Got a few possibilities."

"At least that phone is still on and here somewhere."

CHAPTER 9:

At the Park

QUINCY PARK was one of the smaller ones in the city. It had that broken-in look, with patches of brown pathways and ordinary green grass instead of the supergreen biograss that they had over at the park near Central, but it was still well-kept with some nice mature pine trees and magnolias. It was the middle of the day, and there were people running and walking while others ate their lunches on the benches. A food vendor was doing brisk business over at the entryway, selling wraps that represented a surprisingly wide selection of world cuisines.

Steve was leaning towards the cart. "Mmmm, that tandoori smells great."

Grabbing one of his arms, Amy said, "Catch crooks first, then we feast."

Sighing, Steve turned back. "So, where is this dweeb? . . . Oh, Harris?" He spoke into his headset knowing that Harris was coordinating the search from Central.

Amy heard Harris's response: "Last known position is in the park somewhere."

"You can't be more specific?" Steve asked.

"With your handheld, yes, but not with this cheap-ass disposable stuff the suspect is using."

"Is he on the phone now?"

"No."

"Can you be less helpful?" Steve asked Harris. They had a playful relationship that came out in oddly combative ways.

"Yes," Harris said.

"Oh, shut up."

"Suit yourself."

Amy broke in. "Has that phone moved around much?"

Harris said, "Not from what we can tell."

Amy looked around. "So he's sitting down? Why would he do that?"

Steve said, "Okay, you go to that end of the park and I'll go to the other and we'll work towards the middle."

"And we're looking for people sitting down?"

"Or lying. Maybe he went and got drunk," Steve said.

"Right. Try to be helpful," she replied.

Amy and Lars, walking past the playground and yoga area, got briefly waylaid by children wanting to pet the doggy.

"Yes, he's cute. He's three years old. He's friendly. Likes to say 'Hi,' but he really needs to go on a walk or he's going to become incorrigible." She realized she needed to come up with a better term, but it worked for now and they soon found themselves at the end of the park. Amy asked Lars to walk slowly and sniff around.

"We're at the end of the park. I see two runners, six walkers, five eating lunch. The lunchers are in two groups. One is two women and the other is three people, two men and one woman. The two women are in their thirties, dressed in business pant suits. One navy with a yellow shirt, one black with a white top. Medium build. The three look like they work for a technical firm: T-shirts and jeans or khakis. One of the men is heavyset, but the other two are average size. Each group all seems to work together; the three are talking about baseball, the two are talking about their flakey boyfriends."

Steve said, "Similar over here—mostly the lunchtime crowd, though some walkers. Everyone seems to fit in as much as anyone else. Wait, I see one lone guy just sitting there with a phone in his hand. He has very dark skin with wavy black hair to his shoulders. Medium sturdy, athletic build. Can't tell his height yet. Probably a hundred seventy-five pounds. Wearing a dark blue baseball cap forward—can't see the logo. Sunglasses. White tank top. Nice arms. Old blue jeans. Seems on edge, looking around."

Amy said, "I'm on my way. Look casual. Let's go, Lars." They went back through the park but steered around the playground area, slowing when they could see Steve and Pearl in the distance. Pearl was heavily engaged with sniffing the ground. They got a little closer and then Amy stopped under one of the magnolias to stretch. Lars looked at her with a puzzled look.

Amy said to Lars, /It's okay, I'm just stretching. Relax. Sniff./ Lars's nose hit the ground.

Amy said, "Okay, I see you, Steve, and the suspect."

Steve said, "Moving closer. Slowly."

As Steve came closer, the man spun around on the bench. Steve froze and Amy debated whether to send Lars charging in.

He said to Steve, "Hey, have you seen a blonde guy about five-foot-six wandering around? He's likely in shorts."

"Er, no, sorry," Steve said.

"Well, he's my boyfriend, and I'm not so sure I should be saying that anymore."

"Er."

"What do you do with such people? He's an hour late and it's not like he has a stupid job to go to." He waved his right arm in the air. "He's all like: 'I'm on a break from work right now while I figure out what direction I want in life.' Oh, please, dude. Can you believe this? And does he call to say I'm running late? No, and he's likely not carrying a handheld at all because he wants to be electronically emancipated during this time of reflection. I tell you this is making me reflect a lot myself. Self-involved twit."

Amy said on the line, "Cancel that possible suspect except for possible boyfriend beating."

She could see Steve, who could hear quite well over the headset, cough to cover a laugh.

Steve said back to Tank Top, "Well, maybe he's just tied up somewhere—"

Tank Top replied, "With who, and why wasn't I invited?"

Amy, who had moved closer, could see a helpless look working its way onto Steve's face.

Harris, at Central, said on the headset, "Arrest him, you know he wants it."

The helpless look gained a better hold on Steve's features.

Tank Top said, "I'm sorry I've been bitching at you and there you are just innocently walking your dog." Leaning over, he asked, "And what's your name sweetheart?"

Steve stammered, "P-p-per. Pearl."

"Well, hello there, Pearl, you are a very lucky dog indeed to have a reliable, and I'm sure, punctual man in your life."

Harris said on the line, "I beg to differ on the punctual bit."

Steve, regaining some composure and speech, said back to Tank Top, "I'm sure he's around here somewhere. Does he know how to find you?"

"We meet here all the time. He is not lost, I assure you."

A voice in the headset said, "He's left him for a woman."

Turning her back to them, Amy said into her headset, "Harris! You are not helping."

Harris replied, "Oh, this is all pretty helpless. So Stevo, how are you going to get out of this one? See any blond boys running around?"

Turning back, Amy could see that "I'm hearing things and am trying not to look crazy" sort of look on Steve's face.

Amy noticed Pearl pulling on Steve. *I wonder if he asked her to do that or she's doing it all herself,* she thought.

Steve took a step in the direction that Pearl was pulling. "Well, I hope he appears and this all works out for you all."

"Not likely."

"If I see him, I'll tell him to hurry."

"Thanks. Maybe. And bye, Pearl."

"She says bye."

Steve continued closer to Amy, but before he reached her, he turned and stood beside a tree. In one motion he ripped off his headset and pulled out his handheld, probably so he could speak clearly without anyone thinking he was just another schizophrenic.

"Harris, so help me, you are SO dead."

Harris said, "Can't hear you. Is your headset on?"

"Dead. I'm telling you. Dead. Dead. Dead."

Amy said, "I'm sorry to break into this fine discussion but—"

"I'm not talking to him anymore. He's dead even before I kill him."

Amy cleared her throat. "Referring back to the reason we're here."

"Yes?" said Steve, who was looking pleased about declaring Harris's imminent demise.

"Since it doesn't appear that the suspect is here anymore, I'm going to give Lars and Pearl the scent that I collected at the lab."

"But we don't know if the person who stole the data units and the caller are the same person."

"We don't, but we seem to have hit a dry spot in terms of ideas."

"Why not, we're here anyway. Though let's start on the side of the park away from Tank Top." Steve put his headset back on. "Okay."

Harris back in Central, who had been quiet during this exchange, said, "But you should ask Tank Top for a date first."

"Dead man talking," Steve muttered.

"Hearing voices again?" Amy asked.

"Apparently so."

They walked to the other end of the park, saying hello to the passersby who wanted to greet the dogs.

As they neared the end of the park, they could see a basketball half-court. There were two five-person teams, one with all men, sweaty, partially shirtless and shouting. The other team was coed. There was also an equally enthusiastic audience.

Steve said, "This is hopeless. We're never going to find anything useful here."

"Let's try the sides away from them. This isn't the environment for a threatening call and Beth would have heard this in the background," Amy answered.

Over to one side there were some fairly new, comfortable-looking wooden benches in the shade. The usual complement of pigeons and mourning doves were bustling around looking for lunchtime crumbs, with the occasional robin or crow swooping low at the dogs. Pearl ducked, but Lars started to bounce.

Amy took out her handheld and brought up the scent they got off the data unit. Steve looked dubious in that make-my-day sort of way.

Amy said, "I know it's a complete shot in the dark."

He said, "I'm not sure you have anything to shoot with."

Amy had both dogs take a good sniff and they went right to work, expertly covering the ground in that haphazard-looking pattern that really wasn't haphazard at all. Pearl went off close to the street and Lars stayed more to the inside as they worked their way parallel to the basketball game that, while loud and passionate, was not yet a brawl.

Scenting is slow work, even when you know what you're looking for.

Steve said, "A tandoori chicken wrap is calling to me."

"I can hear it. Lars and I are going to work on the other side while you both continue here," Amy replied.

They had moved a short distance away when Amy glanced up at Steve and Pearl.

She saw Pearl pick up her head as if to move on to another track and then she snapped her head sideways into a magnolia tree trunk.

"Whoa, what's that?" Steve said.

Lars wanted to charge over but Amy said, "Wait, let her work. Let's not muck up the track."

Lars seemed a little put out by this, but blew out a breath hard through his nostrils and hopped up and down in place.

Steve said, "Pearl, is it on the tree?"

Amy resisted yelling: "Duh, ya think?"

"Okay, so Junior Bad Guy put a hand on the trunk of the tree. I'm getting another sample. Now to figure out whose feet belong to it. Amy, could you record the track that Pearl is following?"

"On it," she replied, putting the handheld into record mode.

Pearl's nose was back on the ground. She walked about six feet back in the direction of the basketball court; she turned around and went back to the tree. Then she went in the other direction about ten feet and paused. Lars was starting to whine.

Amy told him, "Patience, enthusiastic one."

He gave another, rather forceful, sigh.

Pearl backed up a step, appearing to vacuum up every molecule she could. Then she took a step forward. Then she stopped and looked up at Steve. "It's okay, honey, just keep trying. I'll make you something special for dinner." This made Lars look pointedly at Amy. "We can talk about that later," she said, scratching the back of his ear. He still kept looking. "You can stare at me all you like, but it's not going to help right now." He went back to sniffing the ground.

Pearl seemed to be considering something, and then she nearly dove forward tracking again. Steve, who had been deliberately lagging behind, had to rush to keep up. She walked quickly with her head moving from side to side, but still going in a straight line right up to a park trash can.

Amy could hear Steve mutter, "A garbage can. Oh, lucky me."

Amy said, "See, Lars, sometimes it's good just to watch and be supportive."

"I heard that," Steve said.

Amy said, "Wasn't talking to you."

But Pearl then continued on, with Steve saying, "Maybe you could do the trash can."

"Maybe not," Amy replied.

Pearl led Steve right to the street and stopped after sniffing in a few small circles.

Amy and Lars had crossed the grass to get closer.

"So he got into his car and flew away?" Amy asked.

Steve said into his headset, "Maybe our dead man in Central can see if there's any video surveillance footage on Steelton Avenue by Quincy Park, cross street Johnson."

"Checking, but it will take a while," Harris said. "What about that trash can?"

"Oh, nothing," Steve said.

"You looked?"

"No, but going back now," he said in that resigned voice.

Steve walked with Pearl back to the trash can, his face scrunched into a trying-not-to-breathe manner. He put on latex gloves, carefully took the top off, and peered into it. "Well, well, well."

He bent from the waist and extended his arm well into the can. When he straightened up, his left hand held what looked like a small, disposable phone. "Ding ding ding. Do I win a prize?"

"Yes, you do," Amy said. "You win the whole can."

Steve dropped the phone into an evidence bag, saying, "I'd like to take the other option."

"Which is?"

"How about the holiday island trip?"

"Nice try."

"Okay, I'm taking the whole bag back and letting the real crime scene investigation people have a look at it while they look for DNA on the phone, which is what we really care about."

Amy said, "Good girl, Pearl. Make him pay up with something yummy."

Lars brightened: /Yummy?/

"Here, have this, and enough, already. Okay?" Amy pulled a treat out of her pocket and gave it to him.

"So why is Yolanda missing all this fun?" Steve asked.

"She's doing another empath dog-and-pony demonstration, where she shows dog-human non-verbal communication without it looking like a circus."

"With Gimli, the corgi, and his matching horse Hal, the Pal?"

"The very same. Hal, the horse, doesn't 'talk' to her, but Corgi Gimli sure does. She claims not to have bought Gimli to match Hal's Palomino coloring, but contends that a corgi-breeder friend convinced her that she had a really, really smart corgi that badly needed a challenging job and just so happened to be that blonde coloring they call red and white."

"Too bad we had to miss it."

"Yeah, I love watching their demos," Amy replied as they got back into their vehicles.

CHAPTER 10:

Investigation Plan

LOOKING AT the large display in the LAI conference room, Harris said, "This is the list of cars that were parked at Quincy Park during the time the caller was there."

They looked at the display, which showed video photos of the cars with a brief description.

Taylor Boxcar 30
Gray
Older 7 letter license—partial—9QHV3 . . .

Galtier Mountaineer
New, Black
License: 12QXH989
Owned by Tom Mayfield
Radiologist and DNA privacy advocate

Fife Robocar 166
Copper
License vanity plate: NOWER2GO
Owned by Rock Capella
Manager at Diamtech

Rincon 2964 Sedan
Dark Blue
License: 13GUJ912
Company Car for Applied Sciences

"Oh, that poor Boxcar," Harris said.

Steve said, "I'll take that slick Mountaineer."

"You would," Amy said. "I kind of like the vintage Robocar."

"Give me my horse," said Yolanda.

Steve started making horse loping sounds on the table.

Catherine Novako, the director of Locate and Investigate, who usually lead these meetings, had turned over the floor to Detective Beth Hanscom.

"Okay, boys and girls, we have DNA on the phone that our caller threw away, and unless we are severely deluded, we have the four possible rides our perp took in front of us. We have immediate owner information on two of them so I'd like us to check them out first. Let's get DNA samples from them if they're willing to offer them."

"Dibs on the Gaultier," Steve said.

Beth smiled. "I'm so sorry, but Dr. Tom Mayfield is a DNA privacy advocate and likely to be extremely sensitive to being asked for a DNA sample. I'm not sending our big, tough guy even if he is gentle."

Steve glowered at Yolanda, who was making "Oh, too bad" faces at him.

Beth said, "I'm going to have Yolanda and Amy double-team Dr. Mayfield, and Steve is going to use his soft touch with Rock."

"Rrrrrrrock," Steve said, punching the air.

"And Harris is going to try to get a line on the owner of the Boxcar and more info on the generic company car."

Steve looked over at Yolanda. "See if you can get a ride in the Mountaineer."

Shaking her head, she growled, "Pfft, you are such a car slut." Looking over at Beth, she added, "Sorry, that was probably inappropriate, but he did deserve it."

Starting to talk with his hands, Steve said, "You know that thing can choose the best route over large boulders, even if said rocks are in a river and rolling around a little."

Yolanda looked at him steadily with her deep brown eyes, as if she was trying to fix him into place. "If I see that, it's the cosmos's message to me to walk."

Continuing to gesticulate, Steve said, "Com'on, you have a horse."

"He has better sense than to go through something like that, unlike some people."

It was actually Amy who said, "Moving right along, and not into the water."

Yolanda said, "Okay, we've got the doctor, and sweetums here," with an underhanded gesture to Steve, "will talk very nicely to Rock."

Beth said, "Thank you. Back to you, Catherine."

Yolanda said in exaggerated sotto voce to Steve, "Maybe you and Rock can have a car programming date using bones and sticks."

"Maybe you should go roll over that Mountaineer."

"I'll leave that to you, honey."

Amy, twenty-two years old and the youngest one in the room, said, "Children!"

CHAPTER 11:

Rock

ON HIS way over, Steve read the report.

Rock Capella drove a copper-colored Fife Robocar. He worked as an administrator at one of the companies near the park. He was five feet nine inches, with brown eyes and black hair that fell just below his ears. During the time of the threatening phone call to Beth, Rock said, he was on his lunch hour, watching his girlfriend play basketball. He was in a hurry coming back from a client appointment, so he parked right beside the park instead of at his work, though it was a timed slot, so he hadn't stayed there long.

Rock had asked if they could meet at a sandwich shop nearby. *Clearly, he's not concerned about being seen talking to LAI,* Steve thought. As Steve walked up with his Labrador, Pearl, a man seated at an outside table matching the photo he was carrying waved.

Steve introduced himself and Pearl, showed his ID, and Steve and Rock shook hands.

"Would you like to get some food?" Rock asked.

Steve sat down at the table. "I don't want to take up your whole lunch hour, I just have a couple of questions." He glanced at his handheld for reference.

"Sure, anything I can do. What happened?"

Steve said, "Someone made a threatening phone call from Quincy Park. We recovered the phone in a particular spot and we're just ruling out people who were parked in the area."

Rock took a bite of sandwich and looked concerned. "A threatening phone call? Yikes. And I was parked in the area?"

"Yes, and we'd like to rule out the obvious people who had nothing to do with it," Steve said, trying to be reassuring.

"Because my saying so doesn't mean enough?" Rock gave him a look that could be taken as an attempt at irony.

"Oh, it means a lot, but law enforcement likes to narrow the field of people they have to look at."

"Rule out how?" Rock had put his sandwich down and was sipping at a soft drink.

Steve took out a small envelope and set it on the table. "We do that by having you rub a piece of test paper inside this envelope between your fingers. It takes a sample of your DNA. There was also DNA left on the phone we found, and we can compare the two samples."

His drink and sandwich apparently forgotten, Rock had a hand on his forehead. "A sample of my DNA? Is that confidential?"

Steve braced himself. This was always the hard part. "It is unless there's a trial, then it might end up in public record."

"For all to see." Rock leaned back in his chair and sighed.

"I'm afraid yes," Steve said.

Rock looked away in contemplation.

Steve looked at Rock more carefully. He had a goatee and beautiful soft lips. His eyes had an open expression, with no heavy brow and no prominent Adam's apple.

Steve was bisexual, and even though he had been monogamously married to a man for ten years before his husband passed away two years ago, he kept his habit of visually admiring both genders. He'd looked at a lot of people, and right now he wasn't sure which he was looking at.

"You're hesitant about a DNA sample," Steve said, not as a question.

"Yep," Rock said, looking down and pushing at his sandwich.

"I'm sorry this is upsetting to you." Steve let that statement hang for a bit, considering. This wasn't a paternity case, nor an inheritance one, so there weren't many reasons left for Rock's reticence. He decided to take a chance. "And I take it there is someone important in your life who doesn't know particular details about your chromosomes?"

Rock shook his head, but it was in agreement. "Yeah, well."

Feeling braver, Steve went on. "Lacking a Y chromosome isn't the end of the world. You haven't killed anyone, and I don't think you're making threatening phone calls anywhere."

Rock smiled ruefully, "She might kill me."

"Or it might just make you more intriguing."

Looking away, Rock said, "I'm really terrified of this."

Steve leaned forward and lowered his voice. "Well, I'll let you in on something. The person we're looking for has a Y chromosome."

Rock looked sharply up at him. "Really?"

"Yes, so since we had this conversation, I don't need a DNA sample from you."

Rock exhaled in relief. "And you won't have to tell anyone?"

"Not yet. But you know there is a catch," Steve smiled. "When we catch the perpetrator, and if it goes to trial, a defense attorney might insist on DNA tests for all those in the investigation."

"Let's hope it doesn't come to that," Rock said.

Steve stood up and indicated that Rock could stay seated, walked around and clamped him on the shoulder. "Let's hope so indeed. Enjoy your sandwich, and consider telling your girlfriend. You might be surprised."

Rock patted Steve's hand. "I'll think about it."

CHAPTER 12:

Sam the Radiologist

AMY, YOLANDA, Lars, and Gimli walked out to the car. Amy opened the back door so that Lars and Gimli could get settled into their respective travel crates. While they had a much larger vehicle that could hold up to six dogs in crates, they chose the smaller van that Yolanda called the two-and-a-half-dog model, referring to the two large crates and a much smaller one that would fit a corgi.

Looking at Gimli's smaller crate, Yolanda said, "Steve keeps saying we should use Chihuahuas since they could sneak into anything."

"Sneaking requires being quiet," Amy replied.

"Details."

Amy closed Lars's crate door and said, "And has a Chihuahua ever talked to a person? I can't think of one."

"Well, there's always someone who claims so, but it's more about 'feed me dinner' and 'I love you' and 'intruder!'"

Getting into the driver's seat, Amy said, "I want to see one in your demos."

Yolanda smiled, giving her a wry look. "A herding demo? Demo what? Chasing cats? Barking at ghosts?"

"Mmm, something like that."

"Dachshunds would be better."

"I've heard of a couple of those working somewhere else."

"Speaking of sneaking, not to diss Harris's fake pigeon, but cats or real birds would work well as surveillance." Yolanda said, "The military has used cats, but I'm sure they won't talk to a person beyond giving them orders."

"*Human. Get thee my dinner,*" Amy said, and took out her handheld, looking over the details. "Our Gaultier Mountaineer owner is Sam Mayfield, radiologist at Anandale Hospital and DNA privacy advocate. He is against automatically collecting DNA from a suspect and published a document on how to control where someone's DNA is left. He's one of those who wipes down drinking glasses while at a restaurant and is careful about who he shakes hands with and what he touches. He recommends that if you sneeze, you wipe down and sanitize your hands, which is great to control spread of disease but seems a touch paranoid."

Yolanda laughed. "Paranoid doesn't even begin cover it. You leave DNA everywhere you touch, and those guidelines were written when our detection tools weren't as good."

Amy continued, "He's active in the Control Your DNA Information movement. It was the movement that stopped the automatic collection of DNA from every person who is born at a local medical facility, and they are the ones who made it possible for you to get back or insist on the destruction of any samples taken from your body. They got DNA included under the privacy act. If you collect DNA, you have to get that person's release unless there is a criminal investigation in progress."

"Or unless you leave it behind in public, which happens all the time," Yolanda said.

"So how are we going to approach him?"

"Not good cop/bad cop," Yolanda said.

"Well that's easy, since we're not strictly cops."

"No good/bad anything?"

"Works for me—should we try the reasonable approach first? That we have this ongoing investigation and we want to eliminate the obvious non-suspects."

Yolanda leaned the side of her head down on a propped-up hand. "That sounds sweet, but you know he's not going to buy it."

"Well, let's just try that first."

"And when that doesn't work?"

"Start with breaking his left little finger?"

Yolanda brightened. "Oooo, start the day off right with a little law-breaking. Off or on camera?"

"On, of course."

"Just for that tour of a jail cell?"

"Be a change in scenery."

Yolanda held up a hand in mock surrender. "Okay, so we act reasonable, but really—then what?"

Tapping the door, Amy said, "I guess we tell him the truth. We can skip him for now, but we might come back with a court order."

Looking out the window, Yolanda said, "Oh, he's going to love that."

"We should have brought Steve to let him try the asking for a date approach."

Laughing, Yolanda said, "Skipping right over that bit about Sam being married to a woman and having kids."

Considering for a second, Amy said, "Yeah, it's better we didn't bring Steve. I'd rather not have any guilt or bloodshed."

Yolanda thought for a second, "Wait, wasn't Steve asked out on a date when he was pretending to be a bad cop?"

Amy laughed. "Yeah, those things can work out entirely differently than you planned. Steve might be buff, but he's really not very scary and he's kind of appealing when he's trying to be."

"Scary? Ha. Big, not so scary bear." Yolanda, still looking introspective, added, "You know, he never did say if he did go on a date with that guy."

The car pulled into the driveway of Anandale Hospital: a remarkably nice-looking, recently built structure with arched, curving lines that drew the eye up and made it look taller than it really was. Green tile highlighted the edges of the windows, and it even had the occasional, simplified, incongruous, almost friendly-looking gargoyle in the eaves.

"Fine, we'll just wing it," Amy said.

"Wait, do we bring the dogs in?"

"Does he like dogs? What did Harris say?"

"He didn't say anything about it."

"Hmmm, usually that means start off without them."

Amy said to Lars and Gimli, "Okay guys, you get to hang here." Amy programmed the car to keep the internal temperature cool. Both Lars and Gimli looked disappointed. "Later we'll go out on that nice grass." Lars laid back down with a pointed *thunk*.

At the desk, they showed their badges and identified themselves to a busy but attentive receptionist. He gave them directions to Radiology and said he'd call down and let them know they were coming.

They headed down the white-tiled hallway with the striped patterns guiding the way to various departments, including Emergency and Intensive Care. Someone had carefully placed larger scenic paintings to give more space to the narrow hallway. In some of the turns of the hallway, a statue of a man or woman appeared in the corner, looking strong yet accessible; they stood with a purposeful, faraway look into a distance that no one else could see, yet somehow managed not to look like any famous dictators of the past.

They entered Radiology, and the person at the desk, wearing a blue hospital scrub shirt and a name tag reading "Alex," greeted them. Amy explained who they were and they both presented their IDs. Alex pressed a button and said, "Hello Sam, the investigators are here now."

"Bring them in," said the disembodied voice.

Alex pushed back from the desk and stood up. "Right this way." They followed him down a smaller, shorter hallway to a door that said, RADIOLOGY: DR. SAM MAYFIELD, M.D.

Alex knocked lightly. The door opened and a trim, tallish man with engaging green eyes, bronze skin, and a mop of short, curly, golden-brown hair extended his hand in greeting. "Hello, please come in." They shook hands and stepped in; Alex took his leave.

Motioning with his arm, Sam said, "Please sit. I don't get a lot of visitors, especially those who are not in a panic about a scan."

Without going into a lot of detail, Amy explained that the cops had received a phone call making monetary demands over some stolen property, that they had traced the source and time to Quincy Park, and that they had found the path of the perpetrator, who had gotten into a car. Video evidence narrowed it down to one of four vehicles, one of which was Sam's Galtier Mountaineer. Seeing Sam's jaw tighten, Amy held up her hand and gave him the best reassuring look she could. "Our hope is to eliminate those who are obviously not involved."

Relaxing just a little, Sam carefully said, "And how are you going to do that?"

Amy took a breath and sent some hopes skyward.

"We found a phone in a trashcan at the scene that was used to make the phone call. It has the caller's DNA on it."

Sam gave a knowing smile. "And you would like a DNA sample to eliminate me?"

Amy said, "Well, ideally, yes, but we are aware of your work on DNA privacy rights, so we know this is delicate."

Leaning back in his chair, he stared at the large monitor with an image of a brain on it.

"Let me ponder this a moment," he said.

Noticing Yolanda looking at the image, he pointed to an area. "You see this white spot? We call them plaques, and they can cause all sorts of erratic symptoms: seizures, memory loss, and other cognitive effects. Fortunately, these days, it's treatable either with stem cells or nanobots."

"That's great news," Yolanda said.

"May I ask you something? How did you figure out the path the person took?"

"One of our dogs followed it."

Sam brightened. "You're the dog people?"

Amy said, "I guess you could call us that—"

Yolanda, completely used to such questions, immediately said, "Yes, that's us."

"I've always wanted to meet them at one of your demos."

Yolanda said, "We have two of them here if you'd like to take a break."

Sam was already on his feet and Amy and Yolanda scrambled to follow.

Back at the car, Yolanda opened the door and introduced Gimli and Lars as she let them out of their crates. Both dogs came right up to a delighted Sam, who petted both of them enthusiastically. "Hi there, puppies." They licked his face in return.

Sam stood back up and Lars leapt out of the car as Yolanda carried little Gimli down.

Sam knelt back down, Lars rubbing his body and thumping his tail against him. Gimli jumped halfway up on his knee and Sam massaged his neck.

"I just lost my lab, Gatsby, so this is very nice," Sam said.

"The dog that found the phone and the trail to the car was a lab named Pearl."

Sam's face brightened. "Oh, what a good dog. Hope she got something good for that."

"I'm sure she got her precious tennis ball and some other goodies."

Looking down at Gimli, he asked, "What does this guy get?"

"He tries to insist on hamburgers and bits of steak, though we sneak veggies in there too; he'll eat anything."

"And this guy?" he said, looking at Lars.

"He's a little pickier, but he has both toys and treats," Amy said.

Sam continued to pet the dogs and chat, and Amy started to get the feeling that he was just stalling. She started considering if an alternative was available.

Sam's phone rang. "Hello?" He paused to listen, then he said, "I'll be right there." He stood up, running his fingers through his hair to try to straighten out some of the wayward curl.

"I need to be getting back. I'm so sorry, but I can't provide a DNA sample." He took a breath before Yolanda could say anything and raised a hand with his index finger halfway pointing up, but with a relaxed hand. "I know it would help things out, but my readers have an expectation of how I would respond. I always say to follow the law, but don't offer anything that isn't specifically required. That they should wait for a court order. I think I should follow my own advice."

While this was happening, Amy had taken out her handheld and asked it for the scent they collected at the park.

/Lars come here,/ she silently said to the kelpie.

Lars wandered over.

/Smell this and tell me if it is a match with your new friend Sam here./

Lars breathed in and started right back over to Sam, wiggling his butt in that "Pet me, Pet me" language that so manipulates humans.

While Sam scratched Lars's butt, Lars bent his neck around to Sam's leg and breathed in deeply enough to make Amy wonder if Sam was going to suspect something was up.

/No,/ he said.

/Thanks Lars. Cookie later./

Amy stood up. "Well, Mr. Mayfield, thank you for your time. Here is our card, please call us if you change your mind. We don't have any further questions for you, but as you know we may have to come back to you with a court order for a DNA sample.

"I understand," Sam said.

They all shook hands and Sam headed back to the hospital.

———————

AS SOON as Sam was out of earshot, Yolanda whirled and asked, "You didn't do something sneaky, did you?"

"Nothing illegal, but Lars says that Sam's scent is not the one we collected off the phone."

"Score!" Yolanda pumped a fist into the air.

Amy put her hands up to the sides of her forehead and ducked her head down. "Ssssh. He'll wonder," but she was grinning. Amy dug out a couple of treats. "Great work, boys," she said, and she gave both enthusiastic dogs treats.

CHAPTER 13:

Discussion of the First Two Cars

HARRIS READ over the reports. "So, after all this careful legwork, we have," he did a drum roll on his desk, "NO DNA SAMPLES."

"Well, mine was close," Steve said.

"Who gave you an LAI license? You think it was close? You don't know. He might have been hiding his DNA for other reasons, like he was just making threatening phone calls."

Steve gave him a harrumph look. "I'm quite sure he is trans. Born woman, switched to male. No Y chromo—aren't we looking for someone with a Y chromosome?"

"Did he tell you that?"

Steve drew in a breath quickly, "Well, no."

Harris had his fingers on his temples, eyes closed in apparent divination.

Steve poked at Harris. "Stop it, you goof."

"And," Harris waved his arm to indicate Yolanda and Amy, "you both have come back saying it's not him because my doggy says so, which may be just fine for you and me, but isn't allowed to stand on its own officially. Dog evidence can justify further investigation, but it can't stand on its own. It needs more rigorous confirmation. You know that."

Yolanda said, "Harris, choir here, stop preaching to us." She folded her hands together in front of her chest, then dropped her hands. "We did the dog thing after he said no multiple times."

Amy said, "Oh, and our radiologist friend doesn't know about the dog sniff bit either, which I'm sure he'd say violates his rights."

"Harris gets to do the next trip," Yolanda said.

Steve and Amy said in unison, "Hear! Hear!"

Catherine, the director of Canine LAI, walked to her doorway and leaned on the jamb, smiling. "How much sweet talking to Detective Hanscom am I going to have to do?"

Steve said, "None, if Harris tracks down car three and finds our caller."

Amy could see Catherine getting her patient look as she put her hands together and said, "Remember that we have to do all the same leg work as everyone else. We can't be perceived as trying to use the dogs as easy short cuts. However, I commend the creativity and possible time savings. We'll move on to the other cars, but keep in mind that we will likely have to revisit this."

CHAPTER 14:

The Third Car, Randall Curtis

DIRECTOR CATHERINE announced during their staff meeting, "We have just heard that the police are already searching for the owner of one of the cars we're looking for in the nanobot data assault and extortion case." A photo of a man appeared. "Randall Curtis owns the gray Taylor Boxcar 30 and is wanted for a robbery of a local tech store. He has fled into the Montague mountains and they've requested us to help track him."

"Yee-haw!" said Steve.

Catherine looked up from her tablet, that she'd been holding with both hands because of its larger size, and stared right at Steve. Pausing ever so slightly, she said, "He is considered armed and dangerous."

"Okay, less yee-haw then," Steve said.

Amy was looking at a photo of a twenty-eight-year-old guy with light auburn hair and a clean-shaven face. His face was angular and his deeply tanned skin had harsh lines, either from exposure or from stress, she couldn't tell which. He had a haunted look.

The description said he was about 160 pounds and was five feet eight inches and in general good health, as far as anyone knew.

THE MONTAGUE Mountains were the lower, less rugged siblings to the Dakors that loomed in the distance: more greenery, lots of trees and ferns, and more forgiving weather, though the sun-facing sides could be rocky.

Randall's last known position was at a small market just outside the mountains. The theory was that he rode a bicycle to one of the trailheads located off the access road. There were three parking areas, so they decided to divide their efforts: one dog starting from each parking area. Amy and Lars were taking the last one in the line. For the search, they were paired with Art, an armed ranger.

Art was lanky five foot ten, with wavy dark brown hair. His face had that open, honest look that smiled easily, while still being slightly weathered from being outside a lot. He had a carefully trimmed beard that look incongruous in an outdoors guy. His look said that he loved the outdoors, but also loved talking about it with people. Amy figured that, essentially, he was a public-facing mountain man with grooming and social skills.

He looked at home in his uniform of khaki, many-pocketed hiking pants, light green short sleeve shirt, and official jacket. His service belt, sporting a radio, flashlight, and gun, seemed bulkier than he was. The gun was the only item that looked out of place. Amy figured he must have been a boy scout as a kid.

The access road climbed very gradually, which made bike access possible, and the trailheads were at a relatively low elevation compared to the mountains above. They were in a dense fir forest with little light seeping through the branches. After they stopped, Amy let Lars out and he scanned the parking lot, sniffing with little result until he moved all the way over to the side.

/Here./

Amy said to Art, "Lars has found what he thinks is the scent. He's already covered most of the parking area, okay if I let him follow the scent?"

Art said, "Sure, let's do it."

Amy said on her handheld, "Central, this is Amy with Art.

Lars has located a viable scent and we're going to let him follow it. Theory is that our quarry ditched the bike somewhere."

"Roger, Amy. Be aware that we can only sort of see you via GPS while you're in the woods."

"Got it. Commencing tracking." To Lars she said, "Go search."

/Search!/ Lars said, and took off along the one available trail, which immediately started to climb up the hillside.

"Slow down, Lars, so we can keep up with you," Amy said. Amy, who was in excellent shape, still had to work to keep up with the long-legged Art.

Where he could, Lars preferred tracking in an S pattern, zig-zagging while continuing in a general direction, but the drop-off of the hillside didn't allow that. Still, he seemed sure of the direction. The trail continued to climb without any switchbacks; the trees grew less thick, there was more sunlight working its way through the branches, and there were some shrubs growing in newly available spots.

As they followed Lars along the path, they broke out of the trees to a hillside nearly empty of trees. After a short time, Lars suddenly turned and started up the rocky slope, which was littered with small pieces of granite and red-brown volcanic rock.

Art said, "Our quarry has been in the trees all this time. Is Lars sure about this?"

Amy said, "Let's mark the spot where we left the trail with a waypoint just in case we need to come back."

Lars stopped. He lifted his head, inhaling deeply, body tensed. Amy was absorbed watching him when she heard a tree-branch-cracking sound. *Wait! There aren't any trees around here!* It seemed like a millisecond later that she heard Art cry out and then start cursing.

She spun around. Art wasn't there.

"Art?"

"Amy!" His voice sounded muffled.

"Art, where are you?"

"Down here."

"Down where?"

"Down in this hole."

Feeling incredibly stupid as she looked around, seeing only a rocky landscape, Amy yelled back, "What hole?"

"Careful!"

Amy reeled in her vision, focusing on the nearer part of the rocky plateau. The grays, browns, and coppers blended in with the sandy soil.

"Art, keep talking."

"I think I'm in a mine shaft."

"You're kidding. Are you okay?"

Amy walked further, taking small steps.

Lars, who had been swiveling his body and head around, suddenly dug his back paws into the soil and charged further up the hill.

Amy, who had been holding the handheld, lifted it and said, "Central, this is Amy. Art has fallen into what we think is a mine shaft. Requesting assistance."

"Copy that—we'll be there."

Amy saw an opening among the stones, with some broken branches. She edged her way closer. She saw what appeared to be fir and pine branches mixed with dirt. Bending down for a closer look, she heard Lars say, /Here, here, here!/

Amy thought, *Great timing Lars, can you hang on a sec?* Right then she heard a distinctive popping that sounded either like an old gasoline car backfiring or gunshots. Suddenly realizing that no cars of that type were around for miles, she spun around from the hole yelling in both voice and brain, "Lars, come! Oh please, come."

The kelpie came charging down the hill, making anguished noises that Amy had never heard from him before. Alarm surged into her mind. "Lars, have you been hit?"

Art was yelling from below, "Amy, don't go up there."

"Hang on, Art. Lars, let me see you." Lars came closer and Amy could see he now had a slight limp on his right front leg.

Looking over his shaking body, Amy found blood on the side of his shoulder. Carefully pulling the fur back, there appeared to be a graze wound from a bullet. *A bullet. A freakin' bullet.* Lars was whining and trembling.

Steadying herself with a lot of effort, willing away the more scary "What ifs" and furious that someone took a shot at her dog, Amy put her hands on the sides of his neck and murmured, "Oh, honey, I'm so sorry, but you're going to be okay. I know it hurts though. I'm going to clean this up." *Who the heck would shoot a dog? A person running for his life I guess,* she thought.

/Man. Scary man./

/I know—it is scary./

/Hurts./

/Yes./

"Central, this is Amy. Lars has been shot, but he's going to be okay." (She realized she was really saying this mostly to herself.) "But we have an active shooter and we're stopping here."

"Roger, we'll let the other units know," came the reply.

Pulling a cloth and some first aid supplies from her pack, she sponged off the blood and put some shielding antiseptic dressing on the wound. "Don't scratch this," she said to him as pointedly as she could manage, "and don't go near that hole either. Lie down here, okay?" Lars appeared happy to lie down.

She looked worriedly up the hill, and then more carefully at the shaft. Amy could see where the pine branches had been laid and covered with debris and then dirt and rocks.

"Someone laid a trap for us, Art. Can you see anything?"

"Not really—my pack came off as I fell. I can't find it and it has my headlamp. Anyway, can you rig a light to shine down here?"

Pulling out her own headlamp, Amy eased closer to the hole on all fours. She usually didn't bring climbing gear as it slowed her down, but she found herself wishing for something she could hammer into the ground to anchor herself to. If they'd had an actual rope she could have possibly set up a pulley system to get Art out, but the crew would bring more appropriate toys for such an endeavor.

Grasping her headlamp in her hand, she switched it on and extended it with her arm.

"Can you see anything?"

"Not quite. Can you shine it further over?"

Amy crawled out just a bit more, extending the beam of the headlamp. Rocks started sliding down the hole.

"Careful, I don't need company."

"Sorry."

"I can see my pack, thanks."

She could hear the sound of crawling and pack rummaging. She worked her way back away from the edge, but not before she sneaked a careful look down the hole. She saw a pit of mostly rock and dirt with the occasional piece of old mill-cut wood which was dusty grey and splintered. The sides were nearly vertical. "Art, are you okay? That was quite a fall. Nearly twenty feet down at a guess."

"It took a while to be able to breathe and I'm banged up, but I'm mostly okay. I don't see a way out of here though. Lots of boulders stacked up here in one direction. The other way appears to go deeper into the ground and is caving in, it looks like."

"Crew is on its way to bail us out of this mess. Art, what is this hole for?"

"It's a shaft of an old mine that's been filled in. It's way dusty. Dirt and sand. Rocky with a lot of old wooden timbers on the ground and some up the sides. I'm not that far down, which implies I'm not that far from the actual mine entrance."

"Would that be a way out?" Amy asked.

"Well it's been filled in with lot of small boulders. Looks like the boulders are more recent, like they used them to close the mine. So yes, that could be the entrance."

Amy glanced up the hill. A short distance away, a wooden opening with stones over much of the entrance seemed to lead into the hill.

"I can see the access you are describing. It's not far, but it's blocked from the outside too. Are you hurt?" She remembered that she has asked that earlier, but it seemed like a good idea to ask again.

"I smashed my left hand up grabbing for something—probably can't climb out on a rope."

"But he can probably move those boulders blocking the entrance," said a voice.

Amy whirled around to see someone she had seen before on a computer display: that auburn hair, that angular face with its harsh lines—and now the beginnings of a beard. He wore a blue flannel shirt that had seen better days, very dusty jeans, and light duty hiking boots.

Lars immediately started towards the man, barking and growling. Belatedly, Amy noticed the handgun he was carrying.

Shit. "Lars. Come!" Amy was caught off guard; she'd never seen Lars threaten a human, but he'd hadn't been hurt by a human before either.

Lars kept advancing, teeth showing, his body hunched down.

"Amy, what's going on?" Art yelled.

"Larson!" The edge in her voice started to lift the pitch of her voice, and she struggled to keep from panicking. Lars paused, appearing to consider the request.

"Come here, now!"

He reluctantly turned back.

"I missed shooting that dog once. I won't again," the man said in a voice that was intended to be confident and matter of fact, but didn't quite sound like it.

"He wasn't trying to hurt you the first time. Just trying to find you."

"Don't want to be found."

"Yeah, I noticed."

"Amy!" Art called up.

"We have company."

"Is his name Randall by any chance?"

"Not telling," said the man.

Art said, "Auburn hair. Five foot eight. 160 pounds. Blue flannel shirt?"

"Well, the blue is starting to go, but I think that's a yes." Amy grabbed Lars's collar and glared at the man.

"And leave my dog alone!" Amy growled.

"I will if he will," the man replied.

"He doesn't want to leave you alone, I must say."

Randall said, "Anyway, I was saying that Art—is that your name?—can move those boulders out of the entryway of the mine and get out eventually."

"He's hurt. Show me where the entrance is, so I can move them for him."

"Well, it's right over there." He pointed with the handgun to the raised section of ground that Amy saw before. It appeared to be partially dug out. As Amy started over, he added, "But you're not going to be doing that."

"What?!"

"You're coming with me."

"No. Why?"

"Because if you don't, I'm going to shoot your dog, and Art, and you, in that order."

Oh gods. I hope those coordinates got through to Central.

Randall smiled. "Consider yourself an official hostage. You are my ticket out of here."

Amy called out, "Art?"

"Best to do what he says, Amy," Art said, obviously trying to sound calming and hopeful as best one could from the bottom of a hole. However, he went on to say, "Randall, if you hurt her, I will slowly kill you myself when I get out of here."

"Fortunately, we will be long gone by that time," Randall grabbed Amy's arm. "Hand me that." He indicated the handheld.

Amy considered for a moment, and then gave it to him. "It won't work for you, it's genetically keyed to me."

"Well, that's just fine with me," he said, smiling as he grasped it. He walked a couple of paces away, set it down on the ground, picked up a large stone, and smashed the stone into the handheld. It caved in very impressively. The handheld was intended to withstand being knocked around and it even floated in water, but it wasn't designed to hold up against being deliberately assaulted. Amy offered a brief prayer of thanks that he didn't carry it someplace else and then destroy it. Central would have this position as the most recently known location so they would be able to find Art and Lars. *Lars*, she thought. She needed to convince the kelpie-cross boy to stay with Art and not to follow her.

"Time for us to go. Tell Hell Hound not to follow us."

"Give me a moment here." She bent down and spoke both aloud and mentally to Lars. "I need to go with this man. Stay here with Art. He needs you." Lars didn't look convinced. Stroking his head and neck and trying to look imploringly into his eyes without being intimidating, she said, "Stay with Art, he needs you to watch for people to come rescue him. Do not follow me." Lars looked unhappy about this, but seemed willing to listen. Amy decided to not tell Lars, "You're hurt moron, you have no business following us. You'll just get killed." Amy sprayed some more anesthetic covering over his shoulder wound and he flinched a little, as if trying not to let on it was still very sore.

RANDALL MOTIONED with his gun. "You are walking in front of me. We're going to be following this trail for a little while. Don't do anything stupid like trying to run, as I won't miss at this close range."

"Whatever you say, Randall." She was grateful that she was getting him away from Art and Lars.

They trudged along the path, heading down the other side of the hill. She walked in front. Just before they got to the bottom, they came to a quietly running stream. Randall tapped her on the shoulder and said, "Turn right."

"Into the stream?"

"Yes."

"But—"

"Shut up and move."

Amy turned down the stream, hopping from rock to boulder to log. Their progress was slow. She realized he was trying to avoid being tracked by the dogs, but a dog paired with a human by a mental connection was tough to fool this way, as they knew to check the embankments when a track suddenly disappeared. She decided now wasn't the time to tell him this. They curved left with the streambed and came to another trail crossing.

"Turn right," he said.

They started to climb the adjacent hill. It was a clever way to switch trails, Amy admitted to herself.

"How many of you dog people are out here?"

Why, so you can shoot at them too? she thought. "A few."

"How many?" His voice grew tenser.

"I don't know. I wasn't the assigner."

"Who else is looking?"

This one she was happy to answer. "There are a lot of people looking for you, Randall, and your picture is on the news by now, too."

"Well, they're going to have to work hard to find me."

They will, Randall, Amy thought. *We don't give up looking. Wonder if the handheld got a clear enough view of the sky to transmit its location, before Randall smashed it?*

They trudged on for what seemed like hours. After some time, she got brave and asked, "So, Randall, why did you hold that store up?"

He walked for a step or two without saying anything, then said, "My mom has vidastock syndrome, and we want to try an experimental treatment that insurance won't pay for."

"The blood disease?" she looked over her shoulder. She could see him nod.

She went on, "It's my understanding that the standard treatment for that is to replace the person's blood with artificial blood, which lets the system have a fresh start."

"We don't want no fake blood," he said with a surprising intensity, and she could hear his foot kick stones out into the air.

Amy said, "But they're having success with it—it could save her life."

"What life would she have?" Randall said.

"Pretty normal, from what I understand—"

Randall grabbed her hair, pulling her back and brandishing the gun, his now-stubbled face very close to hers.

"My mother is not a machine." He spoke between clenched teeth, actually sputtering a little before shoving her forward, hard. "Keep walking."

Amy decided that this was a bad time to try reasoning, and an excellent time to stay very quiet.

"We want to try a radiation-type treatment."

Abandoning her resolve, Amy exclaimed, "What?!"

"They would remove her blood a pint at a time and irradiate it."

"That's crazy, Randall." She instantly regretted her outburst.

She could feel his breath again on her ear. He said in a low, scary, serious tone, "Don't tell me I'm crazy."

"Randall, it could kill her."

"At least she'd be herself."

A dead herself, Amy chose not to say.

Ducking under a tree limb, Amy thought for a moment and asked, "Randall, did someone tell you that artificial blood was bad?"

"Ezekiel William Jebediah says it is not in God's plan. We are to resist becoming machines. Our bodies are the temple of God." Amy held her head in such a way that Randall could not see her rolling her eyes cloudward at the mention of the controversial, self-styled religious leader.

No machines in the temple, I guess, Amy thought as she side-stepped a rock. *And who but this guy calls himself with only first names?*

Amy asked, "Can't you ask the provider of the treatment for help or file a coverage request?"

Randall made a dismissive sound. "Insurance thinks it's a dangerous treatment."

Can't argue with them there, she thought.

"Does, um, Ezekiel know that you robbed a tech store?"

"I robbed more than one, but I didn't tell him."

"So you stole stuff to sell?" Amy figured she might as well make a play at investigation.

"Yeah, small, street-sellable items that haven't been tied to a person yet."

"How about data units?"

"Too big, and not a common thing to buy on the street."

"What about the data on the data units?"

Randall sounded mystified. "What about it?"

"Ever considered selling data?"

"Too abstract. And I have no idea how to sell such a thing. You'd need a whole company to pull that off."

Amy considered this. *He might be playing me, but he sounds sincere. They always do.*

"What do you mean company? Just a group of people, or an actual company?"

"There are companies that have a legit business, but also steal hardware and data to sell, either to the highest bidder or to someone who contracted with them in advance."

"You mean like hackers?" Amy asked, stepping over a series of loose rocks, trying to sound casual, but very intrigued. *Learning something while on the run with a kidnapper, who'd have thunk?*

"More basic than that. Hacking takes a lot of effort these days, so sometimes it's just easier to steal the thing that is holding the data. Go this way," he said, holding a branch for her. Amy thought that was an admirably low-tech approach.

"Do you know the names of these companies?"

Randall paused for a second. "They always seem to have these completely generic, forgettable names. United this, or Allied that, or Strong this. Sometimes they have a bland set of names like law firms do, but that's less common."

AS THEY climbed up a different ridge, the firs grew smaller and more spaced out, and when they reached the top, they could see across to the other hills. On the very next ridge, working their way across, was another two-person team and a dog. The dog was light colored, and after looking carefully Amy could see that one of the people was large, yet moved with a certain grace. It had to be Steve, Pearl the lab, and the much smaller female ranger who was paired with them. She inhaled nervously. Carefully, she resisted calling out to them, though she wanted nothing more.

"Get down!" Randall said, grabbing her arms and pulling her down behind a couple of granite boulders, his fingers clenched and digging into her bicep, nearly breaking the skin.

She tried to pull her arm back. "Ow, ease off."

Randall got back in her face. "Don't argue. Stay down and don't try anything stupid. Don't. Say. Anything." Putting special emphasis on each word, he clenched harder with each word and gesticulated with the pistol in the other hand.

Amy almost said "okay," but caught herself.

"Did they see us?" Randall asked her, glancing just over the rock. His voice was gaining an edge and he was starting to sweat more than he had been when climbing the ridge.

"Naw, they're too far away." Amy leaned back against the rock and tried to think soothing thoughts. *How did I ever get into this situation? Oh, it was me or Lars.* It all made a weird sort of sense then.

Randall glanced back at her and then looked back at the ridge. "But they might have." Amy noticed that his hair was starting to poke out in more directions than it had before.

"No, they didn't see us." She attempted to channel Catherine, their director, at her most calm and convincing.

Randall kept looking over the stone. "I think they're coming this way. They must have seen us."

She worked on her most placating tone of voice. "Randall, there's no way they saw—"

"Shut up." He nearly spit with vehemence and almost panted with nervousness.

"They're coming. They're coming." Now he really was panting. Then he aimed the gun at them.

"Randall, no!" Amy grabbed at his arm and he elbowed her back.

"They can't take me."

"Randall, they don't see you."

"They're coming for me." He aimed the gun again.

"Randall, you can't hit them from this distance."

Randall paused, seeming to consider. Then he bent down, riffling through his pack. Amy was trying to decide whether to worry or not, when he produced a small handgun telescope. It was about the same length or a little longer than the pistol and it looked like one of those high-tech ones that Harris had described to her once. Dread hit her all at once. Handguns were usually not reliably accurate at a distance, but if this was the same type of scope, it could self-calibrate by just sliding it onto the barrel and it could guess at the distance to a target and adjust for that. The accuracy went up tenfold, and now the theoretical threat was shockingly real as he pushed the scope into place.

No more playing along. Amy stood up and grabbed his forearm with both hands. "I can't let you do this. Randall, you haven't killed anyone so far, don't screw this up permanently for yourself."

"Too late," he said with that distant, unreachable look that never turned out well. "Let go."

"No!" She grabbed at the barrel and jerked back, pulling Randall from a crouch over onto his knees. Nearly growling, he struck at her with his left fist, but she was standing. She kept turning her body and the blow glanced off. Randall stood up during the turn and Amy was now between him and the searchers. They paused for a second and Randall resumed taking aim. Realizing that she only had a couple of seconds and regretting being too close for a solid kick, Amy bent down and charged into Randall, hitting him in the belly with something like a tackle.

The gun went off; distantly she could hear the shot ricochet off something, and vaguely hoped it wouldn't hit anyone. Then she realized if she heard a ricochet, the point was probably moot. Their bodies crashed onto the coarse, gravelly scree and started sliding and rolling down the escarpment.

"You crazy bitch! I'm going to kill you."

Amy, who remembered Tom training her that being closer to a gun was better than far away, hung on to him as they continued to roll. Their bodies scraped over the stones, which turned into dirt and then shrubs and more sturdy limbs. Then everything stopped with a *thunk*, and Amy looked up to see that they were semi-entwined in a line of younger pines.

She realized that Randall was still yelling and hoped that the gun was elsewhere.

Full of adrenaline, she tried to scramble to get out of the trees, only vaguely noticing that her body was not quite doing everything she asked it to.

"STOP!" It was Randall's voice.

He still had the gun and was waving it in her general direction.

How the hell did he manage that?

"Get me the fuck out of this tree."

Amy limped over to him, her body only now starting to tell her it really hurt.

Things seemed a little fuzzy and she realized that her left leg was bleeding. She tried to help him up as best she could.

"Tell me why the hell I shouldn't kill you right now."

Amy couldn't think of a response and just shrugged. She just wanted to lie down, and she didn't really care what this crazy-ass guy did.

"Well, you got us down the hill fast, I'll say that much. Get into the trees." Amy started to sink to the ground, but she then hauled herself over to one of the larger trunks before crumpling on her right side.

"I'm not moving anymore."

Randall was rummaging in his pack and was pulling out what appeared to be gauze and tape. Amy stiffened, worrying that he was going to tie her up and leave her bleeding in the woods.

Almost as if reading her thoughts, Randall said, "I should just leave you here, but you're my ticket out of here."

"How, Randall?"

"Because they want you back in one piece, and not with holes in you."

"Yeah, that sounds nice," she said weakly, "though I think I already have something of a hole in me."

He knelt down by her leg, put some water on the gauze and touched the torn skin.

"Ouch!"

"Quiet, it's going to hurt."

"OWWW!"

"Shut up or I put this rag in your mouth and tie it there. Here, yell into this cloth." He tossed her a rag that maybe one day had been clean.

Amy did yell into it.

Then she heard him tearing tape and looked up to see him bandaging her knee with a fresh gauze pad and some cloth tape.

He said, "This is going to soak through, but it will staunch the bleeding and keep it clean."

"Thanks, I think," said Amy. "Hope I'm not lying in poison oak."

"No poison oak here, but plenty of cat claw and other things to scratch you up nicely. I'm going to let you rest here a minute or two and then we have to get going." Amy realized through her brain fog that Randall seemed different than he was at the top of the ridge when he was intent on shooting her friends. She was wondering about that when the fog of the trauma overtook her.

More than a minute or two must have passed when Amy came to. She was outside, and she could feel a breeze. The sky was partially cloudy and peaceful, but she really couldn't remember where she was and all she wanted to do was close her eyes and rest. There was someone lying beside her caressing her side. The other person leaned in further, the stroking intensifying. It must be John, her boyfriend.

"Not now, John, I'm too sore."

"Who's John?"

Suddenly awareness of her situation came flooding in. She was kidnapped in the mountains by an unstable fugitive who smelled of dirt, sweat, and nasty body odor, and not the soap and seawater smell that she associated with John.

"He's my boyfriend."

"I remind you of him?" The voice sounded pleased.

"Only his bad sense of timing is reminding me."

"We could share a moment before we have to move on." The hand was continuing to massage her side. "You do feel nice."

Amy thought of all of the rape defense maneuvers she had been taught and was trying to work up the energy to give a damn enough to do something about it when she heard a hovering sound not far away. Adrenaline shot through her. Opening her eyes fully, she saw it. "Drone!"

Randall rolled quickly, pulling Amy on top of him, his gun pointed at her head. *That must have looked ridiculous with the scope on it*, Amy thought.

Peering out to the open sky she could see a small, black, armed drone about two feet wide hovering there.

"Drop the weapon," a drone voice said.

Drone–gun negotiations never seem to turn out well, Amy thought.

Randall, stiffening predictably, said, "NO!"

Amy, her face frozen in a horrified expression, tried to give the drone a go-away signal, but finally got her mouth working well enough to yell desperately, "Person. Send a person. Please."

"Shut up," Randall said to her.

Amy worked on her pleading look and kept making small waving-away motions with her hands.

She could feel his arm tensing around her neck and she had to focus to breathe.

Then, without any further posturing, the drone flew away. Randall's arm relaxed and she inhaled quickly.

Yanking her to her feet and shoving her forward, he grunted, "Let's go."

"Where?"

"Down the hill. Stay in the trees."

AS THEY moved, Amy could hear a couple of search drones in the distance but they didn't seem to be coming any closer. Randall told her to stop walking often so he could take a look. "I don't think they know where we are, but let's keep moving."

This happened at least three times, though Amy was sore and losing count.

She did notice that the drones could have covered a lot more ground and they weren't coming close, but seemed focused on the area behind them. *What could that mean? Do the searchers really think we're back there? It just doesn't make sense. Unless . . .* Her brain cells felt like they were in a faraway marsh. Amy tried to get an idea of where they were going. Down and they would be walking in a valley soon. They're herding us here, she realized. Oh, this could be bad. She was glad she wasn't facing Randall. *Clueless. I can do clueless right now. That's too easy*, and she stumbled down the incline.

When they hit the bottom of the hillside, they were standing at the edge of a meadow. Randall directed her to walk along the edge of it. "We can get water up here in this stream," he said, pointing to it just a few dozen feet away.

"Stop right there, Randall Curtis," a voice boomed.

Randall grabbed Amy by the arm and dragged her back to him, holding her in front of him, the gun aimed at her head.

"Back off! I will kill her."

"You are surrounded, Randall," said a familiar voice.

Detective Beth Hanscom appeared at the other edge of the meadow.

Amy was terrified, but she had to stifle a laugh—Beth was no outdoors person. Helicopter and even drone use were highly limited in the mountains, so while this drama probably rated helicopter use, Amy got a brief vision of Beth being toted around on the back of someone's horse. The absurdity nearly made her laugh, until she noticed people with rifles on the edges.

"She's not kidding, Randall."

"Shut up," he yelled in her ear. "Do you want to die right now?"

Amy refrained from saying: "No, I'm in no hurry. Take your time."

Randall said, "We need safe passage out of here."

"We can talk about that, but please let Amy go. She hasn't hurt you, and she needs a doctor."

"We need a helicopter out of the area, and cash."

"Okay, but please, I need you to release Amy so we can discuss this."

"No, I love her and she's coming with me."

Dread crept its way into Amy's chest. Trying to think of something to say, she said, "Randall, it's okay. I can help you out, if you let me go."

"No, you can't." The stubble of his jaw scraped against her ear.

Beth said, "Randall, your mother misses you terribly. She wants to see you."

Randall started to weep. "She's not getting better, I can't help her."

"You can't, standing here with a gun on someone, in the middle of the Montagues," Beth said. Amy could see her say something over her shoulder.

Continuing, Beth said, "Amy already has a family here that she loves and wants to go back to. Don't you want that for her, Randall?"

Randall, who was still weeping, said, "Yes." Then he held her tightly and said, "No, she stays with me." His arm tightened on her throat putting pressure on the veins in her neck. The world started to change colors.

"Rrr . . . ran . . . dell," she wheezed. She started to focus inward: *Come to peace. Now. Whatever will be, will be. Peace. Be at peace. I love you John and Mom and Dad and Lars and all my friends.*

One shot cracked the air, throwing Randall's body backwards, his gun firing wide. Thrown to the side, Amy rolled up partially, only to see Randall had a hole where his right eye was. Her vision cleared immediately, and she wished it hadn't.

"WHAT HAVE YOU DONE?" she shouted out. Uniforms were running at her. "What happened? WHY?"

She hurled herself face down. "Why!? He was going to give up."

Hands were on her shoulders. "Amy. Amy. Amy, it's Steve. I'm here."

He rolled her over and she grabbed onto his arm, crying into his shoulder. "Why?"

"I don't know yet. Just hang on to me. We do have his DNA now."

Beating on his shoulder, she said, "I don't care about his flipping DNA."

Steve hugged her. "That's me, master of saying the completely wrong thing."

She sank into him, sobbing and shaking, her tears dampening his shirt, and he sat and rocked her back and forth.

Amy looked up to see Lars dragging Amy's mother, Mary, by a leash that Mary was trying to hang on to.

"Mom!"

Amy, through tears, tried to hug all three of them.

Mary said, "Oh, Amy, honey. You're okay. Thank heaven."

"They shot Randall. They didn't have to."

Mary grabbed Amy's shoulders and shook her a little, then thought better of it and just looked at her. "Amy Callahan, you listen to me. That gun went off. He was starting to pull the trigger when they shot him."

"They don't know that," Amy said to the ground, rocking while still gripping tightly on to first Steve and then Lars.

"Yes, they do," said Steve. "They have a sensor in the rifle sights that can tell when someone's finger is starting to pull."

Trying not to yell, and wiping a tear off her own cheek, Mary said, "Amy, please. I know you're upset and scared, but you need to know that I nearly watched you get shot and killed, and I guarantee you that is every parent's nightmare." Glancing over her shoulder, she noticed a medic right behind her. "I am so happy to be having this conversation with you, but now I want this nice man to have a look at you because your eyes don't look right."

The medic, a guy in his late twenties with an earnest face bent down in front of her. He first asked if she knew the date, and she could remember that it was Saturday but not what day. He then asked if she could subtract seventeen from one hundred. After some thought, she answered eighty-three. Then he asked her to subtract seventeen from that. She told him that would be difficult under normal circumstances, but she was able to figure it out by subtracting ten from eighty-three and then seven from seventy-three, but it took quite a while. She asked him to stop there. Then he shone a light into her eyes and asked her to look up and left and right and then follow his finger with her eyes.

It was harder than she remembered the test being before.

"You have evidence of a concussion."

"Amy, we're going to put you on a stretcher and carry you out. We'll be right here," Steve said.

"But I've come all this way on foot so far."

"And I think you've done quite enough," he said.

"Where's Beth? Who ordered the shot?"

"She's going to talk to you after you've seen a doctor."

"I want to see her now."

"I want you to lie down on this nice stretcher that they brought here for you," Steve said.

"Why did they already have a stretcher?"

Steve said, "Standard procedure, you know that."

"Body bag at the ready?"

"Not for you."

"They knew they were going to kill him," Amy said disconsolately.

"Of course not. Do you know how much inquiry there is going to be over this? Lie down here, Amy," Steve said in his I'm-serious-now voice.

Mary guided and half-pushed her onto the stretcher, with the medic's and Steve's help.

They put a blanket over her and secured her to the stretcher.

They gave her a saline IV and awkwardly strapped the bag in place.

"Okay, Amy, we're going to carry you out to where the helicopter is, and then we're taking you home."

"Lars."

"He's right here," Mary said.

Steve said, "He helped find you."

Mary was trying to keep Lars from jumping up on her chest.

Amy reached out and buried her hand in the furry kelpie.

"I am so happy to see you." Her tears flowed freely now.

He licked her face in return.

LATER, IN the hospital room, Catherine entered, holding a flower vase with a yellow rose, some baby's breath, and a fern. "Hi, Amy. I hope you like these. I wanted to arrange it better, but I also wanted to get in to see you as soon as they would let me."

"Catherine," Amy said flatly.

"How are you doing?"

"I have been better honestly."

"I want you know that I'm putting you on medical leave for three weeks."

"But—"

"And during that time, you're going to be talking to a counselor at length."

"You think there's something wrong with me?"

"You doctors tell me that rest is how you treat a concussion, and to be blunt, this entire experience would screw anyone up, so you need to talk to a professional of your choice."

Amy looked disconsolately at nothing and said, with nearly no animation, "Beth didn't have to kill him."

Catherine inhaled, sighed, and waited a beat. "She told our snipers not to fire unless it was clear he was starting to pull the trigger. The sensors in their scopes can measure when a finger is tightening. Even with that, she tells me she was taking a huge chance, as handgun trigger pressures vary.

"Your mom was there, and she would have killed me herself if you had been shot."

Catherine paused to let that sink in. Amy looked out the window, tears in her eyes. She was so tired of crying.

"Your mom is going to be talking to someone, too. She nearly lost her daughter, and that has her pretty shook, as I'm sure you know."

"Sessions together?"

"It's up to you both, and the therapists. Likely a session or two can be done with you both if it would help, but this is mostly helping you work through being put in this terrible situation."

Belatedly remembering she had forgotten to ask, Amy's head lifted. "Did Art get out okay?"

"Art's fine. The rescue crew found Lars dutifully stationed beside the mine shaft. Art fractured a couple of fingers, and has black, blue, and other colors of bruises, but otherwise, he'll be okay."

Amy sighed. "Glad to hear it, and good boy, Lars."

Catherine put her hand on Amy's arm. "I am so very sorry this happened."

"Yeah, I've had better days. Can Lars come up?"

"He sure can, but he'll have to be escorted so he doesn't unplug you from anything."

Amy laughed. "That he might. I'm glad this isn't life support."

Catherine smiled. "They probably would not have let him come in that case."

Amy sighed. "Survived nearly being shot, but accidentally unplugged by an enthusiastic kelpie."

CHAPTER 15:

Amy Speaks with Charlene
and Then John

ONCE SHE was released from the hospital with her leg and facial cuts bandaged, she sat on the river bank hugging her knees, looking over the river at the park near Central. Lars was checking out the aspen and oak trees for what he considered local news by carefully sniffing the urine on the trunks, and adding his own. Amy ignored him, preferring to watch the dark water slide slowly by, the occasional leaf surfing along to an unknown destiny. A tear was tracking down the side of her cheek, and she suddenly sniffed and wiped her face. As she continued her vigil, the tear would reappear. She could feel an emotional edge she wasn't familiar with—that teetering on a precipice where she didn't know the other side. Could it be more pain? Fear? Insanity? or just a deep darkness that she wouldn't be able to escape? She considered the edge, but just watched it. She didn't have the energy to look closer, much less to consider crossing it.

Amy had been around death before. Sometimes their searches ended with a lifeless body, but she had never had someone killed while holding her. Even though he was threatening her life, and Beth and others said he was in the process of pulling the trigger of the gun at her head, she felt like some of her life energy went with Randall when he died. The bond that Randall said they shared was completely his invention, but his being shot while touching her and feeling his body jerk, twisting back lifeless, robbed her of something that she couldn't identity.

Something brushed her side and she started, realizing that it was Lars rubbing up against her, shoving his head under one of her arms until she gave in and petted him. He looked up at her with a concerned expression on his face. She had never considered the kelpie boy to be that emotionally deep, but this experience was impacting him as well.

Lars looked up and woo-wooed in greeting. Amy glanced up and saw her long-time friend Charlene approaching. Charlene sat down next to her and said, "You look like you need a beer."

Shaking her head and trying to smile while looking back out over the river, Amy said, "Yes, but right now, if I started with one beer, I'd never stop."

Putting her hand on Amy's shoulder, Charlene said, "I could probably stop you, but I can't stop how much this whole thing sucks for you."

Amy leaned into her. "Oh gods, Char, this has been so awful—and I didn't even know the guy."

Charlene hugged her. "Trite as it sounds, I'm here for you."

Speaking to the ground, Amy said, "That's what the counselor says."

Tightening the hug, Charlene said, "Yeah, but I'm here longer than fifty minutes."

Amy laughed and started to cry again. Charlene rubbed her back. "I know you don't want to hear this: you will get through this, but it's going to hurt for a while."

Still talking to the ground, Amy said, "They're offering me medication. I feel like a loser if I take it."

"Oh, Amy." Charlene shook her a little, laughing. "No one is requiring you to be in horrible pain. Consider taking it for a little while. I took meds for a while after my dad died."

Looking back over at her, Amy asked, "Did they help?"

Inhaling and doing a partial nod, the ghost of a painful memory crossing her face, Charlene said, "Some yes, it took the edge off and got me out of this crazy blaming-myself cycle, as if I could save him from a terminal disease."

"You mean you couldn't?" Amy asked with that same half-smile.

Charlene punched her lightly in the arm. "No, that was your job. Superwoman."

Amy made an exasperated noise like "pfffbt" and held up her hand, flicking her fingers outward.

They sat and just watched the river for a while.

AMY WALKED into John's place using her keycode. He slouched on the sofa watching football on TV and drinking a beer. Amy thought it was a little out of character, because he wasn't a rabid football fan, but then again, he did watch it occasionally. Then she noticed that the beer was a cheap domestic one, which was completely strange. She looked more carefully at him. He was sunk halfway down on the sofa with one leg up on the arm, almost half-lying on it. His brow was lower than usual and his lips had a pouty expression that she'd seen before when there was something on his mind.

Amy went into the kitchen and got herself a glass of water. She returned and waited for a commercial break, then switched the TV off. He started, surprised, as if he was in a completely different place in his mind. Sitting down on the sofa, arm propped on the back and facing him, she asked, "Do you want to talk about it?"

He replied, "I don't know what to talk about, it's not like I can change anything."

"You can still talk about how you feel."

Speaking out to the TV he said, "Powerless, impotent, you name it. The great LAI agent nearly gets shot and killed by some jackass, and I'm not even allowed to be there."

"Well it's not like they invite the public to hostage situations."

"You mother was there."

"My mother can move mountains with the strings she can pull, and she very nearly regretted being there. Besides you would have just tried to kick Randall's ass."

"You bet I would."

"Which probably doesn't make for good negotiations."

John grabbed her hand, staring at it while he spoke. "You could have been just as dead regardless."

Amy stroked his curly hair that was sticking out sideways. On good days, their hair was similar. On days like this, his more resembled a shaken mop. He did have a point, she thought.

His eyes were moist as he stroked her hand. "Do you really need to do this LAI stuff? Seems far away from studying psychology."

"There are similarities, and it's not like I get kidnapped every day."

"Once was plenty."

"Yeah, but—"

Suddenly he was looking directly at her. "Amy, you could have died out there."

She took a breath, centering herself. "Aside from crazy kidnappers, I love the work. I love the job. Who else gets to run around with their dog, finding people and getting paid for it?"

John started to make a noise in his throat. Amy put a hand on his shoulder. Tapping his head, she said, "And they're paying for my schooling, which if I finish, means I can do something else."

John looked unconvinced, but slightly mollified.

Leaning into him, she said, "Could you hold me?"

He pulled her close to him and put both arms around her. She relaxed, put her head on his chest, and sighed. "There's something about the kidnapping that I haven't told you yet, as I haven't really figured out what it means to me."

She could feel him shift some, but he kept holding her. "Go on," he said. She thought he was trying not to sound worried.

"After I had shoved us both down a hill to keep him from shooting at Steve and the officer, I got the concussion and was feeling pretty fuzzy. We were lying there resting after running and stumbling for cover." She paused considering then decided to just say it. "He was starting to come on to me."

John sat right up, nearly dumping her off the sofa. "Rape! What the fff—"

Amy grabbed both his arms. "Wait! He didn't."

"Because you kicked his nuts in?"

"I wish. No, a search drone showed up. I was lucky—I don't think I would have been able to stop him because I was feeling pretty awful."

John kneeled in front of her and hugged her tightly. "Oh babe, I want to kill him myself all over again."

She blinked back tears, laughed a little, and relaxed into his arms. "John, that's so weirdly sweet of you." Then she took a breath and started to cry for real as John stroked her head. Her body shook with pent-up tension, as if trying to throw the past few days off.

They rocked together for a few minutes. "I know we don't always agree on things, John, but I do love you."

These kinds of things seemed to leave John at a loss for words, but he gamely said, "Me, too."

CHAPTER 16:

The Fourth Car

AMY CAME charging into the LAI office.

Steve looked up, startled. "Amy. What the hell? You're on leave."

"Who owned the fourth car?" she said, flopping onto her chair.

"What fourth car? And get out of here," Steve said, trying to go back to what he was working on, but he kept looking back to her.

"Herman and Lincoln's case."

"Oh, the stolen data unit case?"

"Yes, unless you have a second Herman and Lincoln."

"What about it?"

"The car, who owned the fourth car?"

Steve turned around and looked at her. "Amy, really, you need to go relax and chill out. Why couldn't you just message me?"

"I will if you will humor me, and this way you can't ignore me."

Steve sighed. "You promise you will go away?"

"I swear I won't be in your sight for a long time."

Steve tapped out a request on his computer, then mumbled into his headset and peered at the screen.

"It's completely boring, why did you make a special trip?"

Amy got out of her chair, walked over to his desk, and poked him in the ribs, trying to read past him. He held her back. "Hang on, I'll read it to you. It was a company car that had just done a delivery in the area. We verified and the driver was on a break."

Amy was nearly standing up with impatience. "The company. What was the company?"

Steve looked closer. "Applied Sciences."

"Randall talked about fence companies that had generic names like United, Allied, or Applied."

Looking concerned, Steve put a hand on her shoulder when she mentioned the dead kidnapper's name. "Amy, I think you're getting worked up about this for no reason. We checked into it."

"How much? What if it's a company with a legit front to cover up that their main business is selling stolen data?"

He turned to face her. "What if you got too much sun on your mountain sojourn?"

Breaking his gaze, she said, "Stop it, I'm being serious."

"I am too, Amy."

"What do we know about Applied Sciences?"

Steve, with that "I give up" look, called out, "Harris, what did we learn about Applied Sciences?"

"The company doing a delivery?"

"Yes, our little sunstroke victim here is just dying to know," Steve said, trying to provoke a reaction.

Amy pushed at him with both hands. "Seems like your sensitivity only goes so far."

Crossing his arms, he said, "It runs out with my patience with impulsive people who don't listen to advice."

Harris read from his screen.

Allied Sciences Solutions
Turn-key Build-in-place Laboratory Solutions
Science Delivered

When silence greeted him, Harris went on to say, "What they mean is basically a lab-in-a-box with builders, too."

Turning back to her, Steve said, "Happy?"

Amy said, after a pause, "No. Can we put them under surveillance?"

Steve threw up a hand. "And look for what?"

"Stolen data units."

"Sure, they'll be right in front in the display window."

"We have the scent of the person that took them. Maybe we could wander around there."

"Maybe we could do something more useful with our time."

Amy said, "It's the fourth car; we've eliminated the other ones."

"I think we might have missed something," Steve said in a serious, placating tone.

"I think we should check into this more thoroughly."

"I think you should go surfing with John."

"I think I will, but think about this."

"Okay, Amy, go away now."

Giving him a brief hug, she said, "Bye for now."

"Bye, bye, Amy."

CHAPTER 17:

———————

Amy Considers the Fourth Driver

AMY SAT on her board just past the break zone of the waves, looking out at the immense ocean and feeling a peace from it—her smallness in complete contrast with its enormity. It would be relatively easy for it to throw her onto the rocks without even noticing, yet it seemed quite happy to let her perch on its top, much like the oxpecker birds that ride around on top of rhinos.

John had just caught a wave and was headed in, but she didn't feel any urgency to stand up amongst the whitewater-edged swells right now. Partly because it took quite a bit of duck-diving through the breakers to get out and she was a little tired, and also because she was trying to get used to the fish shortboard, which was a present from John. She had mentioned that she was interested in transitioning from her old, reliable, stable, nine-foot longboard to something that could play in the surf more, turn quicker, and be able to handle steeper waves. John told her that the seven-foot fish was a good transition board. It didn't even look like a surfboard really; while it had a pointy front tip, it was fairly wide and at the tail end had a horizontal V cut inward. It was sort of like a fish, but not really in her mind. Maybe if she had a fish eye stenciled on its blue-green with pink highlights, it might work.

So she sat drifting just past the lineup of the other surfers, looking out towards the horizon at the approaching lumps that would become sets of surfable waves. The swells rolled under her, turning into pounding whitewater as they approached the shore.

The sun gazed through the light clouds over the ocean. A pelican and a couple of cormorants searched for fish nearby over the greenish-blue, almost brown seawater, floating on the air and then diving steeply down, aiming for what they thought was a fish—the cormorants disappearing for so long that one would think they had drowned. Off on the horizon, in that fuzzy grey-blue area where it's difficult to tell the water from the air, a massive migrating flock of shearwaters flapped southward, undulating like an on-sea ribbon.

She was trying not to think about work and instead just enjoy the downtime, but she couldn't stop thinking about that fourth driver in the Allied company car. Was it possible that the lab-in-a-box people were more than that, and how could she find out—legally and safely? She didn't want to take any further risks. It was only now sinking in that her kidnapper, Randall, really was going to kill her (and likely himself, too, if others hadn't done it for him). She really had no idea how he managed to change from seeing her as a hostage to something to love or lust for. That day was mostly a fuzzy blur.

Amy's thoughts wandered to that holy-man wannabe, Ezekiel William Jebediah, and the peace she had felt disappeared. She struck at the water with a violent splash, then laid face-down on her board, her forehead on her crossed arm, leaving her legs in the water to keep from completely pitching over. She softly struck at her board with her other fist. Picturing his kindly-appearing eyes and his old-man bearded face did not help at all. *You bastard*, she thought. *This is all your fault. You and your kinda-sorta, messed up, pseudo-religious high-mindedness. You don't even think about the effect of your influence over people. Or maybe you do, and you think you're above it all. You're asking people to give up the quality of their lives, or their actual lives, for you. A lifesaving medical procedure and you say, "Oh no, that's not scriptural." There's blood on your hands, asshole. If it weren't for you, then Randall would be alive today, maybe a little less messed up, and I don't know what his mom is going to do.* Many of the world's religions were polytheistic of varying flavors, but it was the monotheistic ones that always seemed to have the over-the-top leaders. The only-my-way types. Amy groaned. *This is such a waste of my time.*

A higher swell hit the side of her face, jolting her out of her internal rant. She really needed to focus on something else, she thought. Anything but Ezekiel Three-First-Names. She hadn't really realized just how much she blamed him for Randall's death. She usually thought that people made their own choices, but Eze-dude seemed, in her mind, to have abused the power that people accorded him.

Okay, either surf or think of something else. Right. What about that fourth driver? she thought, realizing that thinking about work was probably better than thinking about Ezekiel. *We really haven't ruled out the fourth driver, even though the connection was tenuous at best. We should probably do the exact same thing that we've been doing for everyone else. Ask for a DNA sample as a rule-out.*

A pelican flew by, looking at her with a curious look, and she decided that it was time to do what she came to do. She swam out to rejoin the lineup and catch a wave with her fish board.

She realized that what she loved most about surfing was that, despite how difficult it was to master, when she started to paddle hard to catch the wave, it completely took all of her concentration, the world disappeared, and all she could feel was the raw power of the wave as she joined it. When everything came together and she caught and rode the wave, there was nothing quite like it. Surfing had such a powerful draw despite the fact that, while sitting on her board, she didn't travel to any exotic place, and she didn't see that much except for the horizon, or the bluffs over the beach, or the inside of a wave. It was the power that the ocean wrapped up in one wave—once she felt a short, overwhelming burst of it, all she wanted was to feel it again and again. She had never really used drugs enough to be addicted, but supposed it was a similar experience.

CHAPTER 18:

___

Fourth Car Surveillance

AMY SAT in the van with Yolanda. They had tracked the Applied Sciences car that had been out on a delivery.

Yolanda asked, "So how did you convince Catherine to let you out in the field just after coming off rehabbing from your last in-the-field misadventure?"

Amy looked at her sidelong. "Well, she wouldn't let me do it without you or Steve or a cop."

"So it was my winning personality and charm?" Yolanda said, making a face.

"Yep," Amy said, inclining her head in agreement, and then looked back out the windshield.

"So we're assuming that this guy isn't armed and isn't going to just shoot you the second he gets suspicious?"

"Come on, when was the last time you read about a delivery person shooting someone? It's the other way around."

Yolanda acquiesced and said, "Let's go over this again."

Amy said, "After Mr. or Ms. X gets out to deliver something and goes inside the . . ." She paused to double check the sign. "Durango Research building, Lars and I walk casually up to the car and try to get a scent match. If he or she appears again, we move on and go around the block before coming back to the van. If I get a match, I tell you."

"Okay, and don't try anything fancy. I'm right here watching, but a bit far away to ride in as cavalry," Yolanda said.

"Just a sniff test—really," Amy said.

Yolanda asked her, "What signal do you want to use to get Gimli and me to approach?"

Amy tried to think of something she wouldn't do by accident. Brushing the hair out of her eyes was definitely out, so was scratching her nose, or rubbing her eyes, or petting Lars. "I will put both hands on my ponytail as if I'm going to tie it back even though it already is." She mimed it with her hands behind her head, elbows up in the air, touching the back of her hair on both sides.

"Okay, hop out now, so you can be ready to walk in case—I think it's a he—in case he's fast. He won't notice if you stay behind the van."

Amy got out the back of the surveillance van and had Lars hop down to the pavement. Peering around the door, she saw the delivery guy exit out the driver's door in his white and blue, short-sleeve, button-up shirt, dark blue pants, and those sturdy but ready-for-action, flexible, low-cut work shoes with that stick-on-anything sole. "A 'he' indeed," she said more as a microphone check than anything. She couldn't make out the title on his shirt, but assumed that it matched the Applied Sciences that was stenciled on the white van.

He was carrying a box that was just past his shoulder width, and she watched him close the door using the box. Amy exhaled, pursing her lips as she was really hoping he would touch the door. Without that, getting a DNA sample was going to be harder.

"Mic check back to you," Yolanda said into the small transmitter that she had just put in her ear.

"Loud and clear. He didn't touch the van with his hand, so I don't know how this is going to go."

"Good hunting," Yolanda said, with that old expression that Harris loved using; it was rubbing off on all of them.

As the delivery person got further away and closer to the building, Amy gave Lars the scent from the sniff-o-meter and started towards the van in as casual a way as she could manufacture. "In motion," she said into the mic, which she thought was a completely redundant thing to say, but good for reference later in the recording.

The delivery vehicle was parked in that haphazard way that seemed universal to the species. She realized that she had to pull this off in full view of Durango Research and was hoping they were completely absorbed in their work. Fortunately, the driver's side wasn't facing the building. Lars didn't particularly like being on-leash while working and was pulling her around some as he wove back and forth, air-scenting. As they walked up to the side of the vehicle, Amy told Lars, /Sniff here./

Lars, who had been looking in the other direction, walked up and started sniffing the ground around it. He looked interested, but wasn't jumping up and down with excitement. /Sniff the door,/ she said, which she knew she didn't have to tell him, but she wanted to feel useful. Lars had his nose all over the door, but while he was clearly interested, he wasn't signaling a match. "Delivery dude has left the building." Yolanda said in her ear. Amy started to walk in the other direction pulling some on Lars's leash. "Search inconclusive, moving on. Let's go, Lars." She regretted that they hadn't had a chance to go over the van in more detail, but another day.

Amy had gotten about twenty feet away when she heard a voice call out excitedly: "Hey is that a kelpie?" *Ah crud! Look as normal as you can,* Amy told herself, and she said into the mic, "Complications, but don't panic." Turning around, she saw the delivery guy walking up to her with that delighted expression that dog people get when they want to meet a dog. "Yes, he's kelpie with some shepherd." The delivery guy bent down, hands outstretched in what humans and other primates consider to be a welcoming gesture and that dogs over time have tried to adjust to.

Lars charged up to him, dragging Amy along and saying, /Here. Here Here./

Really? Oh shit, this is our guy, she thought, *and I can't tell Yolanda right now.* Lars loved finding the people he was looking for and started wiggling and bouncing up and down. The delivery guy returned the enthusiasm rubbing his head and body.

Breathe, Amy thought.

She said to him, "My dog wants what you had for lunch."

"Boingo's Tacos."

"On 4th Street?"

"Yep, the best carne asada tacos in town."

"I think he would agree."

"I'm Mitch," he said, extending his hand upward to her.

Err, she thought. Amy reached forward, clasping his hand and said, "Marie," resorting to her middle name.

"And what's your name?" he said directly to Lars.

Amy realized that she never had thought of an alias for Lars. Oops. "Right now, his name is Wiggles."

"Hello, Mr. Wiggles," Mitch said, while standing up and starting to scratch the very happy kelpie boy's butt.

Amy was a little panicked that she hadn't come up with a cover story, but realized that when you're walking a dog, you're just walking the dog and normally don't need to justify it at all. With any luck she could just wait this out and move on.

"So you must live in the area?"

Boomerang. She remembered the advice: tell as close to the truth as is safe, but dodge important stuff.

"Naw, I'm a student over at the university. Mr. Wiggles here came along for the ride and wanted a walk."

Mitch was now scratching Lars's ears, and Lars's eyes were half-shut in bliss. "We were on the way over to the park to play ball before he got distracted by the smell of a taco." She said to Lars, /Hello Lars? Ball. Let's go play ball./

Lars ears lifted some, but he was still enjoying his head rub and didn't otherwise react.

Amy said to Lars, /You're kidding. Is this the first time ever that you don't want to play ball?/

"Well, Marie, I'm in this area a lot if you ever want to hit Boingo's. You look familiar, are you in this area much?"

102

"You need to hit the road, woman," Yolanda said into her ear.

Amy put her hands on her ponytail, but she was well used to such dodges. "I may well see you there, but I must tell you that I'll likely be there with my boyfriend."

"He's a lucky guy, as well as Wiggles here. So do you ever go to the parks?"

Amy laughed genuinely. "We're regulars at every park."

She again said to Lars, /Lars. Ball. Let's go play ball./

Lars leaped up as if he'd never heard her the first time and started pulling on the leash. "Thank you, Mitch, you're very kind, and now Wiggles is insisting on his game of fetch."

"See you," Mitch said and got into his van. "Does he ever play with a golden lab in the parks?"

Amy winced internally, but decided it wasn't worth correcting him by saying: *yellow lab*. She also decided a well–placed lie would throw him off.

"Every dog has a lab friend, but his is a chocolate lab."

"Oh, you mean the brown ones?"

"Yeah. See you, Mitch." To Lars she said, /Let's go,/ and Lars pulled on the leash.

Mitch again said, "See you," waved, and started the van.

Yolanda and Gimli were out of the van and heading towards them.

Amy nearly ran up to her, and excitedly said, "Yolanda! He's our guy. Do you have him on video?"

"Who do you think I am, an amateur? Of course, I have him on video. Awesome news, by the way, though that was close."

"I promised Lars a game of fetch. Up for a ball break?"

"We're walking away from this? I guess that makes sense, we know where he works. Walk with me back to the van, so can I relay this back to Central and they can get a full ID," Yolanda said.

A horn blew, and they nearly dove to the ground before they saw that it was Mitch waving at them as he drove away.

CHAPTER 19:

———

Discussing Applied's Involvement with Herman

DURING THEIR staff meeting Catherine said, "We have grounds to detain the delivery person who said his name was Mitch, but Beth thinks we can catch the bigger fish by just paying closer attention to Applied Sciences. She's gotten a judge's approval to bug them; now we have to figure out how. We can bug the phones that we know about, but they have a number of throwaway ones that are harder. I think if we had bugs for general conversation in the building that might help us out, too. But the issue is placing them, as there is video surveillance there."

Someone said in a stage whisper, "Cat burglar."

Others joined in. "Cat burglar. Cat burglar."

Yolanda, knowing what they were getting at, smiled and let it go on for a bit. Finally, she said, "And how might our wee, thumbless, corgi burglar be able to place a bug? Do we tape it to his nose? And he hates it when you call him a cat."

Steve put a small sticky note on his nose and started poking at Harris with his nose. Harris grabbed the note, shoved back on Steve's shoulder, and pretended to read the note. "It says right here that we have new technology that might be able to assist Mr. Gimli with his quest."

Heads tilted, listening. Continuing to pantomime reading, Harris said, "It's not a bug as much as a moth." He fluttered the paper a little, noticed that Amy was making similar fluttering motions with her hand, and tried to ignore her.

"Is this like your spy pigeon?" Yolanda said, referring to one of his ongoing projects.

"No." He paused and the room was silent with that intrigued, disbelieving feeling in the air.

Folding the note into a vague paper airplane, leaning back over to Steve, and holding it near his neck, he said, "The legs of the moth can attach to a special collar that Mr. Gimli, or, what's his tag alias say?"

Yolanda grinned. "Muffin."

He went on, "That 'Muffin' will be wearing. When, ahem, 'Muffy'—"

"He will bite you for that particular nickname, you know," Yolanda said.

"—gets beside the window that we want to bug, you tell him to pause, and then you press a button on the controller and the moth releases and flies to the nearest flat surface and attaches."

Yolanda frowned that special frown that she kept for such occasions. "And, ahem, who presses this button?"

"Mom, of course," Harris said, trying to refrain from ducking.

"And, ahem, where is 'mom' located?"

"Line of sight." This time he did duck as Yolanda threw a small pad of paper at him. The room started to titter.

"Give me a break. Shall I just wave to the camera saying, 'I'm signing autographs right after the show, and come on down?'"

"Well, we'll have to practice to see how we can hide you."

"Me," she said in that flat, *you are a lunatic* way. "Do you have an invisibility cloak in there, too?"

"Yeah, but I lost it."

105

"Harris, is this some sort of whacked invention of yours?"

"No, it's former military." Yolanda kept looking at him. "Really!" he said. Yolanda picked up on the hand fluttering that Amy and the others were making now. Starting to sound a little desperate, Harris said, "Okay, okay, I think I can make this work, but we need to practice some."

Yolanda, shaking her head, said to Harris, "We can practice when you decide to play mom."

"Er, he won't talk to me."

Yolanda looked straight at him, one hand open, palm upward, gesturing at him. "And *why* should he talk to you given how much trouble you're signing him up for?"

"But if you have to do the communication with him while I do that moth release, then two of us need to be there, which increases the complexity."

Director Catherine said, "Okay, I think we have enough information right now. I want you both to work on this and see if we can come up with a workable solution."

Harris said, "Thank you," while Yolanda gave him an unimpressed look.

Amy asked, "Has anyone talked to Herman and Lincoln recently?"

Catherine said, "Herman is out of the hospital, after having the nanobots in his system zapped. Lincoln is still there because he has nanobots that assist with his digestion and they need to figure out how to replace them once they zap the hostile ones."

"I'll drop by and see Herman sometime."

Catherine smiled and said, "I think he'd like the opportunity to have a comprehensible conversation with you. We will likely need to talk with both of them further, as we've learned that Nanology is a client of Applied Sciences."

Harris said, "No surprise there, they probably delivered the original data units."

Catherine said, "And now Nanology has to decide how much they want the disks back. They know they will be sold, but they are of questionable worth encrypted. Nanology, of course, wants to stop working with Applied Sciences, but we don't want them to be tipped off yet, so you all get to go figure out how to place bugs using a corgi."

Harris looked thrilled, Yolanda less so.

CHAPTER 20:

Amy and Beth Speak with Herman and Lincoln

AMY STEPPED out of the car and into Quincy Park. She said to Lars as she let him out, "Well, here we are again." The air was heavy with blooming jasmine and honeysuckle and the sounds of play: children running, playing tag, and calling out, the bounce of a basketball striking asphalt and occasionally the backboard. The kelpie boy barked in excitement. Amy said, "No searching today." He looked like he was physically deflating. "But we have the magic ball." She showed him a tennis ball and he brightened. She didn't tell him that she wasn't going to be throwing the ball very far since he risked plowing into someone; it was more of a distraction.

Beth waved to her from a picnic table that she was standing at. She had a Vinnie Pizza box balanced on her hand. She said, "I did remember to ask if you liked veggie pizza, yes?"

As they walked up, she could breathe the delicious smell of freshly baked dough and cheese. "You certainly did and I assured you that I loved it." Lars came right up to Beth and sat his best sit for her.

Beth said to him, "You'll have to ask your mom."

Amy, laughing, said, "The beggar might get some crust, but he can't have onions, mushrooms, or garlic so it's not worth my having to take the time to edit pizza for him."

"Poor guy." Beth set the box down on the table.

"He loves the crust, don't feel sorry for him."

Beth looked up and said, "And here are our honored guests."

Amy turned to see Herman, his wife Carolyn, Lincoln, and his wife Laura.

Herman looked completely different from the two times she'd seen him before. The first time, she had chased him into a cavern after he'd been beaten up, and he'd sounded completely delirious. The second time he was in the hospital. Now his face had healed and he walked like a healthy man his age should, but the main thing she noticed was his light brown eyes. She had examined his eyes carefully in the past, but now they seemed completely different. They were focused, seeing what was in front of him and not a distant, fuzzy recall of the past. She walked up to him, smiling, and extended her hand.

Taking her hand, he said, "And you must be Agent Amy who found me. Thank you. My memory from that time is hazy, but I do remember an angel who I was calling Mary Jane, though you don't look like Mary Jane at all."

Still holding his hand and his gaze, Amy reached out with her left hand, covering his hand, and said, meaning it, "You are most welcome. It was an honor, and I am so happy to see you doing what I hope is better."

"Much better, thank you."

Amy released his hand and said hello to Carolyn, Lincoln, and Laura. "Beth brought pizza, please have some—and a seat."

Beth said, "There's a cooler there with some drinks, too."

"You thought of everything," Amy said. Beth could be so businesslike, and so hospitable too, probably because it helped with whatever business she was up to, she thought.

Carolyn, who seemed to have her ear to the ground when it came to recent news, said, "We're so sorry to hear about the mess with that young man in the mountains, what was his name?"

"Randall Curtis," Amy said, but she didn't add anything as she wasn't entirely sure how much information Beth had released yet.

"Terrible tragedy," Carolyn said.

"Yes, indeed," Amy said, focusing on her breathing. Just keep it casual, she told herself.

Beth decided to rescue her by asking about Applied Sciences and their involvement with Herman and Lincoln's company, Nanology.

Talking with his slice of pizza, Lincoln said, "They do what's called 'turn-key' laboratory setups. Meaning they'll build a complete lab setup according to a customer's specification. Using them saves us a fair bit of time."

"How much access do they have to your building?"

The pizza slice and his arm extended out sideways. "They have pretty free rein during the day as they need to see where things will fit in and what our workflow is."

"Do they have access to data?"

"No, because that's restricted by thumbprint."

"But they see how you access the data?"

Lincoln looked at Herman, questioningly. Herman said, shrugging, "Sure probably. Since it's thumbprint protected, we never thought too much about hiding the process."

Beth nodded.

Lincoln swallowed and put down what was left of his slice and, after a pause, said, "You think Applied did the theft?"

Amy recognized what she had learned was a cagey look on Beth's face. "Applied Sciences is being investigated for it, but Nanology has agreed, and I'm hoping you all will also consent, to keep things looking exactly as they did before the theft. I wouldn't normally disclose even this amount of information, but I figured you deserved to hear this much."

"So behave as if none of this had happened?" Lincoln asked. "We do have more stringent security protocols in place now."

Beth said, "As much as you can. We're trying to see where this all leads."

Herman said, "Well, I, for one, really want you to catch the twits that did this to us."

"We certainly hope to. It's not likely to happen again, but do be careful when you're out and about," Beth said.

Lincoln laughed, looking at Herman. "And be careful of accepting drinks from strangers."

"Especially pharmaceutical reps," Herman said.

CHAPTER 21:

Yolanda and Harris
Practice with Gimli

IN THE office, Amy bent down and looked through the lower window to see a corgi crawling through the shrubs. Plopping down on a small patch of dirt, he was looking quite pleased with himself with that open-mouthed grin, his tongue hanging part-way out.

Then two humans burst through the door and ran over to the window, Harris saying, "Did you release it?"

"I just did but I can't see anything," Yolanda said.

Harris crawled over to the window. "Could you have him come closer so I can see his collar?"

Yolanda said, "Gimli, walk up."

The corgi stood up and took a couple of cautious steps, negotiating carefully amongst the branches.

"Okay, stop, and lie down."

He plunked back down.

Harris looked closer. "It's tied up in his fur, can we shave his neck?"

Yolanda made her best appalled look. "And what do you think, Einstein?"

"Err, just a light trim?"

"Maybe you should go find a Chihuahua."

"We keep trying that, but none of them will talk to us—remember?"

"Perhaps if you asked nicely—*en Español*."

"*Se habla* doggy?" Steve said.

"We should try that," Amy said.

"Will you two stop?" Yolanda put her hands over her ears.

"Just trying to be helpful," Steve said. When Yolanda glared at him he said, "Well, maybe not that helpful."

After thinking a second, Yolanda said, "Let's try a wider collar. Okay, Gimli, you can come out."

Gimli got up and exited the bushes while Harris and Yolanda went outside.

Steve looked over at Amy. "You think that's going to work?"

Amy shrugged. "Well, not yet certainly, but they are giving it a better try than we are."

Amy squinted back out the window to see that Yolanda had handed Harris what looked like something you'd find on Leroy the Junkyard Dog, only cut to half of its size. "How is that going to fit on Gimli?"

Harris fiddled with it and handed it back to Yolanda, who put the unwieldy collar around Gimli's neck. Gimli's eyes went wide and he didn't move his head at all. In fact, he didn't move anything, just stood there rigidly. They both stood up, assessing, and shook their heads.

Steve said, "He has no neck, he could be a bouncer at the tavern."

Amy laughed at the image of Gimli clamped onto some drunk's ankle. She said to Steve, "You know, I think we have something that would work better. How about a lab working collar?"

He said, "I might have something in one of the vehicles. I guess this means I have to go on record as showing mercy to the wee doggy." He walked out and spoke to them, then headed off to the car, emerging with a smaller collar, while Yolanda removed the collar from Gimli and he raced off in circles, bouncing and shaking his head.

Poor corgi, Amy thought, smiling and shaking her own head, but she knew he was game for anything as long as he was paid in the proper food, which to him was a burger.

CHAPTER 22:

Amy Does PR

AMY WENT into one of the shared offices and shut the door.

They tended to keep their desks out in the shared area because they worked together intensely, but she needed to get some writing done on an article called "Empath 101" that she and Catherine were coauthoring for *On-Target News*.

Many of the *On-Target* audience were fascinated by the empaths' dogs, but they weren't entirely sure what to think about it. "Talking to dogs?" Absurd, but if someone wanted a loved one found, they called the empaths at LAI first, hedging their bets. Since their belief wasn't actually required for it to work, it wasn't a horrible thing to try.

Others struggled. "What does it mean?" "If true, what happens now?" "Talking to cats? Horses? Mollusks? Fish? Primordial ooze?"

Religious leaders were having a grand time preaching that only man can be the communicator, which resulted in a lot of humor from the marine-life academic community, who had been studying whale and dolphin communication for decades.

Setting that aside, she started to dictate, but hesitated, thinking about her writing style.

On-Target liked things pretty easy, but they also liked actual content. They didn't just want pictures of dogs, they really wanted to know as much as the empaths could tell them. She decided to go with the question-and-answer style that they did a lot of in presentations, but thought an intro would be catchier.

> Vet, Dr. Alice Kimble, says dog empathy all started with getting an actual answer to "Does this hurt?" She says she didn't think much about it at first and assumed that she was just getting lucky with intuition, but, over time, she gained the reputation of being able to figure out right where doggy was sore.

> Then Dr. Kimble hired Dr. Annie Parsons. And when Dr. Parsons saw Dr. Kimble do a correct preliminary diagnosis of a knee injury using a method that required communication with the subject, an amazed Dr. Parsons convinced the normally introverted Dr. Kimble to allow some colleagues investigate it further. That is how Canine Empathy Studies began.

Amy paused the dictation to look it over. She wasn't sure if it was too technical, though she was skipping over that it was a torn knee ligament and the fact that Annie was Amy's grandmother. It was tempting to explain just how much Alice had to stretch to tolerate becoming a minor celebrity. She decided to continue on to the Q and A section and come back to it, though she did want to add a bit about how Alice didn't think much either way about animal communicators, who allegedly had long conversations with dogs, sometimes over electronic communications.

Q. How does it work?

A. We don't really know yet. Certain dogs form a special bond with people and it enables them to communicate nonverbally to some extent.

Q. What do they say?

A. Smart dogs are currently about the intelligence of a three-year-old child and what they say is similar. They first just make sounds that dogs usually make, but they can be taught to say the words that they learn. Obvious ones are Sit, Down, Come, Toy. Then they learn abstractions like Yes, No, Hot, Cold, Hurt, Happy, Good, Bad. Then it can progress from there, depending on what the dog's job is going to be. Location dogs learn how to indicate they found someone: Here or Found. Health Diagnosis dogs are similar, though they can now look for multiple things, so they are often taught the names of things they're sniffing for. Police dogs are taught to silently indicate danger: Caution, Warning, Watch out.

Q. Can you breed them?

A. We haven't been successful yet. Many of our dogs we find at the shelter, though some are purebred too.

Q. Will they learn to talk verbally?

A. They'll probably speak more in dog language, which is a little verbal and a lot of signals, and go to more effort about teaching us how to speak and understand dog better. They lack human lips, so for them to suddenly start talking just like humans do is unlikely. Rover is not going to suddenly start saying the letters P or B, which require putting lips together.

Q. Will they get smarter—as smart as humans?

A. Our experts tell us that they would have to grow much larger brains for that. It will likely be a long time unless someone comes up with an augmentation, but that would likely be for humans first.

The door knocked. Amy turned off the dictation and said, "Come in."

It was Yolanda, who bubbled with excitement, "We are so ready."

"That's a switch from 'You do it first.' So, you're gonna place some moths?"

"We sure are."

Amy inclined her head. "Er, good hunting? Be well, regardless."

Yolanda waved as she turned away. "Ta-ta."

Turning back to her work, Amy sighed, smiling, and shook her head. "Ta."

CHAPTER 23:

Gimli Places the Bugs

ONE EVENING, Yolanda and Gimli drove up to the hill just above Applied Sciences. Powering down the car, she got Gimli out of his crate and fitted the black dog coat on him. It was actually a kevlar vest with a small camera on it that would be able to reach her handheld, which could then relay back to Harris and Amy in Central. She put on his wide collar, complete with a tag that said "Muffin" and a generic message ID, and got out the four bugs they were hoping to place on four particular lower windows. She positioned a communicator in her ear, just so she could use the handheld for other things without having to worry about losing the connection to everyone else. She then said, "Hope I'm not late to the party."

"This is your party," Harris said on the line.

"And we're ready to party," said Steve, who was parked further up the road as a backup.

She had earlier found a spot where the fence didn't make it to the ground since it was on a hill. Gimli could easily get underneath it even with his vest on. She had carefully not parked too close to that spot, but a bit behind it where she could see it and the building below.

"You ready for an adventure, my golden boy?"

/Yes!/ came the answer.

"Okay, you're going to go up to that corner of the fence, go under the fence, and go down the hill to the building. Once you get to the building, you'll go into the bushes and crawl right up to the windows and I'll tell you more then." She realized this was a bit much and she would probably have to talk him through things as he got closer.

/Okay,/ he said with that corgi grin, mouth open, tongue out, panting a little.

"Are we ready?"

"We're good to go on this end, we have a camera feed," Harris said.

"Locked and loaded. You go, corgi cat burglar," said Steve.

"You better not be," she said back to Steve.

"Yep, you're right, no lock, no load."

"Pardon me while The Corgman and I have a pep talk."

She put him on the ground and faced him, knowing this was too much information and that it made her feel better while confusing him; she decided to give it a try anyway.

"Gimli, you're going to be going to four locations at this building. Don't worry about trying to count, I'll talk you through all of them. You are going to be going to the side of the building, then two places here on the back, and then one more on the other side. Each time when I tell you, I want you to go into the bushes beside the window and then stop when I tell you. Then I want you to come back out to the edge of the bushes and we'll move on to the next location."

Gimli's brow furrowed in concentration. Petting the sides of his head, she decided to simplify.

"So for right now, just go to the hole in the fence, go through it, go down the hill and then go where I tell you to go."

She checked the handheld to make sure the sensor in the coat was showing up as a red dot, and she finally let him go, saying, "Good hunting." He gave her a slightly puzzled look and ran off in the direction of the fence.

As she got back in the vehicle, she decided to speak her command audibly and mentally, so that others could keep track of what was going on. "I'm saying Gimli's instructions audibly, so you all can listen in."

"We're getting camera and your audio," Harris said. "Oh, and good hunting to you as well."

"Thanks. I think. Okay, Gimli, you're near the fence. Take a look and see if you see an opening in the fence."

She could see him pause and walk back and forth a couple of times.

"Go a little further down the road."

/Here?/ came the question.

Looking at the video feed from the camera, she said, "Yes, that's it, go under the fence."

She could see him carefully wiggle under the fence. Fortunately, the coat wasn't a problem. Then he started to run down the hill.

Sure enough, a motion sensor light came on. Yolanda immediately said "STOP" to Gimli. He skidded to a stop. "Stand there and sniff the ground for a bit."

His nose plunked to the ground drinking in the fresh sod. /Mmmmm./

The lights went back off. "Walk up, slow."

With obvious effort, he started to walk and not run this time.

"The man loves his job," said a male voice on the line.

Yolanda said back, "Thank you, but don't help right now, boys."

She could still see him working his way to the building and didn't have to watch his red dot just yet. "Gimli, go left." She saw him go right. "No, left." He started back the other way. "Walk up." He continued on to the building, but he was headed directly towards the corner of the building. "Go left. Get out," she said, giving him the command to increase his distance away from what he was circling, hoping that a command to go wider around sheep would work on a building. He moved out in an arching pattern. "Okay, stop." He stopped with all feet planted, but parallel to the building. "Go on," giving him the command to move straight ahead. He started to walk, but was coming in too close again; she said "Get out," and he moved further out. They went through about three more iterations of this and then she said, "Good. Stop. There." He stopped, and to her relief he stopped facing the building, which was sort of what the "There" command was supposed to mean.

Yolanda reminded herself to breathe, then said, "Walk up. Slow." Gimli crept up toward the building. She took a look at the camera feed. "Go into the bushes and get near the window." She was now looking at a close-up of a bush that looked like a tangled jungle. *What if he can't get through this?* she thought. She saw the view change to a less dense view and could almost feel him negotiating his way through the wee forest. Then she was looking at nothing and was just about to ask Harris if something was wrong when she realized she was looking at the window. "Turn your head right if you can." The display showed the window on the left and shrubbery to the right. "Hold still."

Say a prayer to the deity of your choice, she thought as she released the first bug. She saw something flicker on the left of the display, and a moment later, Harris said, "First bug is in place and operational."

Hooray, she thought, exhaling. *Now to get out of this.* "Okay, Gimli, great job, you can come out of the bushes, but stay near them." The display went back to a wander through the jungle and then it cleared. "Come back the way you came." She wasn't sure if that was going to translate, but they got it to mostly work and with effort, she got him back to the back of the building.

The next two bug placements went well too. Now for the last one, where he had to work out of her line of sight.

As he came out from the second bug in the back, she said "Go left," and then "Go left" again when he had cleared the corner. By now he knew the drill and was already walking down the side of the building, according to his red dot. When he got into position again, she said, "Go left into the bushes." She could see

ELLEN CLARY

branches bashing into the camera lens. In what seemed like no time he was at the window and had turned his head. She released the last bug and Harris confirmed that it was in place.

Yes! A knot that was in the back of her neck untied and she said, "Okay, Gimli, come on back." She could see the display start to shift, and then it shifted back. Then it shifted again and returned, the branches shaking and trembling. "What's wrong, Gim?"

/Stuck./

"Don't panic, just try moving backwards and forwards." She realized she hadn't taught him quite those words. Rephrasing, she said, "Back. Now, walk," telling him the words that meant go backwards, go forwards. The leaves got smaller and larger, but didn't move. "Try it again." She saw the same thing.

She anxiously worried that she might need to go to his rescue. At least the bugs were in place, and she could get him to bark, which would justify her trespassing.

/Stuck, grrr./

"Don't panic, Gim, just try small movements."

Then she saw his shoulder on the display. *That's weird,* she thought, *I usually don't see his shoulder, he must be twisting his neck way around.* Then she saw that he was biting and pulling on a branch.

/Rrrrr, rrrrrr./

"Easy, Gim," and just as she said that, she heard the *twack* sound of a branch breaking loose and then the *thud* sound of a corgi body hitting the window. She had just enough time to think: *I didn't know Harris installed a mic on the coat,* when every light went on and alarm horns started blaring a shrill two-toned sound.

"Run!" she said unnecessarily.

/Aaaaaaaaaaaaa,/ he shouted, terrified.

"Gimli!"

/Aaaaaaaaaaaaa./ A part of Yolanda's mind was trying to figure out how he was managing to shout telepathically.

The red dot tracking Gimli was going in a circle.

"GIMLI, COME."

/Aaaaaaaaaaaaa./

She said to anyone who was listening on the mic, "Forget it, he can't hear me. Going old school," as she opened the door.

"Leave the handheld," a voice said.

"Done." She pitched it back into the car and relocked it with her hand.

"GIMLI! GIMLI, COME. Talk to me!"

She heard a popping sound though the alarm. *Shit, no!*

A voice said, "Don't shoot, you idiot, there are houses over there. It's just an animal. Go check the window."

/Owwwww./

/Gimli baby, please come./

/Owwwww./

/What hurts?/

/Side./

A teeny, tiny voice in her head said, *That could be good news.*

/I know it hurts, but come up the hill and I'll fix it./

Looking through the taller fence shrubbery, she could see that he was on the edge of the light. He was crab-walking, with his body bent.

/I know it's hard but I need you to come up the hill./

/Ow./

/You can do it./

She saw him work his way up the hill one agonizing hop at a time. He slid back down a couple of feet. /Come on! Gim, I'll buy you the biggest Gonzo Burger they have./ She crouched down, hoping there weren't cameras. What seemed like inch by inch, the corgi worked his way up the hill. She saw Steve get out of his vehicle, and she motioned for him to wait there.

She ran over to the hole in the fence as he got up to it and nearly dragged him, yanking on a part of the coat that caught on the fence. She picked him up and noticed the remnant of a bullet slug buried in the vest. *Oh, thank Dog.* As she opened the door and threw them both in, she put the vehicle on lockdown. The windows darkened, doors and wheels locked. She could have the vehicle lower itself to the ground but thought it unnecessary.

Turning on the interior light, she pulled off the vest and checked him over. No blood, but she had a very unhappy dog. Doing a quick exam showed that he had no broken skin, but his left ribs were bruised, possibly cracked.

"Status?" a voice, probably Harris, asked.

She realized she hadn't said a thing after getting out of the car yelling.

"Sorry. We're back in the car. He's been shot, but the vest stopped it. He's very sore and unhappy. He might have cracked a rib or two. I'm going to give him a painkiller. He has no other obvious injuries, though he might have a splinter or two in his mouth."

Yolanda gave Gimli a painkiller and stroked him while it took effect, and she watched him relax. The alarm had stopped and she could almost hear voices outside near the building, which meant they were shouting.

She said, "What moron would shoot blindly at something?"

"A paranoid, stressed one maybe," said what had to be Steve.

"I'm so sorry, puppy. This wasn't supposed to happen this way." She offered him some cheese, but he wouldn't eat it, which meant that he really wasn't feeling well. His pulse was elevated, but still in the normal range for a dog—it had taken her forever to learn what a typical dog's heartbeat was supposed to feel like. It was like a human heartbeat, but it would pause briefly whenever the dog breathed. His gums were okay and his breathing was getting less ragged.

Yolanda said, "I really want to come home and get our vet to check him, but I need to have a talk with those goons to see if I can learn more about why they're so hair-triggered. I think he's stabilized, so I'm going to leave him in the vehicle and go have a chat."

"And who is going to go have this chat?" Steve asked.

"Why, the damsel in distress who is missing her dog, of course."

"Ooo, they're in a heap of trouble. How are you going to avoid pulling their fingers off?" Steve said.

"With effort. I have to remember that doggy is not bleeding or they would be."

Making sure he was comfortably resting in his crate, Yolanda took the car out of lockdown and got out, pocketed a leash, and locked the vehicle again, but told it to keep the temperature stable and the air flowing.

She mentally rehearsed: *I am looking for my corgi named Muffin. Have you seen him? He might have come over here. He doesn't always come when called. He's very sweet even when he's being a bad dog. He might have been chasing a cat.* And she tried to temporarily forget that they would have killed her dog had he not had the vest on.

Both Amy and Yolanda's wife, Lydia, had told her that her damsel-in-distress routine was just as good as any hetero or bisexual woman's.

Confidence bolstered, she walked down the road to the front of the building, occasionally calling out, "Muffin! Here, Muffin." She saw the guards still standing around outside with that look of just having been really busy, and now wondering if they should be doing something else. She increased her pace, so she could work some urgency into her voice.

"Excuse me, have you seen a loose dog? A corgi?"

One guard, who was younger with short brown hair, weak chin, and a slight build that looked like it was going to take a few years to fill out the uniform he wore, looked completely startled. "A dog?"

"Yeah, I've been looking for him in the neighborhood and he might have come over here. He's terrible about chasing cats. Have you seen him? He's red and white, kinda blonde colored, and about yea tall." She bent over with her hand about a foot above the ground. "I heard the alarm go off, and I was concerned."

The guard's face started to turn whiter than it was before and he looked desperately at the other, older guard, who filled his uniform a little too well. "Good evening ma'am, we saw an animal, but we couldn't identify it."

The other man started to say "I sh—" and visibly rephrased his sentence "shouted at it, but it ran off before we could get a look at it."

She figured repeating herself wouldn't hurt, and added extra love to her voice. "His name is Muffin and he doesn't always come when called, but he's very sweet and will come to you if you have something good to eat in your hand. He's such an opportunist that way." Yolanda could see the younger man's face was going even whiter; it appeared he was about to pass out. She was rather enjoying this.

The older man said, "Our alarm appears to have been set off by an animal, but we can't be sure it was, what is his name?"

"Muffin."

"We don't know if it was, er, Muffin who set the alarm off."

Yolanda sighed. "That dog! What will I do with him? How could he possibly have set off an alarm? He's only a foot tall."

"Glass break sensors went off."

"He *broke* the glass? He's a corgi."

"No, the glass wasn't broken; the window was probably just struck and shaken."

"Struck and shaken? Isn't that quite a long way from breaking the glass?"

"Well, the owner of the business has the sensor set hypersensitive."

Yolanda looked up at the sign. "Applied Sciences. Isn't that the lab-in-a-box people?"

"Yes, it is."

"They putting gold in these boxes?"

The older guard laughed, "Not that I'm aware of."

"Yet they have it set so that something the size of my dog can set it off. Wow."

"Yeah, they're pretty touchy about it, especially in the past year," the younger man said, and the older man shot him a *Shhhh* look.

"Well, if you find Muffin could you call me? My number is on his tag."

"Will do, ma'am."

"Thank you," and she walked off, occasionally calling, "Muffin! Muffin, here Muffin."

Looking over her shoulder, she noticed that the younger man was grasping the other man's arm not too gently, appearing to ask a demanding question in that "What the hell do we do now?" sort of body language.

"Vengeance is mine, sayeth the damsel," she said to anyone who was listening on the line.

"Remind me never to cross you or your dog," Steve said.

"Consider yourself reminded," as she worked her way back to the car while still calling out for "Muffin." After a few steps she said, "Master Gimli is now going to ER to get checked out more thoroughly."

"What are you going to tell them? They have to report gunshot wounds," asked Harris.

"I was tempted to make something up about a rock, but I don't think that would fly, so I'll probably just tell them the vague truth, but say it's an ongoing investigation and I can't discuss it."

"Best to Gimli; he was a great dog today," said Harris, and Amy and Steve added their best wishes as well.

Yolanda said, "He's a great dog every day, but today he gets whatever junk food he wants when they let him eat."

"Extra-large Bongo Burger with double cheese," said what had to be Steve.

CHAPTER 24:

Harris Looks at the Bug Data

HARRIS GAZED at all the captured bug information, and wanted to run from the room and find a gopher hole he could hide in. It had only been a day and data was piling up. They had four working bugs, all reporting multiple conversations. Who would have thought the "lab-in-a-box" people could be this chatty? And so far, it was pretty much all boring day-to-day stuff, except for the arrangements for the clandestine love affair. There was too much for one person to keep up with, and everyone else was busy with other commitments.

He first told his analyzer to look for the word "nanobot," which gathered only a couple of conversations. He tried "nano," but that was too vague. "Data unit" really wasn't getting him anywhere. He took a break to throw a toy for his very bored Portuguese water dog, Boomer. Boomer didn't go out on assignment nearly as much as the others did, since Harris's expertise was more at Central, but given the misadventures that had been happening to the on-assignment dogs, he wasn't too concerned about Boomer missing out on all the hazards.

Boomer splashed into the river with complete abandon after the retriever-dog toy, called a bumper, that Harris had thrown for him. Harris pondered: *What are we looking for? Well, nanobot tech obviously, but these are stolen data units that someone is trying to sell. Given the amount of owner paranoia that Yolanda has uncovered talking to the guards, it seems unlikely that someone trying to sell it would spell out the name of the thing over the phone even if the phone communication was encrypted. They'd probably use a generic term like package or present or maybe gorilla—Or maybe not.*

Boomer charged up, shaking off excess water right onto Harris, and dropped the bumper at his feet. The bumper looked like a short, wide, sewn-up firehose that somehow managed to float, and it had a rope tied on the end. Harris wasn't a hunter, so he had no idea if it came anywhere close to matching a duck. He did know that Boomer didn't give a hoot about real birds. He just wanted to chase after his toy. Harris threw it again, thinking: *So what are we really looking for?*

He thought about what the conversations he was looking for had in common. Someone was trying to sell something. Someone was often on the defensive. Someone was often angry. That's it! Heck with keywords. *What we want to know is who is stressed and talking; that might lead us to someone who is trying to fence the data units.*

"Boomer, come."

They went racing back in. Steve looked up. Harris hit him on the shoulder in what he hoped was a light thump and asked, "Could I borrow you a second or two?"

"Sure, what's up?"

Harris went into a workroom, beckoning Steve in and closing the door.

Harris spoke to the system. "Record on my mark." He turned to Steve. "Talk like you're angry or mad."

Steve's brow furrowed. "Really?"

"Really. Shall I punch you to inspire you?"

Steve said, "Should we put a sign on the door?"

Harris opened the door, shouted to an empty room, "Ignore anything we say right now," and shut the door.

"Give me a scenario," said Steve.

Harris looked up at the ceiling for a moment, then looked back at Steve. "Your partner is leaving you for someone younger."

Steve smiled. "You can do better than that."

Harris looked at him a moment, considering, his eyes getting that malicious, mischievous look. "I am leaving you for someone prettier, and younger, and who gives me better sex." He hit the record button.

Steve's right arm shot out sideways, gesticulating. "WHAT?! You said that I was the one for you. You always said you loved how young I acted. And what the eff do you mean about better sex? Where could you possibly get better sex that you didn't have to pay for, or are you paying for it?" By now Steve was shouting and Harris ended the recording.

"That's perfect, thanks."

Steve took a moment to gather himself. "Okay—I think."

Steve opened the door to find both Amy and Yolanda. For two women who looked nothing alike—Yolanda with her walnut skin, as opposed to Amy's light tan, Amy with her caramel-blond hair past her shoulders versus Yolanda's short-cropped, black hair, Yolanda's very slim build and Amy's more solid body—they were standing there with identical grins, their heads angled the same way, and their bodies in the exact same pose with their arms folded and their weight on one foot.

Looking back at Harris, Steve said, "This is your fault, I hope you're happy," and walked across the room after miming slamming the door.

Harris called back, "Oh, I'm VERY happy. Thank you, Honey."

Harris kept on, "Come on in, and bring your angry, stressed voices with you."

Amy and Yolanda looked at each other, raised their heads in a half-nod, and walked closer.

Yolanda asked, "What kind of romantic interludes are you having in here?"

"I need angry, stressed voices."

"Why?" she asked.

Harris said, "I want to use it to filter all this bug data that we're looking at."

"And you broke up with Steve just for that?"

"I am NOT seeing Steve. Hold that thought."

He pressed record again.

"I am NOT seeing Steve."

Yolanda smiled, catching on. "Yes, you are."

"No, I'm not."

Leaning onto the desk, Amy said, "You sure you don't secretly waaaaant to?"

"NO! Well that came out wrong. I don't hate him."

"Mmmm-hmm," Yolanda said.

Harris decided that this needed a gear shift. "Yolanda, what do you think of the man that shot Gimli?" Harris said.

Her eyes blazed. "That two-bit know-nothing is lucky that I didn't take his gun and shoot his backside up over the building."

Harris said, "Okay, I have enough anger. How about stress? That's harder. Amy, what's the worst final you've had?"

She pinched her forehead with her fingers, released, and then looked off to the side. "Oh gawd, there was a time where I completely blanked on something I knew cold and it took me five long minutes to recover. I'm just glad I wasn't doing a speech."

"What if you were?" he asked.

Amy tensed, and her body shook a little. Pushing out at the air with her hands she said, "Oh, no. We are so not going there."

Harris turned off the recording. "That, my friends, is perfect."

Yolanda said, "I don't think Steve is going to forgive you anytime soon. You should go make amends, lover boy."

Harris, turning back to his computer, said, "Can't hear you."

"Suit yourself, but expect payback," she said.

They left Harris working and went to go find Steve.

CHAPTER 25:

Yolanda Speaks with Mary

YOLANDA AND Gimli walked into Mary Callahan's office. Mary, Amy's mother, was known in common parlance as a "doggy shrink." Her therapeutic specialty was helping people and their dogs work through traumatic issues, such as accidents, abuse, or other anxieties like illness or family breakups. Yolanda figured that being shot at by security guards of a building they were trying to bug was probably a little outside her usual sphere of experience, but trauma is trauma, she decided. Mary was an empath, and she worked alongside her Bernese mountain dog, Sandra.

The room was painted in comforting earth tones and rose pastels. There was a light beige sofa, with a green and blue flowering vine pattern tracking across it, nestled along one wall and a green wing chair on the other side of the room. Each seat had a small table to the right of it and a dog bed to the left. In one corner was a small ficus tree positioned higher up on a table, presumably, Yolanda thought, to discourage boy dogs from marking it. The space between the chair and the sofa had that deliberate, empty look, save for the dog toys that were liberally scattered around the floor. Way off in a different corner was an actual desk and chair with a monitor and a container of what looked like dog treats.

Mary, at five feet five inches, was shorter than her daughter Amy. Her light brown, curly hair was cut short and framed her open face. She had Amy's lighter bronze skin, with dark amber eyes that you could nearly fall into. She reflected both confidence and comfort. Her short-sleeved red blouse was pretty, and yet seemed like it could spend all day in the presence of dogs without falling apart or becoming permanently muddy. She wore khaki pants, which was de rigueur around those who regularly worked with dogs.

Mary said, "Yolanda, welcome, and this must be Gimli, hello. He's welcome to sniff around the office and get used to it."

Yolanda said, "Hello and thank you. Gimli, you can go sniff." Yolanda sat on the sofa, while Gimli said a brief doggy hello to Mary, went over to Berner Sandra for a quick greeting sniff, and started to circulate the room. He grabbed a stuffed dog toy in the shape of a trout and started squeaking it.

Yolanda looked at Mary and smiled. "He doesn't have one of those and I can tell he's going to ask for one later."

Squeak. Squeak.

Mary said, "So I've read the report of the incident, or at least what part they let me see, which seems like enough for our purposes. You both had quite an adventure. Why don't you fill me in? What brings you here today?"

Yolanda inhaled, sitting a bit more upright, trying to relax. "Well, as you've likely read, Gimli was working at night in the bushes near an office building. Things were going well and he was finishing up when he got caught on a branch. He wrestled his way out of the shrubbery, but the noise alerted the guards and one of them, not seeing that it was a dog, shot at him and hit him in the vest. He managed to get out of there without being clearly seen, even though he was screaming bloody murder."

Mary's face was one of attentive concern. "Was he hurt?"

Yolanda made a motion of one hand hitting the other. "It's like being hit hard. It shocked him. It only bruised him physically, but it seems to have messed with his head."

"How do you think?"

Looking at Gimli, who had laid down on the dog bed beside Yolanda, she said, "He's not that communicative. He's subdued."

Mary smiled. "Which is unusual for a corgi."

Yolanda laughed a little. "Like, way unusual."

Mary smiled and said, "Would Gimli mind if Sandra came over and said hello to you?"

"Naw, he's fine."

At a silent request from Mary, Sandra stood up and walked over to Yolanda. Sandra was relatively small for a Berner, but she covered the distance in about three deliberate strides and placed her enormous head in Yolanda's lap.

Yolanda put her hands on either side of Sandra's face and massaged her by contracting her fingers.

Sandra closed her eyes in obvious enjoyment, groaning in pleasure.

"I just love these giant heads," Yolanda said.

"Well, she likes what you're doing," Mary said.

Mary made a note on a pad of paper. Waving the pen, she said, "These aren't anything official, just to help me remember salient things we talk about. I just wrote 'Acts subdued.'"

Looking over her glasses at Yolanda, Mary said, "But subdued is not what brought you into here."

Yolanda tensed her mouth into a line, thinking. "He's kinda freaky when he gets near bushes now."

"What does he do?"

"When he realizes he's near a bush, he runs about twenty feet away, and he starts what looks like hyperventilating."

"Gasping?"

"No, just fast panting, but it's definitely a reaction to being near a bush. It's funny, he doesn't always react until he's standing near the bush. He'll often walk up to the shrub without any reaction."

Mary started chewing on her pen a little. "Interesting. The view has to be just right for him to react. Probably the smell too. Does he say anything to you?"

"Not really, and that has me more concerned than anything."

"Because he's usually . . ."

"Very talkative," Yolanda said, completing the thought.

"Dogs are associative learners, which can have some side effects. Humans are too, when it comes to trauma."

Yolanda frowned, concentrating. "I keep hearing that."

Sandra made her way back to her bed beside Mary.

"Basically, a dog, and sometimes a human, will remember all the surrounding environmental details to a painful incident. How things look, feel, sound, and smell, regardless of whether those details had anything to do with the event."

"The one I heard was a dog fearing hats if he was beaten by someone wearing a hat."

Mary waved the pen in agreement. "Correct. Smells, in particular, can really trigger post-traumatic stress reactions in humans and, we suspect, dogs, too. Gimli is reacting to the look, smell, and feel of a bush. He never saw a person, never saw a weapon. He was just in a bush struggling, and it hurt him. How is he at night?"

"Way worse. I guess it's good he didn't see a person."

"Yes and no," Mary said. "What you're left with is super-stitious behavior about potentially violent bushes." Mary made another note and said, "How much have you told him about guns?"

Yolanda said, "I've described them as something that can throw a rock-type thing really hard."

Mary said "That could work, though I'm sure he's wondering why he didn't see it."

"He hasn't asked yet," Yolanda said.

Mary looked down at Sandra and up at Yolanda. "Would it be okay if the dogs went outside to play? I have a small fenced yard out back."

Yolanda, who hadn't noticed that it was actually a fenced area and not just landscaping, said, "You have a yard? Sure. Gimli, want to go outside?"

The corgi picked up his head, eyes wider, ears up.

Mary stood up. Sandra was already at the sliding glass door, Gimli right behind her. She slid the door open and the dogs trotted out. Looking at Yolanda, Mary said, "There are some bushes on the edges, but Gimli doesn't have to go in them."

Mary closed the door, and they watched through the window. Gimli inspected the yard, sniffing. He didn't go into the bushes, but smelled at the leaves. There were several dog toys on the ground and Sandra picked up a rope toy with multiple rope-branches on it and shook it. The ropes whacked her head, which she appeared to enjoy. Looking over at Gimli with the toy in her mouth, she did a play bow and walked toward him. Gimli wasn't looking at her, but Yolanda could see his body tense. She said, "It's funny, he sees her, but he's almost pretending not to see her."

Mary said, "That could mean 'not interested' or it could mean 'keep trying'."

Sandra crept closer, swaying her head with the ropes of the toy dangling on each side of her head.

Gimli turned his head away. Yolanda said quietly, "Aw, Gim, you're breaking my heart."

Mary said, "Gimli just gave her a 'not interested' calming signal, but dogs are big teases, so he could be convinced still."

Sandra did another play bow, flopping the ropes tantalizingly close to Gimli.

Gimli still ignored her.

Appearing to give up, Sandra stood back up and turned ninety degrees away from Gimli, but still swaying her head low so the ropes kept swinging.

Mary said, "She's deliberately taking pressure off of him. I think she's doing the doggy equivalent of humming innocently."

Yolanda sighed, shaking her head. "He's still not interested."

Then Gimli spun around and launched at Sandra, grabbing a rope, his momentum sending him sailing past her as if he was carried on the wind.

Sandra braced her front legs.

Gimli's body swung around, pivoting on his mouth, still clenching the rope as if he was a kite that Sandra was flying. He hit the ground with a *thump* and started tugging, making play growling noises through his clenched teeth.

Sandra pulled back and shook her head, which forced the corgi to correct his footing and redouble his tug.

Yolanda, with both fists clenched in joy, said, "Yes! Play, my silly boy. Play."

Mary smiled. They watched the tug game for a while. Sandra, who outsized Gimli by four times, both gave and took territory during the game, controlling it for maximum fun.

Yolanda said, "Sandra is really good at this, isn't she?"

Mary said, "She's the most gifted coworker I've yet had."

Yolanda smiled. "It's so good to see him playing again."

Mary turned to her. "So I have good news and bad news."

Yolanda looked at her, inhaling and steeling herself.

Mary went on, "Good news first. Over time he will very likely get better. He might react to crawling through bushes, but it sounds like he doesn't have to do that very often."

"Not so much," Yolanda said with a thoughtful expression.

Sandra had dropped the tug toy and Gimli was now chewing on her jowl as they began a slow-motion wrestle.

Mary cleared her throat politely. "However, the bad news is that you are making his recovery harder with your own anxiety."

Yolanda put her face in her hands and sighed.

Mary put a hand on her shoulder. "The dogs will be fine. Let's go sit down and talk." She guided Yolanda back to the sofa and they both sat down on it.

Mary took a breath, considering. "When Sandra said hello to Gimli, she said to me, 'He's sad.'" Mary paused a moment. "When she greeted you, she said, 'She's scared.'"

Yolanda sniffed. Mary moved the tissue box closer and Yolanda took one, crumpling it in her hand before pulling it back apart and dabbing at her eyes. Mary said gently, "Humans have bigger brains, and they use them to create things to worry about. Your dog may be able to communicate with you, but he is still just like a child. He lives in the now, and right now all he sees is how anxious you are."

Yolanda took another tissue and said, "I'm so afraid of losing him." She started crying in earnest. "Why am I putting him in this danger?"

Mary stayed silent, waiting.

"He doesn't understand the risks I am putting him in. What right do I have?"

Mary said, "That's a decision you have to make for yourself, but right now let's try to reduce your anxiety, as that will help both of you right now."

Yolanda shook her head, smiling ruefully.

Mary said, "They teach you fighting and negotiating skills, but not how to relax. Breathe in. Breathe out. How do you prepare for your demos?"

Yolanda said, "Pretty much the same—breathing and thinking about what I'm going to say and do."

Mary said, "Do you and Gimli like going to nice places?"

"Oh, yes."

"Do it, but with the intention of appreciating the beauty. Be in the moment, just like your dog. If you have trouble with this, you can also take an acting class where you learn confidence by pretending to be brave, which actually does make you relax."

"I don't have time for that," Yolanda said.

"But you do have time to take ten deliberate breaths. Also, I think you should see an individual therapist apart from Gimli for a little while, just to help you work through your anxiety about this."

Yolanda nodded. "I thought about it, but I thought I was being silly."

Mary patted her shoulder. "Our capacity for torturing ourselves is without end. Consider this an investment in yourself and your relationship with your dog. This also will help your job. Okay, work on your breathing and I'm going to call the dogs back in."

She did. Gimli bounced in with a panting smile, and Sandra came right up to Yolanda and put her massive head in her hands.

"Sandra says you're not scared." Mary held up an index finger. "Now that doesn't mean you're not scared, but it means you're not telegraphing it with every touch."

Yolanda smiled at Sandra, stroking her. "You're ratting me out, aren't you?"

Mary smiled. "Yes, she is."

CHAPTER 26:

Harris Analyzes the Bug Data

HARRIS THOUGHT about the time he had spent teaching his analysis system about stressed and angry voices. While the process had been a lot of fun, it was going further that he imagined it would. The system had noticed some other features as well: vowels got louder and longer; the cadence of speech increased if the speaker was angry; cadence could also slow way down during some threats; and cadence also slowed down if they were sad.

So he turned it loose on the bug data that they already had. He learned a few things right away: The couple having the affair was arguing. Though Harris couldn't hear the client side, customers got unhappy when they got the wrong thing delivered at their lab. And Harris was glad he wasn't hearing the other side of the cold sales calls.

He let it run for a while and went out to lunch and to let Boomer run around some.

Coming back in, he waved to Catherine, who was working in her office with the door closed.

He started up the playback and told the system to increase the speed.

"I'm sorry your delivery is late. . . ."

"Your burners will be calibrated tomorrow at the latest. . . ."

"I love you, but I don't want to see you again. . . ."

Harris rolled his eyes. While he envied Amy with John despite their struggles, and Yolanda and her lovely wife Lydia, he really couldn't see himself going through all the heartache that Steve was enduring, searching for that special someone after the trauma of his husband's death. Harris liked his dog Boomer and the elaborate toys that he created. He loved his friends and he hoped that would be enough for him.

The playback continued.

"Fifteen thousand and not a penny more. . . ."

"No, I mean it, I don't want us to keep seeing each other . . ."

Harris increased the volume and went out into the common area and threw a canvas soft toy for Boomer as it droned on. His brain was going to melt. He just knew.

"Your test tubes will arrive at 3:00 p.m. tomorrow. . . ."

". . . are completely iced over and we can't get anywhere with them."

Harris, who had been kneeling down rubbing Boomer's nose, leapt up intrigued, knocking into a chair and startling Boomer, who dodged a few feet away. Shouting, "Stop playback," he ran back to the office. Skidding into his chair, he said, "Reverse five seconds and play."

"Your packages are completely iced over and we can't get anywhere with them."

"We tried that and they countered us."

"We'll sell them to you for a quarter of the price if we can just send them to you along with the other deliverable. Then you can see if you can get anywhere with them."

Harris said, "Stop playback. Computer: Define: iced over."

The computer said, "Frozen water; inaccessible road or bridge; cake frosting."

Thank you, Computer, for your talent for the obvious, glad I asked, he thought.

Trying another tack, he asked, "How about slang?"

"Diamonds; negotiations that are at an impasse."

Interesting, he thought. "Tech slang?"

"Unresponsive computer; encrypted data."

Ah ha, he thought.

"Computer: bookmark this recording. Email Beth and the team that the data units might be on the move and include a link to this clip."

Hoping to hear more, he said, "Resume playback on this bug."

It droned on:

"My wife suspects us."

"But I love you, you should tell her."

Harris put his head in his hands.

CHAPTER 27:

Beth Interrogates Al

YOLANDA WAS sitting in the interrogation observation room.

She had been teaching Beth how to work with Gimli: nothing very serious, just how to walk around smoothly together and have him sit beside her. Beth was no empath, but she was a wizard at manipulating people and creating illusions. Yolanda called this the LAI dog theatre project.

They had figured out the area where the suspect phone calls were coming from and had narrowed it down to the poor guy sweating and fidgeting in the interrogation room. He was on the stocky side, which might explain the sweating, but his demeanor was that of a kid in the principal's office.

Beth and Gimli walked into the room. Beth had Gimli sit off to the side where he could see both of them, and then she walked to the table to sit on the other side of the man.

She looked at her tablet. "Al Beyer, the Director of New Technology and Planning."

Al took in a breath and made a very short nod.

"I'm Detective Beth Hanscom, and," she motioned towards Gimli, "this is LAI Canine Agent Gimli."

Al looked quite askance at the elaborate title. "Looks like a dog to me."

"He is, and he is also my assistant."

Yolanda had to stifle a laugh. She thought, *Beth enjoys this entirely too much.*

Beth said to Al, "As you no doubt know, you have been recorded arranging for the transport of stolen goods. You have waived your right to have an attorney present for this meeting because (a) you are not yet under arrest and (b) you have information that you think would be helpful to us. This meeting is being recorded for review by any legal or other personnel. Do you understand this so far?"

Al nodded.

Beth asked, "Okay, Al, who were you talking to, and was it your client for the stolen data units?"

Al's eyes shifted and he licked his lips. Yolanda could see his regret at agreeing to this, but he had the air of someone who thought there was no other choice. He said, "I don't know, they don't give me real names."

Yolanda quietly asked Gimli, "What do you smell about him?" She tended to talk aloud unless it was necessary for silence. Over time, she had been teaching Gimli to smell the stress hormone cortisol, and also to notice sweat and agitation.

/He scared. Stressed./

Yolanda said into her connection to Beth, who was wearing an earpiece, "Gimli says he's stressed and frightened."

Beth looked at Al. "My dog here is a lie detector and he doesn't believe you, Al. What am I going to do about that?"

Yolanda chortled. Beth had no idea what Gimli the corgi was saying, yet she was learning some neat tactics when a dog was willing to sit beside her.

"Who cares about what some dog thinks?"

"He can smell your fear. Why are you so terrified?"

"You can't get that from a dog."

"He can smell fear, and I can see it, too. There's a light bit of sweat on your forehead."

"It's hot in here," he said.

"Your breathing is different, you can't sit still. What has you so spooked? What's with these people?"

"You don't know what they can do," he said.

"I have an idea, but tell me more."

"No."

Beth leaned forward across the desk. "Don't take the fall for this, Al. You're in a heap of trouble, and you have the opportunity to make it better." She paused. "Or worse."

He put his head in his hands, with one hand on each temple. To the floor he said, "We just build labs."

"What did they have you build?"

"A sort of elaborate setup in two converted storage containers, including DNA sequencers, a semi-large electron microscope—lots of computers."

"What are they doing with it?"

"Something to do with nanobot research, but they wouldn't talk about it much, which makes our job harder."

"What was unusual about it?"

"They wanted lots of hospital equipment that is usually used to monitor people."

"Like what?"

"Like blood pressure and respiration, but also heart rate and brain waves."

Beth leaned back slightly and said levelly. "They want to test nanobots on humans."

"I guess," he said. "But that's not that weird these days."

Thinking back to Herman and Lincoln and what started all this, Beth said, "It's not weird unless it's used to hurt them."

Al looked up quickly, looking shocked. White was showing all around his pupils. "They wouldn't do that, would they?"

"They already have. You already have."

"WHAT?" He tried to stand up and Beth put a hand on his shoulder, guiding him back to the chair.

"Those nanobots raised their heart rates to nearly past their hearts' ability. They were remotely controlled, by you and your people, and stayed that way until we shielded them from the outside world after we got you to turn the nanobot attack off."

Al, looking at the table, said, "But that's not possib—"

"Al, your people activated the nanobots and made threatening phone calls demanding the decryption codes."

"How do you know it was nanobots and not a poison?"

"Because your person told us over the phone and it stopped once they were shielded."

"They were just following instructions from the client. Stand here and press this button."

Beth crossed her arms, looking straight at him. "You expect me to believe that? We have your delivery person who made the phone call in custody and we're not letting him go. He's blaming this whole thing on you."

Al was now very pale, and he was looking intently at the floor. Shaking his head, he said, "Oh, no. No. You can have antennas on nanobots, but it's a close-range antenna. We didn't know." He paused again, looking very hard at a point in space in the room.

"But you chose to use the nanobots to demand the decryption key. That's assault with a deadly weapon at a minimum."

Yolanda thought he was going to cry.

Al said, "This is terrible—a weapon."

Beth was angry now and Yolanda had to reassure Gimli not to run. "How naive can you possibly be? What the hell were you thinking? What did they tell you would happen?"

"They said it might make them uncomfortable, but they didn't say anything else."

"Oh sure, of course they didn't." Yolanda thought she was going to hit him. Beth got right in his face. "Do not lie to me."

"I don't even know how the nanobots got into them. They just told me they were."

Yolanda asked Gimli, "How stressed is he?"

/Stressed./

Yolanda said to Beth, "Al is very stressed, but you knew that." Yolanda could see the ghost of a smile on Beth's face.

"Who are these people, Al?"

"I don't know," he said, looking truly miserable.

"How did they hire you?"

"Through a third party. One of those anonymizer services where they don't know who their clients are."

"Oh, we just love those," Beth said sarcastically. "But you have a deliverable."

"They had us build it into two shipping containers that can be joined together at their site. A different company will then put it together onsite, is our understanding. We had to create elaborate instructions and even a video on the assembly and on packing it to be shipped, which was an enormous pain."

"That's actually useful to know, as they no doubt had to pull permits to transport something like that. Was it on trucks?"

Al looked relieved; he appeared to be thinking that he might not have to contact the other company. "Yes, they will robo-truck it north and from there, I don't know," he said.

"Perfect, and we will need to know the other company, though we might not need to contact them if we can find other documentation. What day is it supposed to move?"

"Tomorrow, actually."

Beth went on, "Please give us the container numbers, so we can track them through the system. You are under arrest, but we're going to let you continue working while the District Attorney decides what your charges will be. The more normal you can make your business look, the easier it will be for us, and that might help you to climb out of this hole you've dug yourself into. On the same note, don't tip them off."

Al's eyebrows went up, and inhaling, he said, "I think I'm pretty done with them. They were bugging me for other things, but I think I'm going to say no."

"We will still be monitoring things and we'd like it if we could get a decrypted monitoring line for your phone in case they call back."

Al looked resigned and said, "Okay, but I'll have to tell the owners."

"Oh, rest assured we'll be talking to them as well. And practice your acting. Everything is normal."

Al looked both relieved and worried.

Beth reached down to pet Gimli.

Yolanda, still in the other room, told him, "Nice job Gim, burger later."

He looked up at Beth with a doggy grin on his face. /Burger. Burger./

Yolanda, smiling to herself, decided not to tell Beth that Gimli's happiness had a lot more to do with food than petting.

———

CHAPTER 28:

Shipping Containers

DURING THE staff meeting, Catherine read from her tablet. "Okay, the Anderson kids have been returned to their parents after their 'let's take the wrong subway train and take a long walk into the wetlands paths' adventure. Now, on to the stolen data unit issue. I'm going to hand it off to Beth."

Beth stood up. "We've made arrests at Applied Sciences. We're now tracking a couple of shipping containers going north to an unknown destination, and we'll find them. I want to thank you all for all the hard work chasing this down. We'll continue things on our end, but I think you all should take a break and do what you enjoy the most, as you're the best at it."

Harris said, "If you've lost someone—"

They all said, "Call Locate and Investigate."

"Hear, hear," Beth said and raised a mimed glass. "And best to all the wonderful dogs, too."

Harris asked, "Before they leave, could we get a look at the containers, just to see how they're put together?"

Beth said, "Sure. I'll let Al know and he can help you figure out how to get through security without leaving a record."

"Geek," Amy said to Harris, smiling.

"For that, you get to come with me," Harris said.

Amy gave him a cautious look. "I feel a teaching moment coming on."

––––––––––––

LATER, HARRIS and Amy pulled up to what appeared to be a staging site next to Applied Sciences. Just before he lowered the window to speak to the guard, he turned his face to Amy and said conspiratorially, "By the way, we're Bob and Cathy."

Amy, stuck for a reply, said, "Er, okay."

But Harris had already reached down on the floor and recovered a clipboard, which Amy thought was a nice, very old-school touch. He lowered the window, lifted a page on the clipboard, and said to the guard, "Could you contact Al and tell him that Bob and Cathy, from A-1 Deliverables, would like to take some last-minute measurements?"

Amy was surprised that the guard immediately nodded and started talking on his handheld. After a moment, the guard nodded, opened the gate, told Harris a couple of long numbers that Harris wrote down, and waved them through.

Once out of earshot of the guard, Amy said, "I do not effing believe this. You just crashed a gate, without even crashing it, and what the hell is A-1 Deliverables?"

Harris handed her a business card that said exactly that, with a phone number on it and no name. Harris, answering her just-about-to-ask question, said, "The number goes to a generic voicemail that just repeats the phone number."

Amy shook her head. "My secret agent boy."

They pulled up to what had to be the Applied Sciences shipping containers in question.

"And why are we here?" Amy asked.

"I wanted to see how they put the lab-in-a-container together. The containers are going to be joined up along the long side," he said pointing at the edge, "but see, you can't take away the whole side of the container or it compromises the structural integrity and you have to add more reinforcements. Instead, they've just taken

151

out a third of each one and replaced it with a roll up door. What's weird is that while there are some smaller added outside doors, there aren't any added windows, which is a common alteration. Someone must be really paranoid about security."

Amy said, "Well the paranoid forgot about someone just letting anyone in to take a look around."

Looking at the door he said, "We can't really see much inside because it's packed for transport, but they tell me it's pretty standard-issue lab fare, save for the human monitoring equipment that's over here." He pointed to one side of one of the containers furthest from the door co-joining door.

Walking to the end of the containers, he took photos of the numbers on the end, which started with four letters and eight numbers plus another number set off at the end.

Pointing at the end number, he said, "See this number?"

"How could I not?" Amy said.

"The first letters are who it belongs to, in this case Minuteman Transport, MMT, and the U means General cargo, then a unique number and a check digit. The check digit is a check to make sure that the number was recorded correctly."

"U because there's no U in General."

"Exactly," he said, smiling and waving a pointed finger in the air.

Amy couldn't resist asking, "Why can't they just put up a giant bar code?"

"Because humans still like to look and see a number. Do you know how the check digit is computed?"

Uh-oh, Amy realized that the teaching moment had arrived.

"Each letter is given a value for its position in the alphabet. A is 10, B is 11, J is 20. Get it?"

"I'm afraid so."

"Then each letter is multiplied by 2 to the power of its position in the number."

"You lost me."

"It's not too bad."

"So you say."

"2 to the 1st power is 1, 2 to the 2nd is 2, 2 to the 3rd is 4. So just remember 1, 2, 4, 8, 16, 32, 64, and so on."

Amy looked at him with eyebrows raised. "I assure you, I'm not going to remember any of this."

"But wait, it gets better." Harris was becoming more intense.

"You add all those multiplied numbers up and divide by 11 and make it an integer."

"This is getting way complicated."

"Now multiply it by 11."

"Harris, you need to stop."

"Almost done."

Amy tried to catch his eye, saying, "Hello? Anyone in there?"

"And the last step is to subtract your final result from adding all the numbers up."

"Harris." Amy tried to put her hands on his shoulders, but he was gesticulating too much.

"AND," he said with a flourish, "that is your check digit."

Pointing at the container on the left, Amy said, "So, you just calculated that check digit?"

"Naw, I just have my handheld optically scan it and do the math."

Looking around for Harris's dog, Amy said, "Boomer, would you bite Harris please?"

"He's used to this."

Looking right at the water dog, Amy asked, "For me please? Pretty please with a cookie on top?"

Both Boomer and Lars started to bounce at the mention of "cookie."

"Now, you've done it," Harris said.

"And," poking him in the chest, "you have to pay up."

Harris reached in his pocket and gave each dog a treat.

Then he reached into his backpack, pulled out a small disc, and looked around. "Do you see something I could stand on? It only needs to help me reach up high and this particular container is eight feet high, so it doesn't have to be huge."

"I see a bucket over there. Will that work?"

"As long as I don't fall through it."

Amy went and got it. "Okay, fess up, what are you up to?"

He sighed and said, "This is such bullshit."

"Please feel free to explain," she said.

He showed her a small disk. "This is a GPS tracking device that I'm going to attach up high on both containers. It's completely silly that I should have to do this at all. All containers should already have GPS tracking built in. I should be able to find out where any container is in the world within a few seconds."

"Well, there have been a lot of privacy concerns about them."

"This is a box, this isn't someone's car. If I were a container shipping company, I'd want to know where all my boxes were at any instant. The only reason it shouldn't be contactable for an extended period of time is if it's inside a building or at the bottom of the ocean."

Harris stood on the bucket and affixed the coin-like device to a place a few inches below the top, using a little of that super glue that he carried around with him.

Hopping off the bucket, he again dug into his backpack and removed a jar about the size of the palm of his head. He opened it and instantly the air smelled of fish. Both dogs spun around and Amy took a step back.

"I'm sure you're going to explain that one too."

"This is a solution of Mulgoo, which is a fish that is only down here and not up north." He started to paint it along the bottom of each container on the end, below the numbers. Both dogs were trying to inhale it, but Harris held them back. "Let it dry, then it won't come off even under a power washer."

Amy was giving him that "Why?" look.

"I just thought a little low-tech backup tracking device might be helpful."

Amy shook her head. "Sure, if you want to attract every animal in the area. With any luck, we'll never see these boxes again."

"Hopefully."

"I think I've had enough education for one day," she added as they headed off.

CHAPTER 29:

The Containers Go Missing

AMY WAS working on an LAI PR "Who we are" type of article when Catherine walked in. She walked over to Harris, who Amy knew was engrossed in working on his spy pigeon. Seeing her out of the corner of his eye, he looked up and said, "Good morning, Catherine."

"Good morning, Harris." Raising her voice to include Amy, she said, "I have some bad news. Beth tells me the Applied Sciences containers have gone missing."

At the same time, Amy said, "What!?" and Harris said, "How!?"

Looking at both of them, Catherine said, "They don't know."

Simultaneously, Amy and Harris said, "But—" and Catherine put both hands up in that 'Hang on a minute' gesture.

"They were supposed to arrive at the northern terminal. They didn't, and they haven't shown up at any earlier terminal, east or west."

Amy said, "But that's crazy; it's not like the robo-trucks make wrong turns."

Harris added, "They don't make much of any turn save for the occasional bend in the route. And they only get turned 90 degrees at stations. Someone definitely saw them leave."

"Oh, yes," said Catherine. "They passed through one station, and they were being tracked with the trackers that you installed, but that's the last time they were seen. They have hundreds of containers up there. Beth knows we've seen them and is wondering if we have search ideas."

Harris looked up at the ceiling, palms raised. "Why on earth would Locate and Investigate know anything about searching?" Then he snapped back grinning, his hair in his face.

Amy asked, "Is it possible to sneak one onto a delivery truck? Can they offload it fast?"

Harris said, "It's a lot faster than it used to be, but there's no sneaking around with anything that large. Plus, they would notice an empty robo-truck without documentation."

Looking at a diagram on her handheld, Catherine said, "Beth tells me that at the way station after it was seen, some of the robo-trucks go west or east to other secondary stations."

Harris said, "That's right. Coolingham to the west and Novaton in the east, with most continuing on to Northstation."

Catherine said, "Once they reach there, they get offloaded onto road trucks to take them to their destination."

Amy said, "Or to a ship if they go to Coolingham."

Catherine went on, "But there's no information to point to them being sent overseas, and there are a lot of land destinations via Coolingham, too."

"So they're looking for an ant in an ant hill?" Amy asked.

Harris said, "Well, right now it's likely an ant in an ant trail, which would be slightly, but only slightly, easier." He ran his hand through his hair, which only served to mess it up further. "I can't believe both GPS trackers went offline."

Catherine asked, "Other thoughts?"

Amy, looking pointedly at Harris, said, "Mulgoo."

Catherine looked at her quizzically. "The fish?"

Amy kept staring at Harris with her eyebrows raised expectantly. Harris finally said, "I painted a Mulgoo solution onto the ends of the containers."

Catherine smiled broadly, genuinely amused. "Really?"

"Well, it just seemed like it might come in . . . handy," Harris said, almost embarrassed.

Catherine asked, "And that's something that a dog can smell from a distance?"

"Would you like a demonstration?"

"No, thank you, I believe you," Catherine said quickly, familiar with the fish's olfactory reputation. "So Agent Harris Consuelo'a, because of the time pressure on this, I think you have just earned yourself a trip north to assist Detective Beth Hanscom."

"It would be easier if I had a coworker with me," Harris said, smiling and looking back over at Amy. "Perhaps Agent Amy Callahan?"

Amy shook her head. "You got yourself into this."

Harris looked at Catherine. "Please."

"I think he's right, he could really use your help, and perhaps the others too when they get free," Catherine said.

Amy ducked her head in acquiescence. "Lars will be thrilled to look for fish smell."

CHAPTER 30:

———

Amy Calls John

AMY CALLED John. "Hi, Honey, Lars and I have to be out of town for a couple of days."

"Working?"

"Yes, it shouldn't be too long."

"Getting kidnapped again?" His voice was heavy with sarcasm.

Rolling her eyes skyward, Amy said, "Been there, done that, didn't really like it."

"Who's running from the law this time?"

"It's sort of a continuation, but a different aspect of it."

"Like how different?"

"It's different. Randall owned one of the cars we were investigating, but there are more."

"But is there a Bob, or a Frank?"

"John, please."

"I'm serious. I'm getting sick of being left out of the loop, and then the hospital calls."

"That doesn't happen that often."

"Once is more than enough."

"I think you've said that before."

"Why you?"

"It's my job, John." Punching at the side window, she said, "Because I might be able to make a difference, dammit." She realized that might have come out a little strong, as he wasn't saying anything in return.

After a beat, he said, "You really believe in this—this making a difference?"

Softening her voice, she said, "Yes, I do, John. I really do."

"Well, okay. I know you don't need my approval, but just so you know, it's okay with me."

"Thanks, John. I really do appreciate it."

"Just don't come back dead, okay?"

"I'll work on that, John. I love you."

"Me too, Amy."

"Happy surfing. Go catch a wave for me."

"Will do."

"Bye-bye," she said, and cut the link.

Looking up at Lars, who was snoozing in his crate, she said, "Could you talk sense to him? Oh that's right, this doesn't make any sense."

CHAPTER 31:

Traveling to the Container Search

HARRIS AND Amy were immediately sent up north to assist in the search for the two containers. Catherine instructed them to be super nice to the Northstation people, as they were not used to using dogs beyond drug sniffing and arrest assists.

Amy marveled at the landscape speeding by. Their vehicle had been slaved to an authorized high-speed police escort vehicle, which was able to broadcast to the other vehicles on the compu-highway to move over for it. They were able to drive 50 percent faster this way. She could see objects like trees in the distance, but as they passed them, they rocketed by and her nearly-hypnotized eyes wanted to follow them, her head snapping sharply to the side vainly trying to keep them in sight.

Amy noticed that Lars was looking out from his crate, also watching. The cars moving over about a mile ahead of them resembled a reverse ocean wave.

Pulling herself out of her reverie, she turned to Harris. "Do you think it's a good idea that we're bypassing Coolingham and Novaton?"

Harris appeared to be contemplating his fingernails while he thought. "Well, it's an odds call. Northstation is double the size of either of the other two, so the numbers are better that our containers are there, but I must admit to being a little uneasy about it."

"How large is Northstation?"

"Right now, there are about 250 containers there and around 100 at Novaton and 150 at Coolingham."

"I hope they're not going on a ship."

"If they do, we're hosed anyway, as they're not going to want us racing around a ship while it's being loaded."

Amy smiled, thinking. "Oh, and doggy, could you sniff this container that's at the top of a stack of six?"

"That might be a bit high even for Boomer," Harris said.

"So, Northstation it is. The dogs are going to have a blast looking for fish smell. I guess we should reward them with real fish."

Harris made a face, implying that fish really wasn't his favorite food despite being willing to paint it onto containers. "Well, I'm not putting it into my pocket."

Amy got a tablet out and flipped through a few photos they had taken back before the containers left. She moved to the back seat, positioning herself in front of Lars. "Since you're awake, I need to show you something."

Lars gave her his best quizzical expression and inhaled, trying to smell the tablet.

Amy sighed. Dogs really didn't get pictures that well. She showed him a photo of the back of the container that had the label.

Holding up the tablet to Lars, and pointing to the characters, she said, "We haven't gotten to this in your training, but these here are called letters. During this search, all you need to be sniffing is the side with letters. No letters means to go to the other end." She showed him a photo of the other side of the container. "That fish smell you like so much is on the same side as the letters on two of the hundreds of containers." She realized there was no way he was going to get that.

Lars said, /Let-ers/

"Yes, letters."

Harris said, "You're teaching him to read right now?"

"No smartass, just to look for letters or no letters."

/Let-ers,/ Lars said, looking at the screen, still trying to breathe it all in. Amy tried to hold the tablet to minimize the amount of dog snot that got on it.

Amy noticed that Boomer was looking intently at the screen.

Harris started to laugh and said, "No, Boomer, it's not a word, it's just letters."

Amused and a little incredulous, Amy said, "You've been teaching him to read? What did he say to you?"

"Just a little. He was trying to figure out what the word in front of the numbers was. He's bright, but still only about like a three- or four-year-old human. He struggles with this weird thing called the written word, which isn't dog pee—that universal communication device used by dogs throughout the world."

Amy smiled and looked back. "Harris, if he spends a lot of time trying to sound out the Carrier's name 'MMTU' then we are screwed, timewise."

Harris gave her a mock-withering look. "I'll encourage him to just sniff below the letters."

CHAPTER 32:

The Container Search

THEY CAME over the rise and found themselves looking down at the robo-truck loading/unloading yard. It was ensconced in a valley surrounded by grassy hills dotted by the occasional tree.

Everything in Amy's mind quieted as she took in the sheer size of the yard. It had the look of a cutaway of an ant hill, where all you could see was just mass activity but each part of the system knew its job.

The robo-truck road forked into six separate, widely spaced roads, each threading under a series of what Amy later learned were container cranes. Each crane would unload the truck underneath it and move the container to the side of the road in a neat row about five or six containers wide. Some were stacked up to four containers high, but many were just a single height. Just past the row of containers was a looping road that came in from the other direction. This was for the conventional, human-driven road trucks and the same crane could also load a road truck. For each robo-truck road there was an equal and opposite road-truck road. It resembled interlacing fingers. Amy realized she was looking at hundreds of containers. And the noise of the containers being set down on other containers, or just whacking into each other, was a little daunting.

When they pulled up to the gate, Detective Beth Hanscom, coffee in hand, walked out to meet them.

Raising her voice over the noise of the yard, she said, "Welcome, and I'm glad you're here. I have people walking around checking the numbers manually in case there's a typo."

Getting out, Harris said, "Typos aren't very likely with that check digit at the end of the number. It's computed based on the number by—"

Amy, who had just walked around the front of the car, shot him a warning glance.

"Um, doing a complicated computation on the base number. They invented this to catch typos."

Crossing her arms and leaning against the car, Beth asked, "So again, what did you paint on the containers?"

"A solution of Mulgoo fish."

Placing her fingertips on her forehead, she said, "Oh gawd, I'm sure my people will be able to smell that all by themselves."

"They very well could," Amy said.

"Though I don't think they want to go around sniffing containers."

"And let the dogs have all the fun?" Harris said.

Beth said, with raised eyebrows, "Yes, I'm sure they'd be happy to let the dogs have their amusement. Okay. Some basics. This is an active loading area. There are vehicles all over the place racing to and fro. They are not used to looking for dogs though I've told them you'll be here. Wear your vests, all of you," Beth said, referring to the bright green LAI vests that both people and dogs wore.

Trying not to sound panicked, Amy said, "Beth, there are a lot of containers here."

"Yes, but the ones that just came in are on this track," she said, pointing over to a track further over to the left. "We've asked if they can slow down the work on this track and they said yes, but only for two hours or so."

Looking at that track, Amy could see some of the containers were stacked two, three, and four high. She asked, "What do we do about the stacked ones?"

Beth said, "Well, it turns out the stacked ones are going to the same destination, so you can get away with just smelling the lowest one. If you want to check a stacked one, we can get an elevator operator, but you probably won't need to."

Harris had slid open the side door of their vehicle and let both dogs out. He tossed Amy a vest for Lars and put one on Boomer. Amy got out three com links and handed one to Harris and one to Beth. "How about Lars and I go halfway down, and you and Boomer start here."

They walked down to the start of the track that Beth had pointed out. The noise dropped off considerably and Amy felt herself relax a little.

"How will I know when I'm done?" Harris asked.

"I'll just put one of our larger marker cones beside the corner of the one we start on," Amy said, holding up a green LAI cone that she had brought from the car.

"Works for me." Looking back at Beth he said, "Anything else, boss?"

Beth smiled, since she wasn't precisely their boss, and said, "What is it you say? Good hunting? I'll be listening if you need me." Looking at Amy, she added, "Oh, and let me get a chauffeur for you."

Amy looked puzzled as she grabbed a shoulder bag that had her handheld, her sniff-o-meter, and some water and munchies for both her and Lars. Beth said into a radio, "Can I get a cart over for one of our agents to travel down line two?"

"Copy, transport on its way to you," a voice said.

Amy huddled with Harris. "Okay, so we're just going to be sniffing the lowest of each container in each row." Harris nodded agreement. "Oh, this should be fun," she said with not much conviction.

Harris said, "Cheer up, you could be being held at gunpoint in the mountains."

Amy, looking away deliberately, said, "Not funny yet."

"Okay, sorry, go find a smelly container," Harris said.

"My limo is here," Amy said, walking over to the golf cart that pulled up.

The driver said, "Hi, my name is Jim, and I will be your tour driver today."

Getting in while Lars hopped into the back, Amy replied, "Hi Jim, I'm Amy, and this is Lars. We signed up for the Whales Tour and we seem to have made a wrong turn."

"We have lots of whales here."

"Why, thank you Jim, I think we would like to go halfway down the whale line."

"Right away, ma'am," he said as the cart began to roll down the lines of containers with the container cranes hovering above. Amy enjoyed some unabashed rubbernecking and Lars seemed fascinated, but wasn't saying anything to her.

The cart coasted to a stop and Amy got out. She reached in and pulled out her backpack and the LAI cone she'd toted along.

"Thank you very much for a wonderful tour, Jim."

"Why, the honor is mine. Will you require a ride back?"

"Well, eventually we will wind up at the end and a ride back would be appreciated."

"Just have your people call my people and we'll be right there."

"Righto, Jim," Amy said, half-waving, half-saluting.

He waved bye and headed off, clearly having something else to do.

Amy placed the cone next to the container she was standing beside, right on the edge so that Harris would see it and know that his part was complete.

Pulling out her sniff-o-meter (*How could Harris remember "olfactory reflectometer" anyway?* she wondered), Amy gave Lars the fish scent. His desire to create an endless snort reminded her of some videos of people who were addicted to snorting a particular drug. She knew that if he could roll in it he would.

"Okay, we're sniffing the ends of the containers with letters," she said, pointing up at the codes.

/Let-ers,/ he said.

"And I want you to sniff in this area," she said. Her hand swept along a strip about a foot off the ground and a handspan wide. "I'll be right here with you until you get familiar with it, then I'll just stand at the end of the row since you're faster than me. Try this one."

The kelpie's head traveled along the container for about a foot and broke off.

"I want you to do the whole thing." She walked over to the first end of the container closest to them. "Starting here and going all the way across."

Lars gave her an 'Oh, please' look, probably because he could smell the fish smell from ten feet away if it was there. However, never one to turn down sniffing, he immediately started sniffing the whole width.

Lars started at the edge of the container and worked his way over to the left. When he got to the end, he said, /No fish./

"Okay, let's do the next one." He started on the next one. /No fish./

"Keep going. This is going to take a while."

At the next one in the row, he said, /Cat./

"What cat?"

Shoving his nose against the container door, he said, /Cat. Cat. Cat./

Oh, cat pee he means, she thought.

"That's okay, Lars, we're not looking for kitties right now."

They reached the end of the row. "Okay, now we're going to the next row, but we're going to go in the other direction to save time." Having just taught him what she wanted, she wasn't sure how well this would work. Sure enough, he ran to the right corner container and did the sniffing from right to left like they did the first row. *Whatever, the containers aren't that wide*, she thought.

/Dog,/ he said.

"We don't care about dog pee either."

On the next one, while sniffing, his head worked up the door. /Big dog./

"Let's move on." She realized that she was going to hear about every animal who ever had peed on the door.

/Human./

"Ewugh."

Lars gave her a 'What's your problem?' look. Having a dog able to talk to you even in rudimentary ways introduced you to their obsession with bodily fluids, which was sometimes a little difficult for a human to handle. *At least this human*, she thought.

They continued down the row. On the next row, Amy decided to stand at the end and just let him work his way down and run back to her. This row had a dog and a cat and "rabbit" pee on it. During the next row he said, /Food./

"What?" She jogged down to where he was.

Lars was trying to inhale what looked like tomatoes that had been smashed against the door. "Good boy, don't eat it, come here." She gave him a couple of treats as a reward for not cleaning the entire door with his tongue. Destroying evidence was bad form, even if this wasn't evidence of anything but a shipping mishap.

They finished that row, and the next one, and the one after that.

"Do you need a break?" she asked, pulling out a favorite tug toy. She knew it was going to look completely absurd, them playing tug in a loading yard, but she needed him to stay focused. To keep out of the way, she moved back into the row they had completed, dropped her pack, and, bracing herself, held out the toy.

Lars threw himself at the toy, bit down on the rope, and shook his head to both sides hard, growling his best play growl, half in his throat and half through his nose. Amy, long used to the game, still had to work to keep from being pulled off her feet. She took a step towards him, and then pulled back. His head was extended and he had all four feet braced on the ground. Amy figured that the game had added half an inch to her biceps. Lars let up and spun in a quarter circle and she followed as best she could. They continued playing tug for another couple of minutes. Amy stopped pulling on the toy and said, "Okay, break time." Lars released the toy, happily panting, and she gave him some water and a treat.

"Ready for more sniffing?"

/Sniff!/ He almost seemed to bounce as they moved on to the next row.

They spent the next two hours working their way down the line, taking the occasional play break.

Lars never seemed to get tired of /No fish,/ but Amy sure was. The occasional reports from Harris told her that they were having the same luck. *Bad day for there to be no fish,* she told herself and tried not to worry about what they were going to tell Beth.

Opening up the comm link, she said, "Harris, we didn't find the container in our section. How are you doing?"

He said, "We're finishing up our last row, but it doesn't look good. I'll call for a cart. We'll come get you and we can talk further."

"Copy," she said. "Okay, Lars, let's go meet our ride."

They were halfway back down their section when the cart with Harris and Boomer pulled up and they got in. Harris got in the back with both dogs and indicated that he wanted Amy to take the front, which she did.

Turning to Harris, Amy said, "So it's actually in Coolingham or Novaton. We lost the gamble, what do you call that in craps?"

"Crapping out. Yeah, we rolled a seven, and we can only hope it's still in station."

"So we're off to the other stations." It wasn't a question.

"I called Beth and she's trying to get them to hold the most recent containers, but they're smaller, so it's a bigger impact. Hence, there's not a lot of time. Catherine is going to send Yolanda and Steve to Coolingham and we're going to Novaton."

"What if it isn't there, Harris?"

"Then they're on a truck going someplace that we don't know. Let's hope it's not a ship."

Amy said, "If it's on a ship, then it becomes someone else's problem."

He shrugged with his mouth and eyebrows. "Well, there is that hope."

CHAPTER 33:

To Novaton

AMY AND Harris and their dogs all got back in the vehicle.

Lars and Boomer collapsed in their crates.

Amy looked at them and said, "You know, I really envy how they can just flop in their crates and all is well."

"Yeah, it makes me want one too," Harris said.

Amy stretched and sighed. "You know, I'm starting to care less and less about these stupid containers."

"Think of what they did to Herman and Lincoln."

"Yeah, but they can already do that."

"Which has me wondering what else they hope to accomplish," Harris said, looking out the window. "This is worrisome."

Their escort began to move the cars and they headed off to Novaton Robo-Truck Routing station.

Amy dozed for the trip. In what seemed like just a minute or two, they were pulling into Novaton and going through the same setup rigmarole.

Amy had again taken the second half of the search and she was soon getting the usual litany of what animal had peed on the doors—be it cat, dog, or what he called "rabbit."

Lars had now started to run to the end of the next row, though he would still sniff each container right-to-left before moving on to the next container, and he was making rapid work using a squared-off S pattern. Amy realized they were getting close to the end of the line when Harris said, "Boomer is done. Negative on fish smell." Disappointment started to sink in. "Shit, Harris, Lars only has three rows left. What are we going to do?"

This yard was noisier since the line beside them was still running. It was hard for her to concentrate in order to hear Lars in her head. It was like there was only so much room in her mind for input, regardless of whether it was in her mind or her ears.

Lars had dashed around the corner to the next row and she was walking to her usual position at the beginning of the next row.

/Cat./

Whatever, she thought.

/Fish. Fish, Fish, Fish./

Annoyed, Amy said to him, /Lars, please, there no way a fish peed on that—/, then her brain kicked in, /FISH! Lars you found it! WAIT./

Amy raced to the next row and turned the corner to join him. He was standing there, bouncing up and down, tail wagging.

/Fish, Fish, Fish./

"Harris, Lars found it! Second row from the end."

Then to Lars she said, "Good boy, Lars. Here's a salmon cookie just for you." She gave him another one, pulled out his tug toy, and said, "Let's play while we wait for Harris."

Harris said in her ear, "That's great, but I just talked to Beth. She's afraid that there might be informants in the yard and doesn't want to let on that we found it."

Amy said, "This spook business is just no fun. The container number is different, FYI."

"Record that number and keep searching. Tell Lars there's more fish."

"We have to tell Yolanda and Steve to turn around."

"Nope, they should continue as planned."

"But it's a shipyard—a dangerous place for a dog Gimli's size."

"You can tell them to be careful, if you choose your words carefully."

While Lars was yanking her around, Amy tried to get a look at the containers. There were two piled up, but the number wasn't the same as before. *How did they do that?* she wondered.

They broke off from the game and Lars put his paws up on the container's rail, looking up as far as he could crane his neck.

/Fish./

"So the top container also smells like fish? That's five or six feet away. I apologize for doubting you."

AMY TOLD her handheld to contact Yolanda. "Hello, Wild Goose One, this is Wild Goose Two."

"Greetings, Other Goose," Yolanda said.

"I know you're on your way to the agility trial."

Yolanda said, "Girl, what have you been smoking? Good stuff up north I hear."

Amy could hear Steve laughing in the background.

"Hear me out. My sources tell me that you're no longer in the running."

She could hear Yolanda say, presumably to Steve, "I have fallen into a wormhole, and I'm talking to Captain Astro."

"But your fans really want to see you on the course."

After a beat Amy could hear her say, "No longer in the . . . Mmm-hmm," in that catching-on sort of tone.

"But go easy, it's a dangerous course."

"How dangerous?"

Crap, I haven't worked that part out, she thought. "They're forever moving the obstacles around and not always paying attention to where they're going."

"But nothing that shoots?"

"Correct."

"Okay, we will continue on to the agility trial and will talk to you later."

"Put on a good show for your fans."

"You know I always do."

"Ta-ta."

"Happy travels, Astro." She cut the connection.

"Amy!"

Looking over her shoulder, Amy was just able to get "Harris" out her mouth, before Boomer nearly ran them over.

Breathless, Harris said to Lars, "Good boy, Lars," and gave him a friendly whack on the side. "Beth is on her way." Lifting up his head after a few gasps, he pulled out his handheld and held it up to the lower number. He frowned. Not only did the check digit on the container with a different number compute fine, but it allegedly contained tires.

He held up the handheld higher, aiming at the top container. "This one too. How can that be?"

Amy noticed that Boomer also had his nose on the container. Harris grinned. "Boomer is saying 'Fish.'"

"How can we be sure?"

"I'm going to scrape off a bit of the fish goo and feed it to the handheld to see if it can match it. It's not that great, but it will give us a guess." Harris took out a small knife and scraped a little of the painted-on substance. Then he scraped it into the small sampler. "It's thinking."

Amy smiled. "As if, but I'm glad it's working on it."

Harris said, "Can you ask them to bring over one of those ladders on wheels?"

Amy walked down to find someone who could bring them one.

Harris looked up at the numbers. There was something that didn't look right around the edges. He said to Amy, "When you get the ladder, just put it at the end of the row and keep searching. If someone asks, we haven't found anything but want to check a few of the higher containers."

Amy went a couple of rows down and found one of the mobile ladders on wheels. Fortunately, they weren't nearly as carefully supervised as they were at Northstation and Amy was able to wheel the ladder down to the correct row without anyone objecting or insisting on helping. Harris came out to meet her and positioned it against the first container in the row. The one they were interested in was the fourth one down.

"Let's go look for more fish, Lars."

/Fish!/

And they headed off to finish the last two rows.

Harris tried to look carefully at the wrong container, taking photos and entering its tracking data. He learned that it was a container labeled "general goods," filled with items that a few families were moving across the ocean. He thought about what a leap of faith it was to just throw all your belongings into a box and hope that you'd see it again someday, instead of it taking a permanent swim in the ocean.

He moved the ladder over to the next box and repeated the charade, then decided that was enough and moved it down to the fourth-position containers they were interested in. By this time, his handheld beeped that the sample was a 90 percent match to the original fish paint, which, given all the dirt and debris that hit the container during transport, sounded about right.

Going up the ladder, he noticed the edges of the numbers had some sort of a residue around the edges. He wasn't sure how close an examination he could give it without someone noticing, but took a photo and placed his fingers on the strip. It was adhesive. What the heck? The other one also had the same tackiness.

Climbing back down the ladder, he worked on a theory. Someone had covered up the numbers with the ones they originally saw. Al, the guy that sent the containers from the lab-in-a-box people, was going to have to do some explaining, but it could also have been the company that delivered the containers to Applied Sciences. Then, at the way station, some very fast person must have been able to get up there to pull the numbers off. That was a little remarkable and implied that either our bad guys had people who worked there, or they paid them off. He made a note to have Beth chat with them, but she might decline, not wanting to tip the bad guys off.

He had been considering whether there was a low-tech way of tracking the container from a distance. Someone had disabled the GPS tracking device. He could still see it up high on the door, so they must have zapped it in some way. It looked like using electronics probably wasn't the solution. He decided to try one of the clear flat paints that contained an element that would fluoresce green when viewed with something electronic, like the newer traffic monitoring cams.

What to paint was now the debate. It had to be something that wasn't already on the container. He considered a big H but decided that was a little too graffiti-like. It had to be distinctive. He decided to do a series of slashes that were like a zigzag pattern or three adjoining mountains way up on the upper left of the container in a blank area.

∧∧∧

He then climbed up to the roof of the container, and repeated the exercise.

Amy had come back with Lars. "Hi, Boomer, is your dad a graffiti artist now? If he is, he needs to learn how to use a paint can."

Harris climbed down the ladder. "Can you help me move this ladder a couple of containers down?"

"Sure, but care to explain?"

"In the car."

"Okay, spook." Amy helped him push the ladder over two containers.

Harris climbed up and repeated the gesture, but Amy didn't hear any painting sounds. "Er, Harris." Then she realized he was faking the marking of this container.

Harris, focusing on the door, held up a hand. He then went up to the roof and repeated the miming.

He came back down again. "Okay, now we need to go over to the previous one you found the tomatoes on and another one."

"Um, okay." Again, she helped move the ladder. They repeated this for three more containers and then moved the ladder over to where they found it and headed back.

Beth walked out to meet them. In a voice that was meant to carry just a little, she said, "I'm sorry that we didn't find anything, so we're off to meet Yolanda and Steve at Coolingham." Harris and Amy nodded and tried to look dejected. Boomer and Lars were no help in the "look sad" business, but Amy figured they just looked like regular dogs, which they did.

They walked back to the vehicle, put the dogs in, and got in.

Turning to Harris, Amy said, "Okay, what's going on, my misguided artist?"

Harris took a breath and then told her what his plan was.

Amy laughed. "And you really think that will work? Are you going to watch traffic cams all day? I can't see even you doing that."

"No, actually, I took a look at it with my camera, and it does show bright green. I'm going see if I can have the computer do the scan looking for the image."

"That's a stretch."

Harris grinned ruefully, "I know, but I wanted to give it a try."

Amy said, "I'm no expert, but image-matching usually is comparing the same size and distance."

"Well I might be able to tell it to look for just the fluorescent green since that isn't a common sight."

Amy asked, "How long before our boxes leave?"

"Should be about a day."

"We don't have an escort going back. Do I give the car permission to speed?"

"Just a little."

"Zoom. Zoom," she said. "Let's go. Hey doggies, it's burger time."

They dashed back, yelling the doggy version of 'Yahoo.'

CHAPTER 34:

After Novaton

AFTER AMY and Harris got back, Harris started to set up his image search program, and Amy updated their status reports. They were both completely engrossed in their work when Yolanda came crashing through the door, followed by Steve and Labrador Pearl with corgi Gimli chewing on her neck.

Yolanda strode up to Amy's desk, dropped both hands on it, leaned in, and, pausing for dramatic effect, said, "The egret eats a fish at dusk."

Without looking up, Amy said, "And the camel spits in the wind."

Yolanda said, "Llama."

"What?"

"Llamas spit."

"I thought camels spit, too."

Yolanda said, "When they do, it's not saliva, it's predigested food."

Amy gave her an appalled look. "How did we get on this?"

"Camels, and you started it by calling me and talking about fake agility trials."

"No, I think it was egrets."

"Egrets don't spit."

"Stop it, I've spent the day with Harris. Have mercy."

Yolanda walked over, put her arm around Amy's shoulders, and, looking over at Harris, said, "Harris, what did you do to this poor woman?"

Harris said, "Nothing. Well, nothing that she didn't want."

Amy leaned into Yolanda and sobbed. "He tried to teach me container check-digit calculation."

Squeezing her shoulders tighter and leaning over to look her in the eyes, Yolanda said, "Do you want to talk about it?"

"NO. And how was your day?"

"I'm sure you can guess. After Gimli being nearly run over twice at the container switching station, I leashed our dwarf doggy friend here and we just walked around the containers together. Next time someone has to waste a couple of hours doing nothing useful, I nominate you."

"I owe you one on that score."

Catherine walked in and asked, "Does anyone want to talk to a reporter about our work?"

Both Amy and Yolanda leapt up. "Yes!"

Indicating both of them, she gestured at the door and both Amy and Yolanda headed out.

Steve wandered up to Harris. "Our role in this container thing should be winding down, but you're working pretty hard on something."

"I painted a marker on both containers that is only visible to an electronic sensor, and I'm writing a program to help the computer scan for occurrences of that image in hopes that we can track it through the traffic cameras."

"Want me to entertain Boomer for a bit?"

"He would love that. Boomer, go with Steve."

"Pearl, Boomer, let's go."

Both dogs leapt up and charged out the door.

———————

Left in the office to some peace, Harris took a sip of tea and thought about what he needed to do.

He diagrammed the structure of the program, part of which he stole from previous code. He hadn't done a lot of image-recognition programs, but enough to be able to get some progress. He had written a test case to see if he could get the system to recognize the green pattern of the marking he'd created.

Looking out the window, he watched Steve throw balls and toys for Boomer and Pearl. Pearl the obsessed retriever always seemed to get the ball, but Steve threw something right after the ball that Boomer would then snag.

Looking back at the screen, he ran the program on his test image, which worked. Then he tried it on some traffic data; that didn't work. His image was too large and it was getting confused by the garish green of a software company's new logo that was showing up on some trucks.

Harris made his reference image smaller and included some of the surrounding maroon of the container's base color. That seemed to work better, though he was still getting the occasional false positive; he decided he could live with that. After some testing, he decided that it would work well enough for his purposes tomorrow. He headed out with Boomer.

THE NEXT morning, Harris appeared dressed in a Chandra the Demon Hunter T-shirt with a couple of Danishes and a large "mega-caffeinated" Buzz drink. Steve looked up and said, "Looks like you're ready to roll."

"And I have the pizza place on speed dial," he replied.

Steve made that "Va-room" engine revving sound that everyone still seemed to understand, even though engines that made that sound were usually only seen at vintage car shows.

Harris brought up a view of the shipping yard on his screen and things seemed to be proceeding much as you'd expect a shipping yard to work. Containers on trucks were lined up at the exit gate for a final check to make sure all the i's were dotted. His containers weren't quite scheduled to leave yet, so he stood up and stretched.

He asked Steve, "How is that Nadine case going?"

Looking over at Pearl the lab, Steve said, "We found the kid, but people are arguing over where she should end up."

"I hate it when that happens."

"Yeah, it kind of takes the joy out of it. I wish I could fix it all for her. She's only four years old."

Harris sat back down; he saw his marked containers in line ready to go. "Show time," he said.

"Good hunting," Steve said.

Taking a drink, Harris watched his containers preparing to leave. They were both attached to one truck. He hoped this would make tracking them easier. He raised his drink in salute as the truck pulled out of the yard and turned north.

He tracked the containers through the highway cams, changing which ones he was looking for depending on the last one he saw. He had written a program to update the onscreen map each time it saw one, and if it didn't see it within a certain amount of time on the next cam, it would beep and start scanning other possible cams. The truck moved steadily north and slightly east. He realized that they could have easily come this far using the robo-truck routes, and decided to call Beth to let her know about this circuitous alternate route. Beth considered putting the truck under surveillance, but decided that would be too hard over such distances with a lot of agencies to coordinate with. After some hours, the truck headed onto secondary highways. It began wandering through the rolling foothills, and Harris was concerned that he might run out of cams.

The truck crossed into Choran on Highway 2217, moving past the foothills into a much flatter landscape. Harris called Beth again. "It's crossing into Choran and I'm running out of ways to track them. I was going to have the Route Patrol folks follow them, but they're still on the road."

"Choran? What is it doing way up there, and why did they do this via a road truck? Are the container numbers the same?"

"Yes, as far as I can tell."

"I'll call their Route Patrol and see if I can get a couple of unmarked tag vehicles, but traffic is lighter up there and a tag might get spotted. I don't really want to get the Feds involved yet, as they tend to take over, but they are the experts at this."

Harris said, "Hang on a minute. You know, we have an office in Orson—a town in Choran. Would you like me to contact them?"

"Sure, a local angle often helps. Just no lights and sirens."

Harris hung up and contacted the Choran office.

"Hi, Markus, this is Harris in Evergreen."

Markus answered, "Hey there, what new and exciting things are happening? They're sure not happening here."

"Well then, I have some good news for you."

"You're doing a TV show about our exciting lives? Why thank you."

"There's a container truck headed for you and I'm running out of traffic cams to keep an eye on it."

"Not a TV truck?" Disappointment colored his voice.

"Sorry, this is a lab-in-a-box truck."

"A what? Really? What kind of a lab?"

"That's what we're concerned about. If you could find a way to track it without giving us away, I'd really appreciate it."

"In person? We're on it. It will get me out of the building. Where is it?"

"It's on 2217 North. I'm sending you photos, the container IDs, and the most recent location I've seen it. I'll keep updating you until I run out."

"We'll head out and put a stake out by the next cam and see if we can coordinate."

"Thanks, Markus, I appreciate it."

"Thanks for the distraction."

"Hope it's not too boring. I can get you fairly close, so you're not sitting around too much."

"Don't worry. Really." He rang off.

HARRIS TOOK a break to stretch and move around, giving them time to get over to the location.

Steve looked up. "And how goes the quest?"

"Would you believe they drove the containers all the way to Choran using a road truck?"

Steve frowned. "That's weird, and indirect."

Harris said, "I think it's another smoke screen."

Markus called in. "2217 is a funny road, I'm just verifying that I'm where I need to be."

"You're close, but keep heading north."

After some more back and forth, Markus told him, "We have your quarry in sight."

Harris said, "Oh, thank you so much. Let me know what you want on your pizza."

"Oh, I will, but let me follow them for a bit," Markus said.

About an hour later, Markus called. "Well, this is getting more curious."

"Mmm?" Harris said inquiringly.

"They pulled off at a truck stop and then pulled into an unmarked warehouse building."

Harris checked the map and the address information. It was just an average truck stop where you could get a meal, a bed, a movie, a restroom, and probably various social connections of varying intimacy. No mention of a warehousing business. He looked at the photos that Markus had sent. Nothing stood out. It was a basic beige metal building, the kind that your eye skips right over. The only curious thing was that its doors were closed and these types of buildings usually had open doors throughout the day. "Markus, were those doors open when the truck showed up?"

"Only when the truck arrived. The door rolled up and then appeared to swallow the truck."

"Hang on while I contact Beth."

Harris called Beth.

"Detective Hanscom?"

On the screen, Beth gave Harris that *Do you have to be so formal?* look and said, "Yes, Agent Consuelo'a. How may I help you?"

"I've had Markus from the Choran office tailing our containers, and they've pulled into an unmarked warehouse at a truck stop."

"Any idea what's going on in there?"

"None."

Beth frowned. "Hmmm. I'm going to ask the Route Patrol if they know anything about it."

"I just sent you the location information."

"Good. Let me make a couple of calls and get right back to you." Beth rang off.

Markus said, "Okay, so I'll grab a burger and watch my beige box. I'll leave the camera on so you can watch with me."

"Wouldn't miss it," Harris said.

Harris brought his own handheld out and took a break to throw a ball for Boomer.

After a bit, Beth called back. "Route Patrol doesn't know anything, but the local police are interested. They're going to send a detective over and they promise to contact Markus first and not give us away."

"What sort of ETA are we talking about? I already owe Markus big time."

"About fifteen minutes."

"Markus is calling, okay if I conference you in?"

"Sure," Beth said.

Both of their images appeared on the screen.

"Markus, I've conferenced you in w—"

Markus looked alarmed. "The truck-tractor is rolling out of the warehouse, but it's hauling a different trailer set."

Harris almost repeated his introduction before realizing that Markus could easily see Beth, and it suddenly didn't matter. "WHAT? Those, those—"

"Sneaky bastards," Beth said.

"Yeah, that. It's definitely the same truck-tractor?"

Markus said, "Most definitely, unless they switched the registration plates."

Harris looked at Markus's camera display. The trailers were now white. He said, "Beth tells me the local police are sending over a detective for a further look. Maybe he or she can come up with an excuse to look inside for our containers."

"That might tip our hand."

"Which is our concern," Beth said.

Harris could see the truck pull out on the highway.

Markus said, "Maybe they could play the part of an inspector."

"But there's no record of a truck business there at all," said Beth.

Harris watched the truck drive off. The white on the trailer shimmered oddly.

"Well, it's not like they can hide the fact that trucks are going in and out of it in full view of a well populated truck stop," Markus said.

"True."

Harris saw a flash of a green /\/\ on the back of one of the trailers, and nearly choked on his drink. "MARKUS, follow that truck."

"Huh?"

"They just put a covering over the trailers—those are the containers."

"But what about—"

Beth cut in, "Just go. The local police can cover this end, and I'll fill them in." The display where she had been went blank.

The world that was on Markus's vehicle camera spun for a moment as the car tore out onto the highway. "I see 'em, but they're turning left on 7498. Good thing that truck is distinctive from a distance."

Harris said, "I want to know what odd thing they've disguised it with. It's white appearing, but see-through at very particular angles. I've seen this type of covering before. You can put it on very quickly—much faster than painting."

They went for miles on 7498, turned on 27, and then on 984. "Have you run out of road yet?" Harris asked.

"We will if they head into the mountains."

"Oh gods, not an evil genius who works in the mountains."

"That would be a little cliché, wouldn't it?" Markus said.

"Yeah, if you're such a genius, you could be a little more creative about it."

The truck went right up to the mountains, skirted the edge, and then turned south again.

"What is going on?" they both asked at nearly the same time.

Markus said, "I haven't spent this much time driving manually since I was chasing a drunk driver years ago."

Digging the base of his palms into his eyes, Harris said, "This has to pay off. If they wind up back in that warehouse, I'm coming up there to shoot them myself."

After what seemed like forever, the truck turned again, onto a very small road.

Markus said, "This is going to be hard to follow on. Stopping to watch for a bit. We're back to the outskirts of town."

Peering at the display, Harris asked, "What's out there? Everything seems flat with the occasional set of trees or buildings."

"Farms and the like. This is not a high-tech place at all."

"Curious."

"Following just a bit more, I can still see the truck. Wait, they're turning in." His voice was incredulous. "Oh, no way."

"Talk to me, Markus."

"Well, your little truckie is now at the Tomasian Farm and Retreat."

"Where? What?"

"It's a religious community that also creates woolen clothing that they call Tomasian Organicwear."

"Right, sure. Are you serious? What the heck do they need a state-of-the-art lab for?"

"Well, they're detaching the trailers. Sending photos. Maybe they're making Super Organicwear."

"Thanks, Markus. This is so weird," Harris said, taking a last hit from his drink.

"I'm headed back. No anchovies on the pizza."

"It will be waiting for you. This is going to become a Fed case. They thank you for the assist, and I'll let our lead detective, Beth, know. And I have some research to do."

CHAPTER 35:

Tomas's Plan

TOMAS SAT by the fire, leaning back in his black leather over-stuffed chair. He longed for a cigarette, but he had opted to quit to be an example to his followers. Trying not to miss inhaling the nicotine smoke's reassurance, he contemplated and brooded. More than ten billion people crawled over his planet, devouring everything like locusts. The places where the darker-skinned people lived were facing starvation and were pressing outward. And yet modern science had been extending lives up to 150 years. Disaster was on the way for humanity, and while the Planet Aires terraforming was progressing, there weren't really enough people interested in living the ascetic life on the cold planet with air that you couldn't breathe yet and sun that you would only be able to barely feel if you could have bare skin outside, which you couldn't. The fire sparked, catching his attention. Ten billion people. The number kept ringing in his mind. It so needed to change, and soon, and permanently. He would rather the population be a hundred thousand, but one million would be okay, and ten million was more realistic. Ten million. That would be a good start-over sort of number. He decided to call it the one percent solution.

He rested his chin on his hand. The nanobot project was finally progressing. It had been so difficult to attract the right sort of smart people to help make it work. His preference was to recruit younger, more moldable people to his religious order and then train them. However, nanotech required a very high level of expertise, and most of the nano-experts weren't who he was looking for. He wanted to start the human race over, and he wanted to be very picky about who got to come along. But in order to start over, he needed the technical expertise, and he wasn't sure he had the luxury to wait around for the expertise to show up in the right package.

He took a sip of his Chardonnay and readjusted in the chair, stroking his chin. Previous attempts at reducing the size of humanity were born of barbarous, genocidal, racial hatred. While Tomas thought of himself as a New Christusian prophet, he was also a realist. While the Ohads were generally hated for their participation in the murder of Christus, the Ohads who had survived had proved to be some of the toughest, smartest people around and the inclusion of some of them in his New Earth was essentially a given.

His preference was for the lighter-skinned people, as he found darker skin distasteful, though again he was likely going to have to compromise on this. It mostly depended on what DNA types he could get the nanobots to distinguish. There just wasn't a simple "look for the smart, fair skinned" criteria in DNA sequencing.

But Tomas was facing a much larger problem. No matter what method he chose for reducing the population, 9.99 billion was a very, very, very large number. Even if he was able to extract the information about the airborne method of nanobot distribution, which was still being researched, and even if it worked perfectly, which he knew there was no way it could, it would take years for nanobots to spread to all the Earth. Right now, with waterborne distribution, he would have to dope every water supply, and even with worldwide water treatment available, there were still many cultures that maintained a suspicion of public water and wouldn't drink it. And to find every major water source would take years.

And even if he were able to get nanobot distribution world-wide, he still had the issue of the sheer numbers. His preference was for every infected, non-qualifying person to have a nano-bot-caused heart attack and immediately fall over dead. If that were to happen, he would have a disposal problem that had never, ever been faced. Even the Devoties of long ago had a disposal problem after they killed thirty-three million people, and that wasn't all at once. Corpses are an immediate health risk, and even if they were to sequester large parts of the world, the hazard would be off the charts.

So square one beckoned again, and he took another sip of wine. Much as he wanted to have New Earth begin as soon as possible, he could see he had two choices. Take out selected geographical areas and risk getting caught. If he was willing to be patient, then it would be far more effective to create attrition. Or, what if he were to make everyone sterile? He actually would only have to make half the people sterile. Women have a lot of help with their fertility but men less so, and they're less inclined to seek help and often didn't know if there was a problem. What if he could find a way for the nanobots to influence the sperm to not even be interested in ova? That way, during a physical exam a man's sperm would look normal. The distribution method could be slower, and it would be a long time before anyone noticed there was a problem. He was forty-five and young enough that he might live to see the effect.

A bit of sap in the log popped, burning blue for a time. He breathed in and stretched his arms. He considered what they had already accomplished. They had learned how to kill with the nano-bots by shutting down or changing a vital body function. Then they had figured out how to make the bot smarter about what they attacked, and they had succeeded in controlling them from a distance. And he managed to do it without his workers actually knowing the criteria of the project. He had turned it around into a health-monitoring project and neglected to tell them about the opposite pole. All this in and of itself would be more than enough for any "evil genius" just looking to kill a lot of folks, but that was too shortsighted for him. Killing wasn't his preoccupation.

He wanted a sustainable future. That was his main goal and his moral obligation, and to have a pile of bodies around seemed an excellent way to bring his neo-future to a new end. No, planned attrition was the best way to achieve this. The tricky part would be to convince his followers to be patient, especially Adam. Adam: so brilliant, so passionate, but so impulsive. What to do about Adam?

CHAPTER 36:

Amy, Markus, and the Feds

AMY, WITH Lars, flew up to the Choran office for one of their regular check-in status visits. When they walked into the office, Markus looked up and said, "Greetings, Earthlings."

Markus had slightly scattered but not unkempt, curly, dark brown hair and bright brown eyes that always seemed to be chuckling at something. He had a permanent five o'clock shadow, even if he'd shaved an hour ago. One time he had tried to grow a beard, but gave up after a week because he wound up with what he described as a series of disputed borders.

Markus had lived in the northwestern city of Soundside until two years ago, when a breakup with his girlfriend prompted him to volunteer for working in the smaller, more inland location. Amy didn't understand his choice but tried to refrain from judging him too often, and he and Steve had developed this teasing relationship that was likely not to go anywhere but was fun to watch.

The Choran City office was in a former bakery that still smelled of bread and sugar. Next door was a bowling alley, with the police station across the street. When asked why they weren't in the police station, the answer was always: they wanted a window.

"Hi, Markus. How goes?" Looking down at his cream-colored golden retriever, she said, "Hi, Chloe," and rubbed her proffered head.

"Pretty quiet up here."

Amy asked, "Steal any drug lord dogs?"

"Not today, we save that for when you're here for a while."

"Oh, lucky me."

"Enjoying your spring?"

"The winter was way cold this time. I am rethinking the wisdom of being here, but you knew that."

"Well, I would be thinking that, but I'm letting you work that out for yourself. But Chloe isn't a Malamute, and I don't see a dog sled yet."

"Nice try. In this area, it would be an ATV or a snowmobile."

Sitting down at his desk, Amy asked, "So tell me something that I need to be here for in person."

Holding both arms out wide, he responded, "The fresh air and wide-open spaces with bits of beautiful mountain around, and the sought-after burning smell of gunpowder."

Looking back at her and dropping his arms he said, "The Feds have us keeping half an eye on those containers that you tracked up here."

"Really? The ones that Harris followed? Why? No dogs in there that we know of."

"The Feds are looking into ways to understand more of what's going on there. The Tomasians are situated on a poorly producing farm, so they're thinking that it's not about growing things."

"Or maybe it is and they need all the help they can get."

"They figured out that one of them is a dog lover and they're wondering if there's any way we can help. I told them I knew just the person for the job."

Amy had that sinking feeling as Markus made that significant, expectant pause. She decided just to say nothing and wait and see how long he could take it. She crossed her arms over her chest and shifted her weight in her chair.

Markus sat there smiling that dumb grin.

"You didn't," she finally said.

"You're the perfect choice."

"Let me count the ways. I don't live here. I don't know what they want, and most importantly: I'm not a spy."

"You'll fit right in."

"Eff off, Markus." She reached down and petted the golden retriever. "Hi, Chloe, let me talk to the sane one here."

"They say they'll give you the training you need."

"Oh right. Instant spy. I don't think so, Markus. Why don't we talk about lost people you've found or something?"

"You know all that already."

"Well, I guess my work is done here."

"Seriously, Amy, I think you're the person for this job."

"Seriously, Markus."

"Really."

"No."

"They want to at least talk to you about it."

"No."

"They'll be here in about fifteen minutes."

"What? I have a job and a life down south, you might recall."

"I'll let you tell them 'no.' I did ask Catherine about it and she said she'd consider it."

"Am I the last one to know about this?"

"Want to take the dogs out for a bit?"

"I'm taking the dogs out and you can stay here. Lars, Chloe. Let's go. Maybe the bowling alley will let us play fetch there."

Amy took the dogs and a couple of tennis balls out to a field that was in the back. She couldn't believe that Markus volunteered her for such a thing. Well, actually she could. She would throw one ball in one direction and the other the other way and it mostly worked, though sometimes both dogs would take off for the one and she'd throw the second one after them. In the middle of all this, she called Catherine.

When Catherine appeared on the screen, Amy said, "Hi, Catherine. Markus is telling me that he volunteered me for some spy thing up here."

Catherine smiled and nodded. "Yes, the Feds are looking to find a way to get close to one of the religious group's followers who works and lives on the grounds and who is a dog lover."

"But why me? I'm no spy and I have to get back down south."

"I'm sure we can work out something part-time once they figure out a pattern that this guy follows."

"I don't know the first thing about being a spy."

"I think they're going to keep it pretty basic. Like some regular dog-park chit chat."

"You know how deep dog park conversations are. 'Look how muddy my dog is. Rover, stop digging that hole.' Or the local sports team. 'How do you think the Mighty Cockroaches are going to do this year?'" Amy went on, "I can't believe you're going along with this."

"You might be able to do some good here," Catherine said.

Amy paused. Catherine knew just how to say the thing to convince her or at least get her to listen. "I don't think I'm the right choice for this."

Catherine touched her thumb and index finger to her lower lip, pinching it a little, looking down as if in deep thought. She looked up and said, "Why don't you tell the Feds your reservations, and they can better tell if you'd be a good fit for this?"

Unable to come up with a reasonable argument, Amy said, "Well, I can at least talk to them."

"Good luck, and call me with any questions." They ended the call.

Amy came back in with two panting dogs and two dirty tennis balls.

Markus pointed to a trash bin that was full of dirty tennis balls.

Amy remembered that this was the balls-to-be-cleaned section. If she remembered, they all got dumped into the washing machine all at once, which made an amazing racket. "You know they have special tennis-ball washers."

Markus snorted. "For the discerning dog, I see." Looking out the window he said, "Our Federales are here."

Amy peered out and saw a fit, forty-year-old, dark-brown-haired man with lighter colored skin, but with hard, dark, shaded features around his eyes and eyebrows. He had a serious, slightly tired, but engaged expression, wore a suit (Amy realized that it seemed like only the Feds still wore suits), and walked with authority. The other person was an equally fit, slightly younger woman with rich, dark brown skin with warm undertones and a more open expression. She was also in dark slacks and a nice coat, though it looked more natural on her.

Markus opened the door. "Greetings, welcome." Amy could tell he was resisting bowing as he let them in.

Amy stood up and they all shook hands.

Showing his ID, the man entering said, "Hi, I'm Agent Jack Hawthorne, and this is Agent Vivian Smith."

Markus guided them into a meeting room.

As they were sitting down, Markus said, "We actually have halfway decent coffee; may I get you all some?"

Jack declined, but Vivian accepted and Amy said, "I'd love one, I already have a cup in there somewhere."

Markus said, "That's okay, I've just given you another one. Cream?" Amy said yes, but Vivian said black was fine.

"Thanks, Markus," Vivian said, accepting the cup.

"Yes, thank you," Amy said.

Jack pulled a tablet out of his bag. "I understand that you have been told a little of what we're hoping to accomplish."

Amy took a breath. "Only a little."

Jack tapped the tablet a few times, turned it around, and slid it across the table.

"This is Mark Johnson, who goes by the name of Tomas and leads a small religious group called the Tomasians. He dropped the 'h,' we guess to distinguish himself from the historical Thomas whose teachings they are focused on. Thomas was Christus's disciple, who Tomas, formerly Johnson, claims was the twin of Christus."

Amy gave him a skeptical look, but didn't say anything. She tried not to think of some smart remark that Steve would have made, like "good and evil twins."

"Tomas has been publicly saying that the world's population is entirely too large and that we should be finding ways to reduce the environmental pressure on the Earth. He carefully hasn't gotten specific, though he says he fully supports the Planet Aires colonization and the Lunar community.

"What's caught our attention is that he seems to be taking quite an interest of late in scientific development, particularly in the medical uses of nanotechnology."

Amy looked up, her eyes hardening. "His group is the one making all those demands? The ones who attacked Herman and Lincoln?"

"We don't know yet," Jack replied.

"But you suspect."

Jack did sort of a half-shrug and nodded.

"This is where you could help us."

Amy, feeling incredulous, asked "How? Markus said something about one of the coworkers liking dogs."

Jack took the tablet back and tapped until another face appeared.

Vivian spoke. "This is Brian Robertson, who goes by 'Adam'—they all seem to have taken on Biblical names. He is one of five people who do scientific work for the order, as far as we can tell. We know that he takes his dog to the park regularly and he loves his dog. We're wondering if someone with a dog would have better luck getting close to him, as he doesn't seem to have much of a social life outside the order's property except for the dog park."

Amy put her fingertips on her temples and pondered the photo. "You've been to dog parks, yes?" Vivian nodded. "And you know how deep and meaningful dog park conversations are?" Vivian smiled and Jack appeared to be attempting something similar.

"It is a long shot, but we're running out of things to try, short of illegal bugging."

Amy said, "And that's tricky with no windows."

"We think no windows was no accident," Vivian answered.

"But why me? Why not some local dog owner who knows how to be a spy?"

"We don't have an empathic division yet."

Amy said, trying to refrain from being flip, "I don't quite see how that makes a difference."

Jack said, "From what we understand, you might not know how to be a spy, but you're pretty good at getting your dog to help you manipulate people." That slight smile played over his face.

Amy looked down, a slight blush starting to creep over her face. Talking to the floor, she said, "I could blow this whole thing."

"We can teach you the basics in the city of Soundside, and help you come up with a cover story."

"I have a coworker named Yolanda who would be awesome at this."

Vivian smiled. "We're familiar with Yolanda, and I agree, but there is one problem."

"With Yolanda?" Amy asked, the incredulity clear in her voice.

Jack bit his lip a moment, cleared his throat, and said, "Not with Yolanda, with them."

Amy looked quizzical. "But they haven't even met."

"You see, and this is awkward, but they have issues with skin color."

"Really? Still? But there really isn't a white or a black anymore."

Vivian lifted her hand, palm up. "And you know it isn't for lack of trying in some circles."

"I've heard of it, but I've never really met anyone who cared that much. So they want everyone to go back to being in one, what's the term, race?"

"Well, they'd like to, but we think Tomas has decided it is time to be realistic and that he wants to hold more to his smaller world population idea instead. Because of this, he's willing to work with mixed-race people, which is most everyone, but they're still prejudiced in favor of lighter-skinned people, which would make you a better candidate than Yolanda."

Amy leaned back, shaking her head. "This is just nuts." She looked up and leaned forward, reengaging. "How much time are we talking about here?"

Jack met her eyes. "You've been certified to use the self-flying plane that the empaths have?"

"Well yeah, but I'd hate to hog it."

Jack looked at the tablet, but Amy could tell he was doing it out of habit and not reading it. "Catherine, your director, tells me that she's applied to buy a second one. If you can use the plane, you can come up here two or three times a week during the day and then go back home the same day. We'll have you spend a day with our trainers in Soundside, and then you'll be working with a local handler here."

"Part-time spy?"

"Part-time spy. What do you think?"

"I think I'd like to think about it."

"Could you tell us by tomorrow?"

Amy, looking slightly panicked, said, "Uh, yes. I think."

Jack reached out his hand and Amy took it. "Thanks for being willing to consider this."

After they shook hands, Vivian reached out her hand, and Amy then took hers, too. "I know this is a lot to take in, but you could really help us out here. You can make a difference." Vivian smiled and Amy realized how genuine she felt. She didn't feel she was being sold on something—at least not too hard.

They stood up. Jack said, "You can talk about this to anyone at your work, but please limit it to them."

Amy also stood up; she had to concentrate on her feet to keep from falling over from incredulity, but managed to say, "Okay."

Markus walked them out. Amy sat on the floor to commune with Lars, massaging her fingers into his neck. His eyes half-closed in appreciation.

Markus walked back in with a slightly mischievous look and said, "I spy a spy with my little eye."

"Can't hear you, Markus," and she buried her face in Lars's fur.

CHAPTER 37:

Amy Considers

AMY LOADED Lars into his plane crate, strapped herself in, and programmed the plane to go back home. The plane, once told where to go, could almost do the job itself, but sometimes decisions had to be made by a person. She had been required to go through training and certification and she had to be in or near the pilot's seat while the plane was flying, but still it was nothing like actually flying the plane, which Harris said he'd teach her someday.

As the Piper taxied to the runway to get in line awaiting takeoff clearance, she considered the whole day. She was glad that she didn't actually have to fly the plane or she'd wind up on an island somewhere.

As the plane climbed into the air, she thought: *a spy*. She wasn't a spy. She stretched, trying to move around in the small seat. She didn't know cloak from dagger. While she was good at some manipulation, she wasn't good at lying. She worried about their faith in her. What if she blew the whole thing? What if he found out that she was with the government and that they were watching carefully? She shuddered, shaking her head, and made herself contemplate the beautiful view.

And how was she going to be able to keep this from John? She was used to not discussing ongoing investigations with him, but this seemed different. He'd probably object—thinking it was dangerous. She had spent a lot of effort trying to convince him that looking for lost people and investigating crime scenes wasn't dangerous. She had almost succeeded until she was kidnapped by Randall and his concern understandably went through the ceiling. John envisioned Amy doing more what her mom did, the "sit in the office and help dogs and people deal with problems of whatever sort" type of thing. She admired her mom, but she preferred something more active, at least until someone pointed a gun at her with intention. Now what her mom did looked very attractive.

ONCE AMY reached Evergreen, she stopped back at the office. Spotting Yolanda, she sank into the chair next to her desk.

Yolanda asked, "So how are the wilds up north?"

"Getting more complicated."

"Halcyon?" she said, referring to a dangerous common drug.

"Nope."

"Bomb factories?"

"Don't think so."

"Alien abductions?"

"Mmmm, naw."

"I'm fresh out."

"Containers."

"Really? Those shipping containers? What's up with them?"

"Precisely."

"Ah. So, someone is trying to figure out what's going on with our mystery containers."

"The Feds. It gets better."

"What could be better than containers?"

Amy sat up and dropped her hands onto her thighs. "They want me to try to go undercover and talk casually to one of those people, simply because the person they're interested in takes his dog to the dog park there."

"Oh, Ms. Bond I presume."

"You do not presume, and when are they going to stop with this Bond stuff?"

"When we stop understanding the references—so never."

Amy shook her head. "I don't get it—why me?"

"What reasons did they give besides you have a dog that you can sort of talk to, and you work for us?"

Amy took a breath. "Well, that's what I wanted to run by you."

Yolanda leaned back, settling in. "All ears."

"I said that I thought you were better for the job because you talk to so many people, and they said that these people still had issues with skin color. They thought that, since my skin was lighter, he'd be more likely to talk with me."

Yolanda bit her lip and nodded, looking down, and with a shrug said, "Yep."

"What do you mean 'yep'? There's not really a white or a black or a whatever anymore, so how could this still be a problem?"

Yolanda looked right at her with that matter-of-fact stare. "Girl, you are just as naive as your sort-of-white ancestors."

"Why?"

"Look, has anyone ever been all white?"

"I don't know."

Yolanda held up a piece of paper. "Has anyone ever been this shade of white?"

"That white?"

"Yes, has anyone alive ever been completely white?"

"I think the answer that you, Socrates, are fishing for is: No, unless they were ill."

"And has anyone ever been all black?"

"Close—"

"No, all black."

"No."

"So, the terms are?" Yolanda drew the sentence out expectantly.

"Incorrect?"

"Approximations."

Amy raised her hands in a partial shrug. "Where are we going with this, besides off course?"

"The point is, your scary people up north—"

"They are not my—"

"Have just changed their approximations. You are closer to white than I am."

Amy shook her head, exasperated. "This is so silly."

Yolanda put a finger to her lips and then held it in the air. "Not to them."

Amy threw up her hands. "I can't believe they even care about such stuff anymore."

"I think the more relevant issue is, can you go through with this while not voicing your actual opinion."

"What? That I think their backwater opinions are completely irrelevant?"

"That's a very good start."

Amy groaned. "I don't know."

Yolanda turned and looked off to the right, raising her voice. "Steve, do people notice the color of your skin?"

Steve, who hadn't been listening to their conversation and whose skin was only slightly lighter than Yolanda's, gave them a quizzical look.

"Is this a test? When do they not?" he replied. "It's all about 'What gradient are you?' Ever had dates like that? I guess not, since you and your wife are the color of tolerance," referring to Yolanda's much lighter-skinned wife.

Yolanda answered, "I sure did a long time ago." After a beat, she said, "Amy's being asked to commune with some white-only-wannabes up north."

Steve brightened. "Oh, the not-quite-cream separatists? Aren't they dead yet?"

Yolanda said, "Or the off-white-wishfuls. And lots of them are long gone, but there are always a few here and there and they appear to be the ones that pair of containers went to. The Feds are very interested, and they want help from the dog squad."

Steve said, "I'm not. Interested, that is. But wow, Amy! What an opportunity."

Amy wrapped her hands and arms over her head. "Why does everyone keep saying that? I don't see you all queueing up to chat with prejudiced asshats."

Steve said, "If those magic skin-color-changing things would work, and work temporarily, I might be tempted to." He looked directly at Amy. "You can nail these people. Are they the ones who attacked Herman and Lincoln?"

"Maybe. They don't know."

Yolanda leaned forward and put her hand on Amy's shoulder. "You can do this, Amy. I know you can."

Amy just groaned louder. "I so don't get this. Yolanda, your skin is a gorgeous mahogany and Steve is a nice sienna, and what am I?"

Steve said, "Runner-up white—"

Amy ran the back of her hand down her opposite arm, presenting it. "Light taupe. Yahoo."

Yolanda laughed, "Taupe is grey, silly. You are so not grey."

"How about warm taupe?" asked Steve. "You can be a house paint color."

"Not even close. Amy, you're more like Gimli's color or Lars's lower half. Amber, or a golden bronze."

Amy kneeled down to Gimli, who was ensconced in a snuggler bed with one eye open. She put a hand on his side and said, "I'm washed out compared to his rich fur coloring."

"And you have blonde hair," Steve said.

Amy grabbed her ponytail. "Sort of blonde hair. I think it's called caramel blonde."

Yolanda rubbed at her short black hair and said, "Compared to me? Please."

"Stop it, I love your hair. I also need to keep this from John, which is going to be hard. I usually can tell him vague stuff without mentioning names, but probably not this one. He is on TownCrier, that lowbrow of social media, and he wouldn't be able to resist."

Steve stood up, hands cupped around his mouth. "My girlfriend is going undercover!" His voice reverberated through the room.

Yolanda joined in. "Up north trying to blend in with a bunch of separatists. Hope she doesn't get kidnapped or killed."

Steve sat back down. "Yeah, probably best not to tell him. This is a business-hours adventure, yes?"

Amy said, "So I'm told. Do I get frequent flyer miles for this?"

Yolanda said, "Just don't manage to crash the plane or you might get a bill."

Steve asked, "Has anyone ever crashed a self-flyer?"

Yolanda said, "Yes, when it was given a bunch of conflicting information, though it was hard to do."

Steve looked pointedly over at Amy. "Don't do that."

Amy put up her hands in mock surrender.

Steve said, "Back to John."

Amy said, "Let's not—"

"I think we need to come up with a cover for your cover story to tell him."

"No, we don't."

Turning to Yolanda, Steve said, "We need a situation and a location."

Using both her hands, Yolanda said, "How about east for location?"

Amy said, "Not that I'm participating in this charade, but I wouldn't go picking any mountain locations to spend much time in right now if you don't want him to worry about someone kidnapping me at gunpoint again."

"South, then." Yolanda said, "Unless he wouldn't worry about a boat. Then you could do west."

Amy said, "He would worry."

Steve said, "South it is. So, let's come up with something that sounds true so it will be easy for you. I know. You're helping out with a cold case and confirming that a lead is viable."

Amy frowned. "Are you testing him? That's about the opposite of what we do. We gather the data, come up with a plausible theory, and hand it off to be confirmed by other people. So much for the ring of truth." She threw a fuzz ball toy at him. Pearl, Steve's yellow lab, looked up hopefully at the throwing motion, but seeing that it wasn't an interesting type of ball, put her head back down, sighing loudly.

Steve said, "How about you're testing more dogs?"

"That's too interesting. Everybody wants to know what breeds you're working with, and have you talked to their dog?" Yolanda said. "We need something boring. I know. Reports. Official ones."

Steve said, "A report on the welfare of the canine paw pads after they've spent a day in the field. Complete with photos and measurements and run over several weeks. You could measure chemical changes in the sweat on the paws."

Amy said, "Zzzzzzzzzzzzzzzzzzzzz."

"That would make it perfect then," Yolanda said.

Amy said, "But how am I going to pull this off?"

"With too many sentences about paw sweat chemicals," Yolanda said.

"Yeah, I'm bored already. He'll stop listening after word six," Steve said.

Amy tilted her head to the right in a half shrug. "That could work—"

CHAPTER 38:

Amy at Soundside

AMY GOT out of the car once she got to the Soundside Fed office. She'd borrowed the car from the Choran LAI office. She'd flown up there and then driven over. It took more time than she wanted, but she was concerned about the logistics of programming the plane to fly into the busier airspace of the northern city. *If I'm going to have to do this more often, I'll have to learn*, she thought.

The air had that fresh feel like at waterside. While it wasn't the ocean, Fairview Sound was large enough that it had a seaside presence of its own, with the usual assortment of bossy seagulls, sandpipers, and their friends. There was even a pelican flying by. She could see a loaded ferry laboriously crossing the water and some pleasure boats, too, and everything was blue and green. The hills and the trees oozed life. The scent of fir trees was ubiquitous. The sun peeked out from behind a set of often-present clouds, and she could see snow on the distant mountains.

She was trying not worry about her meeting with the trainer. She felt out of her depth and was glad that Lars was with her. She had stipulated that Lars had to be there, though his role in this meeting would be more emotional support.

The Fed campus was designed to fit into the landscape, surrounded by trees. Its multiple buildings in dark earth tones were each only about three to four stories high, but the site still had that definite official feel to it. She spotted the general area that office visitors were directed to and headed there.

After the usual official rigmarole, she was given a visitor's badge. There was some discussion about whether Lars needed one, too. It was finally decided that as long as he was with Amy, he didn't need one. They were seated in an area waiting for their trainer. The chair was comfortable, but not one you'd spend too much time in. There was a nice large mural showing the city from a mountain view, and a small indoor waterfall adding soothing trickling sounds, which helped her relax a little.

As she was looking at the mural, a man in his thirties approached her. The first thing she noticed was that he was wearing a suit, but it was one that moved well with his body, and that he was comfortable in it. Suits were rare where Amy worked, so they stuck out in her mind. The next thing she noticed was that he moved with an athlete's grace. As he got closer, he had the look of someone who got up early just to get in that five miles before work, just like her own physical trainer, Tom the Torturer. Amy realized that one day she might introduce Tom that way in an unguarded moment. Looking back at the man, she thought that he and Tom would get along so well that it might be best for everyone else if they didn't meet.

"Hi, Amy, I'm Bill," he said, reaching out his hand. Amy looked him in the eye as they shook hands. Bill's auburn eyes and warm smile helped ease her nerves in the "official-feeling" atmosphere.

He ushered her upstairs and then into a room designed for small meetings. It had a nice table with several chairs around it and a large presentation screen. He had a tablet in his hands, but he wasn't looking at it and instead just set it on the table and looked at her. "So, are you wondering what you've gotten yourself into?"

"More than once. I am so out of my depth on this."

"It's a common feeling, and I'm sure it's no help to say 'Don't worry,' but I'll say it anyway," he said, smiling.

"Keep telling me that," Amy said. "I'm so afraid I'm going to mess this up."

Bill took a breath and said, "The important thing to remember is that there are no expectations. We do not expect him to pour out all his secrets to you."

"But what if he doesn't tell me anything?"

"That in and of itself is information. Someone who never talks about their work usually does it for a reason, often having to do with wanting to keep information secret, or else they think it's so complicated that no one will understand it."

"And what if something goes wrong?"

"You will have a handler in Choran who will be nearby and listening in on your conversation, and who can intervene if necessary. You won't be alone."

Amy nodded and raised her eyebrows while breathing in. "Okay."

Bill pushed the tablet on the table toward her. "Here is that background we came up with for you. Once we agree on the details, you can import it all to your handheld. For simplicity, your name is still Amy, though if you choose to share a last name I would use your mom's last name."

Amy looked down to see Amy Bristol written across the top.

"You are a student at the local community college. We know that in real life you're studying psychology, so we thought that having you working on both biology and psychology might be a nice compromise. You haven't decided on a major, but are looking to transfer to Soundside University later on. You want to be a vet, but are not sure you want to deal with blood and guts, pain, and death, hence the psychology interest. You commute in to class, and live way out of town on your family's organic farm." Bill looked up to see Amy's forehead a little wrinkled with concern, her eyes fastened on him, unblinking.

"You okay?"

"I hope so, it's a lot to take in."

"How much do you know about biology?"

"Er, I know 'My toes itch,' referring to the usual mitosis joke. And I know basic first aid for humans and dogs."

"Well, you're going to get really interested in nanotech if he ever mentions it, but you shouldn't bring it up directly. You've been up here enough to be familiar how the weather usually is there?"

"Yeah, I try not to come in winter."

"Try to come up with some answer to what a farm does in winter. A good basic answer is not much outside, but working on repairing things indoors, and planning crops for next season."

Pointing at the tablet, he said, "Here is a recent photo of Adam. For the first couple of times at the park, just have Lars say hello to his dog so you can greet Adam. Just have the usual dog park conversation. We'd like you to wear a wire, but you won't have an earpiece—is that okay?"

Amy was actually relieved to hear that help would be within earshot. "Wired is fine, but, you're right, hearing voices can be distracting."

"If you get into an awkward place in the conversation, either make your phone ring or have Lars race off so you have to go after him."

"I'm still worried about how to be smooth in this identity."

"Don't overthink it. You're just taking your dog to the dog park. Our hope is that he'll eventually want to share with you what he's working on, but that might not happen. Either way, we'll know more than we know now."

"What if he asks me out? Do I have to date him?"

"Oh no, just politely say you have a boyfriend or girlfriend."

She hoped it wasn't going to sound too paranoid when she asked, "So about this handler backup?"

"He will be in plainclothes, in a nearby vehicle, and can come into the park if necessary. You two will work out in advance whether you know each other or not."

Their conversation went on for much longer, running through various scenarios, but Bill always came back to, "Relax, don't overthink things."

At some point in time, they took a break and went outside to let Lars explore the area. Bill said, "I know you're worried about this, but I really do think you're going to be okay, and from what I understand, you know kickboxing, yes?"

Amy took a step back and looked at him. "Sort of, but I sure hope it doesn't come to that."

He smiled and nodded in that comforting way. "Us, too."

"Just don't make me carry a gun."

"We won't. Now, you get to go back to Choran and meet with your handler, whose name is Tyson Mulhaney. He's a good guy. He'll take care of you. I trust him."

"Thanks. I hope I can help."

They shook hands, Bill petted Lars, and Amy got back into the Choran car and told it to go to the Choran Fed office.

On the way, Amy admired the incredible beauty that lots of rain offered. Right now, she was looking at a mix of deciduous and conifer trees with a rich green undergrowth, wildflowers covering the parts of the hills that the trees hadn't occupied.

She knew the car would be going through the mountains, and it would be all evergreen trees. Then it would get much dryer as they moved inland.

"How are you doing Lars? Did you like where we were?"

/Good smells./

"Kinda boring for you, but we'll have more fun in a bit."

/Fun?/

"Not yet though, time for a nap."

CHAPTER 39:

Amy Meets with Tyson

THE CAR pulled into the parking lot at the small Fed building in Choran. With its sandstone color, it tried to blend into the landscape and failed. It was one of those buildings where you couldn't tell if it was three stories or two, with one sunken-in ground floor. In either case, it was the tallest, most blocky thing around, and while it had windows, they were divided up into smaller panes at just the wrong position that strove to make them completely nonfunctional. The center of the building was a mostly flat grey stone color, with a fake old-looking analog clock displayed on center screen. Harris would have said that you could tell the clock was fake because the time was correct. It was about as imposing as an old post office, though she guessed a post office might be imposing if they were holding your mail captive.

Amy double-checked her notes. She was going to be meeting with Tyson Mulhaney, whose picture showed him to be in his mid-fifties and sturdily built, but probably less imposing than her coworker Steve. The picture showed that he had a large frame, but she couldn't tell if it was muscle or fat. Over time she'd learned not to underestimate larger people. His skin was a dark bronze, and he had light brown eyes and an open, slightly weathered face that smiled back at the camera.

As they approached the building, a man looking exactly like the photograph emerged.

"Hi, you must be Amy." He reached out his hand.

Taking his hand, she said, "Yes, and you must be—is it Agent?—Mulhaney."

"Just call me Tyson, everybody else does. Nice to meet you, Amy, and thanks for being willing to give this surveillance project a try. It is agent, last time I checked, but don't worry about it unless you're trying to find me."

He handed her a visitor badge. "Come on in and we'll do some paperwork, and then we can get out of here and go for a walk and talk about what is going to happen."

After what seemed like signing her entire life away (including providing multiple emergency contacts), they reemerged and Tyson said, "There's a park just down the road, okay if we go there? We can stop and pick up something to drink."

Amy didn't think she had much say in the matter, but said, "Sure. Lars will enjoy it too."

Amy noticed that even though Tyson was large, he moved with a dancer's grace. She wondered if he'd played football, soccer, volleyball, or something that required that specialized coordination.

They walked into the park with drinks in hand. Amy wondered if she was going to need something stronger at the end of all this, and regretted that she couldn't drink and pilot the plane when she flew home. She thought that was a little odd, since she wasn't doing the actual piloting of the plane, but remembered that if John could get their car in all sorts of weird places while drunk, then she didn't want to consider the strange places she could tell the plane to go. It wouldn't let her fly it into a mountain, but it would be happy to take her to anywhere the fuel could reach, most of which were places she didn't want to go tonight.

They sat down at a picnic table, and Lars went to check out the dog pee gossip on the nearby trees.

Tyson took a tablet out and held it up. "This is Adam Robinson. He comes regularly to the dog park around lunchtime to run his golden retriever, Levi."

"A golden? Why isn't Markus doing this? He's the one with the golden."

"He says he'd just want to steal him, and we have to be hands-off about this."

"So Markus admitted to you his creative operational planning when it comes to confiscating drug dealer's dogs?"

"He mentioned that peripherally. I don't think he wants a lot of scrutiny about it. But regarding this issue, we think there's a better chance that Adam might be willing to talk to you."

"About what? Tennis balls?"

Tyson paused and smiled. "I think you're being deliberately obtuse. I know skin color is a hard thing to talk about, but we have to. You are a person with a skin color Adam is more likely to talk to."

Amy's eye widened at his bluntness. She shook her head and said completely without rancor, "You know, I don't think I've ever been quite so objectified in my life, and it's not like I've never experienced it."

"Well, we also need the talents of an agent who is good with dogs as well as humans. Give this some time. Have Lars start to play with his dog Levi, and you say hello and take turns throwing a ball."

"Prepare to be really bored—I hope Lars likes Levi."

Tyson said, "I'm good at the patience thing. Adam is usually here around noontime. You have class three times a week at the college, and you also bring Lars here at noon. The school quarter has just started, so this fits in well."

"What if he asks me out?"

"Politely say you have a boyfriend or girlfriend who lives out of state."

"Oh yeah, Bill was telling me that too. What if he wants to do something after the dog park?"

"You have class, and we have a teacher there whose office you can go to in case he follows you. And," he said in that *ta-da* sort of voice, "we have the most boring, unassuming car for you to drive, complete with campus parking permit. Also, I will be around in case there's trouble. I'll be one of those runners alongside the park, who stops and does some of the parkour course there. We need to come up with a help code phrase for you to say to alert me. What sort of common health problem do you not get?"

Amy thought a second. "Pollen allergies."

"Okay, mention allergies and how bad the allergies are, is my alert to how worried you are."

Amy said, "You mean like 'My allergies are bugging me a little,' versus 'My allergies are horrible, they're just killing me,' while pinching my nose or forehead."

Snapping his fingers Tyson said, "Exactly. The first one means move closer. The second one means hop the fence and run over, possibly with weapon drawn."

"What classes am I taking?"

"We'll give you a course schedule, and you can pick from there. I would suggest a psych class that you've already had, but mention that you're also taking a basic biology class because you have this vet aspiration."

"Isn't he going to figure out that I'm older than a freshman?"

"Just tell him you were helping on your family's farm and entered later."

"I don't know a lot about farming."

"Say you were taking care of the animals."

Amy took a sip of her ignored drink, contemplating the cup.

Talking to the cup, she said, "So many things could go wrong with this."

Flashing that smile again, he said, "And so many things can go right. You are just taking your dog to the dog park. Focus on that, and remember that I'll be right there, though you will have to learn to not be obvious about looking for me. I might be out running and exercising or I might just be in the car." He took a breath. "But you're right, we have to consider contingencies."

Amy thought, *Uh-oh.*

"I know you've been kidnapped before and held hostage at gunpoint. What do you do when you see a gun these days?"

Amy stiffened. Breathing seemed to get more difficult.

Tyson said, trying to reassure her. "He's not likely to have a gun, especially at a dog park."

Amy took a drink and looked at the ground. Lars, sensing her tension, came over and rubbed his body up against hers. "I've been doing more training around guns, both in target practice and disarming tactics."

"But . . ." Tyson said expectantly, leaning back in what seemed to be an attempt to take the pressure off of her.

Rubbing her temple, she said, "I really, really don't like them, and I try not to panic around them. I hate the pain and sorrow they create." She sniffed, blinking back tears.

Trying to be gentle, Tyson said, "Stand up, and let's go through this physically."

Amy stood, looking concerned.

He took out his service pistol, pulled the magazine out of the base of the grip, pocketed it, pulled the slide to eject the round in the chamber, and then turned the gun sideways to show her that it was empty. Then he pointed the gun off to the side, cocked it, and pulled the trigger. The gun just clicked.

Gritting her front teeth, she said, "Can't you just try to hit me instead?"

Smiling, he said, "I could try, but you'd have me on the ground in seconds, and I don't want to mess up my hair. Stand in front of me."

She did, and he brought up the gun to point at her.

Amy quickly looked away with a gasp and half-turned her body.

"You can do this, Amy. The gun is empty. It's just a training tool at this point, and I hope no one in the park calls emergency. I know it's hard, but when there's a gun pointed at you from ten feet away you need to close the distance. This is hard, and it's risky, but it's your best chance if you are not in a position to run or hide. Put up your hands, start talking about anything, and work your way closer. Focus on your training, remember the goal is to get within striking distance, and, in your case, that means roundhouse kick to the forearm range."

"My trainer Tom tells me that kicks aren't the most reliable disarm method."

"True, but if that's as close as you can get, then it's a risk worth taking." Holstering the gun, and miming a gun with his hand, Tyson said, "Let's just work this out without the gun in sight first." He pointed his hand at her in the traditional gun style used by children since the invention of the pistol. "Don't move, or I'll shoot."

Amy asked, "What's his name again?"

"Adam, though you need to forget that after this session."

Amy balanced her weight between her feet, and took in a deliberate breath, and reached her hands up, out, but slightly towards Tyson. "Adam, it's okay, no one is going to hurt you," and she took a step towards him.

Tyson shook his gun-shaped hand at her. "Don't move."

"Adam, you're fine, you're in no danger. Look at . . . what's his dog's name?"

"Levi."

"Look at Levi, he's not worried, and he would know." Amy edged a little closer, then after half a beat, she flung out her hands, exasperated. "You know, he would have shot me by now."

"Well, this is why we want you two to get to know each other, as the likelihood of him just up and shooting you goes down."

"What if there's a friend of his around to be the heavy?"

"Then act helpless, and Adam might come to your aid. Let's do this one more time."

Amy sighed heavily, and repositioned herself.

"And you have to promise not to break my arm."

"Why?" she said with a half-smile.

"Because I have another arm, and I hold grudges."

"Oh, okay." Amy said with the same half-smile.

They spent the next thirty minutes working out scenarios, and Amy only had to reassure two different passersby that she was okay.

By the end of the session, Amy was feeling a little better, and at least confident that Tyson would be right there for her.

They walked back from the park.

He handed her a couple of mics that she could wear. One could clip on to her clothes, one was a barrette. The mics actually came in much smaller sizes, but it had to be something she could find and manage.

Tyson glanced at his tablet. "Are you okay with three times a week at noon?"

"Yes, that's fine, they've cleared my schedule in the middle of the day for this."

"Well, take the weekend and think about all this, forward me any questions you have, and I'll see you next week."

"Thanks, Tyson. Bye now."

Amy headed back to the car, wondering what she and Lars were now committed to.

Once she got to the airport, she told the car to take itself back to the Choran office. Tyson had promised her that she'd be using a completely nondescript car next week. She hoped it was smart enough that someone could tell it to meet her at their airport hangar.

Flying back, Amy wished she could just completely zonk out, but she had to stay in the pilot's seat in case of emergency or radio transmissions. She was able to get a little sleep and catch up on messages. Tomorrow, she would be helping her mom continue the forever-running canine language project, where they try to figure out what would be the most useful portions of the language to teach their dogs.

When she wandered back into the Evergreen office in the afternoon, Steve said, "Hey, secret agent."

"Hi, Steve. Anyone lost?"

"Not so far today, but the day isn't done yet. How is Choran?"

"Kinda still there."

"Are you ready for this?"

"No, but I have a keeper who is going to watch carefully. He reminds me of you."

Smiling, pushing back from his work, and turning to her, he asked, "How?"

"He's big and strong, though probably couldn't lift a horse like you can. He's nice, but a little more official."

"Don't say I'm nice, it will ruin everything."

Stepping forward, she said, "Okay, you're not nice, you big oaf."

"So, you're just going to be chatting with this guy, Adam?"

"Hopefully. Assuming that I can get Lars to arrange our meeting."

"Matchmaking by Lars. Does John know?"

"Not in this level of detail. I was supposed to tell him something else. Remember?"

Looking at her handheld, she said, "Quoting someone named Steve, I'm allegedly going south and doing a report on the welfare of the canine paw pads after they've spent a day in the field."

"I thought of that? Oh yeah. I like it."

She punched his shoulder.

CHAPTER 40:

The Canine Language Project

AMY AND her mother Mary were back to working on what they jokingly referred to as the Canine Language Project, though as time passed, the name appeared to be sticking.

They were trying to come up with a way to teach the empathic dogs English vocabulary that could assist them when trying to communicate with humans.

Amy thought back to one of their first sessions. While they were talking about the idea, she had said, "There are so many ways to approach this."

Now Mary proposed, "Well, let's consider the basics. Some dogs were showing an interest in talking to us, probably because they wanted us to better understand what they want. On the flip side, we wanted to know how having a dog able to talk to us could help us."

Amy said, "Well, didn't it all get started with Alice Kimble, the vet, being able to tell where a dog was hurting?"

"A very dramatic beginning, but a deliberately underreported way to start, I must say," Mary said. "But we've been just letting this evolve, and it would be interesting to see if we can put more structure into it. We've all been good at teaching most any dog particular words."

Amy said, "Sit, stay, down, COME," she added a rising inflection touch with urgency to her voice.

"Which winds up being Come-come-come-please-come" Mary added.

Amy lifted her hand thinking. "Plus the dog's name, and names for things in their environment. And working dogs know words associated with their job. When Lars finds what he's looking for he says 'Here.' And," Amy made a hand rolling 'Ta Da' motion with her hands, "he can say 'Yes' or 'No.'"

MARY SAID, "Being able to answer questions with yes or no is a huge benefit to your work, but let's see if we can move beyond that. So, we have actions, meaning verbs, and nouns. The locator words like 'here' are states of being. Now the challenge is putting words together in to short sentences." Pulling out a paper and pen, Mary said, "I'm going to be old-fashioned and just write down notes; we can dictate them later."

Amy said, "Fine with me, I often end up deleting half of a recorded brainstorming session anyway."

Looking at Amy, Mary said, "Think about your own work. It used to be that when a dog was out searching and they came back to you, you had to follow them back out to see what they found."

"It's still mostly that way."

"Can we improve on that?"

"How?"

"By teaching them more language. When a dog has found something, what do you want to know?"

Amy inclined her head. "Er, well, what they found to start."

"So animal, mineral, vegetable nouns?"

"In our case, usually animal, though what kind of animal is helpful, like person, or dog, or horse."

"Then what?"

"Male or female? Transgender is harder, as they can smell subtleties of hormone levels that humans can't."

"Alive or dead, injured or not. Do you care about how many are there?"

"Sure, though over three is a challenge. Still, I rarely need to know more than that."

"One, two, three, or lots," Mary noted.

Amy thought for a moment. "Moving or standing, running or walking."

Mary said, "Okay, and in my line of work, I care about emotions of the dog, happy, sad, angry, want to bite pushy solicitors."

Looking at her notes, Mary said, "So we have the 'what' they found, which is usually a human, or possibly a different animal. Then what gender, and what state the found person/animal is in, and we can include emotions here if we wish."

Amy said, "Well, that's multiple categories if you will. We have alive or dead, we have in motion or stationary, and we have all the various emotions, and all of these things can be taught separately."

To her notepad, Mary said, "And then, we have whether there is more than one."

Amy looked out the window. Holding a corner of her mouth at an angle and frowning slightly, she said, "It would be useful to know if the person was carrying something like a gun or a knife or a club."

"Weapon nouns," Mary wrote.

Amy shook her head and gesticulated with her hand. "We could write a book, or an entire curriculum."

"We might be."

LATER ON, Amy was in her mom's back area with Lars. Alicia, Mary's very patient assistant, had been nominated as a volunteer. Mary sat in a chair with her notepad at the ready. She read from their list. "Okay, so today we are working on actions like walking, running, standing, lying."

"Alicia, I think we owe you a beer for this," Amy said.

Alicia smiled and said, "We'll see."

Mary said, "Alicia, could you stand on the other end of the yard?"

The yard wasn't very big, so she walked forty feet away and stood.

Mary, who did not have an empathic bond with Lars, said, "Ask Lars what he sees."

Amy looked at Lars, pointed at Alicia, and said, "What do you see, Lars?"

Lars mentally said to Amy, /Alisha./

Amy said to Mary, "He just said 'Alicia.' This might not work for someone he knows."

"It might not," she said, making a note.

"Alicia is a person."

/Pershun./

"Yes. I'm also a person."

/Amy./

Laughing quietly, Mary said, "Let me guess, he said, 'Amy.'"

"Indeed, he did. I think we're going to have to do this exercise with strangers."

"Let's try actions. Start with walking. Alicia, can you walk from one end of that side of the yard?"

Alicia started walking towards them.

"No, just stay on that side of the yard and pace back and forth."

Alicia turned ninety degrees and started to walk across the width of the yard.

Amy said, "Lars, Alicia is walking."

/Wokin./

"Walking, that's good."

/Woking./

"Good, that is: Person walking."

/Pershun woking./

"Good boy." To Mary, she said, "With prompting, he said, 'Person walking.'"

Mary said, "Alicia, can you now jog back and forth?"

Alicia started running very slowly.

222

Amy had to keep a hand on Lars to keep him from running after her. To him, she said, "Person running."

/Pershun ruunin./

"Good: Person running."

/Persun runnin./

Amy said, "Alicia, you can walk now." Alicia resumed walking.

To Lars, Amy said, "Person walking."

/Pershun woking./

"Good boy."

They had Alicia do the running bit again, then Amy asked Alicia to stop and stand there.

"Person standing."

/Pershun andn./

"Person standing."

/Pershun st-and-ng./

"Good boy, close enough for now."

Mary wrote on her notepad, then looked up. "One last term: the one we keep changing."

Amy laughed a little. "Okay, Alicia here is where we owe you a beer. Can you lie down?"

"Back, side, or stomach?" she asked.

What a tolerant woman, Amy thought. "Doesn't matter," she said.

She lay down on her back and Amy really had to restrain Lars from racing over to check on her.

She said to Lars, "Person lying."

/Pershun ling/

"Person lying."

/Person li-ing/

"Good boy." Turning to Mary, she said, "He's going to need a lot of work on this one."

Mary said, "But not now." She looked up and said, "Thank you, Alicia. And Amy, we have some work in front of us."

Alicia got up and Lars charged up to her, nearly bowling her over. Alicia laughed and petted him.

Amy said to Mary, "Unlike the debate about whether we should be teaching 'sit' versus 'sitting,' I do have an answer about distinguishing the meanings of lying."

Mary held up her pen and looked expectantly at her.

Amy said, "It's not up to the dogs to decide if someone is telling a falsehood. They don't care or have enough information to make such a decision, but they can tell us if the person's body is overloading on cortisol, the stress hormone, and we can use that information to determine if someone is lying." Back to Alicia, Amy said, "Next time at the tavern, make us buy you a beer."

"Righto," she said, continuing to pet Lars.

CHAPTER 41:

Amy at the Choran Dog Park

THE PLANE touched down at the small Choran airport and started to taxi back to the hanger. Amy tried to steady herself and repeated to herself for the thousandth time: "I'm just taking Lars to a dog park to throw him a ball. I am a student at Choran Community College, which everyone calls ChorCC or Chorcy. I am studying psychology and also biology, because I'm thinking I want to be a vet. This is going to work fine."

No, it's not, anything could go wrong, that small voice said.

"And everything can go right," she said audibly, taking the best meditative breath she could manage. "Geez, I'm not even out of the plane."

Small voice said, *He probably won't show up anyway.*

Amy said, "Enough worry," and unbuckled once the plane had stopped. As she stood up, she noticed Lars looking at her with concern. "It's okay, Lars, I'm just thinking of something else."

/Worry, sad?/

Damn doggy, being perceptive. "I'll be fine, Lars, we're going to a dog park now."

/Mmm?/

"I know you don't always like dog parks, but this is our job today, and most people don't get to play for a job."

/Job./

"I know you won't completely understand this now, but we're looking for a dog."

/Search!/

Uh-oh, Amy thought, we really don't need Lars charging up to them. Then she realized she was overthinking things—again. *It's a dog park, that fountain of rude doggy behavior. It doesn't much matter what Lars does as long as he doesn't bite a dog or a person or knock over their latte.*

As they approached the dog park, she could see it was about three acres surrounded mostly by a short, low-tech chain-link fence. It was mostly dirt and sand, with the occasional sagebrush and dried native grasses. There were some short hills now and then, and Markus had told her that the scattered, burnt-appearing, black-brown rocks were volcanic.

It was noontime, so there were a few dogs and owners around, but it wasn't very crowded. A pretty typical assortment of labradors, shepherds, bully breeds, terriers, and smaller dogs, though no poodles or bichon frises, or much of anything that required a regular trip to a groomer, and there were a lot of mixes. She didn't see any golden retrievers, which felt a little strange. There was a flat area that was devoid of shrubbery, which looked like the place where people and dogs would go for a grand game of fetch.

She had brought a purple ball because she knew that it was a color that Lars could see and tell apart from all the other balls that littered the ground. She started to throw the ball for Lars, and he was more than happy to oblige. Once in a while, another dog would run alongside barking, but there was, gratefully, no drama. Sometimes Lars would pick up another ball. Then she would say "No, the purple one," and he would drop the other ball and almost grudgingly go get the purple one. After three times of him trying to bring a different ball, Amy was just about to say, "Forget it, let's just walk around," when a voice behind her spoke.

"He knows the word purple? What a smart dog."

Shit, so much for low profile, Amy thought. She turned around to face a tall, pale-looking man close to her age, in jeans, T-shirt and boots, and a baseball cap. His short brown hair poked out from underneath the cap. "Um, yeah sometimes, but sometimes he has other ideas."

Spotting a throwing victim, Lars brought the ball up to him.

"Hi, buddy," the man said, petting his side, and Lars wagged his tail in that body-bending fashion. "What's your name?"

Amy had decided a while back that aliases just weren't going to work for anything longer than an hour for Lars beyond his full name. "His name is Larson."

"Well, what a dignified name: Larson." He pointed a ways off to a type of dog that Amy mentally had always called Generic Brown Street Dog and said, "Over there is Max. What kind of dog are you, Larson?" Lars had started to play-bow now, and Amy hoped he wasn't going to try to crash into this guy.

Amy said, "Shepherd mix," not wanting to have to explain what a kelpie was and not wanting to call attention to that anyway. It took Amy a moment to click into the fact that this wasn't the man she was looking for, and she relaxed a little.

He stood up, offering his hand. "I'm Mike."

Taking his hand, Amy said, "I'm Amy, and I think Larson is going to lose his mind if you don't throw the ball for him, but thank you for shaking hands first before the grubby ball."

Smiling, Mike reached down for the ball and threw it a long way. Amy hoped Lars could find it as he jetted off in pursuit. Then, seeming to remember he had a dog here, he called out, "Max, come."

Up ran a happy-looking brown dog that could fit in anywhere. He came straight up to her and rubbed his body along her legs. She leaned over and patted his side. "Hi, Max." Max panted back and went to Mike.

Amy thought, *Mike and Max. Completely forgettable names. They should be the spies.*

Mike petted Max a little and said, "Okay, go on." Max took off, back to his explorations.

"I haven't seen you before, where are you from?"

Amy, grateful for the chance to practice her lines, said, "I live out of town, but I started at Chorcy this quarter." She was trying to figure out how much to say. Tyson said to share just enough to keep the conversation going.

Mike smiled, "My family are ranchers among a bunch of farmers."

"Yeah, my family are small farmers that came back during the 'Buy In,'" she said, referring to a government program aimed at encouraging small farmers to move into the area and grow organic crops.

"What do you grow?"

Be vague and change the subject if you need to. Tyson's words came back in her head. "Ha, you're talking to the non-farmer in the family. Little bit of everything, as far as I know. How about you?"

"Cows mostly. We're also smaller and trying to become organic."

Amy wondered silently, *You have ranchland and you bother coming to a dog park?*

Mike must have seen the question on her face. "Max here likes to chase the cows, so I take him here. Then I don't have to worry about him getting hurt or killed by a kick, and people don't yell at me as much."

"Yeah, I could see how that could be a problem. Well, I should go find out what my dog is chasing."

She started to leave, but Mike said, smiling just a little, "I was actually wondering if you were in that religious group that lives in town."

Amy paused and looked at him. "What religious group?"

He took his cap off, scratched his head, and replaced it. "I don't know a lot about them. One friend says they think of themselves as Super Christusians, but in this area that's nothing new. They live on the edge of town on this sorry-assed farm that someone must have given away. And they all have biblical names like Adam or Eve or Mary or—What's the leader's name?—Tomas, without an 'h'." Mike had been directing his question to the sky, though Amy was pretty sure that was unconscious, and she had to stifle a chortle.

Amy tried to think of something insightful to say, but wound up with: "Really?"

"Yeah, there's this guy that brings his dog here. He has one of those names."

Amy longed to ask her handler Tyson what he wanted her to say, but she had an idea. "So they'll talk to outsiders? I know some religious groups won't."

"Oh, sure. He has a cup of coffee just like anyone else."

"No talking incessantly about God or asking for money?"

"No, not at all."

"You sure this is a religious group and not a bridge club?"

Mike laughed. "Yes, I'm sure."

"I'll keep an eye out for him. Take care, Mike."

Mike said, "Bye for now." Amy went looking for Lars. She finally found him emerging out of the bushes smelling of sage. She was grateful that that was all he smelled of.

"Hi there, what did you find?"

/Ball Ball Rabbit./

"Rabbit?" She looked at the bush and saw a small hole and a scamper of a prairie dog ducking out of sight. *Ah ha, wrong word*, she thought.

"How about about squirrel?" Which it wasn't, but squirrel was closer than rabbit.

/Squi—./

"Squirrel."

/Squr./

Amy tried talking directly to him: /Squirrel./

/Squirrl./

"Good enough. Let's walk."

/Rabbit/

"Fine, I give up."

They walked all around the park and didn't see any golden retrievers at all. Amy hoped they had the dog breed correct. It seemed out of step to ask team Mike/Max what breed of dog Adam's was, especially since she officially didn't know Adam's name. It was time to admit defeat for this trip.

As they exited the park, she half-expected Tyson to appear, but he had said that he wanted to meet up at the school after she was done, to avoid observers. She loaded Lars into the car and headed over to Choran City College.

CHAPTER 42:

Amy and Tyson at Choran City College

AMY AND Lars wandered through the small but tidy campus of Choran City College.

They found the office where Tyson wanted to meet. It turned out to be a shared office with four desks, but as she walked in, he was the only one there. He was still dressed in sweats and a T-shirt, with a mascot of one of the Choran sports teams on it, and no words—it reminded her of a roach, but she knew not to even try guessing.

"Greetings. So you're a teaching assistant? A 'TA'?"

"I guess so," he said, leaning back in his chair and motioning to the guest chair on the side of the desk. "So how do you feel about your first time out?"

"Pretty uneventful. No sign of Mr. Right and his doggy."

"Yeah, that can happen over many times, so don't get discouraged. You did learn that people notice the religious group, so you get an idea of what at least one person saw."

"Yeah, I wasn't sure how far to go with that conversation." Amy said, distracted by a psychology textbook that she recognized.

231

Tyson said, "What you did was great. I might have chatted or speculated a little more."

Looking back at him, she said, "Such as?"

"Well, I might have said something silly, like don't they offer e-pamphlets or 'God loves you' tattoos?"

Amy looked at him, shaking her head, a smile playing on her lips. "I thought religious types didn't go for tattoos?"

"Well, it's different, now that you can remove them."

Amy looked a little blank, so he went on. "They didn't used to be removable. It was a huge deal, as you were marked for life with either the tat or a removal scar."

Looking down at her lower leg, she said, "You mean if I decided one day that I didn't want running doggies on my ankles, I couldn't just take them off?"

"No, your doggy would be with you always."

She inclined her head, pondering. "You'd think religious people would want a permanent mark."

"It's seen as against the Gods or God and all that. Many of the monotheists worry that during the end of the world, people will be forced to wear a mark."

Amy's religious education had been mostly academic and she wasn't always paying attention then, so she just said, "Oh."

Tyson went on, "I see you missed this fun factoid. There's a story about a bad guy who will try to take over and will make everyone wear a mark or a tattoo. Some of the monotheists think it will be required for someone to have this mark in order to buy or sell anything."

Amy looked incredulous. "Banking?"

"Well, they would call it trading, but yes. Sort of." He held up his hand. "Very sort of."

Amy paused for a moment, considering. "So, religious stuff aside, was this dog park thing really useful? It's kind of pricey for a little field jaunt. Even if it was nice to practice."

"We're going to double-check on our camera surveillance and see if his schedule is still the same. Then we'll have you up again."

"I'm not convinced that you specifically need me."

"Give it a chance," Tyson said, smiling. The door opened and another person, presumably a teaching assistant, walked in, saying hello. They both said "Hello" back.

Tyson said to her, appearing to suppress a wink, "Thank you for coming to my office hours. I hope things make more sense now."

Amy said, "I think so, though I'm going to have to take a closer look at the material to be sure."

They shook hands and Amy and Lars walked out.

On the plane, looking out at the clouds, Amy wrote back to the office, "No big fish today; one smaller, unrelated one."

CHAPTER 43:

Amy Talks with John

JOHN CHOPPED the onions for chana masala, a garbanzo bean dish that they both loved. He was back on with his vegetarian quest. He would stick with it for a while, then couldn't take any more, and he'd scarf down an entire roasted chicken.

Amy got the rice out, and set it and the vegetable broth up to start when things were further along. More the omnivore, Amy enjoyed the occasional hamburger, but usually for lunch when he wasn't around, to give him some space about it; she did eat chicken and fish around him, since that didn't seem to bother him too much. Setting the rice aside, she asked if he wanted a salad and, with his assent, started pulling out various salad-relevant bits.

While peering into the refrigerator, she asked, "So, is that guy who wrote the travel-the-world surfing book going to be stopping by your store to do a reading?" John owned and ran a surf store.

"John Stenner? I don't know if you'd call it a reading, but he'll be coming to hold court or something. Maybe he'll do a presentation."

"You have room for that?"

He poured olive oil into a skillet and turned on the stove burner. "He'll probably have one of those self-standing screens that can unfold. It should work. If not, I'll clear a space for him, but it would require moving some surfboards."

Emerging from the refrigerator with lettuce, hard-boiled eggs, carrots, cheese, and dressing (she did insist that cheese and eggs had to be present in the house, and he did not object), she said, "If so, you should make him help move all the boards."

John added onions to the pan and did one of those pan tosses to spread them around. Amy always envied him being able to do this, as she usually wound up with things all over the kitchen floor. Of course, then she had to argue with Lars about not eating the onions that she'd just flung on the floor; he didn't understand they were bad for him, and he thought she'd done that just for him. So she used a wooden spoon instead. John said, "Oh, he'll have an underling or two around to do the grunt work." He added some garlic, turned down the heat a little to let things sauté, and started mixing the spices, calling them out as he added them to a small bowl, "Chili powder, cumin, coriander, turmeric. A bit of salt. So, how's work? You haven't said much about it lately. Rescue anyone famous?"

Amy had just gotten some tomatoes out and was slicing them into quarters. "Nope, completely boring data-gathering project."

"You're spying on someone?"

Amy inwardly gasped, as she wasn't expecting this, and had to pause the knife for a bit. She tried to remember the tangled thing that Steve and Yolanda had come up with, and was drawing a blank. "Right. Me the spy. No, it's dog data."

"About?"

Fuck, what was it about? she thought. "It has to do with measuring how hard they're working." *What was it? Oh yeah.* "Someone is trying to measure the wear and tear on their pads."

"No way, really?" he said, going back to tossing the onions, adding the spice mixture, and actually getting a wooden spoon out to stir.

"Yeah, well, it's probably not going anywhere. Do you want apples in the salad?"

"Sure. What a weird thing to study."

Dammit, Steve. Amy inwardly said to her coworker, *this needs to be more boring.*

"So, who's doing this study?"

"You don't know him, he's down south."

"Traveling to be bored." He added the tomatoes, some garbanzo beans, and cilantro, reducing the heat to let it cook.

"Lucky me," she said, adding the salad ingredients to a
large bowl.

John walked over to her and stood behind her with a hand on
each shoulder. He reached down, put his hand over her knife-wield-
ing one, and placed it on the butcher block; she released the knife
and then he gently kissed her cheek. "I worry about you."

"Why, John?"

"You seem preoccupied the past few days."

Amy realized that if he actually noticed, she must have been
really preoccupied.

"It's nothing really, I just miss the usual searching for someone."

"Is what you're doing dangerous?"

"I sure hope not." She tried reaching for the knife to continue
cutting up the apple, but his hand tightened on her shoulder.

"South. Where south?"

Turning to him and putting a hand on his chest, she said,
"John, I can't discuss details of current projects. You know that."

"You talk about stuff all the time."

"Yeah, but afterward. Rice, John, we need to start the rice."

"Fuck the rice, I don't want you getting yourself killed
because of some researcher's whim."

Amy waved a hand to the air out of frustration and brought
down her hand flat onto the butcher block with a resounding
thunk. "It's not that way." Amy noticed that Lars decided it was a
fine time to leave the room. Good boy.

"Then how is it?"

Amy took a breath, turned to him and looked directly at
him, and reached out and put her hand back on his chest. "John,
it's going to be okay. Really."

John sighed and stepped over to stir the masala. Amy got the
rice started, then went back to trying to finish the salad.

John said, "You've been brooding lately and haven't said word one about work."

Trying to focus on not slicing her finger instead of the apple, she said, "I'm sorry, John. Yes, it's been a pretty intense project, but I'll tell you all I can when it's over." With a pang of something bordering on guilt, she realized that she might not ever be able to discuss it much.

He said, "I hate how closed-off you are. You're not yourself."

Throwing everything into the bowl, she walked over to him, looked up at him, and said, stroking his cheek, "I'm touched that you noticed."

He put his hand on hers and said, "I'm trying to pay more attention to the squishy stuff."

Amy laughed and kissed him. "My squishy surfer boy."

"Sounds like a song to me," he replied.

—————

CHAPTER 44

Amy and Lars Back at Choran Dog Park

AMY THREW the ball again, saying to herself, *And here we are, exploring the exotic wildlands of a dog park in the sticks.* She looked around again for what seemed like the hundredth time and saw no sign of her quarry. As Lars brought the ball back, she kneeled down and, while petting him, said to the air, "I don't know, Tyson, I don't see him anywhere." She stood up and indicated for Lars to walk with her. She noticed in the distance a runner who stopped to stretch, then pointed at his wrist and held up his hand with five fingers extended. Looking back down at Lars she said, "Sure, I can wait five minutes."

They wandered closer to the entrance and then she saw them. Adam and his golden came in. Actually, it was more of a charge than an entrance, as the golden raced up to Lars, barking, and knocked him over. Lars, who was about ten feet away from Amy, was more than annoyed and howled a complaint. Amy ran over yelling, "STOP!" The golden ceased immediately and looked around confused.

Amy heard in her head, /Whatwhatwhat who you you you?/

What the heck? she thought for a moment. Then she said to Lars, /You okay, Lars?/

She looked over at him.

He shook himself saying, /Weird./

Then the voice in her head again: /What what what./

She realized it wasn't Lars she was hearing.

The realization came suddenly and she reeled. *Oh no, not this dog. Please, not this dog.* To the air so Tyson would hear, she said, "This nutball dog is chattering away inside my head. It's not making much sense though."

Trying to get the dog's attention, she said mentally to him, /Come, it's okay, come./

The golden came over, rubbing his body against her.

Amy said out loud, "You're fine, calm down, Lars won't hurt you. I can't be so sure about your human though."

All she could sense was, /Huh who dog dog dog who/

This dog has never really interacted with a person this way, she thought. *He's like when other dogs first try to communicate with humans empathically.*

Adam raced up, and she reminded herself that she didn't know who he was or his name. He seemed to be a typical angry human, his hand raised partially in the air. "Levi, don't do that!"

To Adam, Amy said, "He's okay now, don't hurt him."

"How do you know?"

"Look at him. He has an open expression, open mouth, and is relaxed."

"He got away with it."

"It's over, he's not thinking about that."

Adam still looked upset, but stopped, paused, and said, "I'm Adam," extending a hand.

"Hi, I'm Amy," accepting the handshake.

Adam's hand was shaking a little and warm.

He looked like his photo: auburn hair, grey eyes, light tan skin, and only a little taller than she would have guessed.

"Are you a dog trainer?"

"No, but I train my dog and I'm a psychology student at Chorcy."

"He's terrible around new dogs."

"You might want to work with a trainer on it."

"This is Levi, and he seems to like you."

Amy looked down to see a relaxed golden looking up at her. She told him, /Hi, this is awkward./

/Awk?/ The dog gave her a blank look.

/Never mind./

Amy looked around to see Lars off at a short distance.

/Lars, come say hi, I think it's going to be okay./

Lars started to approach in a wide arc to Levi, doing his best new-dog approach. He was just about within butt-sniffing range when Levi barked, went into a play bow, and then spun in a circle. Lars broke away and started carefully sniffing the ground, trying to send a calming signal to Levi.

Amy said to Lars, /I'm not sure Levi is interested in calming down./

Lars then ran over to where Amy and Adam were standing, ignoring Levi entirely.

She asked Lars, /If he won't listen then just ignore him?/

Lars seemed to assent with, /Mmmm./

Turning to Adam, Amy said, "This is Larson."

"Hi, Larson, you're a handsome fella. What kind of dog is he?"

She started to say the usual, "kelpie-shepherd cross," and stopped herself. "Shepherd mix."

Adam bent over, thumping his head, which she knew Lars did not like.

"Actually, if you pet his side he really likes that."

Adam switched to stroking Lars's side, and she could relax that Lars wasn't going to just think he was a complete buffoon.

Levi had raced off in a wide circle and now was coming back. Lars paid no attention to Levi, who was starting to poke at Lars with his nose.

Adam asked, "Larson doesn't like Levi?

"Not like this, but give it a little time."

To Lars, she said, while hoping he would understand, /Give the dog a chance./

Lars didn't quite say /Hmphf/ but certainly seemed to, though he did at least look in Levi's direction.

Adam said, "He's such an idiot with new dogs."

"New faces are pretty exciting to some dogs."

Lars turned to Levi, who excitedly play-bowed.

Adam looked at her, "Speaking of new faces, I've never seen you here before."

"Yeah, I just started at ChoranCC, and have just started bringing Larson to the park."

Amy knew what the next question would be and reminded herself to not sound too rehearsed.

"What are you studying?

"Psychology, and I'm considering pre-vet."

"Ambitious, but I'm a scientist, so I say go for the biology bits."

Delighted that he was so forthcoming, she said, "You are? Where?"

He physically started a little, then recovered. "Oh, it's for the Visions Institute."

"Oh, okay, I haven't heard of them, but I don't live in town."

"It's a small group, so you wouldn't of heard of us."

"Seems like most everything around here is about farming."

Adam smiled a genuine smile, and said, "Yep."

By this time, Lars and Levi were racing around the park together.

Amy said, "I think they have mended their differences for now."

"I guess so."

Amy considered a bit and thought it was worth trying to continue the conversation. "So is your lab about farming? Making the best corn ever?"

"Not really, it's different." His brow furrowed a little.

Tyson and others had taught Amy to just stay silent and see what happened, as people don't like silence that much, so she just raised her eyebrows and looked at him expectantly.

"Well, it's a little proprietary, so I'm not supposed to talk about it much."

"Sorry, I didn't mean to intrude, but I was actually wondering if you're one of those famous science publishers."

He put his hands on his forehead and looked up at the sky, talking. "Ha, ha, hardly. Though we've published some really obscure stuff that I guarantee you won't care a whit about."

"So, you are famous."

"No. Really, no." He seemed to want to end the conversation, so Amy decided not to press. "Where have they gone?" He looked around.

Amy said, "The dogs? Their heads are in a hole over there."

"We have the most brazen prairie dogs ever. Levi, come!"

Amy said, "Larson, come." Turning to Adam, she said, "I have to run to class, but it was nice meeting you."

Adam doffed his baseball cap and did a half-bow. "The pleasure was mine entirely, and next time I pray that my dog doesn't bowl either of you over."

Laughing, Amy said, "Bye, Adam. Bye, Levi," left the park with Lars beside her, and headed off to ChoranCC to debrief with Tyson.

CHAPTER 45:

———

Amy Meets with Tyson at Charon Community College

AMY AND Lars entered the teaching assistants' office to find Tyson nearly dancing in his chair.

She sat in the chair at the side of the desk. She said, "I take it you're happy."

Tyson smiled. "That went so well."

"I guess, if you don't mind not subtle," Amy replied.

He started counting out on his fingers. "One, you saw him. Two, you have met each other and know each other's names. Three, you know a little about him. Heck, he even told you he worked in a lab."

"Well, okay." Amy inclined her head, feeling a little concerned.

He leaned towards her a little. "And did I hear you say his dog talked to you?"

She leaned back a corresponding amount, alarmed at what he might be thinking. "Well, not really—"

Tyson started talking to the wall. "Do you know what that means?"

"Tyson—"

He paid no attention, looking at the opposite wall. "What a coup. We have a spy on the inside—"

Amy decided that breaking out of the usual office monotone seemed to be the only choice. "TYSON."

He started and returned her gaze.

Now that she had his attention, she switched back to an office monotone, albeit stressed.

"It doesn't work that way."

"Why not?"

Amy put her head in her hands.

Tyson got up and said, "Let's take a walk."

"Happy to. Come on, Lars," she replied.

Not far from the office was a plaza with a water fountain; there were benches and shade trees around it where people could sit.

Tyson sat on a bench and patted it. Waving his arm at the fountain, he said, "Come into my white-noise booth. It's not infallible, but it's reasonably effective at staving off casual snooping. Now explain to me what I have wrong."

Amy sat down, looking at the water fountain and taking a moment to breathe in and absorb the peace that it offered. Lars looked like he wanted to dunk his head in the water, but lay down near it instead. "I can't be sure, but I don't think this dog has ever successfully talked with a human before."

"What makes you think that?"

Amy asked, "Do you have kids?"

Slightly thrown off, he answered, "I have a six-year-old son."

"Remember back when he was one?"

"How could I forget?" Tyson had that faraway look of someone looking at a memory.

"Was he just making words just to say them or just trying to repeat what he was hearing?"

Tyson laughed, "I wasted so much time trying to figure out what he meant, when it turned out it didn't mean anything at all. He was just enjoying the sound of his own voice."

Amy nodded. "Well, dogs aren't nearly as chatty as human children, but they go through a similar phase where they're just repeating words they've heard, without really knowing what they mean. This dog was like that."

"So no complete sentences?"

"Complete sentences are rare, even from Lars. We teach them a highly abbreviated language, so they can describe if they see a person or animal, and what that person might be doing, like walking or running or lying down, or if they have a weapon. We're also trying to teach them emotions like happy and sad, but that's hard."

Tyson seemed genuinely disappointed—he visibly deflated. "So, you can't have a dog tell you what they're trying to create in those lab containers?"

"Not unless someone ran out the door and tried to hide themselves or something."

Tyson turned his attention back to the fountain. "I couldn't just keep my little dog spy fantasy even for just a little while?"

"Only if you promised not to tell anyone official."

"And what fun would that be?"

"Well, come down south and come out to the bar with us and we all can play then."

He smiled, thinking. "Dog spies. The Intelligence Department and the military would be all over that."

"They are to some degree, but we're not entirely sure what they're working on, unless they tell us—which is never the full story."

He shook his head. "I'm sure they are not giving out the whole story. It would ruin their fun."

CHAPTER 46:

Tomas Speaks with His Technicians

TOMAS REALIZED he needed to meet with his production manager, Karen, to check if there were any issues with the distribution channel.

One way the community created income was selling handmade wool products, like sweaters, blankets, and caps, from sheep on their own farm/ranch. The business, Tomasian Organicwear, was making quite a name for itself, and tourists were starting to find the farm. At first that was problematic, until Karen created a friendly front retail area. Visitors could watch someone weaving, spinning, or hand-carding wool, which was mostly for show as a lot of actual production was done by machine. Fortunately, parking was usually not an issue in their area.

Karen was a fabulous manager. She had kept her original name, which Tomas found he admired in the face of the peer pressure of the others taking biblical names—something that was not his idea. Tomas didn't have to get involved too much in the business, except for the constant, "We need more people, sheep, and space."

The Tomasians worked for room and board and community support, which put a limit on how many people they had. They could get more people, but Tomas would have to be willing to pay them, and that presented its own challenges. He would have to go on record as an employer, which would expose his organization's records to governmental audit. Given that he considered the sweater business only an income provider, he wasn't inclined to go in this direction.

After an hour of talking with Karen, he headed to what he felt was a much more important meeting. He was going to be explaining to his lab techs their new research direction. He knew they were going to be disappointed, as they felt they were just getting tangible results, and they were correct. He hadn't let them in on his make-the-world-smaller plan and he wasn't quite ready to start just yet, though he knew he was going to have to trust someone with the information at some point in time. He didn't know how that was all going to work out.

They gathered in what they called the Small Sanctuary. Allegedly, it was a place for deep contemplation. It had an altar and some sculptures and paintings to go along with the benches. The benches were movable, writing surfaces were subtly attached to the pews, and there was a presentation screen that could easily be unfolded, but even that wasn't quite the full story. It was in the basement, and when you shut the door, you could tell that you were acoustically isolated. There was also an impressible locking mechanism on the door. An observant person would realize that they were in a secure room intended to keep outsiders completely out.

Tomas looked at his technicians, Adam, Ruth, Sarah, and Isaiah. In their eyes, he saw an interested, *what's next?* type of trust. They had followed him here and they would continue to follow. Knowing that helped give him the confidence that he could pull off what he was about to do.

He looked down at his handheld, which was mostly for show since he had memorized what he was going to say. "Welcome. We have received the data back from the outside nanobot experiment, and it was very successful." He looked up, met each of their eyes, and said, "Congratulations, you have earned it."

Everyone sighed, took a relieved breath, and then started applauding, saying "Yes!," and patting each other on the back. Adam shook his fist in the air in a celebratory fashion.

Tomas went on, "I know you all wanted to be the ones conducting the experiment, but we had to verify that an outside party could do it. On human test subjects, they were able to use nanobots to lower" (in his mind, he thought: *or raise*) "heart rates, blood pressure, and anxiety remotely from a distance, which in this case was considerably outside of a building."

They started to break into side conversations, and he said, "You have all done very well. Thank you," which brought their focus back to him.

"In order to move forward with this, we need to secure the services of another researcher who is working in a similar field, and we're currently in negotiation over that. Because of that, we're going to pause this research and start in a new direction."

There was a shocked silence. Adam said, "Oh man, we were just getting started."

Tomas smiled at him. "Take good notes, as we will certainly return to this."

After a beat, it was actually Isaiah who asked, "Okay, what's next?"

"It's one of the world's oldest problems. Reproduction, or more precisely allowing people to better control fertility, to choose when they want to have a child, or prevent it if they don't want to."

Laughing, Ruth said, "We must be the only religious org that wants to help people not have kids."

"Oh no, there have been plenty throughout time, but they died out from attrition, because they focused on controlling their own fertility by frowning on sexual enjoyment. I think this approach is consistent with our smaller, simpler world philosophy."

Adam quoted a common Tomas refrain back to him, "Ten billion people."

"Indeed," Tomas said.

Sarah said, "But there are all sorts of ways to control fertility."

"And nanobots will be another, possibly easier, one," he said. What he refrained from saying was that it might be easier to force infertility on an unknowing someone by using nanobots.

Adam asked, "So, is this what the containers are about?"

"Yes, they are. It will be easy to work undisturbed, and we can move the entire project if we need to."

Adam leaned back, his lower lip pursed. "So, if we're having all the secrecy, then why are we bringing in an outsider?"

Tomas met his eyes with a gentle expression. "This person is further along in his research, and a collaboration with him would be helpful." Tomas declined to mention that his collaborators had likely inadvertently completely ruled out Herman's or Lincoln's cooperation by orchestrating the attack on them and stealing their still-encrypted data.

"So, he can take credit for our work?"

"Now, Adam, I'm sure he'll—"

"Why not? We're all just unpaid drones anyway—"

"Adam—"

"He's probably a devil-worshiping heathen who steals other people's research anyway."

Now it was Sarah who said, "Adam! That's not very nice. We don't know anything about him."

Adam crossed his arms over his chest and looked down. "He's probably a darkie."

Sarah stiffened at the offhand slur and said, "Adam, come on, relax."

Tomas took a breath and said, "I have prayed and spent a lot of time meditating on this issue. This new direction better fits our smaller world philosophy. If we were to publish our work, everyone involved would appear as an author." Tomas got up, walked over to Adam, and bent down to his level. "Brian," using his birth name, "you are blessed with beautiful light skin, but we have to be realistic and work with whoever is in the best position to help us. We are all God's children, and we need to remember that."

Adam seemed to be listening; he kept his head bowed, but he nodded.

Tomas stood back up. "If any of you have any questions, or just need to pray over something with me, please come see me. Let us pray."

Everyone shifted a little and bowed their heads.

"Our heavenly Father, please offer us your love and support as we embark on this new direction. Guide us with your wisdom and help us to discern what is a problem versus what is a distraction. Please help us with this effort to assist those less fortunate than ourselves. We thank you for your continued blessings and abundance. We as Tomasians say—"

And they all said, "Amen."

To end the meeting Tomas said, "May God light your path."

And they all responded, "And walk beside you."

They all stood up and gathered their belongings.

Tomas touched Adam's shoulder. "I mean what I said about stopping by my office if you have questions."

Adam nodded briefly and headed out of the room.

Tomas hoped he would come by later.

CHAPTER 47:

Tomas and Adam Talk

SOME TIME later, Tomas was working in his office when Adam tapped at the door.

"Adam, please come in."

Adam entered and, after a moment's hesitation, shut the door.

Tomas stood up, motioning to the guest chair. "Please, have a seat. May I get you some water?"

Adam shook his head and sat down. There were worry lines in between his eyebrows and it looked like he'd been brooding for a while.

Tomas sat back down. "You appear to be deeply concerned about something. How can I help?"

Adam kept looking down. "I don't understand why we have to change course right now." Tomas took a breath as if to speak, but Adam went on. "I know the reasons you've said, but we're having success on our own. We can help people already without another expert."

"You are, but this is an excellent place to pause while we consider what direction we want to go with it."

"We can help people right now, why should we stop?"

"Well, this researcher has made good progress in airborne transmission."

"So?"

"Meaning it would be much easier to help the person without having to touch them."

"I don't get it. Who cares if it needs to be airborne?"

Tomas paused, considering. "Would you like to continue this project along with the new one?"

Adam looked up surprised. "Yes, please."

Tomas put his index finger to his lower lip. "We might be able to swing that in both labs, but it will take considerable extra effort."

"I think it would be very rewarding. We are now getting to a place where we can actually do some good for people."

Tomas nodded. "And you're right that it would help our group's reputation. What do you envision happening?"

Adam thought for a moment. "We could run a stress-reduction clinic. Start small and go from there."

Tomas smiled. He found Adam's sincerity very touching. "Adam," he said, refraining from saying "my son" since he didn't care for that style, "what you are suggesting has such promise and it could help our group give back to the community, but unfortunately getting to such a place is a very long road."

Adam inclined his head in apparent acquiescence.

Tomas continued. "We are a research facility. We do use human test subjects, but they have to sign away a lot of liability first. We have a lot of steps to get government approval to use our inventions on the general public since they're ingestibles."

"Yeah, that is a reality check," Adam said, sounding disappointed.

"I am so touched that you think we might be able to do this, but it is a years-long process. If you're up for it, we can set that as a distant goal."

Adam looked up and said, "I would like that."

Tomas decided that now was as good as any other time to level with Adam a little. "There are some very serious health concerns with the nanobots." Adam met his eyes, shifting a little in his chair. Tomas took a steadying breath and met his eye. "It's important for you to know that the nanobots can kill just as easily as they can help." Adam just stared back at him, his eyes widening slightly. "Instead of lowering the heart rate, they can raise it to dangerous levels, or they can stop a heart completely."

Adam now looked a little shocked. "Is there a way to prevent that?"

Tomas was a little puzzled, as Adam must have figured this out already, but perhaps he didn't want to admit it yet. "Not yet, but it's something we would have to add. Like many things, there isn't much difference between something that can help and something that can hurt. But we're getting ahead of ourselves. First, I want you to think about how we can pursue both projects, and consider what the issues are about the current project and what steps we might want to take."

"Thank you, Tomas," Adam said, rising almost abruptly.

Tomas said, "You're welcome, Adam. May God light your path."

"And walk beside you," Adam answered as he backed out of the door, almost bowing.

AS ADAM left, Tomas looked down at his desk and then over to a painting of Thomas the disciple he kept in the corner. Now he had a problem. He wanted more help with the new project and he wanted to fill Adam in on the real purpose of it, but Adam seemed determined to find a way to make the old project help others. That was admirable and would be excellent for creating goodwill with their community, but it wouldn't help his particular goals.

He was also a little distressed. Adam was his most experienced and knowledgeable technician. He would be the obvious one to bring into his inner circle, but now he realized that Adam might not be the best choice for the role. Adam was completely onboard with the smaller world ethic, but mostly as a philosophy rather than a plan of action. Tomas realized that he needed to meditate on this for a while.

CHAPTER 48:

Amy and Adam at the Dog Park

AMY AND Adam were at the Choran Dog Park. They had mostly been talking about the wind that had been blowing for a few days and how it frightened the livestock where Adam lived. Over time, Adam had told her that he lived on the Tomasian Farm and Retreat where they made Organicwear woolen clothing, and he would sometimes tell her about the strange drama that happened when the ram would get into the wrong pen or when the sheep all tramped down the fence and went walkabout, which made for lots of exercise for both human and canine stock handlers.

Amy had just thrown the ball for Lars and Levi when Adam asked, "Have you ever tried herding with Larson? He is a shepherd, after all."

Amy stared hard off into the distance, trying to think very casual thoughts and not succeeding. Yolanda had been bugging her for months to go herding with her, subjecting Amy to lectures on how the kelpie's herding style was like the border collie's in that they used their stare or "eye" to intimidate stock into moving. So far, Amy had demurred, as she saw how difficult it was for people to keep track of dog, livestock, and themselves, and then to call out directions while moving and not falling on one's arse. Amy knew that even with her kickboxing experience, she'd be on the ground in minutes with her head spinning. Casual. Think casual. "Um, not really, I don't know if he'd be interested or not." She hoped that Adam wouldn't hear the obvious lie.

Adam said, "Well, I know my fetch-a-holic wouldn't be interested, but every so often at the farm we have herding-instinct testing for people with herding dogs. It's a fun day. They pick some of the more mellow sheep and put them in one of the small pens and the person running the test takes doggy in to see what they think of sheep."

"That does sound fun, someday when I'm less snowed with school. Does the dog ever lose it and start biting sheep?"

"Well, the handler running things usually has a stock stick, or a rake, or a paddle that they can use to get in between Fido and the sheep. It's actually much less dramatic than it could be."

"Sounds risky for the handler."

"Well, they make it look easy. Speaking of which, here come the charging canines."

Levi nearly collided with Adam, tennis ball in a death grip in his mouth. Lars just arced around them, barking and panting.

Adam said, "Want to walk some?"

"Sure, why should they have all the fun?"

Levi started pestering Adam with the ball. Adam tried unsuccessfully to ignore the golden but finally gave in and picked up the dripping, dirty thing Levi kept dropping in front of him and tossed it. "I hope he loses it."

"Good luck with that."

Though they hadn't known each other for very long, Adam did seem pensive and distracted, even if he was chatty enough. She decided to take a chance. "So you know how much biology I'm buried under. How are you doing?"

"Um, okay. Work's a little weird."

Trying to channel her therapist mother, Amy said, "Oh?"

"Yeah, they're changing projects on us and it just makes everything awkward."

In as reassuring a voice as she could find, she said, "I'm sorry to hear that."

"Well, we were really getting somewhere, but they say we need to wait for outside assistance before we continue, which I think is BS."

Watch while I screw this up entirely, Amy thought. "May I ask what it is?"

His face fell some. "I'm not supposed to be talking about it, but we could be helping out our community with it."

Amy thought, *Right now is where I'm supposed to say something like, "Your secret is safe with me,"* but she couldn't bear lying to him. "A community service project sounds like the perfect thing for a religious group."

"Exactly," he said. "Now they have us working in the stuffy shipping container, which I hate."

"That doesn't sound fun at all."

"Well, I like the work, but shoving it all in a shipping container is a pain."

"Why a shipping container?"

"Allegedly because it's more secure, but our new project has to do with contraception and there's nothing secret about that."

Amy needed no acting to do a complete double-take. "Contraception?"

"Yeah, to help with the population problem. We apparently have a new approach to it."

"Wow, fill me in sometime when you can talk about it."

Adam threw up his hands. "Ask me in a few years, after we give up on it as redundant and overdone."

"Sure thing, Adam," she said, and found a cleaner ball to throw for the dogs.

———

TYSON, AMY'S Fed handler, was thrilled and completely puzzled with the new information that Amy had gleaned from Adam, and he promised to get his best Fed brains to work on the details.

Later on, when she was filling her Locate and Investigate coworkers in on the day's information, Harris was completely intrigued. He said, "So he thinks he's doing something good? Do you think it's the same project?"

Amy said, "I have no idea, but I'm sure he wasn't playing me. He was genuinely disappointed."

Steve looked around, shifting with some effort, and said, "Population control doesn't sound very sexy, no wonder he's disappointed."

Amy looked for something to throw at him.

Yolanda wandered over. "Is it possible he doesn't know the purpose of what he's working on?"

Amy said, "Meaning he's thinking he's working on something to help people, but in fact it does the opposite?"

Yolanda continued her thought. "Or perhaps it can do both, but he hasn't been filled in on all the nefarious details."

Steve laughed. "Getting people to work on what they don't fully understand the purpose of? Oh, Yolanda, you would make a fabulous evil genius."

Yolanda smiled, inclining her head. "My next career move. Should I tell my wife yet?"

"Not yet, it will be our little secret until we figure out that we're all bullshitting," Steve said.

"She's well familiar with our bullshit."

"Wow, it does have a poetic malice to it, doesn't it?" Harris said, running his fingers through his hair, which just made it worse. "And it makes this contraception thing sound completely ominous." He shuddered some.

CHAPTER 49:

Tomas Talks to His People

TOMAS WATCHED everyone come in to the meeting room, with many of them talking excitedly, moving chairs around, and getting settled. His chest was tight with tension as he considered what he was going to say.

"My brothers and sisters, welcome in God's love. I bid you greetings."

"Greetings," they all said.

Tomas shifted his weight from foot to foot until he noticed it and made himself stop.

"Some of you have heard that our new project is to assist with birth control to help with reducing the world's overpopulation problem. In light of recent events, we have decided to fast-track that project."

Everyone started talking at once. The obvious question being, which recent news?

"People are starving in areas of Oxia. Ten billion people is more than we can handle on Earth, and the colonization of Planet Aires is proceeding too slowly. We need to commit to our smaller-world goals."

"But those are the darker nations—why should we care?" a voice asked with an edge to it. There were supportive murmurs.

Tomas paused, considering. "Well, for one, the lack of arable farmland has driven the price of hay for our sheep through the roof and may compromise our community's way of supporting itself."

"But birth control is already available," someone else said.

"The solution we're working on lasts longer and requires less maintenance."

Adam said, "We already have too many people. Birth control won't help that, and lots of people want children."

"We do what we can, Adam."

Adam's eyebrows furrowed in a frown, considering.

Tomas looked at the floor, appearing to reflect. "We can't go blaming the darker nations for this problem. We all have to work together on this."

Adam said, "But it is their fault, mostly."

Tomas inclined his head, smiling patiently. "No, we still gobble up most of the resources even after years and years."

"But we're not having all those babies."

"We are God's creatures, and we can't go finger-pointing."

"But you said that God smiled on the lighter nations."

Tomas replied, "Yes, he gave prosperity to the lighter nations, but even the idea of lighter and darker nations is starting to have less power."

"Worry," said Simon.

Now Tomas really wanted to say *My son*, but he said it with his eyes. Simon could derail conversations easily, so Tomas was going to have to be a little careful. "Simon, have you seen older photos of what people used to look like?"

"A little," came the slightly defensive reply.

"Look carefully at them. The differences in skin color used to be much more pronounced than they are now. The concept of lighter and darker is going away."

"Not if I can help it," Simon said.

"Lighten up, Simon," said Sarah, who had been quiet all this time but had had enough. "Not everything is Armageddon."

"We must choose our battles," Tomas said. "Would I prefer

a lighter-skinned world with fewer people? Yes. Is that realistic? I don't think so. What's important is to find ways to sustain our world, but for now we need to focus on keeping our own house in order."

LATER SARAH caught up to Adam in the hallway, her tied-back ponytail askew and her black hair trying to escape from its bonds. Grabbing his arm, she said, "What is with you?"

"What's with what?"

Opening the door, she dragged him outside into the barnyard, scattering a few chickens.

"What's with this 'It's all the dark nations' fault' bit?"

Pulling on his arm he said, "Well, it is."

Sarah glowered.

Adam changed it to, "Well, it's mostly theirs."

Releasing his arm, she crossed her arms in front of her ample chest. "This is not God's way. What would Christus or Thomas do?" she asked, referring to the spiritual leader and his twin brother, whom their leader Tomas was named after.

Adam actually had an answer that surprised even himself. "Well, Christus would be a little perturbed, and Thomas would be questioning the dark nations' motives and asking why they're not being more serious about solving the problem."

"What makes you think they're not trying?"

Adam made as if to kick a chicken and refrained. "Isn't it a little obvious? They all want to live forever through their kids."

"They have restrictions on family size."

"And you see how well that's working."

Sarah said, "Well, they're trying. They have better education. Most people are literate. Women have more rights. Lots of resources for family planning. And governments are giving financial perks to families with fewer children and penalizing those who have additional kids."

"And still it's increasing." Adam whacked a bin with his open hand for emphasis. It reverberated in objection, sending a couple of chickens running in the other direction. "And before they all manage to off themselves, they're going to destroy everything for everyone else."

Sarah tried to put her hands on his shoulders and only half-succeeded. "Adam, that's completely paranoid."

"I don't think so."

Sarah looked at him, shaking her head, but with a half-smile. "Can you help me put the chickens away for the evening? Without kicking them?"

This seemed to bring Adam back. "Sure."

CHAPTER 50:

Tomas Considers

TOMAS WALKED the property. While he had said that people were welcome to approach him when he was out walking, he made it clear that he was using the time for prayer and contemplation, so few people bothered him.

He leaned on a fence, gazing out at a pasture that contained the flock of Merino and Lincoln sheep. His stock managers allowed the fine and heavy wool sheep to flock together as long as a ram didn't make it into the flock, which usually didn't happen. It was important, as the Merinos had beautiful fine wool, best for the more delicate articles they produced, like scarves and handkerchiefs, while the Lincolns had a heavier wool, which was better for blankets. He trusted his managers with this decision, and it seemed to work out. The sheep looked at him curiously for a little while, then resumed munching when they decided he wasn't going to be walking in with a dog to make them move somewhere.

He put his hands on the upper rail and stretched. He needed to get out and do some actual physical labor. Everyone was so quick to help him, and he needed to make it clear that he wanted to feel the sweat on his forehead, his breath laboring as he hauled a wooden tie or stomped on a shovel.

Closing his eyes, he tried to put the details of running the place out of his mind. He breathed in, the smell of the dirt, grass, sheep, and manure reaching into his senses. Exhaling and opening his eyes, he thought: *Big picture. Focus on the big picture. It's idyllic here, but not for long if we don't do something. The masses will find us one day and consume everything we have built.*

He thought about the still-encrypted data units that were in a corner of the lab containers. He had considered having someone work on them, but kept deciding against it. They were tainted in his mind. Every so often, a tech would ask about them, and he said they belonged to an academic who they were hoping to get up here to do some research. He deflected questions about which academic. His partners had convinced him that once the researchers Herman and Lincoln had developed symptoms of disorientation and were suffering from the effects of the nanobots creating havoc to their system, they would give up the encryption key under duress. *Pffft,* he thought. *How naive was that?* The police found a way to shield the researchers indefinitely until the hospital was able to neutralize the nanobots. Now they had the police looking for the data units and there was no way the researchers would help them. *Why, oh why, had he let them convince him to attack the researchers?* The data units were a liability. He had considered just destroying them, but that wouldn't stop the search for them. He needed to have someone drive the useless hunks of metal back down south and have someone else night-drop them on the sidewalk in front of the place.

They were going to have to wait until the researchers published enough information about airborne nanobot transmission for them to recreate it, and that could be years. *If we could get somewhere useful on a different project, we could offer a collaboration, but we can't do it with our current research, as they would be immediately suspicious because of that boneheaded attack.*

So they were going to have to lay low for a while, and he was going to have to convince his techs that the new project really was worthwhile. The fact that they hadn't been arrested yet didn't mean they were okay; instead, it could mean they were being watched.

Time was ticking for the world, but it had been for decades. They were likely only going to have one good chance at a massive nanobot distribution, as others would quickly come up with methods of thwarting further attacks. It had to be airborne or drinking-water transmission, and the nanobots had to be able to duplicate themselves. Those were the hard problems. The preventing-pregnancy bit was probably the easy part. If they could get further on the duplication problem, then they would have something to offer the transmission people and enough time might have passed to allow them to escape suspicion.

So now, instead of two projects they had four. Now he had to consider whether to hire people, which would create resentment, and he really didn't want to go there yet. Plus the additional projects weren't nearly as sexy as the first one, which was why Adam was so attached to it. Adam could see the direct benefit of being able to control heart rates. Transmission and duplication didn't have that direct application, and birth control left everyone a little cold. He wasn't ready to share that he wanted to make it involuntary birth control, as that little factoid, once public, would get them all arrested.

Getting his people stirred up about overpopulation might not have been the best choice. It meant that they were going to have to participate in some of the current family-planning education projects just to give everyone a direction, even if they probably didn't want to travel to the places that needed the education the most. Something dull and humanitarian would be good cover.

CHAPTER 51:

Amy and Mark Talk at the Dog Park

AMY AND Lars walked into the Charon Dog Park to find Max charging around and Mark wandering behind him. Amy had seen the generically named Mark and Max enough times now to think of them as an integral part of the landscape.

Mark's baseball cap was a different sports team this time, and was a little dirty and askew.

"Hi, Mark. How many baseball caps do you own?"

"Lost count a long time ago, especially when a cow steps on one or the wind takes it clean off my head, and I have to run after it."

"Have you seen Adam?"

"Nope," he said looking around. "Didn't see his car in the lot yet. You got a date with him?" he said, grinning.

"Oh, stop it, you know what I mean."

"Actually, I do, and we should take this opportunity to talk," he said, looking directly at her. He had dropped the good ol' boy persona.

Amy, who had given only half of her attention to Mark, looked at him, bringing him fully into focus. "Yeeessss. Go on."

"I'm Agent Mark Hampton. I work with Tyson. I would shake your hand, but I don't want to call attention to us."

Amy whacked her head. "No way! Oh, you are good. Tyson, where did you find this guy?" she said, knowing that Tyson was listening. "You had me from the second you said 'hello,' and something like 'Aw, shucks.'"

Mark smiled. "It comes a little too easy, I must admit."

Looking over at Lars and Max, who were playing a game having something to do with who could kick up the most dust, she sighed. "So there's two of you. What the heck do you need me for?"

Mark adjusted his cap, crossed his arms grinning, and ever so slightly drawled, "Because, little lady, you have gotten me introduced and talking to a guy who would only say 'Hi' to me at best, and now," taking a step back and bowing, "I'm going to run away before you hit me."

Amy shook her head, her mouth open in what was almost a grin, but not quite. "Now I'm really at a loss for words." Mark actually had taken another step away, which made Amy chortle. "Do you really want me to hit you?"

"Oh, hell no, your reputation precedes you."

"What reputation? Is Tyson making up stories?"

"Perhaps a little."

"So if he's starting to trust you, do you think I can go home?"

"Probably. The quarter is ending anyway so it's a good time to stage an exit."

Amy said, "Not that I mind your fabulous company."

Mark put his hand over his heart. "You will miss me, won't you?"

Amy smirked a little. "Terribly, but you probably have a spouse anyway."

He nodded. "That I do."

Adam's car pulled into the parking lot.

Mark said, "Okay, so with the quarter ending you'll be going back to your family for the break. Right now, you're worried about finals, so we can be talking about that when he walks up. Sound like a plan?"

"You bet. LAI is going to be thrilled to get the plane back on a regular basis."

CHAPTER 52:

Adam Talks to Sarah, Then Tomas

ADAM LOOKED at the screen and then leaned back, putting his fingers in a fist to his lips, contemplating. "Hey, Sarah?"

"Yes, Adam," came the reply from the next station down.

"You know those old DNA-testing software libraries, where people were able to tell where their families came from?"

"Yeah, they used to be really common, but, over time, they became less useful as they started looking like a map of plane routes from a major airline."

"Can you derive percentages from them?"

"Yes, why?"

"Can you tell what percentage of their ancestors came from a darker country?"

"Only as a vague guess. I'm sure you can ask the genealogy people as these issues drive them around the bend now." She paused and looked over at him. "Um, Adam?"

"Mmm, yes?"

"Why?"

"Why, what?"

"Don't give me that. Why do you want to be able to tell if someone's ancestry is from the darker nations?"

"Curiosity."

Sarah looked at him harder now. "Has Simon been talking 'bring back racial pride' nonsense to you?"

Adam laughed. "Simon can't find his own shadow."

"But he can work his mouth just fine."

Adam laughed in response.

"Please, just don't do anything crazy."

"Like what?"

"I don't know. Reintroduce a disease or something."

Adam laughed. "Like I could do that. I don't think we have any viruses in the back fridge."

"You know what I mean."

They lapsed back into silence and Adam kept working on getting the sequencing going for the birth control project. "Tomas's first idea was to get the female's egg to generate a not-fertile message or an already-fertilized message, but I like his other idea of convincing the sperm to not even be interested in the egg."

Sarah looked up from her screen, both hands in the air. "There are millions of sperm. That sounds pretty difficult. You'd have to affect the generation of the sperm. If you create the world's first gay sperm, you should get to be the first name on the paper."

Adam smiled, nodding and silently guffawing. "There are sperm that don't work well, but creating them would be a whole different matter. Okay, back to working on making the egg invisible."

They lapsed back into silence with just the radio playing. Adam found himself wondering about the old ancestry library routines. With a few gestures, he found himself in the ancestry testing suite. The routines for estimating percentage of DNA that originated from particular areas were still there. He knew that they had been called into serious question in years past, as travel and mobility became the norm when immigration rules eased.

He pulled up the DNA of a recent test subject whom he had personally met. The person was darker than he was, but not excessively. He wrote a script to run some general estimates of the geographic origins of the DNA. As Sarah promised, it was a rat's nest, pointing everywhere except for the polar regions.

"My heart strings are reaching out to you—" sang the lonely tenor on the radio. Adam thought the guy was a dweeb, but he could definitely sing.

Adam tried with his own DNA. His family had intermarried much less than normal, and while the darker nations were there, his DNA was overwhelmingly from the areas that he and his peers considered the lighter nations.

He could do this, he was sure of it. If he used percentages, he could target the problematic darker nations, whichever method they chose to use. He decided against telling goody-two-shoes Sarah, who would, no doubt, make a strong case for why this was a bad idea, and decided to go straight to Tomas.

———

LATER, ADAM caught up with Tomas outside.

"Brother Tomas, may I walk with you for a bit?"

"Brother Adam, I would be delighted. Come, let's walk over to the farm."

They walked down the dirt access road, the air rich with sheep manure, which was being used as compost for the corn, beans, and what hay they could manage to squeeze in for their own use. Tomas had bought the land very cheaply because it was producing poorly, and that reality hadn't changed much, though the sheep manure helped. His farm manager was struggling with the competing goals of needing to produce more hay for their sheep while needing to grow enough corn and beans to sell at the marketplace. If their land produced better, they could switch over to being one of the profitable, government-sponsored organic farms that grew a huge variety of crops.

Once they had gotten out of the earshot of everyone else, Adam said, "I've been looking at the older ancestry DNA software."

Tomas, who had been looking into the distance and had nearly tripped over a gouge in the road, responded, "Really?" His eyebrows were lifting.

"I know that the usefulness of them is less, with people having now moved around a lot."

Tomas smiled, "And the diagrams resemble decorative knotwork."

"But I started running percentages of lighter versus darker nations and you can still do that with our DNA here."

"The lighter nations being our own definition."

"Well, yes."

"Seems a little risky. Go on."

"Well, someone like me whose family didn't intermarry much is only about 20% DNA that has origins in the darker nations. It can go as high as 30%, but there's a definite pattern."

Tomas stopped and looked at Adam, whose eyes had a certain eureka intensity that one gets with discovery. He could see where this was leading and he wasn't sure what to do about it, if anything. "Okay, and what are you concluding from this insight?"

"The darker nations are causing this overpopulation problem."

Tomas, who was taller, inclined his head down and to the side a little. "Probably."

"We can target them with whatever we come up with, especially once we get the transmission and the replication problems addressed."

Tomas inhaled and looked at the distant horizon. This intensity was exactly what he wanted, but he didn't know if Adam was the right person for it.

"Adam, this amount of initiative and creativity is admirable. We might be able to use this information to fine-tune our target audience, and we could also use it to exclude other groups if possible."

"Thank you, Brother Tomas," Adam said in a noncommittal tone.

"But there's something else you wanted to say. Isn't there?"

"We could make a big difference with this."

"Yes, we could."

"Wouldn't this speed our project up?"

"I think we're getting ahead of ourselves, Adam."

"Yeah, you're right. We have other problems to address first."

Tomas patted him on the shoulder. "Good man. I'm happy that you're on our team; you can make a real difference here."

"Thanks, Tomas."

"And thank you, Adam. May God light your path."

"And walk beside you," Adam responded.

Adam turned to go, leaving Tomas contemplating the beans, corn, and hay, and what to do with Adam.

CHAPTER 53:

Adam and Sarah Head Down South

ADAM LOOKED at the road and idly wondered how they ended up there.

Brother Tomas had asked him and Sarah to hand deliver a package to an associate of his down south. It was heavy and felt like equipment, but Tomas apparently didn't want to say too much about it. Tomas asked him to put it in the trunk. He had asked if it should be on the back seat, where it would be better protected, but Tomas didn't seem that concerned about it and said that it would be more secure out of sight.

The data units that had been sitting around for so long were no longer around and he had a guess that they were in the carton, but Tomas deflected questions about it, so Adam didn't press.

The trip was kind of long but uneventful, traveling out of the flat-with-small-hills area where they lived to more green areas, then over a mountain range and into green rolling hills. The conifer forests had faded into the occasional lone oak. They had passed a lake and now were paralleling a river as they headed into town.

Sarah said, "They asked for an afternoon delivery, so let's stop for a bite first." Sarah punched some buttons on the console. "How about a taqueria? I could really go for a good carne asada taco."

Adam agreed reluctantly, as he worried about the food in the taquerias.

"Oh, come on," Sarah said, sounding a little exasperated. "We don't get down here that often. You can just have a bean and cheese burrito with no salsa if you want to be bored."

Adam sighed. "Okay."

Later, as Adam was cautiously eating a burrito with Levi at his feet and Sarah was blissfully devouring her tacos, she said, "You have to get out more often. We tend to get into our own little world up there."

Adam looked up. "Well, isn't that sort of the point? To draw away into a God-honoring community?"

She happily licked a bit of salsa off her lips. "I know Gregory and Candice cook fine, but they could expand their horizons a little more. For one thing, add a little heat and spice."

He gesticulated with his fork, which he wasn't using to eat with. "And no one but you would eat it."

"Tomas would. You might, with a little more exposure."

"Well, okay," he said noncommittally, inclining his head some.

Adam, amazed that they hadn't talked about it before, looked quizzically at Sarah while reaching down and stroking Levi on the neck and asking, "What do you think is in that box?"

"Some sort of technology, I imagine. Is there something they are going to be testing for us? Something too sensitive to send over the net?"

"Remember those data units that Tomas didn't want us messing with?" He was back to speaking with his fork.

Sarah took a sip of her drink and said, "That's about the right size."

"Maybe they belong to the people we're taking them to."

"Seems a lot of hassle, if that's all they are."

After they were finished and had settled the bill, they were walking out of the restaurant when Levi suddenly took off running and barking. "Levi!" Adam shouted and took off running. "Levi come here! Come, you stupid mutt!"

AMY AND Steve were debating about catching lunch at the burrito place when a golden retriever charged up to them. Pearl was unimpressed, but Lars jumped up and down in excited greeting.

Amy just stared, open-mouthed. "No way."

Steve said, "No way what, or is that the dog's name?"

"This cannot be the dog I'm seeing."

"Say what?"

"This dog lives in Choran."

"Say WHAT? Come on, lots of goldens look alike."

"No really, this is Adam's dog. And . . . ," looking up to see Adam running up to them, "here comes trouble." To Steve, she said, "I'll take the lead while I figure out what to say."

"All yours," said Steve. "Do I get to keep my own name?"

"Yes," Amy quickly said.

Adam said, "Levi! Levi, come here. I'm so sorry, I don't know what got into him."

"Well, I have a guess," Amy said.

Adam slid to a stop and looked up from focusing on Levi. His shock was exactly like Amy's. "Amy?"

"Hi, Adam. Fancy meeting you here."

Adam looked completely nonplussed. "Er, hi."

She decided to forge ahead. "This is my friend Steve." After an awkward pause they shook hands. "Since you're probably wondering, I transferred from Choran to Evergreen here. I'm still studying psychology."

Adam nodded. He had that stuck-for-words look.

Looking down at Adam's leg, where the golden had positioned himself, Amy asked, "And how is Levi doing besides happily throwing you into awkward situations?"

Adam smiled and spoke to the ground vaguely in Levi's direction. "Oh, he's alright, I guess."

"I see that Levi is introducing you to the locals," came an approaching voice.

Adam glanced over and said, "Yes, he is, Sarah."

Sarah looked the picture of poise that Adam wasn't. Amy noticed that she moved with a well-practiced grace despite her heavier frame, her black hair flowing around her.

Adam looked over to her and she gave him that prompting, *introduce-me* look.

Adam, catching himself, said, "Oh yes, Sarah, this is Amy. I know her from the Charon dog park. Amy, this is Sarah, who also lives on the farm where I live." They shook hands.

Amy, deciding to help, said, "And this is Steve." Sarah and Steve shook hands.

Amy, realizing who was in charge, told Sarah, "I used to attend Chorcy and have recently transferred here."

Sarah put her hands together. "And you are experiencing the wonders of the taqueria."

Amy smiled, nodded, and looked at Steve, who nodded too. "Without question—worth transferring, just for that."

Sarah gave Adam a look and put a hand on his shoulder. "Our boy is reluctantly sampling the local cuisine—I think he'll survive."

Adam gave her that patient-but-put-upon look.

Steve made that *I've-got-a-message* body movement and looked at his handheld. Amy hoped that Sarah and Adam couldn't tell that it was completely fake. "Would you excuse me?"

"Your new boyfriend is messaging you again?"

"Yeeesss," he said with a quick, mischievous smile as he stepped away.

Amy also hoped that they could not tell that he had just taken their picture and was no doubt sending it to Central.

Still hoping that Steve could hear her, Amy asked, "So what brings you this far south?"

Adam's facial muscles tightened a little and he looked at Sarah.

Sarah said, "Tomas, our leader, asked us to bring down a couple of packages to an associate of his."

Amy smiled, "Wow, you are all couriers, too?"

Sarah laughed in what felt to Amy like a genuine laugh. "Rarely. I don't know what it is, but I think it's fragile and he's concerned about it getting smashed by delivery professionals playing catch. It's a long enough trip that it's nice with two people."

Or one to keep an eye on the other, Amy thought, but didn't say.

Steve reappeared.

Amy grinned. "He hasn't left you yet?"

He shook his head in a slightly superior manner. "Nope."

Amy said, "Well, Sarah, it was very nice to meet you."

Sarah inclined her head in acknowledgement.

Adam looked up suddenly. "Could I get your contact info?"

Her heart skipped a beat. *Shit, think fast,* thought Amy.

"It's down for today while stuff gets moved around, but why don't you give me yours and I'll contact you when it's back up?" She took out her handheld and held it at the ready. Adam gave her his contact info. "Perfect—I think it will be up tomorrow. And now we should let you all go to your delivery, and we shall partake in taco heaven."

They bade each other goodbye, with scritches for Levi, who seemed particularly put out and was chattering meaninglessly to her.

AS AMY and Steve walked into the taqueria, Amy leaned into Steve and said, "Tell me you have a tail on them."

Steve gave her an innocent look with a hand on his chest. "*Moi?* Who do you take me for? So suspicious." After a beat he said, "I sent in a photo of them and their location and requested a discreet tail to see where this delivery is going to be."

Looking at the menu, Amy sighed. "Too bad it can't be us."

"Honey, we are the last people eligible for such a job. You need Joe Forgettable."

"Who?"

"Precisely," he said, tapping her shoulder with his fingertips.

Amy ordered a couple of small chicken tacos and looked at her handheld. "I need to request a generic messaging ID that I can give to Adam."

Steve folded his arms and put most of his weight on one foot with his fingers to his lips. "Let's see. Let's call it Amy's Super Secret Spy Account."

"Naw, let's call it Steve's Clandestine Rendezvous Address."

With mock hurt, Steve said, "Oh, I wish."

"Your burrito is ready, you big, secret hunk."

Steve did a double take. "Already?" Then he recovered, and gave Amy a wry look, "You big tease, that is someone else's burrito."

CHAPTER 54:

Amy and Steve Back to Central

AMY AND Steve walked back into Central.

"What the hell?" Harris said, clearly having gotten the message about their meeting Adam and Sarah.

Yolanda, sitting on Harris's desk, said, "Some people have all the luck."

"Sorry," Amy said.

Steve crossed his arms, looking right at Harris. "Okay, Tech Boy, you know more than we do—spill it."

Harris raised his chin slightly and arched his eyebrows. "Well, if you really care, your friends delivered two packages to our friends at Applied Sciences."

"Ah, ha!" Steve raised his fist.

Amy said, "What the heck? Are they *the* data units?"

"Don't know yet. Looks like they just dropped them at the front desk."

Amy put her hands on her forehead. "What the heck are they doing?"

Harris said, "Too many choices to even guess. They could be giving up. They could be saying they've decrypted them. They could have wiped them and be giving them back as a message, which would be a little silly."

Steve asked, "Message, like a Mafia message? They don't seem the type."

Amy laughed. "They sure don't, but then again, look what they did to Herman and Lincoln."

Harris said, "They would claim that wasn't their doing, even though they made it possible."

"It was their doing," Steve and Yolanda said almost at once.

The department head Catherine walked in. "Applied Sciences just called. The special package was the data units."

Harris said, "Tell them not to touch them, so we can see what DNA is on there, even though we pretty much know what is going to be there already and they're probably just the innocent workers in this game."

Catherine went on. "I'm going to have them proceed as they would if we hadn't gotten involved."

"Midnight delivery to Nanology by hooded figures?"

"Likely," she said.

Harris said, "Tell them the same thing about not handling the units much."

Amy asked, "So, does this mean I don't have to stay in touch with Adam?"

Catherine looked at her with something that resembled a 'nice try' look.

"Actually, it's very important that you stay in touch with him and also with Fed Agent Tyson Mulhaney. We still don't know what this is all about, and Adam seems inclined to trust you. I have arranged a messaging identity for you, and I've had the set-up details sent to you. Make sure you keep it entirely separate from your other work."

After a beat Amy said, "Has anyone tried to find a way to Sarah? She seems sincere, and I'm sure anything illegal would upset her."

"I think Marcus is working on that. Your story is the same, you're a student, but you're now at Evergreen."

"Here to eat tacos," Steve said.

Amy flashed him bared teeth while still managing to smile. "At least I don't have to fly up there."

Steve started singing an old song about pen pals. He'd actually had to explain the concept to her a while back.

Amy said, "Steve, can you shut up a second while I attempt to do actual work?" To Catherine, she asked, "What am I supposed to say to him?"

"Well, just be his friend, same as before. Tell him how Lars is. How class is going. Talk about your surfing, if you like. If you keep track, you can tell him about how the family farm is doing, but most importantly, ask how Sarah and the others are, and how life on his farm is, and obviously try to get him to talk about his work without appearing to be pushy, which is harder to do in print. Anything you can think of that might make him more comfortable, so he'll tell you more."

Amy leaned her head into her open hand, fingers rubbing her furrowed brow.

Sensing Amy's ambivalence, Yolanda walked over and put a hand on Amy's shoulder and to Catherine said, "It's okay, I'll give her chitchat lessons."

Smiling, Catherine said, "Thanks."

Amy looked at her handheld and at her new messaging identity. She wasn't convinced that this was going to go anywhere.

Catherine said, "It's very subtle, slow work, but it's pretty essential. The Feds want to keep a connection to this group without having to directly infiltrate it. You've helped them out so much."

Amy blew out a breath and shook her head. "I don't feel like I've done anything, really. Mark, remember I mentioned generic Mark in a report? The one with generic Max the dog? Eventually, he would have gotten Adam to talk to him."

Catherine smiled. "But that extra social connection helped, and look what you just learned outside the Taqueria."

Amy raised a hand halfway. "Which we would have learned of anyway."

"And we have a recent photo now, too."

Amy dropped her gaze. "Okay, but can I go chasing after someone soon?"

"The very next missing person is yours."

"All mine!" Amy said in triumph, raising her fists shoulder-height.

CATHERINE WALKED back to her office, and Amy tried to think of something innocuous she could say to Adam. *Well, best get this out of my system now.* She positioned her headset so she could easily dictate.

> *Hi Adam,*
>
> *This is Amy, I'm a secret agent who has been assigned to keep track of you and all your religious nutcase friends, and your impulsive dog, too. Okay, maybe not.*

"Message command: delete message."

"Entire message?"

"Confirm."

"Message deleted."

Amy settled more deeply into her chair, steeling herself. "Message command: new message."

> *Hi Adam,*
>
> *I wanted to give you my current messaging address.*
>
> *Hope your ride back to Choran went smoothly for you all.*
>
> *Please give my best to Sarah, and a scritch for Levi.*
>
> *I have a busy schedule at school planned. I get to learn about abnormal personalities and therapeutic methodologies. And,*

of course, there's the math and writing classes I have to do also. How is life on the farm going? And how is your work doing?

Larson says hello.

Take care, Amy

Amy put the handheld down to look it over. *Looks innocuous enough.*

"Message command: send."

"Sent," the voice said.

Oh, this should be a ton of fun, she thought ironically.

CHAPTER 55:

Adam Contemplates

ADAM SAT listening to the newscast. He was in the common area, trying to relax on one of the sofas, drinking a soda, watching the news.

"Choran is preparing for the arrival of ten thousand immigrants from its sister city Konstana. In an attempt to ease some of the population pressure, several sister cities are accepting new arrivals."

"This isn't going to do anything," Adam said. He threw his arms in the air out of frustration, pulled back to rescue his drink, and raked his free hand through his hair.

"Solve what?" Sarah asked, as she walked in.

Motioning at the newscast, Adam said, "They're bringing in a bunch of darkies from Konstana."

Sarah sighed. "You've been spending too much time with Simon. This is a way we can help."

Adam looked away. "This is a way we all can sink together. What do we do when there's nothing left?"

"We work on the problem," she said, sighing, in a voice that said that they'd had this conversation more than twice.

"We need to make them not want to come," Adam said, looking at the ceiling.

Sarah smiled. "And not dream of a better life? Doesn't sound very realistic. It's everyone's dream, well, many people's."

Adam slouched back, taking another drink.

ADAM LATER walked outside and looked down at one of the border collies moving the sheep to a different pen. A corgi was doing the close-up sorting and Raphael was yelling ineffective instructions. He usually really enjoyed the comedy inherent in the situation of sheep wanting to go one way, the dogs another, and the human trying to direct, but it wasn't touching Adam at this moment. He walked away down one of the fence lines. His fears came at him with every step. This could all be taken away from him, this life that he had come to treasure: the space, the time to contemplate and to meditate—all overrun by thousands of needy people who didn't know how to take care of themselves. He stopped and leaned on a fencepost.

A wild turkey called in the distance. It was such an incongruous place to do cutting-edge science, but to him it was perfect, despite the struggles with dust and sanitation—the incongruity of running a farm and a laboratory side by side. As the turkey's calling died away, clarity sank in and Adam knew what he had to do.

CHAPTER 56:

Adam Writes Amy

AMY SAT down at her desk, hoping to help Steve dictate some notes from the Sammy Malcolm case. He had found the errant wild child, but not without some unfortunate detours through the sewer lines. She was going to suggest that in general, they should consider staying above ground first and checking the closest exits.

She checked her messages. Five staff-related messages. One message from Adam Robertson.

"Noooo," Any said, dropping her head in her hands.

"Bad news?" Yolanda asked from across the room.

"I have a message from Adam," Amy said, glancing back at the screen, hoping that it had gone away like a bad dream.

"Oh, your other problem boyfriend."

Amy put a hand on each temple and said, "Do not go there."

"What's he say?"

"Let me read it first."

Dear Amy,

This is Adam. I miss seeing you every week at the dog park. Life here is much the same, but we're getting 10,000 new

*people from our sister city Konstana, so life here might change
permanently after that. Work progresses and Levi says hello.*

Adam

Amy said to Yolanda, "Choran is getting ten thousand immigrants and he doesn't sound very happy about it."

"Anything specific?"

"No, except that they're coming from Konstana."

Yolanda and Amy consulted their handhelds.

Yolanda said, "Which just so happens to be in a—"

"Darker area," Amy said. "Oh great, now I don't know what to say."

"Just like Catherine said, 'be his friend.' Chitchat."

"Tyson says that, too. It's supposed to relax them but it feels awkward to me."

"I know you don't want to hear it, but this guy is holding a torch for you and you may as well use it."

Amy slowly shook her head. "You're right, I didn't want to hear that."

Throwing one of the soft squishy balls at Amy, Yolanda said, "Come on, this is easy. Just talk with him."

"Say what?"

Yolanda gave Amy her best *duh* look and said, "*Ten thousand people, wow that sounds hard. How is your area going to cope with that?* Ask about how the farm is, and what's going on there. Ask how people you know there are." She paused for a moment. "What was the woman's name?"

"You mean Sarah?"

"Yeah, her."

"And slip in questions about his work since that's what we're interested in."

Amy looked at her dubiously, inclining her head.

"Stop that. Just treat him like a human being and not a suspect."

Amy nodded in surrender. "Okay. I think I'm going to retreat to think about how to do this."

Yolanda smiled. "Away you go," she said, waving a hand.

Amy went and got a glass of water, walked into one of the private meeting rooms, and closed the door. Instead of sitting down, she paced the room, every so often looking at a scenic painting on the wall as if seeking inspiration. The woods in the painting weren't supplying any answers, but she entertained herself with the idea of escaping into them and their peace.

Be his friend, Yolanda said. Just chitchat like I was talking to a friend.

Hi, Adam, you crazy bastard. Maybe not. She kept finding herself wanting to say that.

Amy continued staring at the painting, hoping for a muse or inspiration to appear out of the woods. Not even a squirrel chittered. She looked harder at the painting. It showed woods over rolling hills with a creek in the distance. The painter had put the point of view up on a hill where Amy could envision someone setting down a blanket and spreading out a glorious picnic feast. Everything about the scene said peace. She could feel herself relax a little. Breathing in and then out, the bunched muscles in her neck and shoulders relaxed. *Bucolic, that's the word. That's what this is.*

Then she understood. Prejudice aside, this was what Adam didn't want to lose: that space, that serenity, the opportunity to reflect. *Well, and not to be hungry or cold,* another part of her mind filled in. *Or surrounded by all those 'dark' people who will take everything. Slow down,* she told herself. *Back to the picnic on the hill. Okay, I'd like a turkey with pesto sandwich, with a salad, orange juice, and a brownie for dessert.* She shook her head, and said, "Argh. Stop. Focus." *This is a man who is worried about losing a way of life that he loves.* She started to dictate.

Hi Adam,

I hope you are doing well. It sounds like you are facing some challenges with your area's population increase. I trust there is a plan in place on how to adjust. While it's an imposition, it's a very admirable thing that your area is doing to help spread out the population.

How is your farm and your work? You mentioned that you were working on a different way of doing birth control. How is that going?

How's Sarah? Has she gotten you to eat more tacos and burritos?

Classes here are going fine, but keeping me very busy. I have at least one crazy professor, but that's pretty standard.

Lars says hello.

Take care,

Amy

She played it back and then sent it to Yolanda for her insight.

CHAPTER 57:

Amy Speaks with Yolanda

THE NEXT three weeks involved several back-and-forth messages between Amy and Adam. Amy was just sitting down in the office to read his most recent missive when Gimli charged in with Yolanda behind him. Referring to the exuberant corgi, Yolanda said, "I swear he likes chasing down rats and squirrels more than anything else."

"Any success on the Meyers search?"

"Eventually—they had climbed into a neighbor's storm cellar and when the door closed, it was too heavy for them to move." After a beat, Yolanda looked over and asked, "So, what's lover boy say now?"

Amy shook her head. "I do wish you wouldn't call him that. I was just about to take a look. He's finally talking some about his work."

"Really?"

"He's been saying that he thinks he's gotten an old technique working again. The one where you could track down where someone is originally from using their DNA."

"I don't think that works anymore."

"Neither does anyone else but him. He's not going into detail, but he thinks he's found something in DNA that doesn't change with interbreeding."

Yolanda got an impatient look on her face and crossed her arms. "Everything in DNA changes with interbreeding, or is there something I'm not following here?"

"You got me."

Amy returned her attention to Adam's most recent message.

Dear Amy,

I hope this message finds you well. Sarah and Levi say hello. I have really been making progress on my project at work and I would love to tell you more about it, but I very much want to do it in person and not via message. Could you let me know the next time you're going to be up here and we can get together?

Regards, Adam

Amy put her head down on her desk and groaned loudly enough that Lars raised his head off the bed beside her desk.

Yolanda asked, "That good, huh?"

Amy put her forehead on her palms. "He wants to tell me something about his work project, but he wants to do it in person up there."

Yolanda smiled, looking down. "That's not that terrible. It's not like you haven't done it before."

"I was sort of hoping I could be done with all this."

Yolanda walked over to her desk. "I know it seems never-ending, but this could be important."

"Or it could just be one of those 'Would you like to come up and see my etchings?' sort of moves."

"Which is why you wear a wire and know Tom-Fu," Yolanda said, holding up her arms in a fight position.

Amy glared back, but slowly broke into a smile and mimed the *en garde* position. "Hii-yah! Don't come any closer, you paranoid, prejudiced dweeb."

Yolanda dropped her arms and put her hands on the desk and

leaned forward. "Or else you're going to sic your ebony-colored friend on him."

Amy held her hands folded to her chest, breathlessly asking, "Would you do that for me?"

"Let me check with my wife, but I'm sure it will be all right."

"How much time do I have to ignore his message?"

"Until the other people who monitor the exchange notice. So maybe a few hours."

Turning to Lars, Amy said, "Time for a quick run." Lars jumped up, and out they went.

Harris poked his head in. "Er, what's chasing Amy?"

Yolanda said, "Just reality up north. She'll be okay."

"Ah, I see—or do I?"

"I think we'll all be talking about it in a couple of hours. You have access to that account, take a look."

Harris sat down at his desk and spent some time taking a look. "I wonder how serious this is."

"Or is it an elaborate ploy for a date?" Yolanda asked.

Harris, who understood obsessing on a technical issue, pursed his lips, putting a finger to them. "Well, he seems pretty dedicated to his work and sounds excited about it, so it's probably not just a romantic thing. Sounds like Amy gets a field trip."

"Hence, the running out the door."

Harris laughed. "Well, I'm glad that it's her and not me. I'll flag it for Catherine's attention."

Yolanda thought for a moment. "Amy's going to say that it's in character to play hard to get."

Harris said, "Amy's going to say it's in better character to play: I don't give a fuck."

"No, really, she's going to say that she shouldn't go running up there right away since she's a busy student."

"Quarter break is coming up; maybe that works." He stretched and messed with his hopeless hair. "It's so much easier to plan out someone else's work schedule."

"Great, do mine, too. On second thought, don't."

CHAPTER 58:

———

They Arrive at Choran

AS THE sound of the plane engine started to die down, Amy, Yolanda, and Steve exited down the side stairs. The sky was clear, with a few scattered, light-duty cumulus clouds. Tyson the Fed was standing on the tarmac. Markus from the Choran office of Locate and Investigate was beside him.

Amy walked up, an inquisitive look on her face. "Meeting on the tarmac?"

"I didn't want us to forget in the confusion. Here's your wire," he said, handing her a soft zippered bag.

"I guess I still have to wear that?"

"Especially now," he said.

She noticed that, while he again was not in a suit, he was wearing rough-and-ready khaki pants and a collared short-sleeve polo shirt that he was filling out very nicely. She also realized that, in their entire crew, probably only Yolanda, who reserved her appreciation of the human body to just women, wouldn't notice. Amy said a silent prayer that they'd be on good behavior.

Indicating with her arm, she said, "Agent Tyson, this is LAI Agent Steve Holzar and LAI Agent Yolanda Danimeyer."

They shook hands and Tyson immediately said, "Please call me Tyson."

"Likewise, I'm just Steve and this is . . ." Yolanda stared at him, daring him to make a smart remark at his peril. "This is . . . Yolanda."

Yolanda said, "Pleased to meet you, Tyson."

After a pause, Markus appeared in Steve's peripheral vision.

Steve turned his head, looking right at him and holding his hands outstretched. "Sweety!"

Markus held out his hand loosely in the air in front of him, as if to preclude a frontal assault. "Darling. It's been so long."

Steve bent down to take his hand. "My heart aches at your absence. Counting the hours."

Yolanda turned to Amy, arm bent, pointing at them with an upturned palm. "And how many seconds did it take them to undermine any credibility we've built over the years?"

Amy looked at a smiling Tyson. "Negative four seconds."

Tyson said, "Don't worry. It's not like we're serious all the time."

"Yes, but you're serious at least part of the time." Amy said to Steve and Markus, with a lift of her eyebrows, "While you two are trying to figure out what to do about your doomed non-romance, would you unload Pearl, please?" They could hear the Labrador's tail whacking the sides of her crate. Yolanda had already carried down Gimli's smaller crate, and Amy was heading back in for Lars. The pilot had been unloading some of their bags.

As they headed out to the vehicles, Tyson said, "Quite the party we have here."

Amy said, "Yes, we had to take a real plane with an actual pilot. I'm trying not to worry about the spectacle we're causing. This is likely the most excitement that's happened for six months and word will get around."

Tyson said, "I'm here because this is my case, how about everyone else?"

Amy replied, "I can't do the monthly check-in with the Charon office while I'm working on your case, and Yolanda and Steve couldn't decide who should go, so they both decided to come up, citing that they'd feel better if they were here."

Tyson smiled, gesturing to the surroundings. "I didn't know we were such an attraction."

"Somehow I think a side trip to Soundside is hoped for, but I can't be sure," she said, grinning.

They headed over to the Choran office and squeezed into the small meeting room.

They went over the details that Adam had sent. Amy was going to meet him at the Strongwill Reservoir. Tyson was going to be listening somewhere nearby.

Tyson said to Amy, "I can't get close enough to quickly intervene, so be careful."

Yolanda said, "We'll be there, too, hiding in the faraway bushes."

Amy looked down at the table with her brow furrowed.

Yolanda said, "What's up?"

Amy looked at her and said, "I want you to keep Lars with you, so he has to be far enough away that he won't start barking."

Yolanda gave her that *Really? Please explain* look.

Tyson asked, "Why don't you want Lars along? It takes more explanation not having him there."

Amy said, "Dogs become targets when people aren't in a stable emotional position. Lars has been shot once, and while I don't think anything weird is going to happen, I just want him out of the picture so I don't worry about him."

"But he would keep you more centered."

"Not necessarily. I tend to go unhinged when I think he's in danger."

"Fair enough, then. What's his cover story?"

"He's just at a friend's house."

Tyson smiled, playing devil's advocate, "What friend and why haven't you introduced him before?"

"Okay fine, he's at the local doggy day care center."

"Funny, I don't think we have one."

Amy shook her head and touched her forehead, then flung her hand off like her forehead was on fire. "WHAT-ever."

"I'm serious, you have to think this through. This is what cover is."

"I've abandoned him to roam the streets." She put her hands back on her forehead, but peered out between them.

Tyson crossed his arms over his chest. Amy tried not to find that distracting.

"Okay, he's with Steve, a friend of my family who just moved here and was wanting company."

"Is he a farmer?"

"Yes, but he's not farming right now, and is looking for property here."

"Better pray they never meet, as Steve will have all sorts of farming questions to answer."

Lifting her hands from her head, she said, "They actually have met down south. Okay, I give up, I'll take Lars along." Her voice had the sound of a decision made.

Tyson seemed surprised. He raised his eyebrows. "Are you sure you're okay with this decision?"

"As okay as I'm going to be with this whole thing," she said.

"Okay, Markus tells me you can use the small car from your office. That's it, right?" he said, gesturing to the parking lot. "It doesn't look too official, but one issue is, it's not quite new enough to be a rental car, so try not to call attention to it."

Taking a breath with an inclined head, Amy said, "Okay, I can do this."

"You can. Don't forget your wire."

Steve and Yolanda, smiling, said, "Good hunting."

Amy shot them a withering look.

———

AMY LOADED Lars into the car, got in, and noticed that the navigation system was an infamous older model. *Oh, this should be fun,* she thought.

"Destination?" it asked.

"Strongwill Reservoir."

The screen showed: *Stronghill*, *Strongview*, and *Stenvell*.

"No, Strongwill."

Stronghill, Soundside.

Resting her head on the steering wheel, she was thinking that she was going to have to just drive herself. "No, we're not going to Soundside." *Much as I may want to,* she thought.

Grumbling, she found the map display on the console, and with some hunting around located Strongwill. She hoped this would work, as she wanted to reread all of Adam's messages before their meeting. She really didn't want to have to do all the driving.

"Strongwheel Recreational Reservoir," it said, in what she thought was almost a proud tone of discovery.

Putting her head in her hands, she said, "Go."

CHAPTER 59:

Amy and Adam

THE CAR pulled into the Strongwill Reservoir parking area, happily announcing, "Strongwheel."

Whatever, Amy thought.

She could see Adam sitting on his car. She was a little relieved to not see Levi, concerned that Levi might start mentally blasting her with random words. She realized he could just be off chasing a rabbit or a squirrel, so she tried not to get her hopes up.

"Hi, Adam," she said, getting out of the car and letting Lars out. Lars immediately started to sniff around, looking for a good place to pee. Amy asked, "Where's Levi?"

"Oh, he's with Sarah. I think he likes her better in some ways."

Reflecting on the times where Adam wanted to punish Levi for just acting like a dog, she thought, *What a surprise.* "How is Sarah?"

"She's fine. She's busy on our new project and seems to be enjoying it. Wanna take a walk?"

"I'd love to."

They walked away from the parking area, down the dirt access road that ran around the reservoir. Then the road started to climb. The water came into view, sunlight playing over the blue-green surface surrounded by the green and brown shore. Amy breathed in the smell of the water, which offered a peace that was eluding her. She was starting to feel like this was one of those awkward dates where no one admits to what's going on. Adam had been telling her about the goings-on at the farm, and she realized she was only half-listening.

". . . and then Sarah had to head the sheep off before it went running out of the pen."

Amy asked, "Where was one of the dogs?"

"She thought she could do it herself."

"My friends tell me, 'That works fine until a sheep has other ideas.'"

Adam laughed. "Yep."

They stopped at an overlook, with the slope receding into the water below them.

Amy thought about the verbal code that she and Tyson had gone over. The ones about allergies that they had decided on at the dog park, or she could mention the weather. The weather ones were sunny, windy, and rain. They went over and over them, and now they just seemed silly. She was wearing a wire and could probably just say something in plain English and get away with it.

Adam looked out over the water, clearly preoccupied. He continued on over the rise, dropping down to where Amy could see a stream coming down a gentle slope. Amy tried not to worry that she was out of visual range, in case they had decided to tail her.

Adam turned right, edging along by the creek. He started to climb what looked like an old trail, skirting along beside a large berry bush.

Amy said, looking at all the overgrown grass along the narrow, faded path, "This trail doesn't look very government-issue."

"This is an older section that has some preexisting features from when it was private property."

Say what? Amy thought. She hoped her backup could figure out where they were. "Er, features?"

"Like this," he said, half-turning to her and pointing with his arm extended, palm up.

It was a wooden bridge about fifty feet high going over the stream. Pale with age, it was once robust, but now it seemed less than stable. From this distance, the walkway looked sturdy enough, but the railings, held up by X-shaped cross pieces, looked like something large had been chewing on them. Amy's eyes tracked across it. She could see the bridge went over what was now a huge berry bush and some large boulders, crossing the creek over to a more forested area. For her listening audience, she said, "Looks like a really old bridge, Adam."

"This is the only way to access the other side of the creek, where there once was some instrumentation that they used to monitor the creek flow."

Amy, feeling like she had a talent for the obvious, said, "I take it they don't do that anymore?"

"Naw, it's now further downstream."

Walking up to the base of the steps, he said, "Let's climb up and head to the other side."

Amy looked up again, evaluating, and turned to Lars. "I need you to wait here."

Lars put his feet up on the steps and whined.

"No, it's too dangerous, you don't have hands."

He blew out his cheeks and *arrooo*'ed in protest.

"I'm serious. I would be worrying about you the entire time, and we'd both fall off. Here's a chewy stick."

He sniffed, considering.

Amy took a few steps over to a clearing and dropped the chewy. "Wait here."

He sighed in what certainly looked like reluctant acquiescence, and plopped down with his prize.

"Good boy."

Adam put a hand on the railing and raised his foot up to the first step.

Amy asked, "So where are we going?"

"I want to get to the other side of the creek and this is the best way." He took another two steps.

You said that already and that's not exactly an explanation, she thought. She looked back at Lars to see that he was happily working on his chew stick. *Well, at least one of us is happy.*

Amy looked at the steps going up. It was more like a ladder. Each step was worn in the middle, but they looked like they would still hold their weight. The railings were darkened with the oil of many hands, but time had also greyed the wood. The rails rocked gently when she pulled on them, but they held as she put her weight on the step, steadying herself with the handrail. She took another step and her confidence started to increase. *Just get up this section,* she thought. She was usually fine with heights, but had little experience in less-than-rock-steady bridges.

While Adam was ahead of her, she started quietly talking as if to herself, hoping her listeners could hear her. "I'm on an old grey bridge that's just off the main property. We climbed up a creek to get to it. It's a little rickety. Lars is waiting on the ground at the base."

As she climbed, Amy looked down. The berry bush was huge and had climbed over some large boulders. She could see the other side of the bridge descending beyond the bush. While there was an easy access to the creek, with a clearing nestled in front of some bay trees, it occurred to Amy that people looking for them would have a difficult time finding them even using dogs. To Amy, this suddenly felt even more risky than it already was.

Adam had reached the top of the steps and was starting to walk across.

"Adam, stop a sec." *Should she fake being afraid to cross? That actually wouldn't be hard to pull off,* she thought.

Adam stopped and looked back. "We just need to go right down there." He turned and pointed to the creek bank just on the other side. He started up again.

"Adam, stop," she said.

He resembled an impatient horse just wanting to go. He stopped, but he was still leaning forward, looking ahead.

"You need to tell me what this is about," Amy said.

"I'll show you when we—"

"You'll show me right now, before we go any further on this scary bridge."

He sighed loudly. "It would be easier if—"

"Now, Adam. Show-and-tell now. I'm not going any further unless I know why."

Shrugging, he put down the canvas tote he was carrying, knelt down, and unzipped it.

Amy took the time to step carefully closer to him.

He drew out what looked like a large sealed bag. Inside that bag was a smaller, similar bag that held liquid.

"The water in this bag contains nanobots, similar to what we use to lower blood pressure and heart rate. Turns out, they can be switched around to increase blood pressure instead. It will make someone ill."

Amy tilted her head, eyes squinting. "Why would you want to do that?" She was trying not to panic about the memory of Herman and Lincoln fighting for life in the hospital. Their brain scans red with too much activity, and their BP's climbing steadily.

"If enough people get ill, then they'll think there's something inherently wrong with the place and won't want to live here."

Amy took a slow deliberate breath, "Er, wwwwhhy?"

"Well, if they just moved here, they would easily blame it on the location."

Amy had a dreadful feeling that started in her head and continued to work its way down to her stomach. *Oh this is so not good. Call for help. What was it that we'd agreed on? Mention allergies, that's right.* She had to get her mouth working again. "I'm sorry, but I don't understand. Can you spell it out for me? And is there something in bloom? My allergies are just killing me." She pinched the bridge of her nose. Then she remembered she was supposed to mention bad weather. She looked up at the perfectly clear sky, and said, "Do you think it will rain?"

Except for giving her a confused look, Adam didn't seem to notice that the nonsense she was babbling was actually a code that pulled a fire alarm. It was his turn to take a calming breath. He resembled someone who was trying to explain why the sky was blue to a four-year-old. "We just had 10,000 people from a darker nation arrive. If something mysteriously makes them sick, then they might all just leave."

Amy scratched her head. *This is so weird, it doesn't take any acting.* "How?"

Adam held up the bag. "The bag inside this bag will dissolve slowly in water, releasing the nanobots into the water system."

Oh Gods. Oh Gods. Amy didn't even know where to begin talking, so she took a different tack. "Did Tomas ask you to do this?"

"No, he explained to me that it could work this way, but this is my project."

"Don't you think he'd be unhappy with you doing this?"

"I'm hoping he likes my initiative. He's always been encouraging me to explore the possibilities."

Ah-ha, here's a chance. "Adam, Tomas doesn't appear to like doing anything high-profile, especially mass sickness."

"They won't know it's us, that's the beauty."

"I think you're being naive. They will figure out it's nanobot-caused, and there aren't many organizations doing that kind of research in this area."

Adam looked at the bag and didn't seem to hear.

Amy, having to resist punching him out of frustration, said, "Have you even tested this? I thought you were a researcher."

"Well, I did a lot of modeling."

"You haven't tested it?" Amy's voice started to rise. *This is a completely stupid conversation I'm having about testing mass murder.*

"It will work. I've already placed three other bags like this," Adam said, and started forward.

Oh, fuck! She grabbed his arm. "You WHAT?! Adam, stop. There's something you don't know."

"Can we talk about this later?" He shook his head as if she was talking about something inconsequential.

"NOW," she said. He looked back, with a quizzical expression. Amy said as levelly as she could manage, "The nanobots can kill."

Adam said, slightly defensive, "How do you know that? What do you know about my work?"

Okay, time to jump off this cliff, she thought.

"Adam, I'm with the police, and we've been tracking a serious assault where someone used nanobots."

His face dropped in shock. "You're a cop! You're a fucking cop!" He punched at the air. "I trusted you. And so what if some other doofus used nanobots?" He leaned away from her as if to leave.

Amy gripped his arm harder.

"We traced the nanobots back to your organization."

Adam laughed, looking away. "That's impossible. You're completely wrong. We haven't assaulted anyone. You people always blame us for everything, why do you think we try to get away from you all?"

Haven't assaulted anyone yet, she thought. "The assault was done by a third party, but it leads back to you folks."

"This is nuts."

Amy leaned into his face, yelling and nearly sputtering. "Do not talk to me about nuts. You're the one who's trying to justify murder."

"This isn't murder," he said, trying to lean back.

Lars, back on the ground, had stopped chewing, /Okay?/

It took Amy a moment to realize Lars was saying something. She replied to him, /I'm okay./ She said to Adam, "You don't know that. I have seen what the nanobots can do when they're set to raise blood pressure and heart rate. If not stopped, the brain circuitry will fry, which is pretty dead in my book."

Adam said, "I don't believe you. You're probably with some company who wants our research."

"Hardly."

He wrenched his arm free. "Leave me alone." He started forward.

She grabbed his elbow again.

"Adam, if you do this you will bring down a world of hurt on your group. This could end your group's existence. This idyllic life will stop. Believe me, Tomas doesn't want you to do this."

Adam stopped, considering. "I don't believe you. I don't think you're a cop. I think you're with a competing lab."

Amy heard barking, whining, and scratching. She glanced over the frayed railing to see that Lars was trying to climb the stairs.

Amy hurriedly said to him, /No, don't climb./

She saw him scramble up two steps. /Lars, stop, you'll—/

Lars's rear foot slipped and his front feet slid forward through the opening. He tried to right himself with his back feet, but instead he wound up twisting and tumbling to the ground.

"Shit," Amy said, then remembered to speak empathically so Adam didn't realize what she was up to. Desperately hoping Lars would listen, she pleaded, /Go get help. Go back. Get help./

Lars stood up, wobbling some, whined, and looked up at the ladder.

She begged again, /Go! Get help. Please!/

Lars paused, considering. Amy thought she could hear him whining, but decided it was her imagination. After a very long moment, Lars took off running back down the hill.

In the meantime, Adam had pulled away and had taken two more steps.

She ran up, grabbing his jacket. "Adam, please stop. The police are on their way. This is over."

"There are no cops!" he cried.

"I assure you there are."

"You just want this!" He brandished the bag.

"You can keep your stupid bag, if you come back with me."

Rats, I just lied to him. Ah, well.

"No. You're just trying to scare me."

Amy shouted, "What part of 'over' do you not understand?"

Guess those fancy allergies distress codes aren't that important anymore? she thought.

"Forget it, go away." He started pulling her along.

Amy grappled for footing. Adam had gotten one arm out of his jacket and had his other arm halfway out. He shifted his bag between his hands.

Amy readjusted her hold on the jacket, using it to get a lock around his right arm, which was still in the sleeve. They were now leaning on the railing, but trying to get better footing against one another.

Adam may have lived on a farm, but he hadn't done farming or heavy lifting, and Amy's training was helping her hold him in place.

He said, "You can't stop me."

"I think I am." *Just hold on,* she thought.

They were stuck in a tableau. A sort of tug-of-war, with sweat included as a bonus. Amy could feel the railing bending with their weight.

Adam was twisting, and Amy had to keep readjusting her grip.

"Let me go."

"Sorry, can't do that."

"Why'd you lie to me?"

"I'm sorry, Adam, we're concerned."

"No, you're not, you just want my research."

"Adam, I couldn't possibly understand the complexity of your work. My understanding ends somewhere before organic chemistry."

"So, you have to let me go?"

"No, I can't let you go."

This continued for two more rounds, Amy nearly losing Adam's arm a couple of times. Then she heard a bark, and she heard, "Amy! Amy!"

They both looked over to see Lars leading Steve, Yolanda, their dogs, and Tyson up the hill.

Adam cried, "No!" and he lifted the bag with his left arm, cocking it back across his chest in order to throw it.

Dropping the arm she was holding, she cried out, "Shit, Adam, no!" She dove for the bag and both of them slammed against the railing. Their combined weight cracked the already weakened wood. She had her hand on the bag and pushed it towards the bridge floor, but the world was shifting. They were falling. "Fuck. Adam, grab something." Amy's motion propelled her forward to the next section of the railing. She grabbed at it with both hands. Pain seared through her palm, and she realized she'd impaled it on the broken section. Trying to focus on keeping her hold, she looked down to see Adam just falling. "Oh Gods, no. ADAM!" She watched him fall, almost like he was skydiving, but he didn't land in the water. Instead he fell on his side on a boulder. His head whipped down in a frightening way. Amy heard herself crying as she hung in the air, wrapped around what was left of the railing, wondering how much time she had before she fell, too. The railing groaned with the sway of her weight. Someone was shouting at her, but she didn't pay any attention. She had to get herself up before she or anyone else fell.

She looked at the bridge walkway and could see that the bag was safely on it. *Small favors,* she thought. Grimacing with effort, she swung her right foot back on the walkway. There was a creaking sound underneath her arm. Working through the pain in her hand, she slowly edged her foot closer. When she was able to put some weight on it, the railing started to lean away from the bridge. Readjusting her grip, she got her knee up high enough to hold purchase, but the handrails continued their quest to free themselves from the bridge. *Almost,* she thought, and shifted her weight so she could wrap her arm around the railing, relieving some of the throbbing in her hand. Gasping a couple of breaths, she crawled up the X section, and then she was able to get her other foot back on the walkway. She launched her body at the next railing just as the one she had been bracing against came completely off. It screeched and fell to the ground, flattening the berry bush, and then careened off the boulders, pieces tumbling into the creek. There was a voice calling her name and she tried to wave that she was okay, but she suddenly thought, *The bag. Don't step on the bag.* She edged past it and sat down, her head spinning. All she could do was lie down, sobbing from the exertion and the vision of watching him fall. "Adam, Adam. Adam."

———

"AMY, DAMMIT, you're scaring me to death. Stop with the aerial stunt work," said a familiar voice. "Hang on. Crap, and you're bleeding."

Amy looked up to see Yolanda coming towards her fast. Amy took a sharp breath and pointed. "Stop! Watch out for that bag."

Yolanda froze, trying to arrest her feet. "Is it a bomb?" Her face tightened.

"No, it's fragile and toxic."

"Oh, what fun. Central, or anyone else who's listening, we have a bag of toxins up here that appears to be sealed."

A commlink voice said, "Copy that, Yolanda, do you want us to come up?"

Amy said, "No! No more people on this bridge. We'll bring the bag down."

"We have to get you past this broken railing first."

"Move the bag first. Carefully."

"How carefully?"

"Adam had it in a canvas tote, so it must be transportable."

"Okay." Yolanda, put a hand out and grasped the bag at the top, lifted it and moved it further back up the walkway, and set it down gingerly. "Now the hard part," she said, looking pointedly at Amy while she walked back to her, and knelt down in front of her. "Let me see your hand."

Amy offered her bleeding hand.

Yolanda frowned. "This is gross. Didn't your mother teach you to wash your hands?"

"Leave my mother out of this. This fuckup is entirely mine," Amy lifted her hand and starting to shrug.

"Give me back that hand, and stop splattering me," Yolanda pulled a towel out of her bag and wrapped it around Amy's hand, and grimaced. "Yick, if you give me a blood-borne disease, I am not going to forgive you."

"I'm clean. Well, as far as blood goes. Can we just go?"

"I'm just going to wrap this enough to get you down, then a medic can fix my bungling." She wrapped gauze around the hand

and covered that with a self-sticking elastic wrap. She pulled a waist belt also out of her bag, and started guiding it around Amy's waist.

"That doesn't look like standard issue."

"It's for damsels in distress."

"I am not an effing damsel. I got myself back on the bridge." Amy tried to get up.

"I am more than a little impressed with that, by the way." She pushed Amy back down. "And stop trying to fly down."

"Hurry, Adam has info we need."

Yolanda clipped a rope to Amy's waist belt and wrapped it around her own waist. "Let's see if you can stand."

"I'll be fine," Amy teetered to her feet, her teeth clenched.

Yolanda looked down, her face grave. "I don't think he's going anywhere."

"You don't understand, we have to get to him. He's hidden bags in the reservoirs, and he didn't tell me where they were."

"I really don't think—"

"I have to try. Please help me walk," Amy unsteadily took a step.

Yolanda pulled her up to full standing. "You don't look like you're in any shape to—"

"Help me get off this thing," Amy wobbled, trying to take another step.

Yolanda guided her past the broken railing, keeping tension on the rope between them.

"I need to get down," Amy said, half-dragging herself back along the walkway and stopping to pick the bag up.

Yolanda took hold of her arm. "Fine, bleed to death, pushy girl. Don't make a mess on your way down the ladder." Amy only tripped twice and Yolanda righted her each time. Yolanda said into her handheld, "Steve, can you call for a medic? We have one cut-up hand, and one fallen body of unknown status."

"Already on their way," he said.

AMY GOT to the ground and headed towards the berry bush.

Yolanda tackled her. "Stop, dammit."

"We have to get to Adam. This is my fault."

"Bullshit! Not while you bleed to death or get an infection courtesy of our wooden friend here."

Not really listening, Amy said, "Both of us leaning on the railing is what broke it."

"I saw it happen, remember? This is not your fault. It was an accident, and you were trying to stop him."

"This whole situation is so screwed up." Amy handed her the bloody bag.

"Gee, thanks, you shouldn't have, what the hell is this toxin?"

"It's a dissolvable bag of killer nanobots."

"Do we have any place to put this bag?"

Tyson, came forward and took the bag.

Amy repeated, the urgency in her voice increasing, desperation making her voice start to screech, "We have to get to Adam, he's hidden three other bags, and he didn't tell me where they were. And how are we going to get through this bush?"

Tyson had already called the maintenance people, and they were cutting back the bush.

Steve and Yolanda physically restrained Amy from trying to help. A medic unwrapped her hand, took a look, and said the wound was messy but superficial. She painted a substance on it that could act as a bandage, a disinfectant, and another layer of skin. She offered to numb the surface some to help with the pain, but Amy declined, not wanting to lose coordination.

The workers had cleared just enough of a path and Amy charged in. One guy called, "Careful, there are stones out there with a steep drop-off."

AMY APPROACHED Adam's body. She'd seen dead bodies before, with their grey pallor from no blood circulation. Adam looked alive, but in sorry shape. The right-hand side of his face was partially caved in and his arm was bent the wrong way. She could hear him quietly gurgling. "Adam. Adam, can you hear me?" She put a hand on his left shoulder. He was still warm and he was breathing, wheezing with effort. He started to shake. "Adam!" She looked over her shoulder. "He's seizing."

A medic moved in to hold his head.

Steve appeared at her side and said. "I'm not terribly surprised."

"Adam, it's Amy, where did you hide the bags?'

Steve said, "His head is caved in, I don't know if you're going to get a reliable answer—"

"Shut up for a sec," Amy said, cutting him off and leaning in, trying not to be completely horrified by the appalling sight. "Adam, did you hide three other bags? Adam?"

Adam stopped shaking, and started sputtering. "Yssss."

"Yes, three?"

"Ysss."

"Where, Adam can you tell me where?"

"Waahter."

"Which water? Which reservoir?"

"Waashter. Bags disssolvvve . . . T-T-Twelve . . . hours." Adam's sputter became a rattle. His body spasmed once and then stilled. All of his remaining animation just stopped.

Realization sank into Amy. "Twelve hours? Shit! Where, Adam, where?" Clenching her teeth, blinking back tears, Amy started hitting Adam's shoulder. "Dammit, Adam, where are they?" Steve moved in to pinion her arm.

Amy said to the medic, "We have to keep this man alive. Revive him if at all possible."

The medic looked doubtful.

Steve said, "Just humor my crazy colleague."

Sniffing, Amy said, "Don't call me that. This is important."

"But you are acting a little crazy, but fine." To the medic Steve said, "Please do what you can for this man for my nutball partner."

Steve pulled Amy up by force, nearly lifting her off the ground. She pulled back, "No."

ELLEN CLARY

Now he did lift her, saying, "You need to stop, so we can regroup and come up with a plan to locate the bags."

"No. No. No."

Putting her back on her feet and taking her arm, he asked, "We have hours?" Amy nodded. "Well, get your gear and let's go regroup. Pound on me if you like."

Amy looked up suddenly. "Lars?!?"

Steve said, "He's okay, he led us here, and—"

/Amy. Amy,/ Lars said.

Amy could see that Tyson, of all people, was trying to hang on to the collar of the excited kelpie boy. He and Steve were probably the only ones who could contain him.

Tyson saw Amy and said, while being bounced up and down, "Agent Callahan, can you come fetch your beast before he throws himself onto the berry bush?"

Amy charged back to Lars and threw her arms around his neck. Hugging wasn't Lars's favorite thing, but from Amy, he treasured it. He shoved his head up to her and started licking her face. /Amy, Amy,/ was all he would say, and then would butt his head into hers. /Okay?/

"Ow, you silly beast. Stop. You are sopping wet, but I am so happy to see you, and I'm fine," Amy said, rubbing his neck. "What a good boy."

Steve said, shaking his head and trying not to laugh, "He was in such a hurry that he overshot the turn up the hill and ran into the creek, and then raced back to us barking, letting us know we were too slow."

Regaining her composure, she combed through his black, sepia, and golden fur with her fingers, and examined his legs for cuts, abrasions, and swelling. He seemed remarkably fine, except for— "He's drooling, has he drunk anything?

"No," said Steve in a scolding tone with a scowl at Lars.

Amy could hear the 'dammit' he implied.

"He wouldn't drink anything from anyone." Steve knelt down, too, with a collapsible bowl of water dripping over the sides.

311

To Amy he said, "Why don't you have a go before I pour water over his head?" He leaned down to Lars, and in his ear said, "Fool."

With that admonition, Lars immediately started drinking the water.

Still scowling, but only in play, Steve continued, "At your warning, we ran down the access road, but we couldn't see where you were. The bridge was obscured by the trees, but Lars appeared with that *follow me* dance. He knew where to turn up the creek. Well, after that brief swim in the creek to completely confuse us."

Amy sighed, looked at Lars, and told him a private, /Thank you./

Still drinking, he said a contented /Mmmmmm./

Steve looked over at Tyson, who was rubbing his sore hand from holding the struggling Lars. "Okay, now we really need to plan."

"And I need a drink," Amy said.

"How about a nice juice?" Tyson said.

"Can it be a smoothie?"

"I'm sure we can arrange something," he said.

CHAPTER 60:

They Devise a Search Plan

AMY, STEVE, and Yolanda, along with Choran locals Markus and David, crowded into the Choran LAI meeting room. Beth, the lead detective, was waiting for them at the front, her hair windswept, as if she had flown there using only her arms and had run into turbulence. Fed Tyson was up in the front on the side, looking unruffled as ever. Harris and Director Catherine were on the datalink video monitor. Harris, who was not the most comfortable being on camera, was looking off to the side, probably talking to his dog, his normally straight hair pointing in several different directions. Someone had thought to get bagels, coffee, and juice delivered, for which Amy said a silent *thank you* to the bagel and juice gods. Steve and Markus appeared to be genuflecting to the god of coffee.

Amy leaned over to Yolanda and asked, "Do you think Harris minds always being the one to hold down the fort at Evergreen?"

Yolanda shook her head. "He likes it that way. He's the one with all the power there anyway, and with this amount of chaos, I'm sure he's happier down there."

Sipping from a coffee cup, Beth said, "Hello, and welcome to you all. I can honestly say I wish we were meeting under better circumstances."

The room filled with murmurs of assent.

"Just to recap what everyone already knows. Agent Callahan met with Suspect Adam Robertson because Adam said he had something he wanted to discuss in person." Adam's photo appeared on the large screen and Amy shuddered and looked down. Both Steve and Yolanda put a hand on her shoulders. Beth looked at Amy and said, "Amy, I'm so sorry that we have to go over all this. I have not included any further photos of him."

Breathing in and nodding, Amy said, "Thank you."

"Agent Callahan went in wired and we have a recording of much of the conversation. Adam took Amy to an old bridge at the Strongwill Reservoir. He told her he intended to place a bag of nanobots that were set to increase blood pressure and heart rate. Adam was convinced that the nanobots would just make targeted people ill. His hope was that they wouldn't want to live in Choran anymore. He said that he had already placed three other bags. Amy refused to fully cross the bridge and called for help over the wire, while she held Adam in place. When help appeared, Adam tried to throw his bag off the bridge and Agent Callahan dove in to prevent him from doing so. Their resulting struggle broke the bridge railing and Adam fell to the rocks below. Amy was able to cling to the remaining railing and climb back on the bridge, and Agent Yolanda Danimeyer helped her down from the bridge."

Amy was carefully studying the floor, trying to stay present, and unsuccessfully attempting not to remember Adam talking from his shattered, leaking skull. Yolanda rubbed her back.

"He was still able to speak, and he again confirmed to Amy that there were three bags of harmful nanobots in the reservoirs. But he did not disclose where he hid the bags. Agent Callahan requested that he be kept alive in hopes of reviving him, but such efforts have not proved successful. He has been pronounced brain-dead and the decision what to do now goes to his family." Looking at Amy, she said, "He is an organ donor, so the effort has not been futile."

"Heartwarming," Amy said, just to Yolanda.

"It's good karma, you did the right thing," she replied, readjusting in the folding chair.

Beth touched a control and the display showed a map of the surrounding reservoirs. Amy groaned. "Definitely more than fifteen."

"Seventeen actually. We don't think he went outside this area, since there were so many choices and it would have taken too much time."

Studying the map, Amy could see a group of three larger reservoirs, a group of two—one being quite large—and another group of three, with four smaller ones to the north and five even tinier ones further to the south.

"Markus and David, since you know the area and can move faster, I'd like you to do the set of southern and northern lakes."

David smiled and said, "Ponds."

"Tyson and I don't think he used those areas. My hope is that you'll be able to rule those out and come back to help Steve, Yolanda, and Amy search the larger reservoirs."

The display then showed circles drawn around the larger lakes with their names on them. Steve would get the set of two with the very large reservoir, and Amy and Yolanda would each get a set of three. "It's entirely possible that one reservoir has all three bags, so please keep that in mind.

"While it's possible that Adam may have walked to three different places, in the interest of time, we think he drove there. I don't think he did any sneaking in from a hole in the fence. So check the parking areas first before walking all the way around a reservoir.

"As you might guess, we descended on the Tomasian Farm and talked to everyone there. We have brought Tomas and all of the lab techs back for further questioning, and they're all crowded into the police station next door."

"The cheery, windowless, brick cube," Markus said. "That should make them confess to anything."

"A couple of you have met Sarah, and she is being very forthcoming about her growing concern about Adam. She also tells us that Adam is exploiting a side effect that they noticed a while back while trying to control heart rates and blood pressures. None of the techs have made any reference to what we saw down south, where Herman and Lincoln were brought down with a racing heart rate and out-of-control blood pressures. We're grilling Tomas, but he's claiming not to know anything about that. I don't believe that for a second, but I don't know if I have enough evidence to hold him for longer than a day. I will be able to confiscate the containers, at least for a while, because of the stolen data units being transported in them.

"Tomas is a slippery eel. He's up to something, but he hasn't tipped his hand enough. I don't think what Adam did is directly related to what Tomas has in mind, but they are cut from the same cloth. In my opinion, Adam embodies a more impulsive, less patient Tomas. You can tell that Tomas is very concerned, but it seems to be more about its effect on him and his operation than about potential harm to people.

"I have let the Choran water district know that we might have a very serious contamination issue if we can't get this resolved in five to six hours."

Beth readjusted her position. "Markus tells me there is a deli across the street that can make us lunches, since we won't have time for an actual lunch later. Any questions?" There were none, but she could tell it was all a little too much. "Please all, stay in touch with us so Harris can track progress. If you find a bag, please contain it in one of the lidded buckets that we've provided. Also send out a photo, so we can all get a better idea of how he's hidden the bags. Good hunting to everyone."

Yolanda turned to Amy. "Are you sure you're okay to go back out?"

"I'm more than sure. I want this to end soon."

CHAPTER 61:

Steve and Pearl Search

AS STEVE'S car approached the parking entrance, he shifted it into manual mode and parked it on the side of the road before the actual turn because he didn't want to compromise any scent that might be left.

Steve let Pearl out of her crate and she started dancing in a circle.

/Where Gim? Where Lars?/

"They're working, like we're supposed to be doing."

/Oh. Go sniff?/

"Yes, wait a second."

She spun around more and drank in the area where they'd parked.

"Stop, come here."

/Mmm?/

"Don't move around too much as I don't want us to walk on anything."

She blew out her cheeks as if to say: *Amateur.*

He called in. "Agent Holzar and Canine Pearl are at Little Stainley Reservoir, about to sweep the parking lot."

"Roger," came what had to be Harris's voice. "Four hours to deadline."

Steve laughed to himself. *Just a little pressure*, he thought. He had chosen the parking area of the smaller of the two reservoirs, hoping if Adam had been here, there would be less ground to cover. Looking out across what must be a half-mile of water, he realized that even a find here would take some time. He got out his olfactory reflectometer storage device, which would forever just be called a sniff-o-meter in his mind, and called up Adam's shoe smell. It felt weird that they had taken this smell from a recently dead man, but he hadn't been technically dead when they took the sample, so he hoped the smell wasn't compromised with that distinctive smell that a dead human has.

He held it out to Pearl and she took a long inhale. It reminded him of getting high in college, which they all still did even though there were less hazardous methods available now.

And then she was off.

"The parking lot. We need to cover the entire parking lot."

Pearl said, /Pffft./ Clearly, she thought she knew exactly what she was doing, and who was he to argue?

First, she scented the air, then put her nose to the ground and moved in a weaving pattern, occasionally stopping to blow out through her nose and shake her head.

Every so often, he would ask her to move to a spot and start again, but for the most part he just let her work.

When it was clear that there was nothing to be found he got a tennis ball out and told Harris over the radio, "Big goose egg on Little Stainley. No sign of Adam, moving on to the Big Stainley lower parking lot."

"Roger," came Harris's voice again. "Let the record show that Agent Holzar will be moving on to Big Stainley Reservoir lower parking lot."

Steve put the handheld down and turned and threw the tennis ball for a delighted Pearl, who bounded down the access road with her hindquarters bunched underneath her.

After a few throws, Pearl and he got back in the car and he drove it manually down the street to Big Stainley.

Though the parking area was paved, the entry was dirt, so Steve tried a track analyzer that he had connected to his handheld. It had an image of Adam's car tire and it could compare a current photo to the stored one. It could even compensate, within a certain tolerance, around an image damaged by the car tire going too fast though the dirt.

He got out and left Pearl in the car at first. He ran the tire analyzer on a couple of tracks he could see. It pinged, indicating a partial match on one of the prints.

"Central, I have a possible match on Adam's car tire, though it appears he was going at speed. I don't think he stopped. Will check further."

"Okay," Harris said.

They did the same exact search routine that they did at Little Stainley, and wound up with the same results. *Geez, I hope we're not doing this wrong.* he thought.

"I think that Adam cruised through here, but didn't stop. Off to our last destination."

JUST BEFORE setting out, he looked at the last lake. The reservoir looked like a real lake, with smooth curving shoreline, and not like a stopped-up drain whose shoreline had a ragged edge. This particular reservoir wasn't a perfect lake-like shape, as there was a point that jutted in on one side, and the lake was smaller and more pinched in near it.

Pearl headed off, nose to the ground, stopping every thirty seconds or so, lifting her head and sniffing the air. They were traveling along an access road that approached the lake and turned into a trail that circled around it. She took a side trail that led out onto the point which looked like a fine picnic spot. There were a dozen footprints going in all directions. Steve hoped that they weren't tracking a walker and his lunch and that for all their work, they would find the remains of a half-eaten turkey on rye or sourdough.

They worked their way down to the water and Pearl said, /Here,/ and looked up with her mouth open, panting with an excited expression.

"Good girl, Pearl." He threw her tennis ball back in the direction they had come.

With Pearl fetching her prize, he looked down to try to figure out what had happened. "Central, Canine Pearl has tracked Adam to the edge of the water and I'm trying to assess what's here."

"Any sign of a bag?" asked Harris.

"Negative. I'll send you some photos."

"Roger."

Pffft, he thought while he took some images. *Adam stopped here and from the shoe print, knelt down, but why? In contemplation? Confusion? Admiration? Probably not on the last one,* he guessed. *Adam's feet seem to shift around in a few places in this spot.*

Pearl had returned with her ball and handed it to him.

/Ball? Ball?/

"Not now, we still need to work."

She seemed to deflate a little, but he gave her a liver treat, which perked her up.

While Steve sent the photos, she poked around some, sniffing, then looking out over the water, then back where they'd come from and took two steps and resumed sniffing.

/Here!/

"What?" Steve said.

Pearl walked further along the water, but she wasn't on the path. She was walking carefully right on the edge of the water, weaving out and back in following the water's edge. Her nose was on the ground. She wasn't air-scenting, she was following his track.

They continued in this manner all the way around the pinched end of the water. *This is weird, why would Adam do this,* he wondered, but Pearl seemed so sure. He couldn't resist asking, "Pearl, are you sure about this?"

/Search./

Which was her way of saying: I'm busy, talk to the tail.

"You're the boss."

She ignored him and continued on. Steve backed off the squishy edge; it supported her weight easily but, with his weight, he just sank.

Steve was just about to update their status when she stopped. Her head came up and she turned back sniffing on the track she'd covered, then went forward and turned again.

/Here./

"Here what? What do you mean? I don't see anything, nor is it likely he's standing here."

/Here,/ she said and looked over the water.

Steve sloshed over to where she was. She was telling him the trail around the edge ended here. Anything else would just be Adam leaving. So what did this mean, he wondered? He wanted not to sound like a complete bumbling fool when he called in, so he wanted to have at least a theory.

He looked around the shore. No sign of a bag anywhere, just like the last place that Adam had stopped. *Is it possible he took the bag away from the water? Naw, that doesn't make any sense. It has to be close to the water.*

Pearl kept looking off at the water. He got out his binoculars and slowly scanned the surface. There was a bump out in the middle. Zooming in, he could see what looked like a small tarp that was close to the color of the water.

Pearl was wiggling her butt in anticipation.

/Fetch?/

He reached down and rubbed the back of her neck. "No, sorry, I don't know what it is, and we need to look at it closer first."

She looked disappointed and blew out her cheeks.

"We will go take a look." He wasn't sure if she would understand that, but she knew that she couldn't just swim out, chomp on it, and bring it back, which is all she wanted to do.

He got out his comm. "Hello Central."

"Hello there."

"There is something small floating out on the water that I want to get a closer look at. Could we get someone with a boat out here?"

"Checking—"

The line went dead and he threw the tennis ball a couple of times for Pearl.

"Agent Holzar?"

"Yes?"

"One of the Choran water district employees will be there in a couple of minutes to get the boat out."

"Roger," he couldn't resist saying.

———————

A FEW minutes later, a district vehicle appeared and headed down the access road. Steve looked up to see a woman, her shoulder-length hair waving in the wind, driving quickly towards them and sliding to a stop. "Hop in, my name's Janet."

They bumped down the road a very short way to a small low building that was beside the water.

Pretty small building for a boat, Steve thought. *Wait a minute, aren't boathouses on top of the water? Where do you put the actual boat?*

Janet leaped out of the truck in a practiced fashion and jogged over to the door, old fashioned keys in hand.

"No keypad."

"Kinda low tech here," she said as she pulled open the door, went in, and started tugging on something.

When Steve got to the door, he nearly fell over laughing. "A canoe!"

"We don't use power craft on this water."

"Well, it's not like we're in a hurry or anything," Steve said, hoping he didn't sound snippy.

"If you grab that side, it will go faster."

Steve thought, *Well, she does have a point there.* He stood on the side and they each grabbed a gunwale, lifting the canoe out of its storage spot and setting it on the ground at the water's edge.

Janet disappeared for a moment, emerging with two paddles

and two life jackets. She put the paddles in the boat and handed him a life jacket. "The PFD is required," she said.

Frowning at it, and looking for the adjuster so he could make it bigger, he muttered, "Pure Effing Delay device."

Janet didn't object to his tone, but just said, "Personal Flotation Device, and I grabbed the biggest one we had. Let me help you." She grabbed the adjustor, pushed a button on the latch to release the tension, and fitted it to him.

"I get to row, too?"

"Actually, we'll be paddling, and yes, it would help."

She did a little bit of prep, closing the door of the boathouse, and they put the canoe in the water. She got in the back and held the boat in place while Steve and Pearl got in.

She handed him a paddle and asked, "Do you know how to use this?"

"An oar?"

"It's a paddle. Oars are in a row boat and you pull on them. We do this instead." She demonstrated a forward paddling motion.

"I think I can manage that."

"Good, because going in a straight line is harder than it seems."

"Er."

"Don't worry, I can fix things from the rear of the boat."

They started off towards the tarp that was floating on the lake, the boat moving in a haphazard zigzag direction.

"This is hard," Steve said, feeling a little frustrated.

"Try to paddle when I do and on the opposite side of the canoe."

He looked over his shoulder at her paddling and noticed her pushing the paddle out away from the boat and the end of her stroke. "Am I supposed to be doing that?"

"The J stroke? Naw, it's just for the person in the back."

They eventually got to what was floating in the water. Janet kept her paddle in the water, steadying the boat.

"Okay, Pearl, let's have a sniff." He offered her the sample smell, which she sniffed at, then he put the handheld down and picked her up and put her on his lap.

The canoe rolled some with the shifting weight.

"Is this a good idea?"

"It's okay, for now, but don't let her lean out too far."

Steve held Pearl in his lap and Janet brought the boat closer.

Pearl took a sniff and another. No reaction.

Janet moved the boat a little further.

No reaction. Steve thought, all this effort for nothing.

Janet guided the canoe to the other side.

Pearl extended her head and said, /Here./

Yes! He thought. "Good girl. Check again."

She tried a different spot. /Here./ A different spot. /Here./

"Excellent. Good girl, Pearl."

He gave her a liver treat, which she gobbled down and asked, /Swim?/

"Not yet. Soon though."

She sighed and flopped down into the canoe, making it shudder.

He got out the comm. "Central, Canine Pearl has confirmed that Adam has touched the tarp. I'm going to pull the tarp off slowly."

"Okay, Agent Holzer. Proceed with caution."

"Roger."

He handed the handheld to Janet. "Could you record this while I pull the tarp off? The camera is on right now and sending to Central."

"I'll need to clamp it to the gunwale." She did so and aimed it at the covering.

Steve narrated: "I'm picking up the corner of the tarp."

He lifted a corner. Leaning closer, he could see a plastic bag with a colored stripe along the top.

"Um, Central, I am looking at a small drybag."

"Dry as in waterproof?"

"Correct."

"Does the bag look intact?"

"From this angle, yes; checking closer."

He stopped and looked up at the far shore to steady his vision. While Janet was doing a good job of keeping the boat stable, concentrating on the small bobbling bag was making him a little dizzy. He looked down again. The bag was floating in the water. There was a strip of something along the side of the bag and what appeared to be a small piece of tape at the bottom.

"Central, I'm going to pick it up using the bucket, as that seems safest."

"We can see it on the screen. Go ahead."

He got the ungainly bucket out and put it partially in the water, hoping to coax the bag in. No such luck. He pushed the bucket down further and maneuvered it under the bag. He had it lined up but now he was moving five gallons of water from the side of a canoe. The canoe rolled to the left. "Pearl, move away." She had a concerned look on her face, but did so.

He worked the bucket to the surface with the bag contained in it. Laughing, he said, "I can't believe what I'm looking at. Water inside a waterproof bag, that's sitting in water. There is a stripe of something along the side of it and there's a string attached to the bottom. There's probably something not good about the water inside the bag, huh?"

Harris said, "Secure the bag and then examine the string very carefully."

"I'm hanging off the side of a canoe, how am I supposed to secure it?"

"Can you lift it into the canoe?"

"Probably not without capsizing. Wait, I have an idea."

He took off his flotation vest, wrapped it around the bucket, and then tied it to the canoe. "I wrapped my PFD around it and tied it to this cross-piece-thingy of the boat."

Janet said patiently, but trying not to laugh, "It's called a thwart, for the record."

"This thingy?" he said, inclining his head towards it. "It can call itself Harold for all I care as long as it hangs on to the bucket."

Steve reached down and picked up the bucket lid. "I'm going to put the lid on as best I can without sinking us." He lined up the lid and reached down into the water, his fingers pulling up while the other hand pushed down. "Brrr, this water is cold." The boat started to roll, but the life vest attached to the bucket helped counterbalance. Switching arms, he pinned down the other side of the lid. "Bucket is secured."

He could hear, "Yaaay," over the comm.

Steve said, "This string appears to be kite string. I'm pulling it in and I really hope there's not a bomb on the other side." Hand over hand, he slowly started pulling the string in, letting it pile up in the bottom of the canoe. "I'm feeling some resistance, but it's not like a treasure chest."

After what seemed to Steve to be a few weeks, he could feel the string tugging more. Looking down, he saw a white round shape. Pulling it closer revealed it was a roll of the rest of the string. "Central, I'm holding a ball of string. I didn't realize he was flying a kite."

"Acknowledged."

"We're heading back in. I'm working on a theory about this."

"Come back in, and we'll be all ears."

As they carefully worked their way back to the shore, Steve looked back at the first point that Pearl had signaled. Then his eyes traveled over to the second place. It made perfect sense. In his mind's eye, he could see Adam setting the bag and its tarp down in the water and securing the string to the bag with a piece of tape. Then he watched Adam walk around the edge of the lake playing the string out. When he got to the second spot he carefully pulled the bag into the center of the lake. Once there, he then wrapped the rest of the string back onto the roll and threw it into the water.

It was a cleverness he had to admire.

CHAPTER 62:

Yolanda and Gimli Search

YOLANDA AND Gimli were walking in the parking lot of Cromwell 2 looking for Adam's scent, when Gimli said, /Here./ *Phew*, Yolanda thought, feeling both relief and excitement. They had struck out at Cromwell 3 and she was afraid they were going to have to try number 1. This lot was paved and large. They had been methodically scanning it for five minutes when Gimli found a sign of Adam on the far side of the worn paved area. It was a surprising location as it wasn't right by the wide hiking trail that surrounded the water body. "That's weird, it's almost like he's trying to be sneaky," she said to no one. Adam hadn't struck her as the sneaky type. *Wrong again*, she thought.

"Central, this is Yolanda. We're at Cromwell 2 and Gimli has indicated a spot that has Adam's scent."

She heard Harris say, "Good to hear, Agent Danimeyer, please keep us updated on your progress." *That was sort of a pointless thing to say*, she thought. But she realized that his statement of the obvious combined with the formal address form meant they were doing for-the-record references.

Just to be a smart ass she said, "Thank you, Agent Consuelo'a."

"Oh, and Yolanda?"

"Yes, Harris?"

"The lab analyzed the bag that Steve and Pearl found, and they revised the deadline when the bags might start dissolving to two and a half hours."

"It's so nice to hear your voice sometimes. Such a nice, relaxing time."

"Good hunting."

Oh, eff off, she thought.

She looked at Gimli, who was still drinking in what he found on the damp, paved ground through his nose, but he looked up and danced in place in anticipation. *Time to go my boy.* "Go search," she said, and with a bark he was off.

Because he was low to the ground, he could easily alternate between smelling the scent that was in the air versus actually putting his nose to the ground. Once in a while, his head would come all the way up and he'd look around, sniffing in several directions. "Gimli, do you still have the scent?"

/Mmm,/ came the noncommittal response, which essentially meant: *Hang on a moment.*

Then he put his nose to the ground and said, /Here,/ and was off again.

He worked his way halfway around the perimeter of the lake. There he stopped and started moving around to the left and the right. He took a few steps ahead, then turned around, and came back to the same spot. Yolanda could swear she saw smoke coming out of his ears, but decided not to interrupt him. Harris knew where she was and would eventually notice that they weren't moving anymore, but he would let them work for a bit first.

Then Gimli was standing on a rock beside the path. It was beside a small stream coming into the reservoir. The water went from the stream into a pipe and then presumably into the larger body of water. He was standing there with his head extended out from his neck, which looked very odd on a dog with such a small body. His body length appeared to double, though she knew that wasn't possible. Then, at what had to be his maximum stretch, he folded his body in an accordion and leapt up the stream.

"Whoa, slow down, let me catch up," she said as she located a boulder that would support her weight and not roll. She didn't weigh much compared to the average human, but she was no corgi. She wanted to keep him in sight, but didn't want to compromise the scent track.

She looked up to see Gimli working his way up a creek. "This is called a stream. It's a small river," she said, using a word they'd worked on before.

/Pof/

Which meant: *I'm busy, no time to learn a word.*

"Fine then, don't mind me helping you evolve." *Actually, we really don't have time for school right now anyway*, she thought.

/Pof/

"Central, Canine Gimli has discovered that the suspect's trail is leading up a small stream. He's working his way up it."

"Roger, Agent Danimeyer," Harris said.

Yolanda smiled, remembering Steve's penchant for saying, "Roger who?"

Gimli kept working his way along the stream, first going on one side and, when that seemed to run out, discovering the scent on the other side a little ways down. It wasn't easy for a human to stay in this stream. It was clear that Adam wasn't experienced in evading a tracker, and he was trying things he had probably heard about in the media.

As they progressed, the embankments on each side seemed to grow, and she had to raise her head to see the top of them. Then they went around a corner and ran into a shrubbery. But it wasn't a shrub, or at least not just one. There were branches of possibly four different trees, one pine, one alder, and a couple of other ones, and some manzanita and other bushes facing them. Closer examination showed they had been recently broken off. Gimli was shoving his nose all over the bushes. /Here,/ a head turn, /Here,/ a step to the right, /Here/.

Relieved he wasn't freaking out about the bushes, she said, "Okay, stop. I get it. Good boy. Adam placed these branches. Is it to slow us down or to hide something, I wonder? Want to climb?"

He barked in assent.

"And how did I know you'd say yes?"

He barked again, bouncing.

She amused herself thinking that this was a weird place for a herding command, but she looked at him and said, "Go bye," which was the herding command to circle out clockwise. Gimli charged up the embankment, circling around the branch barrier, and then careened down to the stream on the other side of it. She peered over the branches and asked, "Any scent there?"

/Huh?/

"Go search."

/Search!/

He sniffed in the stream, then to the left and back to the right in larger and larger arcs. Then he stopped and looked at her. Nothing. Adam hadn't gone over there. The branches were covering up something.

"Come on back," and he repeated the half-circle.

She said to the handheld, "Central, Adam has created a large pile of branches over a stream. Gimli verified that he hasn't walked past this point."

"Roger, Yolanda. Can we look closer?"

"I'm sending photos now. I'm going to start lifting off the branches."

"Be extremely careful. I'm checking to see if Markus and David can come help," Harris said.

Yolanda finished the thought. "We probably don't have time to wait for them, so I'm going to start."

"Acknowledged."

Yolanda picked up one branch, which had the red bark of a manzanita. She levered it up and set it to the side. No bombs yet, fortunately. This would be one of those "dumb ways to die," she thought, but then again, they would find a way to make it sound heroic. She picked up another branch, an oak this time, awkwardly tangling around the others. With effort, she freed it.

It didn't appear to be booby-trapped either. She set it aside. *Shit, this is going to take forever,* she thought.

Gimli chomped on the first branch, dragging it further away, clearly wanting to help. This wasn't a good time for him to help yet, so she let him continue doing what he was doing to keep him occupied. Branch by branch, she picked them up and put them to the left.

She progressed for a while in the same fashion, the air redolent with the smell of rotting leaves, when a thorn snagged at her skin. She froze in mid-heft. She knew the bag was plastic and vulnerable, but she couldn't see it. Looking closer she could see some of the branches had a lot of vicious-looking thorns. She proceeded even more slowly. Her progress seemed glacial to her, but when she stopped to reassess, the pile was indeed getting much smaller.

She was getting closer to seeing the water and still couldn't see a bag. From what she understood, it had to be in contact with the water. As she progressed, and things got less hazardous to a corgi, Gimli had worked his way closer. Extending his nose to sniff the latest branch he said, /Here./

Yolanda said to him, "Well, now we know he picked this branch up." She picked up the next one and let him sniff it. He sniffed at the base and said, /Here,/ and pointed his nose higher on the branch and again said, /Here./

So Adam was more carefully placing the branches now. I have to be getting close, she told herself. She lifted one of the last branches to reveal a bag partially poking up out of the water, balanced on a couple of small branches.

Gimli sniffed at the bag and said, /HERE./ He opened his jaws to retrieve it, his eyes alive with joy in anticipation of seizing onto his prize.

Yolanda's mind flashed on all those exercises they'd been working on recently where what they were looking for was poisonous or a bomb. She also remembered all of the times the exercises ended with "*Boom.* Game over. Everybody is dead. Start over."

They had switched to not having the doggy retrieve the found item and instead using a mental /Here,/ or lying down beside it, or running back to the handler. But Gimli was from the older times and he loved, just loved, retrieving. But this was no longer a test or a game, and she hoped he would listen. Adrenaline poured into Yolanda's system and she shouted, "Gimli STOP!" Then she belatedly added the closest thing that he would understand: "Poison." Gimli froze with his jaws open, his tongue touching the bag.

He said, /Hmphf,/ lifted his head a little, and closed his mouth, just away from the bag. Relief flooded in and Yolanda had to resist dropping everything to kiss him. "Good boy! We get to live for a little while longer."

Looking closer, Yolanda could see that the bag was carefully balanced on a V of shaped sticks. Her eyes traveled downward. Just below the bottom of the bag, where it would fall if it lost its perch on the sticks, was another branch. One with thorns. Not the teeny tiny pinprick ones but large nasty spikes. It was a booby trap. She said as evenly as she could, "Gimli, stop." Which meant don't move your feet, but she hoped he would just hold still.

She set her branch down and said into her handheld, "Central, I have located one of the bags. It's balanced above some thorns in a booby trap."

"I see your image. Are you requesting assistance?"

"There's no time. The branches aren't holding it down and the current is going to push it into the thorns, so I'm going to have to give it a go."

"We're with you. David and the lab tech are on their way."

She reached over for the bucket they'd brought along. With it in hand, she crept closer. The bag was swaying back and forth with the pulse of the water. Without the branches restricting it, she realized she probably didn't have much time. While she was considering how to lift it out with the branches, a wavelet rippled down the creek, the twigs holding it up fell over, and the bag started to camber forward.

"No!" she said, splashing into the water and grabbing at its top, praying it was sealed and wouldn't break open. The bag held, just grazing past the spiked pike awaiting it. She nearly lost her balance and pushed down with the bucket to keep from falling. *Ouch,* she thought. *Stand back up dammit. Crap, this water is cold.* She got her feet under her with the bag teetering in her going-numb fingers. *The bucket,* she thought. *Get the bucket over there.*

In what felt like sheer force of will, she got her body to obey, and as gingerly as she could, she worked the bag into the bucket with her freezing, shaking hands. She carried it to the side and put the lid on it.

Almost in relief she said, "GOOD BOY!" and remembered to give Gimli a piece of liver. "Hamburger tonight. Let's go back."

He bounded down the creek. /Burger. Burger./

"Central, we have found a bag, it is in a bucket, and we're on our way back. And I'm wet and very cold."

"Excellent work, Agent Danimeyer. We'll get a blanket for you and the lab tech will meet you and exchange buckets. Please have David finish your search of the area."

"Okay," she said, though she was quite sure there weren't going to be any more bags here.

Gimli was still dancing along saying, /Burger. Burger/.

He so wants to be a fat corgi, Yolanda thought.

CHAPTER 63:

Amy Calls John

AMY DEBATED sending John a message saying that she wouldn't make it home tonight and realized there would be hell to pay for such a dodge, so she called him. His smiling face appeared, looking as disheveled as usual. "Hi, Amy. Nice to actually see your face during the day."

I need to call him more often when there's nothing serious going on, she thought. "Hi, John. How are you doing?"

"I'm wondering why I'm the lucky recipient of a phone call. What's up?"

"Bad news, I'm working on something and won't be able to make it home tonight."

"Not at all? Well, no hoisin eggplant for you then."

"I know, I'm really sorry."

"What are you chasing now?"

"Can't talk about it yet, unfortunately."

John peered into the phone. "Where the heck are you?"

"Up north." Trying to appease him, she held up the device, so he could see better.

"Middle of nowhere?"

"Yep." She looked back into the phone.

Then John leaned closer to the display, which made him look absurd, and she had to refrain from laughing. "Hey, you look like you've been in a fight."

Oh, here we go. "I'm okay, John."

"No, what happened? Did someone try to hurt you?" His voice grew agitated.

Amy ran a hand over her head and along her face. "We caught him. He's not a threat anymore."

The muscles around his eyes tightened. "Have you seen a doctor? Come home."

"Yes, I have. I'm fine, and I can't come home yet."

"What happened to you?"

"I can't talk about that now, John."

"Well I hope the other guy is more messed up."

Amy looked away from the phone, her eyes filled with tears, her breath coming in ragged gasps.

"Amy!"

Without looking she said, "I'm okay, John, really. Steve and Yolanda are up here too."

"You're not okay."

"I have to be. I have to follow this through."

"Come home."

"I will, but not now."

"Are you in danger?"

"No. Not anymore."

"I don't like this."

"I'm really sorry, John."

"I want to come up there."

Amy paused, collecting herself. "I'll be home soon, I'm okay. You have to believe me. I'm not in danger, so I'd rather you not close the shop to come up."

She could see him cross his arms in front of him. "Don't like."

She said to him, as steadily as she could manage, "I'm a big girl."

He ran both hands through his hair, sending it everywhere. "One that I like and want to see again. Come back alive and in once piece, please."

"Will do, John, love you."

Giving up, he leaned back, blowing her a kiss. "And I, you."

CHAPTER 64:

—————

Amy and Lars Search

AMY AND Lars tracked Adam's path along the edge of the Lagoonas reservoir back to where a creek fed into it.

"It can't be this far out, can it? Lars, are you sure you're tracking Adam?"

Lars, who had been air-scenting up to this point, had his nose on the ground.

/Yes./

"Okay, then."

They were on the far side of the reservoir from the parking lot. The place had an isolated feel to it. Even the birds that were flitting around them at the beginning seemed to fall away, except for a vulture, cruising by with that hopeful *Are you dead yet?* look.

Lars started to climb the rocky incline of the creek.

Amy, halfway sliding down the hill, worked to keep her footing.

"Are you sure?" she said, balancing on a rocking boulder. "I don't have four legs, and I left my trekking poles in the car."

/Yes./

They worked their way up the creek and reached the top of a rise.

Lars said, /Here./ He was pointing to what looked like a small cave.

"This doesn't look municipal at all."

/Huh?/

"It's okay, keep tracking."

They went inside.

Lars nearly immediately said, /Here./

"Where? Stop. I can't see anything." Amy got a glowstick out of her pack.

Holding it up, Amy could make out dimly in the gloom an underground pond with a small beach on the right. The pond wasn't making much noise compared to the creek, and Amy figured the cave surroundings must be damping the sound. Lars walked over and was sniffing at footprints.

"Good find. Let me record this." She switched the camera mode on and let it adjust to the low light. "Agent Callahan here with Canine Lars. We have tracked Suspect Adam to this cave, and have found footprints that appear to match his. Lars says that these footprints belong to him. I will take scent samples to double-check. I am standing beside an underground pond in a cave. The pond's outlet is a creek that travels down to the reservoir, though I don't see the outlet of the pond." Peering into the dim light she said, "There appears to be something floating in the water further out." She tried to focus the camera on it. "I can't tell what it is, but we will investigate it. I'm shutting this off for now, so it can transmit."

She realized there was no way to transmit without a view of the sky and a satellite, so she told Lars to wait while she set the handheld and pack outside, but kept the glowstick.

Outside, she looked around for a branch that might reach that far, but there weren't any obvious choices so she went back in. The palm that she had impaled on the bridge stanchion ached, and she tried to concentrate.

She thought about the other two bags. The one Pearl and Steve found was way out in the middle of the reservoir, and they had to commission a canoe. Gimli and Yolanda's was anchored with a branch in a small side pocket. Amy peered more closely.

If this is a bag, it's not moving, which is unusual for anything floating in this water that has a creek outlet nearby. It could just be a piece of equipment like something that monitors the water level, she thought. *Wish I could just conjure up a canoe. Must be nice. Steve even had an official canoe pilot.* While Amy looked, she listened to the quiet gurgle of the water flowing past her. Looking down the pond, it didn't have an obvious connection to the stream, but it had to have one. There must have been a pipe connection lower down that she couldn't see. Holding up the glowstick, she looked again at the bag. It would move a little and then stop abruptly and then drift back. Then it repeated the process. *It must be anchored to something.*

Steve and Yolanda said their bags had both been sealed, so removing an anchor shouldn't open it, but it seemed risky.

Calling back to him, Amy said, "Lars, do you remember how to push a ball with your nose?"

/Ball?/

"See that bag. Could you push that with your nose?"

/Fetch!/

"No, stop. No fetch. Push." Miming with her hands, she inhaled and made herself refrain from adding, "This is important," knowing it would confuse him.

/Poosh./

"Right, but go slow."

/Poosh./

Lars entered the water and started to swim out, heading directly to the bag or whatever it was.

"Go out. Out further," she said, realizing that Yolanda would have just used a "Go bye" herding command. "Around the bag. Out."

The kelpie boy passed the bag and swung around.

"Slow."

She heard him give a watery exhale. He said, /Cold./

He's not going to last long, but let's try for a few seconds, Amy thought.

He was within a foot.

"Touch. Slow."

The bag moved a little and pulled back.

Amy gritted her teeth. "Touch again. Gentle. No bite."

Amy could tell this was taking a lot of effort. The bag appeared to do the same thing.

"Never mind, just leave it and come back. It's too cold. We'll have to think of something else."

Lars had touched the bag one last time and swung back around and headed back.

"Good boy, Lars. Come on back."

Amy tried to think of what she was going to do beyond drying Lars off.

She looked up again at the bag. Then she looked again. She could swear it was moving. "No way." She visually lined the bag up with a rock she could barely see on the other side of the pond. It was slowly drifting towards them.

"Lars, you did it!"

The bag kept drifting in what seemed to be a preordained path. Amy positioned herself in its path. Lars shook off and some of the water splashed on her. "Wow, that's cold, go outside and warm up and I'll dry you off once I get a hold of this."

Lars went outside and she could hear him shaking more. The bag crept onward. She looked at the bucket she'd had to lug up that stupid hill. *Just a few more feet and we can call it a day.*

As it drifted on its way the bag seemed to rotate, then it was smaller, and then it disappeared. Amy lowered the glowstick and in the shadows she could see there was a vortex. Then she thought about how the water was getting to the creek. "No!" she cried, pointlessly grabbing the air where the bag had been.

She put the glowstick in the water, the cold sending a jolt up her arm. She could see the bag being pulled down towards a pipe. *Okay, I can catch it on the other end,* but looking again she could see a metal grating over the pipe. *Shit, the bag could rupture,* she realized.

With no hesitation, she jumped into the water.

Amy nearly passed out from the shock of the frigid water. She could feel her heart pause before beating even harder. She told herself, *Focus. Look down. Find the bag. Swim down. Get the bag. Get. The. Bag.*

Amy was surprised that she still had the glowstick clenched in her right fist. She could see the bag twirling in the water inside the whirlpool on its way downward. She marveled in the back of her brain how the bag still appeared to wander even while inside a whirlpool. *Gods, this is cold. Swim.*

She could see the bag and reached for it while it shyly slunk its way out from her grasp. The water was pressing on her ears and her lungs were starting to complain about oxygen. She remembered Harris expounding on how it was the buildup of CO_2 that your lungs were complaining about, and not oxygen debt. She made a note to tell Harris just how unhelpful this information was right now. The bag floated by; she grabbed and missed. She could see the pipe, but it was beginning to blur and her vision narrowed. She reached out, but there was nothing there. She couldn't see any farther. Despair seeped in. She had lost, and now she had to apologize to several thousand people who were in mortal danger. She wondered just how many there were. She blindly struck out in frustration and felt the bag. She reached out with her other hand, dropping the glowstick, and braced the bag between fists that she could hardly feel. She had the bag, she'd done it, but there was something else she needed to do. What was it? Her brain just wasn't responding and she started to drift. Part of her brain said, *SWIM UP, KICK. Oh yeah.* She started kicking, even though she couldn't see anything and could only hope that she still had the bag.

Her head broke the surface, and she could hear Lars barking. Her breath forced its way out of her lungs and she tried to breathe, gagging on water. She coughed out a mouthful of water and gasped for air. She still had the bag, but she couldn't see yet and was trying to tread water with only her legs. The temperature of the water was making it very difficult to breathe.

Lars started whining and she was able to head towards his voice. She found the side. With her arms, she could feel the sand on the beach area. She placed the bag up on the sand, as far away from the side as she could reach. Lars was licking her face. She pulled herself farther down the side, so they were away from the bag, but that was all she could do. "I can't do this, Lars."

/Grab./

Where did he learn "grab"? Amy wondered. "I'm sorry, Lars, there's nothing to hold on to."

/Grab./

She could feel his head on her chest and his body tensed. "I'm just going to pull you in," she said, but she put her hands on his collar and around his neck. He pulled, and her hands slipped off of him. "This isn't going to work, Lars." He put his head back, this time grabbing some of her shirt with his teeth, and started to pull harder. "You're just going to rip the shirt or get dragged into the water," she said, but he just dug in further. She was able to work her hands well enough to grab his ruff and, with his help, she was able to drag herself onto the beach where she could crawl a little farther away from the water. The glowstick was floating in the water and Amy's eyes started working well enough that she could see the bag was out of danger.

But that was the end of her energy. What she had left, she spent coughing while lying on her side. Her clothes were glued to her skin, robbing her of what little body heat she had left. She closed her eyes and gave into the uncontrollable shivering that had been waiting in the wings.

Lars leaned up against her, whining. He was still wet and the warmth of his body made no difference. He pushed his head against her.

/Move?/

"I . . . can't . . . Lars."

She distantly thought about her handheld, but realized she had put it outside the cave so it could upload data. She gave herself again to the shivering.

Lars butted into her.

As she drifted, a thought occurred to her. Unable to speak any further, she mentally asked him. /Lars, could you go outside and bark?/

/Bark./

/Outside,/ she said.

No longer feeling cold or shivering, Amy felt herself floating away to the sound of his barking.

CHAPTER 65:

Steve Finds Amy

AMY WAS out surfing with John.

She asked him, "How am I supposed to enjoy this if you keep stealing my waves?"

Laughing, he said, "Let's swim to the islands on our boards."

"But that's hundreds of miles."

"It's okay, it won't take long," he said and started off.

She started after him. "What kind of trouble is this going to get us into?"

"You'll be fine, don't worry. You're safe now."

Surprised to find herself believing him, she followed.

The ocean swell was reassuring as it carried her board. She could feel the warm breeze and saw how it tousled John's hair in that cute way that she always liked.

There was an island in the distance that was getting closer.

John stood up on his board and held out his hand. She didn't realize she had stood up. She looked down to find herself standing on the water. Worried, she looked up at him. He said, "Don't worry, the water will support you."

"John, what's happening?"

"That's up to you. You can walk to the island or stay out here on the water."

"Would you stop with the Zen crap and explain to me what's going on?"

He held both her hands. "I love you, but I can't make this choice for you."

She felt understanding seep in. "Thank you, John, I love you."

He bent in and kissed her, and then he was gone.

Looking at the island, she realized she didn't have to rush, so she lay down on her board, feeling the air stirring around her. She did think it was odd that she wasn't hearing any birds, but she didn't worry. She could see the sun, but she couldn't feel it. She thought about Lars. She would miss him, but knew he would be well taken care of. She hoped he'd adjust to his new life, be it with John or Steve or someone else.

She could feel the island calling. She sat up to look at it. She could tell it wasn't just an island, but a pretty representation of an island, with a new world behind it, waiting. She hadn't expected to be in this position, but did anyone ever, really? She thought age almost didn't matter, as she could see an eighty-two-year-old thinking the same thing she was with her twenty-two-year-old perspective.

A sea lion appeared. It jumped up on the board and said, "Amy! Amy!"

"If I wasn't hallucinating before, I'm obviously doing it now. I don't have any fish. Would you please go away?"

The sea lion touched her arm with a flipper. She tried to pull her arm back and said, "Go away. Please leave me be."

It said over its shoulder, "Pulse is 48, body temperature is 95 degrees Fahrenheit. We have to get her out of here and wrap her in a warming blanket."

"Oh Gods, go away, you stupid sea lion."

It started laughing.

"What's so funny?"

He dived into the water and the ocean waves began to swell, some of them breaking on her.

She asked, "What's happening?"

HARRIS HEARD Lars's barking, and said, "Agent Callahan? . . . Amy? . . . AMY! . . . Hello, Amy?" After repeating himself and getting no response, he contacted Steve and Yolanda, who raced over from their impromptu command post.

Harris sent them the coordinates, and Steve and Yolanda ran the entire way from the parking lot to the creek. They worked their way up the hill, guided by the racket that Lars was making.

Having found Amy's handheld, Steve, breathing heavily and wiping sweat out of his eyes, saw the cavern at the head of the creek above the reservoir. Lars was barking, shivering, and covered in debris, probably from rolling to dry off. Lars was signaling for him to go into the cavern by running back and forth with an urgency that Steve rarely saw in him. In the gloom of the cavern, Steve could see Amy bunched in a ball on the small plot of sand by a pond. "Oh Gods, Amy, what happened?"

She didn't say anything, didn't move. He shook her. "Amy, Amy, please." *Her skin is like touching a frozen*—he broke off his thoughts, and dove in his pack for a medi-patch. He placed the patch on Amy's arm. There was a glowstick floating in the water that supplied some light, but he switched on his headlamp. She moved her arm. "She's alive!" he shouted.

Then he saw the plastic bag, the same exact kind that Pearl had located. He yelled back to Yolanda, "Amy found the last bag. I need that bucket over there to secure it.

"Amy! Amy!" he shook her shoulder.

Amy's voice was thin and raspy, but he could make out her words. "Go away, you stupid sea lion."

He started laughing. "Sea lion? What the fuck? For the record, let it show that Agent Callahan is delirious, and anything she says should not be considered official record. She's too cold, we have to get her out of here."

The patch started to blink red.

"94 degrees Fahrenheit—we're losing her." He rubbed her

sides vigorously. All he wanted was to gather her up in his arms and get her to safety. But he realized that Amy, protocol, and common sense all said to deal first with the threat of the dissolvable plastic bag and its payload of nanobots just waiting to kill thousands of people. She was putting her life on the line for this and he had to do his part. "We have to get the bag secured first."

Yolanda crawled in. "I need to get the bucket, let me move past you." She slipped around him and grabbed the bucket. "Adam's bag looks intact." She picked it up, placed it in the bucket, and put the lid on. "Now, I need to get around you again."

The reading was now 92 degrees. Steve said, "I really don't like this, we need to get the bag and then her out ASAP. Is there someone else out there? You go first and watch the loose rocks." He held up his headlamp.

"Got it covered. Don't worry. Just get her out of here alive," Yolanda said.

As Yolanda exited, she grabbed her handheld and said, "Harris, we need a medic ASAP."

"They're already on their way," said Harris.

Steve gathered Amy's body up as best as he could. She was stiff, which made things both awkward and easier. He talked almost continuously. "Amy, stay with me. Wake up. Stay awake." Tripping over her legs, he half-dragged her out of the cavern.

AMY HAD lost her board, and the waves kept pounding her. She thought, *Could I drown here? How could that be?*

She could feel hands on her. "Amy, it's Steve. I'm here. We're going to wrap you up and get you warm."

His words didn't make any sense, and she lay back down on her board and let herself drift in surrender.

WHEN STEVE laid Amy down, the medic wrapped her body in a warming blanket that would both dry her skin and gradually warm her.

The patch now said 87 degrees Fahrenheit. He didn't know the fine details, but he knew this wasn't good. He and Yolanda sat at Amy's head and rubbed her shoulders, trying to stay out of the way but still wanting a connection.

The patch reported 86 degrees, and it beeped a couple of times. "What the hell does that mean?" Steve said.

The medic, whose name tag said Calvin, gave him a steady, questioning look while pulling something out of his bag, looking like he was trying not to be grim.

Steve understood. "Yes, we want the truth."

Calvin showed him a small tool with a sharp probe on it and what looked like a small display on the top. Steve shuddered. Calvin said, "Her heart is starting to seize. I am going to insert a field defib, but they often don't work when the body temp gets below 86 because things just don't function well at that temp." He looked over at the waiting medi-chopper that had arrived. "And the bad news is that transporting her in this state can kill her." He pulled the blanket back from her chest and carefully positioned the defibrillator. The display came to life with what appeared to be positioning information. Pausing a second, he said, "You might want to look away if you're squeamish."

"You're putting a spike into her heart?"

"That's just to get it close and then electrodes will deploy around the heart," Calvin said.

"Does that work?" Steve asked, tension creeping into his rising voice.

Calvin gave him another *Do you want the truth?* look, and Steve said, "Never mind, please continue."

Steve wasn't normally sensitive, but it was entirely different watching a person carefully insert something that resembled a spike into someone he cared about. He kept a hand on her, but looked away and said what was slowly dawning on him. "So, if she's going to live, it has to happen here?"

"Yes, indeed. If we could get her to drink something warm it would help, but she's not responsive."

Steve looked at Yolanda and, with tears in his eyes, said, "I guess drowning her accidentally in warm water would be counterproductive."

Yolanda hugged his shoulder in response and the three formed a triangle, with each of them holding on to each other's shoulders, with their outside arm on one of Amy's shoulders, and Lars's head on her chest, licking her face.

Calvin said, "When the defib beeps, you need to let go of her for five seconds, because it is about to shock her heart."

They waited for what felt like hours. The display on the defibrillator changed into a heart rate readout. They could see the medi-patch, which showed her body temp. Each time the defib beeped, they'd all jump and look at the very slow heart rate, which would briefly go to nearly zero and then back to the low forties. Her internal body temp had dropped to 85 degrees.

Steve said, "Come on, Amy. I don't need two dogs." Guilt flooded in. "Wait, I shouldn't talk like that. Lars will always have a home with me even if he doesn't like to talk to me."

At his name, Lars picked up his head, glancing at him. Steve rubbed Lars's neck. The kelpie fully understood that something was very wrong. He put his head back on Amy's chest, though they had to keep him from touching the defib. Yolanda wrapped her hand around his head, so she could pick him off Amy's chest when a beep came.

Steve said, "Come on Amy, I'll buy you a case of whatever you're drinking."

Yolanda cut in, "Hey, Amy, that reminds me you owe me a beer—don't think you can weasel out of it this way, girl." She patted Amy's shoulder with each word for emphasis.

Everything hung in suspended animation. Waiting. Waiting for something to change. But there was only more waiting.

Calvin was in conversation with the hospital, apparently talking strategy.

And they waited.

Their usual jocularities had left them. Steve said with a long sigh, "Amy, you're only twenty-two, please don't leave us. Please don't leave me."

"Your mother does not want to outlive you," Yolanda said.

The patch made a different type of sound. "Oh Gods, what now?" Yolanda said.

Both Calvin and Steve said, "Look!" pointing to the display. It said 86. Steve hardly dared to hope. Then it was 87, then 88. When it hit 90, Calvin said to the hospital, "Her body temp is increasing."

Yolanda and Steve, at the same time, said, "YES!"

Calvin was more cautious, checking her vital signs and looking at her heart rate on the display for any abnormalities. "Heart rate is improving and no arrhythmia."

When her temp hit 95, Calvin said, "She's coming back." Everyone cheered.

Calvin removed the defib.

Steve started shaking Amy as hard as he dared. "Amy, Amy. It's Steve."

Amy's eyes opened a little and closed again.

"Steve? . . . Steve? Where's the seal or sea lion or whatever?"

"I'm here too, Amy. Yolanda that is."

It was all too much and Amy, eyes still shut, leaned her head back on what felt like a sandy beach. Hands were on her, but they seemed to be moving in very brisk ways that said they had a job to do. She was cold again. "Cold."

"This isn't going to be fun, unfortunately," a voice said.

"Hurts."

"You were completely numb and life returning is going to be painful."

"Metaphor," Amy said.

"Ah, so you're not dead after all."

"Fuck off, Steve."

"And you knew it was me."

"Go away."

"You already told me that, you also called me a stupid sea lion."

"Well, you were."

"Body temperature 96 degrees," a voice said. "Heart Rate 52. She's breathing and conscious."

Everything hurt. She shook.

Then she remembered. "The bag!"

"It's okay, we have it here and intact and on its way to join its friends in isolation."

Amy exhaled, and passed out in surrender. They let her this time, after some long hugs. Someone was mentioning something about beer.

CHAPTER 66:

Amy Meets with Dr. Jill

AMY WALKED into Dr. Jill Friedam's office, having absolutely no idea what she was going to say—which she figured was exactly the plan. Amy hadn't seen her since the Randall Curtis incident, and she was concerned about being back here.

"Amy, come on in."

"Hi, Dr. Jill," she said, using the title the doctor had become affectionately known by.

"It's okay, you can call me Jill. Please sit," she said, motioning to the small sofa that sat opposite her own chair. To the side of the office, next to the wall, was a short table that had some roses of various colors with sprigs of rosemary and a vine of holly that wrapped through them. On the other side was a window with a nice view of one of the city parks, and below that was a dog bed that Lars plopped onto. Beside her chair was a table with a closed notebook on it.

Jill sat in her chair. "I've read the report. You don't do these things halfway, do you?"

"Er." Amy smiled awkwardly and looked at the carpet, which she noticed was one of those blend-with-everything greys with hints of blue, green, and a little pink.

"It's okay, Amy, you're not on trial here. I'm here to see how you are doing after these extraordinary events. I know we've seen each other after the Randal Curtis case, but this is completely different."

"I—"

"But first," holding up a hand, "I want you to know that while you have to meet with a therapist at least four times over this coming month, it does not have to be me. It can be any certified therapist who has access to the official reports."

"I'm more comfortable with you than a stranger."

"The devil you know. Works for me. Even though it's not always very fun?"

Amy smiled weakly, lifting her upturned hands. "It's never fun."

Jill settled into her chair. "Okay, talk to me. How are you doing?"

"Everything has been such a blur. Everyone is being so supportive, it's actually been a little overwhelming."

Jill nodded and didn't say anything.

"The media attention has been pretty intense, once they released information."

"What was that like for you? This is not just an average PR thing."

"Catherine has been doing much of the talking, but she brings in Steve or Yolanda. They haven't talked to me much yet, because I was undercover and they don't want Tomas to see me on the news with an LAI label by my name."

"What is that like?"

"A relief, but I feel like I should be doing more."

"You're on official leave, and I want you to take it seriously. You have the death of the person you were investigating, and you put yourself in serious peril."

"But—"

Jill opened the notebook and looked at a page for a moment. She read slowly out loud. "Body temperature as low as 85 degrees Fahrenheit. Started coding at 86 degrees." Jill paused and looked at her steadily. "You know this means you died." It wasn't a question.

"Your heart stopped, more than once." She let silence sink the moment in. "If it wasn't for a device restarting your heart each time it stopped, you would not be here. We would not be having this conversation."

Amy's eyes teared up, and Jill offered a nearby box of tissues. Amy took a tissue, balled it up in her hand, looked at the carpet again, and wept, rubbing her eyes with the back of her hand, the tissue still crumpled. Lars padded up to her and she put her head in his neck fur. "I didn't have a choice."

"About what?"

"I had to get the bag, and it was sucked down a whirlpool towards a metal grate. I had to dive in."

"This isn't about that, Amy."

"What?"

"Forget the nuts and bolts, let's talk about mortality."

"I don't know. I just did what I needed to do. I didn't have a chance to reflect."

"That's fine, but how are you sitting with it now?"

"Feeling kinda stupid. Like, how did I let that happen?"

"Amy, I don't think anyone is questioning your decision."

"I can hear it beneath their words."

"Hear what?"

"Being so brazen to jump into freezing water."

Jill sat back in a *please continue* body position.

"It's like they think that I had a second to think about it. To consider."

"Amy, they admire your bravery. Your willingness to do what you thought was necessary. No one is second guessing you. Right now, they're treating you gently to give you time to start to recover."

Amy slowly nodded, looked out the window, only now remembering the tissue. "I'm realizing, not many people get a choice when they die . . . in an accident, that is. It's like a consequence they didn't think about, if they have a choice in it at all. This whole situation felt completely out of my control."

"And is that an issue?"

"I have no idea. I think I will feel better when they stop treating me like I'm breakable."

"I'm quite sure they will stop once everyone gets more comfortable. At that time, they will realize that you're not fragile, but right now you are vulnerable, and that's okay. You need to heal. There is no shortcut." After a moment, Jill asked, "How's life at home?"

"John is being so kind to me."

"How is intimacy?"

Amy's face reddened, and she looked away.

"More or less sex?"

"More, and more intense."

"Life-threatening situations can definitely bring that about. Okay, I won't bug you about sex anymore. How are your parents handling this?"

"They worry. They respect my decisions, but they want to know if this work is something that I really want to keep doing."

Jill said, "And?"

After a brief pause Amy said, "Yes. I think it's something I can make a difference in."

Jill said, "Well, that certainly seems to be the case, but I want you to relax for this next month. Go surfing down south. Go climbing. I'd tell you to lie on the beach, but I know you're not the type."

"Okay, I can do that, but I have to attend the wrap-up meeting."

"After the month is over, you can ask yourself all these questions again, and you get to talk about it with me all month, too."

"Oh, boy."

"Consider it," she paused for a moment, almost smiling, "*quality time.*"

"Can't wait."

"Oh, I'm sure you can, but come anyway."

Amy smiled in surrender. "Okay."

CHAPTER 67:

Wrap-up Meeting

THEY ALL gathered in the meeting room. Catherine and Beth were up at the front.

Beth said, "Welcome, everyone. I want to thank everyone for their help on this very important mission. And I am really glad that everyone has made it back safely."

Amy saw Beth glance very briefly in her direction, but Beth didn't make a point about it, for which Amy was grateful.

"As you know, Adam Robinson, the subject of our immediate concern, during a struggle with Agent Callahan, fell from a service bridge above a tributary that feeds into Strongwill Reservoir. He was gravely injured when he struck the rocks along the water. Agent Callahan gave orders that he be put on life support in hopes of gaining more information about the location of the nanobot bags that he had hidden, but he never revived." Now Beth was looking right at her. "However, the organ donor people thank you for this foresight, so your request was appreciated."

Amy had to restrain herself from looking skyward in a defensive *who-cares* motion, and she hoped Adam's eyes didn't end up with someone she ever had to look at.

Steve leaned over with his hand on her arm. "You okay?"

"Fine," she said without any inflection, except a sigh.

"Using the dogs in the hidden bag search made the success of this endeavor possible, and potentially saved thousands of lives. This is not lost on the Feds. While they may not be entirely convinced that you all can directly communicate telepathically, there is no doubt that communication between an empathic dog and his or her handler is very enhanced and is a significant advantage." She paused. "They were impressed, and you can expect them to request your services in the future."

Amy wasn't sure if that was good or bad news.

"The prosecutors have not decided whether to charge Tomas with a crime."

Now Amy couldn't stand it. "No? He's going to get away with this?"

Beth, prepared, smiled. "Tomas is canny and careful. He put a lot of people in between himself and anything illegal. The people who arranged the theft and the attack are left standing caught in the spotlight, especially because he eventually returned the data units, claiming they weren't supposed to be delivered to him. And Adam's plan was not Tomas's plan. We figure that Tomas has something much more devastating in mind. But keep in mind that the community that Tomas set up is not a cloistered one. They are well-liked in the area in which they live, and not just for fabulous hand-woven wool scarves, though that helps. If we are going to go after him it has to stick, because he has gathered a lot of supporters."

Beth took a sip of coffee. "But I do have some good news. Some of you have met the Tomasian named Sarah."

At the mention of Sarah, Amy sat up, tuning back in.

"Sarah has agreed to help us, by giving us information updates on what is going on inside the Tomasians."

Amy said, "Excellent."

"Tomas is a smart man, so he may figure this out quickly. He's not known to be violent, so we are thinking that Sarah is not in physical danger, but he might just stop telling her anything. When in contact with us, Sarah will use her given name: Lisa Gernois.

"Sarah also has custody of Adam's dog Levi, so we're hoping that Markus in the Choran office can teach her some things about how to communicate with him."

"Oh that poor woman. Levi's not a trained dog," Amy said.

"Well, we'll see what Markus reports."

Steve leaned over to Amy and said, "HiHiHiHi. Wag Wag. WhoWhatWhere." Some people started laughing softly.

Trying to contain her own laughter, Amy hushed him by gripping his arm. She looked up. "Sorry, Levi is a very silly dog."

Catherine stood up and Beth took a step backwards and headed for her chair. "Thank you, Beth, for providing us with a more than exciting time. We are all glad to have survived and we'll hope to be returning to more routine activities for a while. Before I go further into our future plans, I want to say that you all are getting a well-deserved paid week off . . ."

There were cheers to that.

" . . . and Agent Callahan will remain on medical leave for the rest of her thirty days."

Yolanda said, "Sounds like a jail sentence."

"It is. Okay, not really," Amy said.

Catherine went on to cover future training plans, and they adjourned.

CHAPTER 68:

———

Yolanda Toasts Amy

BEFORE THE party, Yolanda pulled Amy aside, hand on her arm. "Are you ready to party?"

"You bet I am," she said, covering Yolanda's hand in thanks.

"Do I have permission to tease you some during the toasts?" she said with a mischievous look.

"Sure, of course."

"No, really, I need to know if it's okay. Where shouldn't I go? What topics should I steer clear of?"

Amy looked off, thinking for a moment. "Don't talk about Adam, try not to be too hard on John. Everything else is fair game."

"It's a deal. Thanks." She squeezed her arm.

———

At the party, the food and drink flowed freely and everyone from Evergreen was there, including friends and family. Lydia, Yolanda's wife, and Amy's parents, Mary and Stan, were there. Even Markus had come down.

Eventually people started toasting, congratulating everyone on a job well done, and offering thanks for everyone's safe return.

After a lull, Yolanda said, "Well, I guess it's my turn now."

"Yes!" someone in the room said.

"Well, I hope everyone has their drink in hand. I have mine right here, because I need a little time with this." She held up her beer bottle, waving it in that way that showed she'd already had a couple before this one.

"Now, I want you all to know that I have permission for the following toast. Okay, I didn't spell out every word, but I did receive some latitude to fill you in on this."

Amy leaned into to John. "Oh, here we go."

John said, "What's up?"

Looking up at the ceiling, smiling, Amy said, as she turned her head back to Yolanda, "Ms. Danimeyer is just getting warmed up."

Yolanda said, "Amy has told some of you the sweet story that she experienced while she was unconscious. She was surfing with John out to an island. It's all very peaceful, and gives you this nice warm fuzzy feeling, and makes being in a hypothermic coma sound like something that should be a tourist thing." She had been waving the beer bottle around and Amy was concerned that someone was going to get a hops shower. "Well—" After a stylish head shake, she looked pointedly at Amy. "Let me assure you that the reality was anything but peaceful and fuzzy. The medic is hustling around with barbaric looking instruments, the helicopter is landing, Lars is agonizing, Steve is offering to buy her a case of whatever she wants to drink. I, on the other hand, am remembering that Amy owes me a beer and she can't just leave. Plus we need to get the last plastic bag secured. It's anything but peaceful. All this bustle and what is Amy doing? Surfing. Surfing?! Girl, you picked a not-so-fine time to go surfing. Wake the eff up." People, who had been tittering hesitantly at first, started laughing out loud. "So," raising her bottle in a dramatic pause, "let's hear it for our favorite slacker."

"Hear! Hear!" Someone started chanting, "slacker, slacker," and everyone joined in, including, Amy noticed, her mother. She tried not to consider any meaning to that.

Amy walked over to Yolanda and hugged her. "I love you, you embarrassing drunken wench." She looked over at Lydia, Yolanda's wife. "Is she always this impossible?"

Lydia smiled and inclined her head noncommittally.

Amy said, turning back to Yolanda, her hands on her shoulders, "So, you *are* always like this." Over her shoulder and still hanging on to Yolanda, she said back to Lydia, "Let us know if we should arrest her."

Yolanda said, "Next time you want to go swimming in freezing water, use a wet suit."

CHAPTER 69:

Amy and John Go Surfing

DURING AMY'S medical leave, Amy and John were spending the afternoon surfing in the moderate surf. It was mid-week, and even though it was a gorgeous day, it wasn't crowded.

They were both beyond the breakers, letting their boards rise and fall with the swell.

Amy stretched, taking in the breeze.

John looked at her a moment. "I know you're sick of this question . . . "

Looking back at him she said, "Go on, ask."

"Do you want to keep working for LAI?"

Looking off at the horizon she said, "I really don't know yet, John. I have some time to think about it, and I'm kinda-sorta under orders not to worry about it too much yet."

"You like people aiming guns at you? Or doing to-the-death wrestling matches on rickety bridges? Or the hypothermic bag diving?"

She splashed water at him. "That's not fair, though I am impressed with your vocabulary."

"Just thought I'd ask."

Just so I know you don't approve, she thought. "I know you don't like it, John."

"I don't like the almost-dying part."

She leaned forward, gently grabbing his hair and pulling his face close to hers. "You know what? Neither do I." She kissed the air towards him and released him, pushing him backwards.

"Hey, get back here."

She leaned away from him, paddling her board backwards. "Beg."

He swam forward. "Begging."

"Mmmm, not good enough."

John rolled on his back on his board, his hands clasped. "More begging."

"Nope."

He rolled back over and levered himself up into a kneeling position, one knee up, the other knee on his board.

Amy let her board drift over to him and kissed him gently.

He put both knees on his board. "Mmmmm," he said, and when he leaned his head back and closed his eyes, Amy shoved him hard into the water.

He came out of the water, sputtering and shaking his head. "HEY, what was that about?!"

"You may stop bugging me for a decision about 'What do I want?' right now."

Still spitting water, he got back on his board and said, "Yes, ma'am."

"You know what I really want?"

"Yes?" he said, keeping a cautious distance.

"Hoisin eggplant."

Smiling, he said, "I think we can arrange that." He repositioned his board in the water but still kept his distance, which seemed a little unusual to Amy. "Race you back," he said, and started paddling hard to catch the wave that was building under them.

"Hey, you stole my wave, you stupid kook," Amy shouted.

Laughing, he waved as the board went with the breaking wave and he popped up into a crunch. She could still hear him laughing.

She shouted into the wind, "You're hand-feeding me that hoisin, dammit."

She watched him go. She had missed the wave entirely, and would wait for her next opportunity.

She saw a shadow, and looked off to the right.

A sea lion poked its head out of the water and studied her a moment. Its eyes were lidded, but it looked at her; its small ears seemed to be carefully folded in and its whiskers drooped expressively. "Oh, hello, there," Amy said.

It rolled in the water and barked, head nodding, like a dog that wanted her to throw a tennis ball, though she figured that a fish was closer to the request.

"Sorry, no fish in my pocket."

It barked more.

"I am not telling you to go away this time, stay as long as you like."

It swam in a circle around her, lifted up its body with flippers waving, and dived down. She could see it swimming off into the distance as she swam for her wave back to the beach.

Acknowledgments

THIS BOOK began as a NaNoWriMo (National Novel Writing Month) dare back in 2012 from my friend Jan Curtis Williams. As with many participants, I found there was no way I could keep up with the frenetic pace you need to write even a short novel in a month; however, I did find that I could write a little each day, and from that comes a surprising amount of progress and a love for the craft. Thank you for the push, Jan.

A truly heartfelt thank you to my copyeditor, Diane Puntenney. You made this possible.

Patricia Minger created a trail for me to follow by being brave and publishing her book *Magic Flute* through She Writes Press, which is one way through the morass of the publishing world.

Along with Patricia and Diane, my sister, Anne Clary Warner, and also Hew Wolff and Bill Cox, provided early insights with first read-throughs.

As I worked, I gathered around me a group of advisors and sages who were excellent at helping me keep perspective and at fielding many random questions. Betsy Sutherland, Bobbie Mayer, Ellen Levy Finch, Elizabeth Trail, Marcia Kennedy, Mary Mactavish, and Mary Tillinghast Leneis, thank you.

Thank you to my advance readers (some of who have already been mentioned), Cheryl Bavister, Debra Losey, Rick Peterson, Susan Arthur, Trish King, and Snitch's Mom.

Brooke Warner and Samantha Strom of SparkPress/She Writes Press have demonstrated enormous patience in dealing with my frequent newbie questions.

My publicist, Crystal Patriarche of SparkPoint Studio, is providing me wisdom and reassurance in an area which I know little about.

Thank you to all the dogs who let me watch and study them without objection.

And lastly, but which should be firstly, thank you so much to my wife, Terri Hauck, who gives me love, support, and much essential levity.

About the Author

ELLEN CLARY is a dog-owning computer professional who has both literary and technical college degrees. She has a love of dog behavior and training and a dog sports habit. While she enjoyed being a humor writer, she now wants to write dog-related novels that she, and others, would like to read. A California native, she now lives in a Victorian house in the San Francisco Bay Area with her wife and dogs.

SELECTED TITLES FROM SPARKPRESS

SparkPress is an independent boutique publisher delivering high-quality, entertaining, and engaging content that enhances readers' lives, with a special focus on female-driven work. Visit us at www.gosparkpress.com

Resistant, Rachael Sparks, $16.95, 9781943006731. Bacteria won the war against our medicines. She might be evolution's answer. But can she survive long enough to find out?

Hidden, Kelli Clare, $16.95, 978-1-943006-52-6. Desperate after discovering her family murdered, a small-town art teacher runs to England with a handsome stranger in search of safety and answers in this suspenseful, sexy tale of treachery and obsession—perfect for fans of Sandra Brown and Ruth Ware.

Trouble the Water, Jackie Friedland, $16.95, 9781943006540, When a young woman travels from a British factory town to South Carolina in the 1840s, she becomes involved with a vigilante abolitionist and the Underground Railroad while trying to navigate the complexities of Charleston high society and falling in love.

A Dangerous Woman from Nowhere, Kris Radish, $16.95, 978-1-943006-26-7. When her husband is kidnapped by ruthless gold miners, frontier woman Briar Logan is forced to accept the help of an emotionally damaged young man and a famous female horse trainer. On her quest to save her husband, she discovers that adventures of the heart are almost as dangerous as tracking down lawless killers.

The Absence of Evelyn, Jackie Townsend, $16.95, 978-1-63152-244-4. Nineteen-year-old Olivia's life takes a turn when she receives an overseas call from a man she doesn't know is her father; her mother Rhonda, meanwhile, haunted by her sister's ghost, must face long-buried truths. Four lives in all, spanning three continents, are now bound together and tell a powerful story about love in all its incarnations, filial and amorous, healing and destructive.

About SparkPress

SPARKPRESS is an independent, hybrid imprint focused on merging the best of the traditional publishing model with new and innovative strategies. We deliver high-quality, entertaining, and engaging content that enhances readers' lives. We are proud to bring to market a list of *New York Times* best-selling, award-winning, and debut authors who represent a wide array of genres, as well as our established, industry-wide reputation for creative, results-driven success in working with authors. SparkPress, a BookSparks imprint, is a division of SparkPoint Studio LLC.

Learn more at GoSparkPress.com